Guardians of Water

Guardians of Water

Amy Wachspress

Woza Books
Books that Raise the Spirits

Guardians of Water

Woza Books
Oregon City, Oregon
(707) 468-4118
www.wozabooks.com

Cover design: Anjelica Colliard
Book design: Amy Wachspress

Publisher's Cataloging-in-Publication Data

Wachspress, Amy
  Guardians of Water / by Amy Wachspress – 1st ed. –
Oregon City, Oregon : Woza Books, 2024

Paperback ISBN: 978-0-9788350-3-3
Hardcover ISBN: 978-0-9788350-4-0

Summary: Six diverse women friends struggle to survive when the systems that support contemporary life collapse after an oil-eating bacteria unleashed to contain a spill goes rogue and devours all the petroleum in the world.

1. FIC028000 FICTION / Science Fiction / General. 2. FIC044000 FICTION / Women. 3. FIC070000 FICTION / Disaster. 4. FIC130000 FICTION / Diversity & Multicultural.

Library of Congress Control Number: 2024904356

Printed in the United States of America

10 9 8 7 6 5 4 3 2 1

For all the women dear to me throughout my life,
in memory of Elena Castañeda,
for Gaia.

"Something happened. They want everyone in the conference room," said Angela's coworker from the doorway. Angela looked up from her computer, ready to complain about the interruption, but one look at the woman's face changed her mind.

She set her phone on vibrate and slid it into her pocket in case one of her boys tried to call her. She joined her coworkers streaming down the hallway like a school of fish. The entire Child Protective Services Division, where Angela worked as a social worker, assembled in the conference room. The division director held up her hand for silence. "If you follow the news, you know that an oil spill occurred off the coast of Louisiana a few days ago. To clean it up, the oil company released oil-eating bacteria into the ocean, which is apparently a common practice, I don't know, sorry, I don't follow this kind of scientific stuff much. According to the news, the bacteria ate the spill and jumped to land, where it's spreading across the country, eating crude oil. The scientists who created the bacteria can't seem to stop it. I have no idea what this means, people. But they're saying we'll have no more gas. Could get crazy. I'm closing this CPS office for the time being. When this blows over, you have a job waiting for you here. It has been an honor..." She choked up and simply put her hand over her heart.

For a moment Angela thought the whole thing was a prank set up by a warped reality show. Everyone looked confused and stunned. The director's words sunk in about as swiftly as water poured on concrete. The room bulged with professionals trained to assist people in crisis, but this wasn't your garden-variety crisis. At first no one moved, and then, as if instantaneously zapped out of a frozen state, everyone moved at once in a million directions.

Angela needed to reach her sons and see them safe home because the world had just cracked open.

PART ONE: Reunion

Reunion: Rachel
Green Creek Rancheria, California

E ven after the catastrophic events that subsequently occurred, Rachel continued to think of that summer as Bobcat Summer because it began with the death of her aged border collie Rusty, which left her cats easy prey for a marauding bobcat. The bobcat would have picked off the cats one by one with calculating efficiency if the tribal police from the adjacent Rez had not shot the malicious predator. Sadly, the bobcat eluded the tribal police long enough to make a dinner out of Sinclair, Rachel's gorgeous calico tabby. Several days had passed since anyone in the family had seen Sinclair when a vicious pounding overhead jolted Rachel's husband Vince from his peaceful breakfast. He ran outside and in the early morning light he witnessed the bobcat chasing Cinders and Roosevelt across the roof. Vince ran the bobcat off before it could eat their two remaining cats and then Rachel kept Cinders and Roosevelt indoors until the tribal police hunted down and killed the bobcat.

Rachel and Vince lived with their daughters, Sophia and Abigail, on a ten-acre parcel bordering the Rez, and their ability to depend on the tribal police to eliminate the bobcat was one of the many perks of living next door to the Green

Creek Band of Pomo Indians. Rachel worked at the Green Creek Health Clinic as the only fulltime resident doctor, and Vince taught fourth grade at the country school in nearby Oak Valley, so they knew most of the members of the Tribe, especially families with young children.

When Rachel began working at the tribal clinic and they moved to their land, she worried about raising children in such an isolated location. Their house was the last house on the county road leading to the Rez before the road entered tribal lands. Rachel could walk to the clinic from her house on a path through the forest. There was no fence or other distinct boundary delineating the Rez from their property, so Rachel and Vince felt as if they were part of the community, and didn't feel isolated at all. They attended community events. Their daughters played with the Pomo children and learned Pomo dancing, regalia making, and other traditional arts alongside their friends in the afterschool program.

The Green Creek Band of Pomo had not joined the frenzy to build a casino like surrounding tribes, largely because of the strong opinion on the matter of their longstanding chief, Marjorie Firekeeper. The Tribe operated a fairly lucrative organic farm and a goat milk dairy that produced gourmet goat cheeses, yogurt, and kefir. They sold their products through regional natural foods outlets and at farmers markets. Few outsiders came to Green Creek, and the place was rather difficult to find. Rachel valued living in a remote location. She felt certain they had made the right choice when they decided to raise their girls in a quiet place, close to the beauty of nature and immersed in the culture of a vibrant Native community. Rachel had grown up in a moderately observant Jewish home and, while many aspects of Judaism still resonated with her, she found that many aspects of life among the Green Creek Pomo fed her spirit in ways that Judaism had not. Vince was a lapsed Methodist who didn't find as much spiritual food in the Native culture as his wife did, but he embraced the culture anyway. A worldview grounded in an awe and love of the natural world resonated with him.

Tom Kaweyo, the chief of the tribal police, gave Rachel and Vince a courtesy call to inform them when his men had eliminated the bobcat. The day after the demise of the bobcat, Rachel left for the reunion. Rachel had recently turned forty, and her circle of women friends, with whom she grew up in Syracuse, New York had either just turned forty or would reach that milestone by the end of the year. The last time they had all been together was at their tenth high school reunion. Rachel remained in close touch with a couple of the women, but not all of them. In January, when Maxine turned forty, she sent an email to the group to commemorate her birthday. A subsequent flurry of emails resulted in a consensus to celebrate their collective fortieth year by having a reunion. Robin picked the date because she believed that the Summer Solstice contained positive energy, which was characteristic of Robin, who lived on a commune (she called it an "intentional community") in rural Kentucky. Rachel, though skeptical about the auspicious properties of the Solstice, respected Robin's beliefs and, if pressed, might even go so far as to admit that she viewed them as refreshingly pagan.

Once they settled on the Summer Solstice for the time, Angela, who lived in Oakland, suggested Capitola for the place, because of its proximity to her and Rachel, because it was one of her favorite vacation spots, and because the beaches in that area were some of the most beautiful in the world. The only one of the friends who couldn't travel to Capitola for the reunion was Callie, who remained entrenched in her anthropological field work in Brazil. She would join the others via screen chat. Rachel talked with Callie on a regular screen chat once a month. Compared to Rachel's quiet life hidden away in the majestic oak forests of Mendocino County, Callie's life studying isolated indigenous people seemed exotic and adventurous.

On the Friday of the reunion weekend, Rachel drove to Oakland to collect Angela, who would catch a ride to Capitola with her. Angela and Rachel had remained friends after high school when they both moved to California to attend college at UC-Berkeley. They visited one another as often as possible within the context of their busy lives, and always spent Thanksgiving together at Green Creek. Angela's boys and Rachel's girls thought of one another as cousins. Rachel and Angela had seen both Maxine and Callie recently because their globetrotting friends traveled to or through San Francisco on business. But they had not seen Robin, Melanie, or Jo in a dozen years. Everyone eagerly anticipated the reunion.

Reunion: Angela
Oakland, California

Angela's phone rang, but she didn't hear it because she had left it on the kitchen counter when she stepped out to put her letter to Winston in the mailbox. She played the message back and heard Rachel informing her that she had just left Green Creek. Winston had a year to go to finish his eighteen-month sentence, and that seemed like an eternity to Angela, who struggled to manage on her own with the boys. She worried about the future, since Winston would have a felony on his record, which would make it more difficult for him to find work. They definitely wouldn't take him back at his old job. The familiar anger at Mickey rose in her throat. Angela thought, I'm not going there, I'm clearing my mind of anger, which is a useless and destructive emotion that has no positive value and it does not serve me. She often asked her therapy clients how their anger served them. She held her right hand up in front of her face, palm outward and made a pushing-away motion. She refused to dwell on Mickey's instrumental role in Winston's arrest for being in the wrong place at the wrong time. How could her intelligent husband have been so oblivious to the danger posed by consorting with Mickey? Since Winston's arrest, the family had erased Mickey from their lives, and Angela refused to allow him to invade her thoughts. She struggled to forgive Mickey, and let go, whenever she thought about him. "May Mickey enjoy an excellent life far away from us," Angela said aloud.

In her head, she ran through what she had to do in the two hours before Rachel would arrive. She needed to go to the grocery store and then organize the boys' things for them to stay at the various friends' homes where they would spend the weekend. She had taken the day off work. Her boss hated it when she took a day off because Angela was the only African American woman on her service provider team who spoke Spanish. She kept telling them to hire another bilingual African American caseworker. Well, not her problem. Even though she had taken the day off, she felt rushed to get everything done. She had run two loads of laundry, packed her suitcase, cleaned the bathrooms, picked Winston Jr.'s saxophone up at the repair shop, put together a bag of gluten-free snacks for Jamal, sewn up a tear in Suleiman's favorite pair of shorts, and written the letter to Winston. She decided to eat a salad before she ran out to the store because she knew the dangers of shopping hungry.

Angela was so looking forward to three glorious days away from her responsibilities; three days filled with nothing more than visiting with her longtime women friends. She wished for the umpteenth time that she had a daughter, but she wouldn't trade any of her three noisy, messy sons for one. Thinking about Win-J (short for Winston, Jr.), Jamal, and Sulei made her feel blessed. She sometimes wondered what it would have been like if she and Winston had chosen to raise their boys in a rural community like Green Creek. No way. She loved Oakland and the vibrant African American community there.

Reunion: Robin
Rainbow Farm, Kentucky

S tanding in the security-check queue at the airport, Robin remembered, with a nauseating wave of recognition, how much she hated to travel. The air in the airport was laced with disease. She fought an urge to hold her breath. She could not feasibly hold her breath until she arrived in San Francisco. She wore two face masks and still felt exposed. She had emptied her water bottle before joining the security queue and would now have to depend on outside water, which tasted plastic, despite the high-quality filter in her superior water bottle. Noxious perfume worn by other passengers wove its fingers into her hair and clung to her, while the stench of their aluminum-contaminated deodorant penetrated the mask and bombarded her nose. The fluorescent lights contributed to her irritability as they sucked all the calcium out of her body through her eyes (she could feel it getting sucked out), despite the fact that she wore sunglasses. She didn't want them to X-ray her or the food she carried in her backpack, but she couldn't avoid it. She imagined she was absorbing hordes of toxic molecules every second, and it would only get worse once she boarded the closed environment of the plane with recirculated air. She hoped her friends appreciated the sacrifice she was making to travel to California, far from her clean and healthy communal home. Next time she would lobby harder for the reunion to take place at Rainbow Farm, where she worked as the community's nutritionist and dining hall manager. Her friends had no idea how delicious Robin's homegrown meals tasted.

As she approached the security checkpoint, she removed her ID from her wallet, and regarded the photo she carried of Ken and Willow. In the photo, a two-year-old Willow sat atop Ken's shoulders while eating an ice cream cone, which dripped mercilessly onto Ken's head and down the sides of his face. Ken was laughing, his eyes turned upward in the direction of their daughter. The photo was grossly outdated, but it always made Robin smile. Ken was such a great dad, and she loved her temperamental sixteen-year-old daughter to bits. She wished that she and Ken had more children, but then she reminded herself that a population explosion threatened to destroy the planet and having more than one child was selfish, irresponsible, and unsustainable. She had made personal sacrifices to save the earth, she thought self-righteously.

Robin was the product of a Norwegian mother and a Chinese father, Ken was pure Korean, and Willow had inherited her tall, slender Scandinavian build from Robin's mother and her straight, dark, glossy hair and dark-brown almond-shaped eyes from her Asian ancestors. She's too beautiful for her own good, Robin thought. Willow loved animals, and Robin had left her in charge of their two cats, four rabbits, and tank of tropical fish while she was away at the reunion.

After subjecting herself to the security check, Robin refilled her water bottle at a water dispenser before proceeding to the gate, where she sat in the lounge to wait until the flight boarded. She especially looked forward to seeing Maxine, who would meet her in San Francisco and drive her to Capitola from the airport in a rented car. As juniors in high school, during a time when Robin was exploring her sexual identity, Robin and Maxine had a brief affair. The affair confirmed Robin's heterosexuality for her, while Maxine, on the other hand, graduated to full-blown lesbianism and never looked back. Maxine continued to jokingly refer to Robin as her "first love," which Robin liked since it made her feel adventurous and unconventional. She and Maxine had remained close during all the intervening years leading up to forty. Maxine was the only one of her high school friends who had made the effort to visit Robin at Rainbow Farm. Robin thoroughly approved of Maxine's wife, Theresa. She wished that Theresa was coming to the reunion, but they had agreed on no spouses, no children, no pets.

Reunion: Maxine
Washington, DC

While boarding her plane in DC, Maxine couldn't stop thinking about Roo, her geriatric dachshund. She fretted over Roo throughout the flight and the instant the plane landed in San Francisco, she called Theresa to check in. Roo had developed a respiratory infection earlier that week. Although they had two young and healthy black Labs, Roo remained Max's beloved baby.

"Ay, mija," Theresa chided, "you're on vacation. Don't worry about us. Roo is fine. I'm fine. Minnie and Moe are fine. Have fun and forget about us for a few days. Can you do that?"

"I'll try," Max promised. She never grew tired of her wife's clipped Puerto Rican accent. If truth be told, the Latin twirl at the edge of her words turned Max on to this day, even after more than fifteen years together. Like Gomez in the old Addams Family Show from the Sixties, Max would say to Theresa, "Tish, your Spanish drives me wild." Unfortunately, Max couldn't understand what Theresa said in Spanish. She could just hear Robin (in her head) chastising her, "You're so *white* Maxine. You're married to a Puerto Rican and you still haven't learned Spanish." But Max was hopeless at learning languages. She had taken a full year of beginning Spanish on three separate occasions in her life and she still couldn't even order food in the language at a Mexican restaurant. Not everyone was a linguist. She had other talents. As a labor attorney, Max often traveled on business. One would think she would have gotten used to spending short stints of time away from Theresa and the dogs. But she always missed them, no matter how interesting the people she met or the places she visited. She was a homebody at heart.

Max retrieved her carry-on suitcase from the overhead rack and deplaned. It felt good to not have to hurry for a change. She had plenty of time to rent a car before Robin's flight arrived from Lexington and Melanie's from JFK. She decided to grab a sandwich at an overpriced airport café before hopping the shuttle to the rental car agency. She caught herself wishing that she had not agreed to give Melanie a ride to Capitola with them. It was a selfish wish. It made sense, of course, for the three of them to drive together from the airport. But Max would have liked to have had that little window of time alone with Robin. Dear Robin was such a purist; so true to her beliefs in the way she chose to conduct her life. By contrast, Melanie's life offered a cautionary tale about what happened to disorganized people. Melanie had never left Syracuse, married her high school sweetheart Ned in a shotgun wedding after she got pregnant, and given birth to the oldest of her five children at the age of eighteen. It came as no surprise that Melanie's daughter, Jennifer, also became a teen mom, so Melanie was the only one of them who was a grandmother already. Plus she and Ned had a "surprise" baby only a few years ago. Max wondered how many of their babies Melanie and Ned actually planned. She couldn't remember if Melanie's surprise was three or four years old. Once upon a time, Melanie was a lot of fun, the instigator of more than a few wild and hilarious escapades. But the last time Max saw Melanie, at their tenth high school reunion, Max remembered thinking that Melanie seemed to have lost her sense of humor. Enough about Melanie. Max resolved to extend generosity to Melanie and to make an effort to stop judging. She turned off her tablet, bussed the remains of her lunch into the nearest trash bin, and headed for the shuttle to the rental car agency.

Reunion: Melanie
Syracuse, New York

Melanie aggressively (and a tiny bit maliciously) left her phone turned off when she landed for her layover at JFK. Let them figure out any problems on their own. The world would not fall apart if Mom went on a retreat with her girlfriends. The entire weekend promised to be such a vast departure from her everyday life that Melanie felt like a character in a movie. She would never have been able to afford the trip if Jo hadn't offered to pay for her airfare and accommodations at the upscale resort in Capitola. God bless Jo and her solid gold hit *Can't Miss You If You Won't Go Away*. Few people knew that Melanie had thought up that name for Jo's award-winning song.

Melanie had bought some new clothes especially for the weekend, including a white muslin summer nightgown. She didn't want her friends to perceive her as dowdy. She had put on a few pounds, and she had all good intentions of going to the gym, but her nonstop duties caring for her rambling family and unkempt household left her no time for the luxury of attending an exercise class. Even though she weighed a little more than she should, she was in good shape for a woman who had gone through childbirth five times (seven if you counted the two miscarriages between Tracy and Stella) and who had breastfed babies for a total of nearly nine years. Running after children all day long at her job as a preschool teacher kept her active. Ned liked to say "children keep you young." If that aphorism held any truth then Melanie would be about four and not forty.

She got in line at a fruit smoothie stand and stared at the technicolor pictures of the different drinks, trying to decide which one to buy. They all looked delicious, shimmering in sherbet-shades of orange, purple, pink, and yellow. Even the green one looked appealing, but who drank a spirulina-spinach smoothie for fun?

Suddenly, a beefy man at a dining table across the way began to make choking noises as he clawed at his throat with puffy fingers. Bystanders stopped to stare at him, but no one galvanized into action to come to his aid. The overdressed jewelry-bedecked woman who shared his table squealed incomprehensibly. Melanie bolted from the fruit smoothie stand, wove her way through the paused bystanders, who acted as if shot with tranquilizer darts, and vaulted a low metal railing surrounding the dining area where the drama of the choking man continued to unfold. She dropped her large handbag unceremoniously on the ground at her feet, encircled the man with her arms, and lifted him partially out of his chair with a strong Heimlich Maneuver jolt. A hunk of ham flew out of his mouth and bounced off the squealing woman's left boob, landing in her soup with a splash. The man coughed like an old radiator as Melanie slid him back onto his chair. If he was coughing then he was breathing. She hoped she hadn't put her back out.

The bystanders transfixed in the walkway clapped, as if Melanie had staged the entire life-and-death episode for their benefit to relieve their travelers' boredom.

Melanie retrieved her handbag from the floor and brushed it off absently.

The squealer came to her senses and rose from her seat to thank Melanie profusely. Melanie considered saying, "I'm a preschool teacher, ma'am, and it's all in a day's work." But she restrained herself. In truth, Melanie had to take the full refresher course in CPR and emergency first aid every year to keep her teaching certification. At least she had made good use of this year's refresher by saving the choking man from death-by-pork.

Although badly shaken by his brush with asphyxiation, the ham-eater recovered enough to thank her. She modestly disentangled herself from the encounter and hurried away from the scene. She had lost her appetite for the smoothie after seeing that piece of ham land in the soup. Honestly, they don't pay preschool teachers enough, Melanie thought.

She walked to the gate for her connecting flight, sat by a window, and dug in her enormous handbag for her e-album of photos. Tracy hated that handbag. "You look stupid with that suitcase on your arm, Mom," Tracy complained. "Why do you need to carry such a big bag everywhere?" She carried it because it held everything she might need. It was her security blanket. She opened the e-album and brought up pictures of the children. Jennifer was twenty-one (already?) and doing a great job raising her two-year-old son Cody. Lisa, at eighteen, exuded success. She attended community college and planned to transfer to a four-year for pre-med in a year. Don, Melanie's only son, had just turned fourteen. He was angry at Melanie at the moment because she had once again refused to allow him to play football. But it was too dangerous. What mother in their right mind allowed their son to play a sport at which an ambulance parked at-the-ready on the sidelines with a stretcher and a paramedic team suited up for action? He would have to make do with soccer and basketball. Tracy, now twelve, and Baby Stella, who would be four years old in a few short weeks, grinned at her from a recent photograph Ned had taken of them baking cookies in the family's large, chaotic, comfortable kitchen.

Finally she brought up a photo of Ned. He had started to go bald, but he still looked good. Dang, she was supposed to be on a vacation from the family and here she was looking at photos of them. Ned, who worked as a paramedic, would be proud of her for saving the ham-choker. She decided to turn her phone on after all so she could tell Ned about her heroic gesture. When the phone lit up, she discovered a text

from Jo. MUST CATCH LATER FLIGHT. I'LL BE LATE. SAVE
ME SOME TEQUILA!

Reunion: Joanne
Chicago, Illinois

After Jo went online and changed her flight, she
texted Melanie to give her a heads up that she
would arrive in California later than expected.
Then she pulled her lush, straight, black hair into a ponytail
and took the elevator down to the fitness center to work out.
No one had any idea how hard she had to work to maintain
her slender figure. Italian women were hard-wired to absorb
massive quantities of pasta and swell into bloated middle
age. Not Jo. She resolved to fight it, beating back the fat inch
by inch. As a result, she lived in a state of chronic hunger.

Robin and Max would probably think she changed her
flight so she could breeze in celebrity-style, just to reinforce
the point that she was famous. They could think that if they
wanted. Jo refused to dwell on what Robin and Max would
think. In fact, if they found out the real reason she postponed
her flight, they would level even more criticism at her. Tim
insisted he needed her presence as eye-candy dangling from
his arm at some stupid reception his producer was hosting in
his honor that afternoon. She didn't want to do it and had
already refused several times, citing the reunion and that she

needed the weekend off. But Tim kept pestering her about it and then, this morning, he had thrown a tantrum. What a drama king. Oh well. It would only take a couple of hours and it obviously mattered a lot to Tim to have her accompany him. Neither she nor Tim had a history of success in maintaining relationships and they were both trying hard to improve their record. Tim had unruly, out-of-control, spoiled children from his previous two disastrous marriages. Jo had been married only once, but she had done her best at two other long-term relationships that had crashed and burned as completely as her marriage. Fortunately, she had no children. Having a child would have stripped her gears. She could barely tolerate Tim's difficult offspring as a tangential feature of her life, let alone taking full responsibility for a child of her own. She had fortunately dodged that bullet. She shuddered and rolled her brilliant green eyes toward the ceiling at the very thought of motherhood.

Jo wondered if any of the girlfriends knew she was dating Tim, a rising country music singer eight years her junior. She had only been seeing him for a few months. Melanie knew, of course, and teased Jo mercilessly, calling her a "cradle-robber" and, worse, a "cougar." The sensationalism-seeking journalists (if you even considered them journalists) smeared Jo and Tim across the tabloids a few weeks ago for a wild night of partying in Atlanta during Tim's most recent tour. Jo doubted that any of the girlfriends read tabloids. Perhaps they might have glimpsed a distorted image of Jo on the cover of one of those rags at the grocery store checkout. She hated the media. They were a pack of sharks circling with bared teeth.

Jo had calculated the timing so she would know when she needed to leave the reception in order to downgrade her appearance and catch a taxi to Midway for her flight. She had packed her bag. In fact, her bag was always packed. She needed to find a way to slow down and stay home more. She wished she could just blink and time-travel to Capitola, without having to deal with airports and rental car companies, driving on strange roads late at night, and camouflaging her appearance so no one recognized her. Ever since *Can't Miss You*, she felt as if she had lost control of her life, as if her fame had torn her up into little pieces and doled her out to strangers. People she didn't know (and didn't want to know) had access to intimate details about her life from her songs, her website, and the media sharks. She had wanted fame and fortune, she got it, and she didn't like it. Be careful what you wish for.

Taking up with Tim had probably been a colossal mistake. She truly had not expected it to turn into anything. But he kept after her, wanting to see her again and again. And he was so damn sexy that she couldn't resist him. Plus, it flattered her that a younger man found her forty-year-old self attractive. He had a delicious body. His firm double-bubble butt melted her into a puddle; and he knew it so he always wore those tight-fitting jeans. With no underwear. Jo needed to go back upstairs and shower off. She needed to cool down and transform herself into Tim's glam-girl for the media sharks.

Jo wondered how to explain her life to her high school friends. Rachel the doctor, Angela the social worker, Robin the nutritionist on that throw-back hippie-commune, Max the do-good lawyer; none of them could possibly imagine the bizarre reality in which Jo had to function, the reality that usually seemed either unreal or hyper-real. Melanie understood. Dear, wonderful, maternal, down-to-earth, sensible Melanie, who kept Jo grounded more than Melanie would ever know. Jo resolved to steal a little one-on-one time with Melanie during the reunion. Maybe she would change her return flight and go to Syracuse for a few days following the reunion. After all, she was Cody's godmother.

The Girlfriends Reunion
Capitola, California

Rachel and Angela arrived at the Pacific Haven Resort in the afternoon, before the others landed in San Francisco. They checked into the large beach house they had booked, which had a deck overlooking the sparkling expanse of the Pacific Ocean. Rachel and Angela would share one of the rooms, Max and Robin another, and Jo and Melanie the third. After unpacking their bags, they made a trip to a grocery store to stock the refrigerator and they picked up Thai take-out on the way back and ate it on the deck, groaning with pleasure over the spicy peanut sauce.

"I could go for a spicy peanut flavor of ice cream," Angela declared, as she opened a frosty bottle of Chardonnay. "They could call it Spicy Icy."

Rachel laughed, tilting her head so that the late-afternoon sun shot luminous, amber threads through her curly dark-brown hair. "Wouldn't that contradict itself? How can something be hot spicy and creamy frozen both at once?"

"Well then what about Chocolate Peanut Spicy Icy?" Angela suggested, amending her idea. She poured the Chardonnay into two long-stemmed glasses, passed one to Rachel, and took a sip from hers. She mustered her willpower and resisted calling or texting any of her boys to see how they were doing without her.

"That has potential," Rachel said with approval as she rolled the cold wine on her tongue. She admired her friend's mocha-brown skin emanating a golden glow in the sunlight reflected off the water as the evening approached. Rachel liked Angela's new dreadlocks. They were only a few inches long, but they suited Angela. "How long do you plan to grow your dreads?" she asked.

"They aren't dreads. They're twists. It's a different technique. I'm not sure how long I want to grow them," Angela replied as she leaned back in her deck chair. "It takes a lot of work to keep them twisted." More than committing to the work of twisting them, she was still deciding if she wanted to assume the persona of someone who wore twists. People made assumptions about you when you had them. She risked increased scrutiny by the police with the twists. She wondered if they would stop her more frequently. Maybe she was overthinking because of what had happened to Winston.

"Whatever they are, they look good on you. What do the boys think?"

Angela rolled her eyes and took another sip of Chardonnay. "The boys. Win-J refers to them as 'retro', if you can believe it."

Rachel laughed. "Retro? No, I can't believe it."

"You know I'm jealous of you."

"What'd I do?"

"Because you have daughters."

"Well I'm jealous of you for having sons," Rachel countered.

"And because you have those wash-and-wear Jewish curls that require so little work," Angela continued.

"Don't even go there with that good-hair-bad-hair crap, girlfriend. You could be a goddamn model with your slender, perfect curves in exactly the right amount in all the right places. I, on the other hand, with my wash-and-wear curls, have not had a glimmer of slender since junior high school."

"I need you inside my mirror talking to me on a daily basis." Angela laughed.

"I'll make you a vid you can play on your phone and you can prop it up against the bathroom mirror while you get ready for work in the morning."

"I don't spend much time getting ready for work," Angela responded, with a sigh. "Mostly I just try to remember everything the boys and I need to take with us for the day and to get a decent breakfast into them."

"Not getting any easier?"

"A little. Win-J has really stepped up."

"Vince will help out for that week when he's down there next month for that conference," Rachel reminded Angela.

"I'm looking forward to having another adult in the house, even if just for a week. Hey, what time does Melanie's flight get in again?"

Rachel glanced at the time on her phone. "I think she got in at around four."

"Let's take a walk on the beach," Angela suggested.

"Sounds great. Let me change my shoes." Rachel polished off the last twinkle of wine in her glass, gathered up the remains of the Thai take-out, and headed inside.

In San Francisco, as the shuttle pulled up to the door, Robin saw Max through the window of the rental car office. Max sat in the waiting area, typing with furious concentration on her computer. Her preoccupation with work prevented Max from noticing that Robin's shuttle had arrived and afforded Robin a moment to observe unnoticed. Tall and broad-shouldered (from swimming almost daily), Max had sandy-brown hair worn in a smooth pageboy that curved to the contour of her jawbone. Robin could not remember Max ever wearing her hair any differently. Max was solid and muscular, with no flabbiness anywhere on her large frame. When viewed from behind, Max could pass as a linebacker. A pair of fashionably slim, black-rimmed glasses balanced on Max's nose, obscuring her soft, brown eyes.

If I was a lesbian, Robin thought, Max could have been mine. But even as she thought it, she knew it wasn't true. She and Max had pursued completely different lifestyles. Life at Rainbow Farm would have bored Max, and Robin could never live in a city. She needed peach trees and rich rows of greens to feel centered and connected to the earth. Max glanced up, saw Robin, and her face broke into a delighted smile. Robin waved. She tried not to inhale the fumes from the departing shuttle as she wheeled her suitcase up the ramp and into the rental car office. She parked the suitcase to receive a warm bear-hug from Max.

"Silly girl," Robin teased. "You look like you're going to a business meeting. Why so dressed up?" Max wore a beige linen suit, a simple button-down cream-colored blouse, and sensible flats.

"Habit," Max replied with a shrug. "Naturally, you look like you're going to a save-the-world convention," she parried playfully. Robin wore a sleeveless forest-green tie-dyed jersey dress, sandals, and a straw hat. She had traveled in her most comfortable clothing. She had brought the hat to protect her skin from the California sun, and the best way to transport a hat from Kentucky was to wear it. People failed to comprehend the full danger of melanoma, in Robin's opinion.

"Oh shut up," Robin said with a laugh. "In some parts of the world, people consider a green jersey dress quite fashionable."

"Do you want water or some popcorn?" Max offered, with a wave of her hand in the direction of a cooler stocked with water bottles and a table where red-and-white striped bags of popcorn stood lined up in a row.

"Yum. Delicious," Robin replied with disdain. "Stale genetically modified chemical-soaked freak corn and toxic water with carcinogenic plastic molecules leached into it." She laid her suitcase flat on the floor, unzipped it, and searched inside.

"Excuse me for offering toxic refreshments," Max responded, chuckling.

"I brought you something special."

"What? An air ionizer? Giant crystal?"

Robin extracted a cardboard box from her suitcase, lifted the lid, folded back some tissue paper, and displayed luminous, gold-and-rose-kissed peaches. They looked touched by fairy dust.

"You grew these?" Max asked, awestruck.

"Of course," Robin replied proudly. "You'll need a towel. They're juicy. Be right back." Robin retreated into the restroom to collect paper towels and to wash her hands. When she returned, Max had shut down her computer and put it away. They each had a wondersome peach. That taste of home rejuvenated Robin.

"This is the best peach I have ever eaten in my entire life," Max declared, partly because it was true and partly because she knew how much it would please Robin to hear her say so. "I already got the car and Melanie's flight should have landed right after yours. As soon as she gets here, we'll roll."

"How's Roo?" Robin remembered to ask.

"I called Theresa when I landed and she assured me that Roo-girl is fine. Do you want to see a picture?" Max held up her phone, which displayed an image of Roo as the wallpaper.

"She has so much white in her muzzle," Robin noted.

"Yeah, she does," Max agreed with a wistful note in her voice. "But I think the old girl has a couple more good years in her."

"I can't believe you showed me a picture of Roo before I showed you pictures of Willow."

Max shrugged and squinted out the window. "Oh my gosh, I think that's Melanie getting off the shuttle."

Melanie wore her long, straight, blonde hair in a perky ponytail that hopped out the back of a New York Mets baseball cap. Her bangs curved over a large pair of maroon plastic sunglasses that obscured her blue eyes from view. She wrestled with her suitcase, which she had secured with rope because she didn't trust the zipper. The night before, Jennifer had helped her paint her fingernails and toenails deep purple to match her swimsuit, and Ned had teased her that she looked like she'd slammed her fingers in the car door. She was trying too hard to make her life look like a success, and she suddenly wished she had not painted her nails.

But when Robin rushed out of the rental car office and hugged her enthusiastically, and Max followed right behind flashing a big smile, Melanie felt loved and welcomed, even with the lurid purple nail polish. Robin brushed away tears as she exclaimed, "It's so good to see you, it's been way too long."

Melanie removed her sunglasses. "We should have done this a long time ago. Hey, Jo's gonna be late, by-the-way. She said to save her some tequila. I'm not sure what's up, but I have no doubt we'll hear all the juicy details later."

"You know Jo," Robin replied. "She needs to make a grand entrance."

"It isn't like that," Melanie defended Jo. "Her life is complicated."

"Everyone's life is complicated," Max commented. "Let's get in the car where we can turn on some air conditioning and music." Max clicked the remote on the car key and the rear lights on one of the cars in the lot flashed. "Must be that one."

They stashed Melanie's lassoed suitcase and Robin's over-sized bulging suitcase in the back with Max's compact carry-on and climbed into the car. Robin sat in the front with Max. Melanie, in the back, leaned forward to catch the conversation as they pulled onto the highway.

Some time later, when they rolled into the Pacific Haven, they found their beach house empty. A note on the countertop informed them that Rachel and Angela had gone for a walk on the beach, and a half-empty bottle of Chardonnay in the fridge informed them that those two had already started to party. Max put her bag in her room, hung her jacket in the closet, changed into a pair of sandals, and helped herself to a glass of Chardonnay. Meanwhile, Robin unpacked so much stuff from her suitcase, including food grown at Rainbow, a pillow, a water purifier, and a portable juicer, that Melanie accused her of purchasing the suitcase in Diagon Alley.

"Where's that?" Max asked. Robin and Melanie regarded her as if she had just landed from Mars.

"You obviously spend no time around children," Melanie said.

"It's from Harry Potter," Robin enlightened her. "You do know who he is, right?"

"Oh, yeah, boy wizard," Max mumbled as she peeked into Melanie's room, where it appeared to her as if Melanie's suitcase had spontaneously regurgitated its contents onto the floor.

Robin opened the refrigerator and closed it shut quickly with a snap. Then she opened cupboards and cabinets, making a mental note of the kitchen equipment and the food Rachel and Angela had purchased. "I can't work with this," she complained.

"Hey, Julia Child, are you going to plot a kitchen makeover or can we go for a walk on the beach?" Max asked.

Laughing, Robin grabbed her hat off the countertop and followed Max and Melanie out the door. The ocean glittered in the magical, orange-rose glow of the late-day sun. "Look, look," Robin called to the others excitedly as she pointed, "dolphins." A school of dolphins flashed in and out of the waves, amazingly close to the shoreline. "Hello dolphins!" Robin shouted. "So pleased to see you!" She spread her arms wide as if to embrace the entire landscape.

Melanie stopped in her tracks and her jaw dropped as she stared with unabashed touristic enchantment. "I've never seen a real wild dolphin in the ocean."

Max smiled indulgently. She had seen dolphins in the ocean many times and even swam with them in Hawaii when she and Theresa had gone snorkeling.

"It's a sign," Robin asserted.

"Of what?" Melanie asked with childlike curiosity.

"A good omen for the weekend and continued good waves of energy spreading from the reunion," Robin explained in a matter-of-fact tone that defied argument. Max laughed, as she usually did when Robin spouted her woo-woo ideas. Before Robin could reproach Max for making fun of her spirituality, they caught sight of Angela and Rachel approaching. Robin took off across the sand at a run, met up with Angela and Rachel, and flung her arms around each of them in turn.

"Now we just need Jo," Rachel noted, as the five of them strolled along the water's edge.

"About that," Melanie said. "She's going to be late."

"Has to make her entrance," Robin added.

"It's not that," Melanie insisted. "Honestly. You guys are so critical it makes me wonder if you're jealous."

"Us guys?" Angela asked with raised eyebrows. "Did I say anything? I did not."

"Seriously," Rachel said. "I don't care when she arrives as long as she does arrive."

"She'll make it by tonight," Melanie promised them firmly. "She's been looking forward to this weekend. Something probably came up with Tim." Melanie worried about Jo in that relationship. In her opinion, Jo was too star-struck when it came to Tim, and she thought Tim would use Jo and then dump her.

"Who's Tim?" Rachel asked.

"I call him Tim Tabloid," Melanie answered, with a giggle. "I guess you guys don't follow Jo's career much."

"Not my kind of music," Angela said, with a shrug. "But a lot of people like it. More power to Jo."

"Tim's music is even less your kind," Melanie assured Angela. "Jo's been going with Tim Cooke for the past few months."

"No!" Max exclaimed. "Seriously? Tim Cooke? Isn't he like ten years younger than us?"

"Eight," Melanie corrected. "I don't want to gossip about Jo. She'll tell you about her life herself. Let's talk about something else. Like, what are we doing for supper? I'm hungry."

"I think Robin has supper in her suitcase," Max informed them.

"Shut up," Robin told Max. "I brought a few things from my garden. It's totally not enough for supper."

"Let's order pizza," Angela suggested. "So we don't have to cook."

"Are you crazy?" Robin demanded incredulously. "I love to cook."

"And Robin would probably shoot herself if we ordered pizza," Max added. Robin attempted to grab Max and drag her to the water to dunk her in an act of feigned fury, but Max was far too strong and much larger than Robin so that plan swiftly failed. Max planted her feet in the damp sand and laughed her head off like a jolly giant in a Scandinavian saga. Robin gave up and stumbled back up the beach, breathless and tousled, to announce that she would make vegetarian burritos for supper and it would only take her fifteen minutes to put them together but she needed to run to the grocery store first.

"That will take fifteen hours," Max said, rolling her eyes.

But it didn't. Robin ran to the store, returned, and prepared delicious organic burritos in record time. Later, while Max was mixing up the second pitcher of margaritas, the front door opened and Jo breezed in with her sleek black hair unfurling behind her like a flag and her silver hoop earrings winking in the candlelight from the lit tapers on the table. She dropped her bag and swept her girlfriends up in hugs all around.

"Now we're all here!" Melanie stated with satisfaction.

"Robin made the most yummy dinner," Rachel told Jo. "Fix yourself a plate."

Jo surveyed the remains of dinner and said, "I'll just make a salad with those vegetables."

"Not a chance. You're not on a diet this weekend," Melanie scolded. "You're eating. I'm putting beans and cheese into one of these tortillas and heating it up for you."

"Put it in the oven," Robin ordered. "The microwave will damage the proteins and fats."

Max rolled her eyes. "Professor, it's recess, knock it off."

"Microwave," Melanie mouthed silently to Jo from behind Robin.

"Thanks Mom," Jo told Melanie with a laugh. "I'm hoping that's a pitcher of margaritas I see." She pointed to Max's handiwork. Max retrieved a glass from the cupboard and poured a tall drink for Jo. As she handed her the glass, Angela passed the plate of limes and Rachel passed the plate of salt.

"Now I'm on vacation," Jo declared.

"What kept you?" Melanie asked as she put a plate of food in front of Jo.

"Guess."

"Tim Tabloid, huh?" Melanie suggested with certainty.

"You betcha," Jo confirmed. "And don't call him that. Seriously. We hate those tabloids. What happened was Tim couldn't handle this reception-thing his producer set up for him without a sparkly babe on his arm. It's OK. I went as his bling, caught a later flight. I'm here now."

"What's he like in person?" Max asked.

"What do you mean?" Jo replied cautiously, as she considered how much she wanted to reveal about him or her life with him.

"I have a couple of his CDs. I just wonder what he's like in real life."

"You don't seem the Tim Cooke type," Angela told Max.

"You've probably never heard his music," Max countered.

"True that," Angela confirmed.

"I like that soppy stuff," Max admitted. Then she attempted to pry more out of Jo, who had piled vegetables, guacamole, salsa, and sour cream on her burrito and was digging in with gusto. "So what's he like?"

"Melanie, please grab my bag." Jo pointed vaguely in the direction of the hallway between chews. "I have photos on my phone. Robin, this burrito is heaven. Where did you get these tortillas? They taste like real corn."

"That might be because they *are* real corn," Robin replied with satisfaction. "Organic, nontoxic, and no GMOs."

"What's a GMO?" Jo asked.

Robin rolled her eyes and Max explained "Genetically Modified Organisms."

"Sounds like sci-fi," Jo said as she wiped her hands on a napkin and took her bag from Melanie.

"Oh no, it's real alright. Don't get me started," Robin said grimly.

"We won't. Trust me," Max promised as she threw a "look" at Robin.

Jo thumbed through her phone and found photos of herself and Tim taken on a recent trip to Aruba. She passed the phone to Melanie while the others crowded around to see.

"He looks like a regular guy," Max commented.

"A really handsome regular guy," Melanie observed.

"My photos are probably boring compared to all of yours," Jo lamented. "I have no kids, no pets, no garden, no hobbies. Just a toned body and songs inside my head." She laughed self-consciously. She was extremely proud of her career and had worked hard for it, but sometimes she felt deficient because she didn't have a family life. "C'mon, let's see. I'm sure everyone brought pictures. Show and tell."

They took turns flipping through their pictures, explaining who was who and what was what. After sharing the photos, which required another pitcher of margaritas, they tumbled into bed exhausted from travel, exhilarated from each other's company, and looking forward to their upcoming day at the beach together.

Robin set her alarm and rose early to work her magic in the kitchen. The others roused from sleep to the delicious aroma of fresh-baked applesauce-spice muffins, artichoke frittata, and coffee.

"This is the best coffee ever," Max announced. "What am I drinking?"

"Dark roast songbird coffee from Columbia with organic cream from pastured cows," Robin answered.

"What does that even mean? Did they put a bird in the coffee?" Max quipped.

"How do you pasteurize a whole cow?" Jo asked.

"You ladies are hopeless," Robin responded with a mixture of irritation and amusement.

"Everything tastes delicious," Angela complimented, biting into her second muffin.

"Of course it does. This is what real food tastes like," Robin informed them with smug condescension, which they overlooked since they didn't want to deter her from further cooking. "Songbird means the coffee is grown in the shade of trees that provide homes for songbirds, which, translated, means it's organic and grown using sustainable practices that support the local economy of the indigenous people who grow the coffee beans."

"You can't make this stuff up," Jo muttered.

"Speaking of indigenous people, I'm going to get Callie on a screen chat at six o'clock," Rachel informed the others. "So we have to plan accordingly."

They lingered over breakfast, insisting that Robin make a fresh pot of coffee after they practically inhaled the first pot. Finally, when the fog had burned off the water and the sun appeared, they changed into their swimsuits, slathered on the chemical-free, fragrance-free, dye-free, approved sunscreen that Robin produced from her suitcase (she actually made Melanie throw out her commercial spray-bottle of sunscreen and made her swear an oath never to put it on her children again as long as she lived), and headed for the beach. "It will not only give your kids cancer but it'll give cancer to all the sea creatures within a fifty-mile radius of your kids," Robin asserted. Rachel very much doubted this to be true, but she chose not to go into battle against Robin over sunscreen.

They spread their patchwork of colorful towels and beach blankets on the sand, set up folding chairs and umbrellas, dipped their toes in the chilly Northern California water, took a walk for a couple of miles, pointed in excitement when they saw a pod of dolphins swim past, gossiped about people who went to high school with them, ate grapes and cheese from the cooler, collected shells and sand dollars, and gazed out to the horizon as if they could read the answers to life's pressing questions in the bright distance.

Jo took a nap. Robin described in detail how to make a blueberry galette. Rachel put on a wet suit and went for a swim. Angela painted a picture of her hectic life as a temporary single mom. Melanie shared the story about the man she saved with the Heimlich Maneuver in the airport and had them in stitches laughing. Max talked to every dog and dog-owner who passed by.

Robin searched in her bag for a sweatshirt and produced a collapsed tent pole. Waving the tent pole aloft she exclaimed, "Oh my gosh! I almost forgot. I brought a visioning activity for us to do and I want to do it here on the beach. We should do it before it gets any later." The others observed curiously as Robin removed a spray of colorful, shiny ribbons from her bag and attached them to the top of the tent pole with a clip. She unfolded the tent pole, which extended to eight feet, and sunk one end in the sand so it stood upright. The ribbons dangled from the top of the pole.

"Everyone take the end of a ribbon," Robin instructed, "and stand in a circle around the pole." The ribbons were the six colors of the basic color wheel. "Now, we're going to weave the ribbons around the pole. Max, Jo, and I will go under first and the rest of you will go over. Each time, before we do a weave, we go around and everyone says something they wish for the future. When we finish, we have a pole of wishes. I'll start. I wish for a good harvest at Rainbow Farm." She pointed at Rachel to go next.

"Health for those I love," Rachel wished.

"More opportunities for us to get together," Max wished.

"Safety and protection for my boys," Angela wished. "May no move of theirs be misinterpreted by the police."

"Amen to that," Rachel agreed softly.

"Peace of mind," Jo wished.

"I wish that all my children will love the lives they choose to live," Melanie wished.

"Now we weave," Robin instructed, and they each took a step forward, going over and under with their ribbons. "We'll have lots of wishes before we finish, so you don't have to pack everything into your first couple." It took them many weaves to wrap the tent pole all the way to the bottom. After they wished for the big things, like all the best for their loved ones, their wishes touched on a wider range of desires. Financial security. Professional success. Healing for those in need. Relief for communities and countries in distress. A viable plan to protect the environment from further destruction. Motivation to go to the gym. More time for travel. A healthy, delicious, low-calorie ice cream. The perfect little black dress. More days at the ocean. By the time they reached the end of the pole with the ribbons, they had exhausted their wishes for the most important things in life and had managed to wish for a lot of small pleasures to boot. Robin tied off the ribbons and handed the pole to Rachel. "I can't take it back on the plane now that it's opened up. You keep it. Put it in your yard at Green Creek. It's loaded with positive energy. Let the wind and rain take the wishes out to the universe."

The air turned chilly when the fog rolled in so they loaded up their bags and headed back to the house, sun-soaked, sandy, and content. They showered off and changed to warmer clothing for the evening.

At six o'clock, Rachel set her computer on the dining room table and opened the screen chat program. She saw that Callie had gone online and she sent her a connect-message. The others crowded around behind Rachel's chair and cheered when Callie appeared, a stunningly beautiful woman with long dreadlocks and a silver ear cuff. Callie's mom was African American and her dad was Nicaraguan, and she spoke several languages fluently. She had a doctorate in anthropology and a tenured position as a university professor; although it seemed she rarely spent enough time stateside to actually teach any classes.

"You all look wonderful," Callie exclaimed. "Can you believe we're forty? I wish I could be there."

"You would want to be with us even more if you had any idea how delicious Robin's cooking is," Rachel told her. "Girl, you need to plan a trip to Cali."

"No, you need to plan a trip to the Quarana," Callie countered.

"What's that?" Jo asked.

"That's the name of the tribe she lives with," Rachel informed Jo. "She's been studying them for a couple of years."

"Hey, what did you do with your hair Angela? I love it."

"It's twisted," Angela answered.

"I might try that," Callie said with a grin. "I'd have to chop it all off first. I look like a stoned-out Rasta, don't I?"

The girlfriends objected and told her how great she looked, but Rachel thought that Callie, who was small in stature to begin with, seemed a little frail. She worried about her health.

"Where's Max?" Callie asked.

"Here," Max said as she leaned further into the range of the computer camera's eye. "How's your research going?"

"I'm not sure who's studying whom anymore." Callie laughed. "I've learned so much from the Quarana. I'm writing a book, but it's slow going. I think that the leaders in the U.S. should come down here and have a conversation with the Quarana elders, you know, to set them straight about a few things."

"I think the same thing about the children in my preschool class. They could teach the leaders of the country a thing or two," Melanie piped up.

"What's up with Poiry?" Rachel asked. "Is he still trying to convince you to marry him?"

"You would ask that, Ray," Callie answered. "Embarrass me in front of everyone, why don't you?"

"Who's Poiry?" the others chimed in.

"What's this about marriage?" Robin asked.

"He's a friend," Callie clarified firmly. "He's a great help to me and we're fond of one another, but it stops there. He already has two wives and a slew of children."

"Then you would be the trophy wife," Jo teased.

"Hardly. His other wives are younger than I am. So is he."

"Younger men are the bomb," Jo replied.

"She's seeing a guy eight years younger than her," Melanie informed Callie. "Can you believe it?"

"Absolutely," Callie replied. "That's our Jo. You go girl."

"I have a question," Angela interjected. "What do you love about your life?"

"Seriously?" Callie asked.

"I'm going to get everyone to answer that question at dinner," Angela informed them. The others groaned. "But you won't be at the table so you have to go now."

"No fair. I won't get to hear your answers," Callie protested.

"Nevertheless, answer the question," Angela persisted.

"You can have more than one," Melanie told her. "Right Angela? We can have more than one thing. No way we can choose only one."

"I can go with that," Angela agreed. "You can have more than one thing you love best."

"I'm thinking," Callie said. "I love learning about different cultures. I love the Rainforest. I love tropical fruit and pure water. I love that Poiry keeps asking me to marry him and that the guys in the tribe don't usually wear clothes." She dissolved into peals of laughter.

"You're such a pervert!" Rachel exclaimed. "Poor Poiry. You're ogling him, aren't you?"

"Naturally," Callie confirmed with a sly smile.

"He's going to wear you down, girl," Angela warned.

"When will you come back home?" Robin asked.

"November," Callie told them. "In time for the holidays. I love it here, but I'm starting to feel a little homesick."

"Come to Green Creek for Christmas," Rachel suggested.

"It could happen, Ray. That'd be nice. We'll talk. So. Now you guys. You have to tell me all about yourselves and what you're up to." Each of the others took a turn in front of the screen sharing with Callie a morsel from the banquet that was their lives. After they finished, Rachel took her seat back to sign off.

"The usual, two weeks from Sunday, OK?" she confirmed with Callie.

"See you then. Give your girls a sloppy smooch from Aunt Callie. And love to Vince too."

"I love you sister-girl. Take care of yourself," Rachel signed off.

"Love you back." Callie disconnected.

After the screen chat, Chef Robin gave instructions and they helped her prepare a scrumptious dinner. A fresh apple pie was baking in the oven when they had spread their feast on the table and filled their wine glasses. They took their seats.

"We have to say blessings," Robin announced. Jo raised an eyebrow but didn't protest. "Take hands. Everyone gets a turn. I'll go first. I'm grateful for this nourishing food and I hope that it brings everyone joy, health, and wellbeing. I'm grateful for these friends who have known me since I was a girl and who renew my spirit. I'm grateful for the positive energy in the world and my ability to add to it. I feel blessed with good fortune."

Max went next. "I give thanks for friendship and for the company of women." That said, she choked up and couldn't continue speaking, so she looked helplessly at Melanie, who sat beside her.

"Oh gosh." Melanie laughed nervously. "I don't know where to start. I have received so many blessings." She paused to gather her thoughts. "OK." She closed her eyes. "I give thanks for Ned, Jennifer, Lisa, Don, Tracy, Stella, and Cody. I give thanks for these good friends and the good times we have shared and for this opportunity to spend time together. I give thanks to God our creator who gave us life and preserves us and watches over us." Melanie opened her eyes and looked in Jo's direction expectantly.

"I'm not very good at this sort of thing," Jo apologized self-consciously.

"Sing something," Melanie suggested. The others chimed in with their encouragement. So Jo sang a song she had written about the beauty of having a good friend. She had written it with Melanie in mind, but she didn't say anything about that. Maybe she would get up the courage to tell Melanie later in private. Her clear, pure voice carried across the room and out toward the ocean through the screens of the sliding doors.

Max's eyes welled with tears as Jo's song concluded. "I don't know what's wrong with me this evening," Max mumbled.

Angela went next. "That's a hard act to follow." She paused. "I'm grateful for the years of friendship and especially lucky to have had your support these past months after everything that happened with Winston. Thanks for that. It has meant a lot to me to have women friends with our history together. And thank you Robin for this incredible food."

Lastly, it was Rachel's turn. She squeezed Angela's hand on her right and Robin's hand on her left. "I'm grateful that we live in our charmed lives here in this country and that we grew up unharmed and our children are thriving and our husbands were not killed in battle, that we live in a place where our homes and communities were not destroyed by the instruments of war. There are so many places in the world where a group of childhood friends would never live to see forty years together, where women die young and lose their loved ones early. I'm grateful that we live amidst such abundance and safety. I'm grateful for our health, our love for one another, and this super amazing meal, and that we are here at this time in our lives to share it."

"Amen," Melanie and Robin said together, as if in church. Max used her napkin to wipe her eyes.

"We must do this again soon," Jo said, as she loaded her fork. "You guys are so grounded. My life gets so crazy. Sometimes I even wonder if I'm awake and if what I see is real. Being a celebrity is frightening and weird."

"You must like something about it if you keep doing it," Robin pointed out.

"This seems like a good time for my question. What do you like best about your life?" Angela asked Jo.

"What do I like best?" Jo echoed.

"Yeah. What do you like absolutely the best about your life? It can be more than one thing. Just answer without thinking about it too hard," Angela pressed.

But Jo did think about it real hard. "I love that I can lift other people up with my voice. The best thing about my life is music and being able to sing in a way that means something to people, makes a difference for them. When I'm in front of an audience that's into my music and I'm in the zone, I don't need anything else in my whole life. That's everything right there." Melanie rubbed Jo's back affectionately.

"What about you, Melanie?" Angela asked.

Melanie cocked her head to one side, took a bite of food, and chewed contemplatively while those who had not yet answered the question considered how they would respond when the question came to them. "Before I answer, I have to say that these are the best green beans ever. Robin, you have a serious gift."

"Thank you very much. They're real green beans. Organic. Local," Robin replied complacently.

"Of course," Max commented.

"When you eat real food, it tastes like food," Robin continued, ignoring Max.

"My first-off answer," Melanie said, "would be my children, of course. I love having a family. When everyone sits down together to dinner or crams onto the couch to watch a movie or on Christmas morning. OK, that's a cliché, but I love Christmas morning with my children. I could watch them forever, talking all-at-once, teasing each other, and eating everything that's not nailed down. That's my number one favorite thing about my life. But I also love children in general and I love my work as a preschool teacher. It's not a romantic or glorified profession, but it's one of the best things in the whole world to do. Nothing makes me feel better than making a difference in the life of a small child. So I love my own children, and their dad too, of course, and what I love most about my life is that it's full of children."

"That's why you're the best teacher in the world," Jo pointed out, "and I can testify to that firsthand because I'm your biggest and most devoted child."

"Oh sweetie, you're pretty grown-up," Melanie contradicted.

"So Rachel. What do you love best about your life?" Angela persisted.

"Definitely more than one thing," Rachel stated. "First my marriage to Vince and our daughters, and also I love helping people feel well and healing them when they're sick. I love to see people get better and to know that I helped, to see people make changes in their lives. I also love where I live. The land is... how to describe? You would have to see it, to walk among those ancient oak trees. Living in a Pomo community, I feel the connection to the land every day. I don't think I could live anywhere else ever again. I love having that place as my home."

"I feel you," Robin responded excitedly. "I would say the same thing myself. Sorry, I'm interrupting."

"Not at all, I'm done. That was it. Your turn, Robin."

"The landscape at Rainbow Farm is different from Northern California, but we have beautiful land too, and I know what it's like to befriend a place and to have it feel like home. Like a deep home that I have belonged to for centuries, that it took me time to find and return to in this incarnation. I love Ken and Willow of course, and also helping people feel well from healthy eating. I have to say more about the helping people feel well part because I love cooking delicious nontoxic real food for people so that they don't get sick. I love picking plants from the garden and cooking them right up and having people eat them all in the same day. If I look at a really beautiful head of cabbage then I want to eat it. I want it inside of me. I want it to become part of my body. I love turning clean, gorgeous plants into delicious, nourishing food."

"You've got it bad, girlfriend," Jo commented with a shake of her head. "I guess you never see a donut with pink frosting and sprinkles and say, 'gosh that is so cute I want to eat it right up', huh?"

"Never," Robin replied emphatically, laughing. "Donuts don't look edible to me. My brain doesn't recognize them as food."

"I wish I could bottle that and inject my kids with it," Melanie said mournfully.

"What about you, Max, what do you love best about your life?" Robin asked.

"I have to get political and say that one of the most important things in my life is that I am married to the woman I love. Until recently that was not possible. The fact that we were able to marry each other and have that recognized by the law is huge. So I love that I live in a time when I have that right and that freedom. And I love my community, my neighborhood, where Theresa and I fit in as a couple, the family of us and our dogs. I also love practicing law. Sure, some of the law doesn't work and doesn't make sense and isn't fair, but so much of the law does work and comes from a commitment to justice. I love the ongoing process of evolving the law so that it advances justice. I love that I get to work toward justice. As imperfect as the law may be, it represents the struggle to promote justice, and I love being part of that struggle."

"Was that your Nobel Prize acceptance speech?" Robin joked.

Max blushed. "I also, by-the-way, love my dogs," she added. "I even let them lick me on the mouth."

"Ewwww," Angela groaned. "Too much information."

"And incredibly unsanitary," Jo added.

"Now you," Rachel demanded of Angela. "We answered your question, now you tell us."

"This isn't the best time in my life for me to assess what I love about it," Angela replied sadly. "Things are kind of hard right now." She took a breath. "My boys are my bright, guiding stars. I love my husband and pray that he survives inside and that he doesn't let prison change him from who he is, from the man I know. I love my work helping children recover from trauma so they can find joy again. I have great friends, like you, who support me and help me through hard times. So, yeah, thanks."

"Winston will be OK," Rachel reassured Angela. The others agreed. Still, Angela wondered.

"I say, bring on the apple pie," Melanie suggested. "There better be ice cream to go with it. Someone snuck some past Robin, right?"

"I have nothing against ice cream in moderation when it's good quality," Robin defended herself. "I'm not a complete prude."

"I take that as a yes. Woo-hoo," Melanie exclaimed. She hopped up and went to raid the freezer. Max put some coffee in the coffee maker and went to get her laptop while it brewed. Robin chastised her for bringing an electronic device to the table. "I'm just putting that photo of all of us up as my wallpaper," Max defended herself. They had asked a stranger to take a photo of them with Max's phone. She turned the computer around so the others could see.

"I look like I did my hair with an electric fan," Robin complained.

"Nah," Melanie disagreed. "You just look windblown, like the rest of us. Except for Angela, who looks like a model. It's a good picture. Send it to me, Max."

After dessert, Angela put on some old R&B and they danced. Then they sat on the deck and listened to the ocean and waxed philosophical. Jo sang again. Eventually, one by one, they turned in for the night, until only Melanie remained. She didn't want the reunion to end. For one weekend, Melanie had felt like a star, with her affluent and successful friends. She had arrived at Pacific Haven feeling inferior. She was the only one who never left Syracuse. She wasn't a doctor or a lawyer. She was a preschool teacher. People perceived her as one step up from a babysitter even though she worked hard to earn her college degree in early childhood education. She arrived at the reunion feeling unaccomplished compared to her friends. But over the course of the weekend, she came to realize that she had accomplished a lot. She did important work. Very young children grow up and have agency in the world and she knew how to teach children to be good people. What work was more important than that? She dug out her phone and studied the photo of herself and her daughters serving dinner to the homeless at her church's soup kitchen. I wouldn't change any of my life, Melanie thought. If the world ends tomorrow, I will die content.

In the morning, the women returned each to their own lives.

Three weeks later, life as they knew it ended.

PART TWO: Collapse

Collapse: Rachel

At ten-fifteen on a blazing-hot July morning, tribal Chief of Police Tom Kaweyo uncharacteristically barged into the clinic and insisted on speaking with Rachel. When he arrived, she was in the middle of a patient consultation with Christina, one of the most beloved tribal elders. Rachel had recently diagnosed Christina with diabetes; however Christina regarded suggested dietary changes with contempt and balked at increasing her level of exercise. Rachel had never seen her so subdued and apathetic, and she wondered if Christina had given up on living. She had to find a way to help her understand that if she made some lifestyle changes, she would enjoy many more years of her life. She considered her conversation with Christina a life-and-death situation, so she did not take kindly to the interruption when she heard Tom's voice booming in her waiting room. She took even less kindly to the commotion when Tom burst into the examination room without so much as a courtesy knock on the door.

"This better be important," she stormed.

"Oh it is," Tom countered. Her anger suddenly became alarm. "Come with me." He waved his arm to encompass everyone in the clinic. "Everyone come with me." Tom had never interrupted her when she was seeing patients before. Not even when his wife died. Her heart pounded in her ears.

Christina stood up calmly, took Rachel's hand in hers, and said, "Let's go." Although it seemed unusual for Christina to take her hand, holding Christina's hand made her feel more prepared for whatever catastrophe loomed. Everyone from the clinic followed Tom across the parking lot to the community center next to the tribal office building.

Many tribal community members, both Native and non-Native, stood and sat in the large community room, transfixed by what they watched on a large-screen monitor. Tom edged toward the front. Rachel and Christina followed him, still holding hands. She saw an aerial view of the Gulf of Mexico, covered in an oil slick. She remembered that an oil tanker had spilled many gallons of oil off the coast of Louisiana just a few days before. Several oil spills had occurred in the Gulf in recent months. Surely an oil spill would not have prompted Tom to interrupt her at the clinic.

As she listened to the reporter's words, her stomach lurched and she felt light-headed. The reporter explained that scientists had developed a bacteria they called C. enviroensans that "ate" oil and they had released it into the ocean at the Gulf Coast in an effort to mitigate the damage from the oil spill. The bacteria did indeed eat the oil. Then it went rogue and moved inland, where it ate through the entire oil supply of Louisiana. It ate crude oil, refined oil, gasoline, and natural gas. After the bacteria consumed the oil and gas in Louisiana, it moved up the coast, and so far had eaten its way through the gas and oil in the Southeast United States. A map appeared on the screen and showed a graphic of the entire country that depicted the progress of the rapidly moving, hungry bacteria. The commentator reported that the C. enviroensans did not appear to eat products made from petroleum, such as plastics. It seemed to have an appetite limited to gas and oil from petroleum.

When the same broadcast they had just watched began again from the beginning, Rachel asked Tom, "What does it mean?" Christina still held Rachel's hand, and she gave it a comforting squeeze.

"It means we're screwed," Tom answered grimly.

"You mean it's coming here?" Rachel asked in horror.

"I have no doubt that it is," Tom replied. "You saw how fast it's moving. I figure in a coupla days we won't have any more gas or oil either, same as Louisiana, same as the Eastern Seaboard. When that happens, we'll be wrestling alligators on top of alligators."

"Vince is in Oakland at a teachers' conference."

The look of sympathy and concern that Tom cast her frightened Rachel. "He better head home right away. I expect the roads will be a mess in a minute. Call him and tell him to get his ass back up here ASAP."

"The children," Christina said. "Someone should collect our children from the summer-school and bring them home."

"Good idea, I'll get right on that," Tom agreed. He seemed pleased to have a useful task on which to focus his energy. "Listen up," he called out over the murmur in the room. "I'm going to take Deputy Gibson and we're going to drive into town in the bus to pick up our children who are at that summer-school program." A murmur of approbation passed through the room.

"Tom, please bring Abby and Soph home with the others. I don't know if they'll release them to you without a note since they aren't members of the Tribe. Here, take this." Rachel pulled her prescription pad out of the pocket of her white coat. She scribbled a hasty note giving the school permission to release her daughters to Tom.

Chief Marjorie Firekeeper rose and spoke in an authoritative voice that carried throughout the room. "We must prepare for the possibility that we will have no or limited access to the outside for an unknown period of time. We must prepare for the possibility that we will lose access to fossil fuel and probably electricity from the outside too. Tribal Council members please meet in the conference room. Everyone else please spread the word that all voting tribal members should come to the community center for an emergency general membership meeting at three o'clock. We will discuss how best to secure the safety and wellbeing of every person living on tribal land." The chief turned briskly, with purpose, and marched off to the tribal office building.

Rachel wanted to continue watching the monitor, but she knew she had to return to the clinic. She had to discuss with her staff what these events might mean for the clinic. She also had patients in need of attention.

Her phone rang and she answered.

"Are you watching this?" Vince asked.

"Are you OK?" she replied, relieved to hear his voice.

"So far, but I so wish I wasn't in Oakland," he lamented.

"I wish you weren't there either. What bad timing."

"Don't worry about me. I'll get back home. I'm on my way to Angela's right now. If I can't drive home then I'll walk. But I'll get back to you and the girls one way or another," he promised. "What's going on at the Tribe?"

"We just found out about it. Tom pulled me out of the clinic to come over to the community center to watch the news with a lot of other people, but I'm heading back to the clinic now. Chief Firekeeper is about to meet with the Tribal Council and she called an emergency general membership meeting for this afternoon." Rachel rarely referred to Marjorie as "Chief Firekeeper." She could feel herself undergoing a tectonic shift in her thinking, as though she had completely left the United States of America and entered entirely into the country of the Green Creek Band of Pomo. The term "sovereign nation" came to mind and she felt, in a way that she had not felt before despite her years working at the Rez, what this term actually meant and why it mattered so much to Native people. "What's going to happen, Vince? I'm scared."

"It's not good. Our future depends on how they handle this situation at the Tribe, Ray. You're their doctor and we belong there. We're part of that community. You're strong, sweetheart. You always manage to see your way clear to doing the right thing. The community is lucky to have you. I'm lucky to have you," his voice caught and he paused to compose himself. "I'm not going to let a ridiculous apocalyptic systems meltdown keep us apart."

"Please come back to me."

"I'll be home before you know it."

"I love you so much."

"Love you the same."

Rachel called her parents in Florida. Her mother couldn't put a sentence together for crying. Her dad promised they would call her that evening when they had more information about their situation, and when they could talk to the girls. After she hung up, she pocketed her phone and walked to the clinic. She couldn't remember when Christina had let go of her hand and vanished into the crowd. She met with the small group of patients who congregated in her waiting room to determine which of those present had pressing health issues and which of them could wait. She asked the staff to meet with her at one o'clock when they usually broke for lunch. She met with the patients in need of immediate attention and looked at her afternoon schedule. The burden about to tumble onto her shoulders began to come into focus when she realized that she couldn't effectively write a prescription. How would she practice medicine without access to pharmaceuticals?

When she met with her staff, they divided up tasks to prepare for the clinic to function if the Tribe became isolated. Rachel wanted a list of everyone in the community who had diabetes, heart disease, high blood pressure, asthma, and any other life-threatening health conditions. At the general membership meeting, she would propose that a group go into town to the pharmacy. If they could actually procure meds, they would have to keep them under lock-and-key. Could Tom's small tribal police force secure life-saving medications? The more disturbng question was how to decide who would receive the meds and who wouldn't whenever they started to run out if it came to that. Who among them had the right to make such decisions? Not Rachel. Not anyone. She forced herself to focus on specific pressing tasks immediately at hand.

She felt lucky to belong to this community that was a small sovereign nation with many years of experience at self-government, which, however rocky or conflicted, however imperfect, was independently functional. This crisis would test the leadership ability of the Tribal Council.

Rachel's staff called her afternoon patients and rescheduled so everyone could attend the general membership meeting. Shortly after noon, the children arrived at the Rez on the bus, confused, scared, and requiring a great deal of attention. Abigail and Sophia cried and clung to Rachel, asking about their dad. They wanted to know what would happen to him and how he would get home if his car wouldn't work. Rachel told them about her conversation with Vince and promised they would call him that evening so they could ask him their questions. She sent them with the other children to the Youth Center.

When Chief Firekeeper called the general membership meeting to order, they began with a blessing, a gratitude, and brief drumming. A microphone had been set up to ensure that everyone could hear. About six hundred people lived at the Rez, including children, and about four hundred of them were tribal members enrolled in the Green Creek Tribe. The rest of the community was either non-Native or they were enrolled in other tribes. Most of the non-Natives were partnered with or married to Natives, or belonged to Native extended families. She considered the fact that she and her daughters were probably the only Jews in the community.

Chief Firekeeper had served as the elected tribal chief for more than twenty years. Whenever her term ended, the Tribe re-elected her. She commanded tremendous respect within the community. To their credit, and unlike many other tribes, the Green Creek had not experienced excessive destructive internal family feuding, disenrollment of tribal members, and disruptive changes in leadership.

The chief's first order of business demonstrated why she was their chief. She knew the various family units within the Tribe and she also knew that everyone who wished to be represented in the meeting would not fit in the community room. A large gathering of tribal members filled the parking lot and field adjacent to the community center. The chief wrote a list of the family groups that constituted the Tribe on a dry erase board. Then she asked if there was a representative from each of the groups present. For those not in the room, she sent messengers out into the outdoor crowd to find representation. Then she assigned a spokesperson for each of the family groups and created something she called the "Spokescouncil." She charged the spokespersons with taking notes on the proceedings and then sharing information with their family group. She explained, "When the time comes to make decisions, you will discuss the issues with your family group, gain their input, and then report on their thoughts and represent their wishes at the Spokescouncil. I will rely on the Spokescouncil to make all key decisions from this point onward. The Tribal Council will work with the Spokescouncil to ensure that community decisions come as close to consensus as possible. Spokescouncil will meet every day at one o'clock in the community center annex. Tribal Council will meet every day in the conference room at ten o'clock." The chief instructed the directors of the various tribal programs to meet with her the following day and she formed subcommittees to oversee each of the areas of community life that would need attention under their newly unfolding circumstances. She tapped Rachel to represent the medical clinic and she formed a health infrastructure subcommittee.

Rachel was the most qualified medical practitioner in the community. But without the backup of community resources, such as specialists, the hospital, a pharmacy, and mental health professionals, she had no idea how she could function effectively. She was a family doctor. She knew how to treat a host of everyday maladies, how to help people manage chronic diseases (in general, but not like a cardiologist or endocrinologist), how to help parents raise healthy children under ordinary circumstances, and she delivered babies. She was not a surgeon. She had not set a bone since her residency. The enormity of the responsibility foisted upon her overwhelmed her and tears sprang to her eyes. Tom patted her arm, sensing her panic. "We're in the same boat," he whispered in her ear. "Don't ask me how I'm going to maintain law and order with two sworn officers and a youth programs junior cop. We'll do the best we can. Can't do more than that." She rested her head on his shoulder for a couple minutes, grateful for his friendship and his support.

Chief Firekeeper and the other leaders on the Tribal Council demonstrated astonishing organizational skills and acted with impressive good sense as they set about restructuring systems to support the community in isolation from the outside world. Before the chief adjourned the meeting, Christina stood and spoke to the Tribal Council. "We have gone too long without an active Elders Circle," Christina said. "It's time." She remained standing, silent. The chief looked at each of the other Tribal Council members in turn, to check for agreement, with no words passing between them, before she turned her gaze back to Christina. "OH!" the chief said. A vocalization arising deep in the center of one's being, it was the Native form of "amen." Rachel had heard OH! used many times as an emphatic pronouncement of agreement. "Interested elders please come to this room this evening at seven o'clock," the chief instructed. "We will convene an Elders Circle. We are adjourned."

Rachel hurried to catch up with Christina, excusing herself as she pushed through the throng of people. When she caught up with her, she took her elbow. "Let's reschedule our consultation," she suggested.

"Not necessary," Christina replied with a sly smile. "I'm new. The diabetes will go away."

"I don't understand," Rachel replied, bewildered and concerned.

She patted Rachel's arm affectionately. "You will, child," Christina said. "In time, you will."

Collapse: Angela

Angela called Win-J, who answered on the first ring. He never answered on the first ring. "Hey Mom," Win-J greeted her in a voice so serious that he sounded older than his sixteen years. "Don't use your phone to call, Mom. Text. It uses less juice."

"Where are you?"

"They told us to go home, but the buses aren't running. The streets are a hot mess. Don't try to drive. I'm walking over to King Elementary to get Sulei right now." Win-J and Sulei, who was six, were in school-based summer programs. Jamal, who was eleven, was attending a two-week basketball camp at the junior high.

"I hope they will keep Sulei there until you get him." Angela tried to keep her voice as calm as possible.

"They announced at school when they released us that the elementary schools will hold kids for relatives to pick them up. You get Jamal and I'll get Sulei and I'll meet you at home." Jamal's basketball camp was near Angela's office and Sulei's elementary school was close to Win-J's high school. In the six months since Winston had been sent to the state prison, Win-J had tried to step in for his younger brothers as the man around the house. Win-J was furious with his father for getting arrested over such foolishness, and then convicted on a trumped up charge for something he hadn't done. One lapse in judgment for an African American man in Oakland could have serious consequences. She told herself all the time not to look back, to look forward. She felt a familiar pang of regret that Win-J had been forced to grow up so fast. And now, well, this situation went over the top.

"OK, baby. I'll see you at home. Please be extremely careful. I love you." Angela's voice trembled.

"Don't worry. I'll be careful. I'll be strategically careful, Momma," Win-J said softly. "Remember to text." She couldn't recall the last time he had called her "Momma."

Standing in her office, overwhelmed, she turned to the pictures of Winston and the boys on her bulletin board. She removed a photo of the family in which Winston still had his shoulder-length dreadlocks, and admired her handsome husband. She removed a few other photos and slipped them into her purse before taking a last look around and deciding she didn't need anything else. Only the essentials mattered now. She walked to the parking lot, sat in the driver's seat of her minivan, and turned the engine over just to hear it hum. She collected a few things from the van before she turned the engine off, locked up, and set out on foot to collect Jamal. Leaving the van behind was a tough goodbye. But when she saw the state of the streets, she knew without a doubt that she couldn't expect to drive anywhere. The main intersections had deteriorated into gridlock, with cars bumper-to-bumper, as stuck as bugs in tar. Many cars sat empty, abandoned in the middle of traffic. Some people still tried to drive on the side streets, but pedestrians were on a mission to reach their destinations and would not yield. Frustrated drivers became aggressive. Angela saw a man in his car hit a man walking, who toppled to the ground clutching his leg, and the driver kept going without stopping. Several people rushed over to the fallen man. Angela felt guilty that she didn't help, but her first and most important responsibility was her children.

Even if the gas-gobbling bacteria never ate its way to Oakland, it would be useless to try to drive anywhere in the snarl of unmoving vehicles. Angela wished that this catastrophe would bring out the best in people, but it looked like that would not be the case as most people panicked and focused on themselves and their own loved ones. But who could blame them? She hadn't stopped to help the man hit by the car because she had to get to her boys as quickly as possible. She broke into a run. She wanted her boys safely at home, while at the same time realizing that home would probably not be safe for long. Then she remembered Vince.

Angela slowed her pace in order to check her phone, where she discovered a text from Vince. He said he was on his way and would meet her at home. Poor Rachel! She must be beside herself with Vince so far away in the midst of this; and in Oakland of all places. The cities would certainly be the first places to fall apart if the systems they had come to rely on collapsed. Could any authority step in and salvage this situation? Government? Law enforcement? Scientists? Who was in charge? Would they lose electricity, and if so, how quickly? If all the petroleum products vanished, then, she reasoned, the safest places would be isolated rural communities, like where Rachel and Vince lived. The chance of survival in Oakland did not look good to her. For one thing, where would they find food? Even if she knew how to grow anything edible, which she did not, where would she grow it? She could stock up on canned food, but it would run out. In a flash, she saw her way clear. She wished she could stay in her home, but wishing wouldn't change anything. She would take her boys to Green Creek.

Vince would obviously want to get back to Rachel and his girls, and Angela would go with him. They could stay with Rachel until things blew over and if they didn't blow over then Green Creek would provide the best home she could secure for her boys. They would have to walk the one hundred miles to Green Creek, but they could do that. Her boys were strong. They would walk with Vince. She began a list in her head of things to take with her from her life in Oakland. The list was much too long, and the thought of paring it down brought tears to her eyes. She wept as she ran, thinking of all that she could not take with her, most of all her husband.

The best in people that she had hoped for just a few minutes earlier manifested itself at Jamal's basketball camp. The counselors had remained in the gym with the children, where they were singing Woody Guthrie's "This Land Is Your Land" when Angela arrived. She found Jamal, who burst into tears as he ran into her arms. Normally Jamal would have been embarrassed to be seen crying, but normal had sunk from view and most of the children were too terrified to worry about appearances. Angela kissed the top of his head.

"Where's Win-J? Where's Sulei?" Jamal asked anxiously, wiping his eyes and gulping for air.

"They'll meet us at home," Angela reassured him. She thanked his counselor for staying with the children.

"Absolutely," the young counselor replied. "We'll get out of here soon enough. No worries."

No worries? Worry did not begin to describe Angela's feelings at that moment. She took Jamal's hand as they wove through the crowded gym and into the chaotic street. Jamal tightened his grip on his mother's hand and his eyes widened with fear as he saw his familiar world crumbling into chaos. They ran.

By the time they reached home, breathless and trembling, the list in Angela's head had overtaken her thoughts. She grabbed a pen and paper and catalogued things furiously. Jamal stood transfixed in front of his computer, watching newsfeeds. He still had his lunch, uneaten, in his backpack, so she sat him at the dining room table and told him to take out his lunch and eat it. "I need you to do something for me, baby," she said, as she closed his computer to lock out the wild images. Jamal didn't protest, but took out his lunch and watched her curiously as she grabbed photo albums off the shelf and slammed them onto the table.

She took the wedding album; albums with photos of the children when they were babies, toddlers, younger than they were now; the album with photos from when she was growing up in Syracuse; and Winston's album of his family from L.A. She left the albums with pictures from her college years, vacations, and old friends on the shelf. She regretted that she had not printed out more of her digital photos. She placed two large manila envelopes at Jamal's elbow. "Take the pictures out of these albums and put them into these envelopes for me. What we can't fit in the envelopes we won't take, so no duplicates. Make good decisions."

"I will, Momma," Jamal assured her.

"Make sure I look good in the ones you choose," Angela added, which elicited a wan smile from her son.

Angela opened the laundry room closet and took down the sleeping bags. She unlocked the bicycles and wheeled them in from the back yard. Bicycles would be valuable and she didn't want them stolen. She opened the kitchen cupboard. While she was taking stock of how much food she had on hand, the front door flew open and Win-J and Sulei swept in. Angela wiped away tears as she clutched first one and then the other of her sons to her. "You're a rock star, Win-J," she told her oldest. "Lock the door. Don't open it for anyone except Vince."

From where she squatted with her arms still clasped around Sulei, she looked up at Win-J and then over at Jamal. She could see that all three boys understood that their lives were about to change completely. "I have a plan," she told them evenly. "I've thought about it carefully. Things will get pretty bad here if all the gas disappears. People living in the cities will have it the worst because of the problem of finding food and water. We need to get out of Oakland. Vince will head home to Rachel and the girls, and I think our best chance is to go with him. It's about a hundred miles. We can walk that. Even if we run out of food, we can walk that. We're all strong, right? Are you down with that?"

"What about Dad?" Jamal blurted, putting into words what they all had on their minds.

"I'll leave a note here for him to tell him where we went. He's strong too, just like his sons. And he loves us very much. If he can make it out," Angela's voice broke as she tried and failed to suppress a sob. "He'll make it out, guys. They're bound to release him under these circumstances," she continued resolutely (not thoroughly believing her own words but saying them anyway to allay her sons' fears). "Then he'll come home and find the note and he'll follow us to Rachel's. He'll find us. I have faith that he will. Can I count on you boys to make a run for it with me?"

She felt a rush of relief as she saw the approval in Win-J's eyes. "That's a good plan, Mom," he said. "But we need backup."

"What do you mean?"

"Safety in numbers," Win-J replied. "We should get a group together to make the walk. We need more men. No disrespect to Vince, but he's only one guy. We need more protection than that. A lot of people will have the same idea as you. All kinds of people will hit the road. Good and bad."

Angela hadn't thought about that aspect of her plan.

"I'm going back out," Win-J informed her, with that new manly determination she had glimpsed earlier when he told her to go get Jamal while he collected Sulei.

"I don't think so, mister. You see what it's like out there," she snapped.

He put a hand on her arm to steady her. "I have to," he said. "I'll be OK. I promise. I'm not going far, just over to Rosie's." Rosie was his girlfriend. "Her dad's a cop and a big guy, six-foot-four, and he knows how to shoot a gun. He actually *has* a gun, Mom. I think they would go with us. Her uncle's also a big guy who's a cop. I gotta talk to them before they make other plans. We need that kind of protection and I bet they need a safe place to go. They're all from around here, their whole family. They probably don't know anyone outside of the Oakland area well enough for them to go live somewhere else."

"Plus you want to take Rosie with you," Angela noted. A hint of a smile crossed his face because he knew she had called him out.

"That too." Win-J's little smile was so loaded with adult wistfulness that it took her breath away. "But equal to our need to enlist reinforcements," he reasserted.

"Can't you just call them?" Angela pleaded, even though she understood that he had to do this in person. If they joined forces, they would agree to have each other's backs, become one family. He shook his head negative and unlocked the door. He vanished in an instant. Angela remembered reading somewhere that having a child was like tearing your heart out of your body and watching it walk around outside of yourself for the rest of your life. She prayed silently for his protection.

Sulei had started crying in big hiccupping sobs and she picked him up and sat him at the table next to Jamal. It scared her to feel how heavy he was; too heavy for her to be lifting him, too heavy for her to pick him up and run with him. Rachel had told her once that many Native families spaced their children four years apart because back in the time when the colonizers were slaughtering the Natives, the Native mothers could only carry one child while on the run, so they didn't have a new baby until the next-oldest child had grown big enough to make a run for it on their own. The spacing of children often persisted, even decades after they had been massacred and herded onto reservations. Rachel frequently saw that four-year spacing at Green Creek. Angela shivered. She went into the kitchen, made a peanut butter and jelly sandwich, and put it in front of Sulei with a glass of apple juice. He sniffled while he ate.

Jamal concentrated with a fierce intensity on the photo project.

Angela's phone rang. She remembered Win-J's caution about conserving the charge on her phone, but it was her brother Kevin so she answered.

"Are you and the boys OK?" Kevin asked anxiously.

"Is anyone? I'm safely at home with Sulei and Jamal right now. Win-J had to go out, but he'll be back soon. Rachel's husband Vince is in town for a conference and he's headed here right now."

"I'm glad Momma and Daddy didn't live to see this," he said bitterly.

"Agreed. It's a circus here. How is it there?" Kevin lived in Brooklyn.

"Pretty crazy here too. I'm leaving tomorrow with some other people. We're going to start walking to this place I know in Connecticut. I have friends there who live on some land. Cousin Ben is going with me. What about you? Can you get the hell out of Dodge?"

"Yeah. I'm going to take the boys to Rachel's in Mendocino. We'll make a run for it with Vince. Win-J is rounding up more people to go with us."

"This whole thing could get real ugly." Kevin's voice grew husky. "Love you Angie."

That set Angela off crying again. "I love you too, Kev. I'll text you as long as my cell charge holds out. You take really good care and we'll see each other again one of these days."

"We sure will. Life is long, Angie, and anything can happen. Let me talk to the boys." Angela put Sulei on the phone. She couldn't bear to listen to what might be her son's last-ever conversation with his beloved uncle so she retreated to her bedroom to ponder what to take with her. Could she take a pillow? It was bulky, but she really wanted to take her own pillow. She opened the closet and stared inside like a person on a diet staring into the refrigerator while trying to decide what to eat that had no calories. Should she take winter clothes in case she was still at Green Creek when the weather turned cold? Jacket? Boots? She started pulling a few things out. Should she put them into a suitcase? A backpack? The framed wedding photo of herself and Winston on her dresser caught her eye and her legs turned to jelly. She sat down hard on the end of the bed.

Sulei appeared in the doorway, holding Big-Dog, his worn stuffed animal and favorite comfort object. "Can I take Big-Dog with me to Rachel's?" he asked anxiously.

Angela pulled herself together. "Of course you can, baby. Let's see what else you want to take." She stood, took Sulei's hand, and returned to the living room, thinking that if Sulei could take Big-Dog then she could take her pillow. "C'mon Jamal," she said. "You can finish that later. Let's have a look at what you want to bring with you to Rachel's. Sulei is taking Big-Dog."

Jamal caught her in the high-beam of his solemn eyes. "I'm almost done with the photos," he informed her, as he rose from the table and followed them into the boys' bedroom.

She instructed them to pack their belongings in their school backpacks because they seemed the easiest to carry. She'd let them take a few of their personal precious objects, but mostly they would need to take clothing. Spare shoes, she thought. And boots, yes they would take boots. She wondered where she would find shoes for them when their feet grew into a new size, but she consciously put that thought aside. If she thought that far into the future, she would become too overwhelmed to make any good decisions. I will not look back, she told herself. I will look forward. She discussed which clothes to take with the boys and asked them to start laying things out on their beds. "I'll be back in a few minutes, I gotta pack some other stuff," she told them, with a sense of purpose that she did not feel.

She would take the first aid kit, cooking pot and deep dish frying pan, sleeping bags, flashlights and all the batteries in the house, canned beans, can opener, rain ponchos, utensils, plates, cups, towels. Swiss army knife. Which books? Definitely not Winston's car diagnostic manual, she thought with a twinge of gallows humor. Langston Hughes's complete poems, yes, absolutely. How could she organize herself to care for her boys in stark survival mode in the space of a few hours? She needed Winston. What would happen to prisoners? Would they release them as she had assured her boys they would? They couldn't possibly leave prisoners locked in their cells. That would be inhumane. Winston will take care of himself and I will put one foot in front of the other and take care of our boys, she commanded herself. Just then, the lock in the front door turned and Vince entered. Angela rushed forward to greet him and, without meaning to, fell into his arms and cried. If Rachel's husband was OK then hers would be too, she thought, even though she knew this did not follow logically. She was relieved to have another adult in the house to help her make decisions.

"It's going to be OK," Vince said soothingly as he stroked her back. "We're all going to be OK."

Angela stepped back and wiped her eyes. "Did you talk to Rachel?"

"Of course. She's good. Just worried about me, and you too. The Tribe will take care of her and the girls. I'm going to have to walk home from here. What fun," he said soberly. "You should come with me."

"I know," Angela agreed. "I figured that out already. Oakland is about to dissolve into lawless chaos. The boys agree completely, and they're prepared to walk. We can do it. Our chance of survival is much greater at Green Creek than here."

"We should leave as soon as possible. A lot of other people will have the same idea and will be on the road. I think it will be safest to head out in the first wave, before people become desperate, before the reality of the situation sinks in." The authority in Vince's voice calmed Angela. "How soon can you be ready to go?"

"Whoa. Rewind a little. Win-J went to Rosie's to enlist her family to come with us. Her dad and her uncle are cops. They're big men with guns. Win-J thinks, and I agree, that we'll be safer if we go in a group and if the group has some muscle."

"Great idea. But they need to be ready to go immediately. Like now," Vince replied urgently.

"I can't be ready to go like now, Vince," Angela responded, expressing more irritation than she would have wished. "I need a little time to think carefully about what to take, and I don't just mean the family lace, although I do want to take a few things to remind me of my whole life up to this point; but I mean that I need to think about what we'll need to survive on the road and in the weeks ahead."

"You don't need that much," Vince argued. "Clothes, food, and a few special mementos. Once we get to Green Creek, we'll have everything you would have. We'll share. The safest thing is to go before panic sets in; before people start flipping out and misbehaving."

"Please don't rush me. I have to pack my entire life into a few backpacks. This is not easy. And I need to think about things that will run out and are important to take to contribute to the community at Green Creek, like batteries, candles, matches, aspirin, needles, pens, thread, soap, cinnamon, flour, and coffee. Oh my God, coffee! I don't think coffee even grows on this continent. When it runs out we may never get it again."

A horrified expression crossed Vince's face. "Absolutely take the coffee. I'll carry it!" They both laughed, which relieved some of the tension.

"Seriously, though, can we go today?"

He was trying her patience. Angela wanted to spend one last night in her own bed, even though she imagined she would probably not sleep. "Negative. Think about it. It will take me a few hours to figure out what to take and to pack it up. Then we should eat dinner. Look at the time. We wouldn't get far enough out of the city to find a reasonable place to sleep before dark."

"Sorry. Yeah. You're right. I can't seem to shake this sense of doom," Vince confessed. "It does make more sense to leave first thing in the morning."

"I think I can be ready at first light."

"OK, first light, then," Vince agreed. "Deal."

"But we have to see what Rosie's family can do," she added.

At that moment, Win-J returned, flushed with excitement and high on the success of his mission to recruit Rosie's family. On behalf of their extended family, Rosie's father, Darren, had accepted Win-J's offer to accompany Angela and the boys to Green Creek without hesitation. They did not want to risk remaining in Oakland, but they didn't know where to go instead, and the family seized the opportunity to escape when it presented itself. Rosie's mom, Tanisha, declared Win-J's invitation a gift from God. Win-J called Darren and put Angela on the phone with him. She asked Darren if his family could be ready to leave at first light and he guaranteed her they would make that deadline.

"Then we'll meet you at your house at sunrise."

Vince called Rachel to give her a heads up that he would be bringing people with him to Green Creek. She was relieved that he would have a group to travel with him. Angela talked to Rachel briefly, but they had too much to say, no time to say it, and both of them started crying when they tried to speak. If all went well, Angela would spend a lot of time with Rachel in the future.

She then called a handful of her closest friends to invite them to join the group. Some of them she couldn't reach, others she managed to reach but they had made other plans. She cherished having a minute to say goodbye to a few people dear to her heart, and she found a couple of friends who wanted to go with her. Her friend Julie was single with no family to speak of, and she leapt at the chance to join a group in which she would feel protected. Angela's co-worker Margaret (who was pregnant) and her husband had decided they needed to take their two very young children out of the city, but they had no idea where to go. They welcomed Angela's invitation and agreed to meet her at Darren's house at dawn.

The rest of her evening evaporated quickly as Angela and her boys prepared for their departure. Just before midnight, after the boys and Vince had gone to bed, when she had everything packed up and organized, Angela sat on the couch. If she didn't draw the line on packing, she feared she would continue to take things out of the bags and substitute other things into the bags all night long. She watched images on the monitor from earlier in the day of people streaming through the streets. She wondered how much longer the journalists would continue to broadcast. She turned the news off and went to bed.

Contrary to her expectation that she would lie awake all night, Angela quickly fell into an exhausted sleep. She dreamed of slow dancing with Winston. She felt his hands running up and down her back and she nestled her lips into his neck. She wore a tight silver dress and she felt his hand slide to her behind, which he squeezed. He undressed her slowly, turning around and around in their dance. Then they were no longer standing but lying on a bed, naked and tangled in one another. She ran her hands over his body, feasting on the feel of his creamy chocolate skin under her touch. He rolled her onto her back and entered her, making slow love. After their mutual release, he held her in his arms. She drifted with Winston, floating on their marriage bed, far from the pragmatic world, just the two of them, entwined, as one.

When Vince woke her before first light, Angela swam up to consciousness smiling softly. It took her a moment to realize that making love to Winston had been a dream. She slowly and reluctantly returned to the alarming state of affairs in which she found herself. She didn't want to leave her bed, but she forced herself to get up and face the day. She decided definitely to take her pillow.

Everything she did brought tears to her eyes; the sense of finality rising in each simple task like foam rising on the crest of a wave. Last morning waking up in her bedroom in the marriage bed she and Winston had shared. Last hot shower in her bathroom with the lemon soap she liked. Last look at the artwork on her walls, so lovingly selected. Last time rousing her beautiful sons from peaceful slumber in their own beds. Last time playing her favorite Coleman Hawkins record, real vinyl, on Winston's turntable. Last bacon and eggs cooked on her stove. Last cup of coffee made in her coffeemaker, just the way she liked it. The accumulation of the volume of goodbyes tumbled down all-at-once, burying her.

She insisted on washing and drying the breakfast dishes and putting them away in the cupboard. Vince called her crazy, rolling his eyes in exasperation, ready to be on their way. But she knew her mother would never have left a dirty kitchen under any circumstances.

Vince helped the boys roll out their bicycles. He had scored a couple of shopping carts on his way back to Angela's house the previous day and Angela had packed her household items in them the night before. She and Vince would push the carts while the boys wheeled their bikes, which they couldn't ride without putting a dangerous distance between themselves and the adults. Even though it never rained in California in the summer, Vince pulled a couple of plastic tarps tight over the top of each of the two shopping carts and tied them down.

Angela wrote a note to Winston that read GONE TO RACHEL'S AT GREEN CREEK. THE BOYS AND I PRAY THAT OUR LOVE WILL LEAD YOU TO US. HOLDING YOU IN MY HEART ALWAYS, ANGELA. At the bottom of the note, in smaller letters, she wrote, IF YOU ARE NOT MY HUSBAND, I BEG YOU TO LEAVE THIS NOTE HERE FOR HIM. HE IS THE FATHER OF MY CHILDREN. She put the note in the middle of her bed along with a photo of herself and Winston with the boys. She hoped the photo would give intruders pause and encourage them to leave the note in place for Winston. She weighted down the note and the photo with a souvenir Raiders football they had acquired when they took the boys to a Raiders game the previous year. If Winston returned home, if he was lucky enough to get that far, and if the note was still here for him, that football would give him a laugh.

Angela knelt on the floor next to her bed, closed her eyes, put her hands together like she had as a little girl, and prayed for Winston's safety and that one day he would return to her. Then she took a final, loving look around her bedroom and closed the door gently on her former life. In the living room, Vince asked her with forced gaiety, "Ready to roll?"

"Let's do it," she replied, setting her mouth in a grim line of determination.

Angela closed the front door behind her and locked it. She stepped onto the sidewalk and gripped the handles of her shopping cart. The moment tasted like dirt in her mouth. Overhead, the underside of a chain of fluffy clouds glowed with the rose-orange light of sunrise that penetrated the indifferent blue of the early morning sky. Angela felt a brief wave of rage at the obliviousness of nature to human misery. The sun would cruelly rise every morning whether humans walked the planet or not. She wished she could float up and walk across that chain of clouds like so many stones in a stream and arrive at a different planet where humans were universally benevolent and caring, and where science and technology had taken humans down a path for survival and progress in which fossil fuel remained a non-participant, absent from existence.

She felt cut adrift. She considered the tenuousness and fragility of life, which was what made life so precious. She thought about when her sons were babies, and about the stockpile of memories she had of good times raising her children so far. She wished she could remember every treasured minute of the past with her boys and with Winston. Her life was sweeping by much too fast; too precious, mysterious, challenging, and miraculous to grasp. To what purpose? It didn't seem to make much sense. All she could do was go through it; enjoying a super delicious cup of coffee, the transcendent slant of orange-golden light at sunset, the embrace, the fragrance, the laugh, the song, or simply the quiet voice of the man she loved. It was all so complicated and yet so simple. Here we are, she thought, people thrown together on this planet. One day there was gas to be had and the next day there was not. She would keep on trying to make her life matter for as long as it lasted.

Collapse: Robin

Robin's lunch crew had just finished loading the dirty dishes into the industrial dishwashers, and Robin was putting together a three-bean salad to marinate for dinner, when Ken appeared. "Come with me," he said grimly.

"Willow's OK, right?" Robin asked in alarm.

"Willow's fine," Ken hastened to reassure her. "It's not Willow, it's the world outside."

"The world outside" was how the residents of Rainbow Farm referred to the chaos, toxicity, and insanity that permeated the lives of those who lived in the outside world, and that the residents of Rainbow had fled from when they originally established their intentional community. The world outside was where people ate processed, genetically altered, chemical substances instead of real food and spent their days in front of largescale monitors and computer screens; it was where nations slaughtered one another over religious dogma or access to oil reserves and where children grew up without ever seeing a forest, the stars in the night sky, a tomato growing on a vine, or a slice of authentic cheese. Robin wondered what the world outside had gotten itself into now. She wiped her hands on her apron, untied it, left it on the countertop, and followed Ken to the community room where people gathered around a screen to watch the online news.

After watching for twenty minutes, with hardly more than a murmur passing among them, people began to converse quietly in small groups. Peter muted the report and commanded everyone's attention. Peter was one of the founders of Rainbow Farm and the current president of the Decision Association, which was the leadership body for the community. "This mess is one of the reasons why we live here, folks. We're prepared. For years, we've expected something like this would happen. That's why we're set up for survival. We're fortunate because we can close our gates and become self-contained in a heartbeat. We have everything we need right here at Rainbow, so let's roll up our sleeves and get to work."

"Ain't it the truth," Peter's wife Kristy called out. "We'll figure out how to handle this in no time flat. We're so much more evolved than those unfortunates stuck in that quagmire in the world outside." Kristy, a fanatical survivalist, was also a founding member, and she had not left the Rainbow property in more than ten years. Being separate, independent, and prepared was her religion. "First off, we have to inventory our stock," she announced.

Robin knew exactly what Kristy meant by their stock, and it wasn't their livestock, their canned food, the wool they had spun, the candles they had made, or the amount of water in their holding tanks. She meant their munitions stored in the armory. Thank goodness Willow and the rest of Rainbow's children were in school and not present to witness exactly how their community went about organizing to survive this crisis. Robin understood the necessity, and had no quarrel with Kristy prioritizing their ability to defend themselves and protect their land; but it made her queasy, and she didn't want Willow to see this aspect of their community.

Peter formed a delegation that he dubbed "the defenders" and sent them to inventory the weapons. Kristy headed up the defenders and strode off with purpose. He charged another group with the task of checking the fence lines and securing the entry gates. They would ride the solar-powered golf carts along the fences to check for weak spots. Most of the perimeter fence was wired so that it could be electrified. Robin wondered what people in the outside world would do if they lost electricity and to what extent their power grid still depended on petroleum. At Rainbow, everything ran on solar and wind. Electricity wasn't her area of expertise. Ken was an electrical engineer and he knew about that stuff. She knew about food, nutrition, and gardens.

"We need to think about food," she called out to Peter.

"Is anyone else hungry?" he asked, which drew laughter. "Seriously, that's a good point," he continued. Robin had a well-established food and gardens team that she could rely on to help her make decisions and get the work done. Peter asked the members of her team to meet with Robin in the dining hall. Rainbow bought only a few things from outside, like coffee, chocolate, and bananas, which they would sorely miss when they hoisted the drawbridge. Robin didn't drink coffee. Ken, on the other hand, would be heartbroken.

As she hurried back to the kitchen, Robin felt oddly elated. They had prepared for this sort of situation during the years they had lived at Rainbow. This event justified the intent of their community. Peter's words rang in her ears. They all believed, somewhere deep down, that this kind of thing could happen. Most of the people in the world outside had chosen to remain oblivious and unprepared; but Robin's people had made a place of safety at Rainbow where they could survive a catastrophe of this magnitude.

Robin and her gardening team were in the midst of a discussion about planting a late summer vegetable crop, when Katie, the community's veterinarian, appeared. "Excuse me, I need to talk to Robin for a minute," she interrupted, anxiously. Katie's skin was weathered from the many hours she spent outdoors. She had a passion for horses and she rode almost every day, rain or shine.

"Come into my office," Robin said, as she steered Katie out of the dining room, through the kitchen, and onto the back porch. It was an old joke. Robin referred to the herb garden behind the kitchen as her office. She sat on the top step of the stairs leading down to the fragrant garden. "What's up?"

"We have a situation with the farm animals," Katie began. "I just talked with the Decision Association about it and we agreed on a plan."

Any issue with the animals would impact their food supply. "What's the problem?" Robin asked, on high alert.

"Everything's fine right now. Like I said, it's a situation. Not a problem." Katie sat down next to Robin so that their shoulders touched.

"You know I'll be seventy in March," Katie began.

"Everyone knows," Robin interjected. "Seventy is the new fifty. What does your age have to do with this?"

"You're sweet." She paused before continuing. "The situation is that I won't live forever and Rainbow doesn't have another veterinarian. As you know, I have a few apprentices with whom I started working last year."

Of course she knew, because one of Katie's apprentices was Willow, who had loved animals since before she could walk. Willow had hung around Katie and helped her with her veterinary work for years. Robin put two and two together and understood. "Willow," she said softly.

"Yes, Willow. Even though she's the youngest of my apprentices, she's the best and most knowledgeable. She has a sixth sense about animals. It's a gift." Robin didn't need the reminder. She knew her daughter's talents.

"She's only seventeen," Robin unnecessarily pointed out since Katie knew Willow's age.

"But if something happens to me, she knows more about caring for the animals than anyone else. Some things we think ahead about at Rainbow and others we have not planned for quite so well. Now we have this crazy drama playing out in the world, we need our animal buddies more than ever to help us sustain our community, and the only veterinarian among us is old and has high blood pressure." Katie gazed off to the horizon, as if she could read a message about her mortality where the clouds met the trees.

"So what exactly are you proposing?"

"I would like to take Willow out of school and have her work with me so I can teach her everything I know. You must realize that Willow would love to do this. Please talk to Ken and let me know if you will agree to it."

"So it has come to this," Robin reflected. "The Rainbow contingency plan for the care of our animals depends on a teenager. On my teenager."

"Well, I hope not. I hope to live for many more years. And there are a few other people who have certain veterinary skills. But Willow will be a good insurance policy. She won't have to go it alone. She'll have the help of the other apprentices. I just think we need to step up our game in light of recent events."

"I'll talk to Ken and Willow this evening. I'm not overjoyed about taking her out of school or putting this on her shoulders, but I see your point."

"She'll continue her education with me. It will simply become more specialized. Believe me, she will have to learn a lot of science a lot faster than she would have learned it in school."

The two women stood.

"Please join us," Robin invited. "We have not yet discussed a plan for our meat and dairy supply. We could be looking at a hundred-and-one ways to cook a rabbit by next summer," Robin quipped, with a note of irony in her voice. Katie chuckled as she nodded in agreement and followed Robin into the kitchen.

By the time Robin left the dining hall and walked home to check in with Ken and Willow, she felt as though she had begun using twenty percent more of her brain capacity. She had a dozen different to-do lists started, and she had assigned several of her kitchen staff the task of systematically inventorying food on hand as well as food coming up in the gardens. When Robin walked in the front door, Willow flew across the room and into her mother's arms. Willow, who towered over her diminutive mother, had to hunch down to bury her face in Robin's shoulder. Willow cried and Ken rubbed her back, soothingly murmuring "hey, hey."

Robin gently lifted Willow's head so she could look into her daughter's eyes. "Daddy and I moved to Rainbow Farm because we wanted to be prepared in case something like this happened. We moved here because we wanted to stay safe, and we are. We're OK here, honey. We'll be just fine," she reassured her daughter.

"What about Grammy?" Willow asked with a sniffle. "She won't be fine, will she?"

"We don't know," Ken said with a sigh. "I'm about to call her and try to convince her to come live with us at Rainbow," he informed them.

"How will she get here?" Robin asked

"We'll talk about that later," Ken said, glancing in Willow's direction.

Robin turned her attention back to her distraught daughter. "I have something to share with you that will cheer you up," Robin told Willow as she led her over to the couch. Willow pulled her long legs up and tucked them behind her. Robin refrained from scolding her for putting her feet on the couch. Instead she filled Willow and Ken in on Katie's plan for Willow to become her successor as Rainbow's veterinarian. Willow would leave high school but high school wouldn't be relevant anymore if things continued to spiral. The need for Willow to assume her role in the community took precedence, and veterinary skills would remain valuable no matter what happened.

The prospect of spending her days caring for animals and working with Katie perked Willow up. Ken suggested she go talk to Katie. In her excitement about this new development, Willow seemed to forget her anxiety. Robin had no doubt the fear would return, but she felt grateful for the momentary distraction that had lifted her daughter's spirits for the time being.

Right after Willow left to find Katie, the phone rang. It was Max. Robin tried to convince Max that she and Theresa should pack up the dogs and head for Rainbow Farm, but Max wouldn't agree to it. The call ended tearfully, with both of them saying how much they loved one another. Max promised to call again if the phones kept working. Robin did not feel optimistic about that. After she hung up with Max, she began shaking uncontrollably and Ken held her in his arms until she managed to calm down.

"I keep thinking of everyone I know, everyone I love, who does not live at Rainbow. I'm losing all of them."

"Me too," Ken sympathized.

"Call Diane and help her figure out a way to get down here," Robin said. Diane was Ken's mother. "Tell her that Willow needs her Grammy badly right now. Tell her she doesn't need to bring anything with her, just Stubby." Stubby was Diane's aging beagle.

"I'll see if I can convince her. I should go get her. I can take the wagon, go on back roads, it's only forty miles. I can be back in a jiffy. I don't want her traveling alone."

The thought of Ken leaving Rainbow frightened her, but she knew he was right. They couldn't let Diane travel alone.

"I know, I know," he reassured her when he saw the look on her face. He put his arms around her again. "I don't relish the thought of going outside. But I need to keep her safe. I'm going to call her now."

"I want to meditate before I go up to the kitchen to get dinner on the table," Robin informed him, with a weary sigh. "Give me fifteen."

"Sure." Ken held her close and she could feel his heart beating against her own chest. "We're gonna be OK."

"Oh we are," Robin agreed. "It's everyone else I'm concerned about."

Collapse: Max

Max had sunk her teeth deep into writing a complex deposition on the afternoon that the systems collapse parked its tank in her yard. She had closed her office door. The comforting fragrance of leather emanating from the book bindings drifted to her from the floor-to-ceiling bookshelves that covered the wall behind her. She gazed out the windows facing a panoramic view of DC. She had worked hard to sit in this office in her favorite city.

When her phone rang, the ringtone alerted her it was Theresa, which was puzzling because during the summer, when she did not teach, Theresa usually swam laps at the health club at that time of day. Max answered warily. It crossed her mind that something might have happened to Roo. "Hola. What's up?"

"Turn on the news," her wife commanded grimly.

"How come you didn't go to the pool?"

"Live stream any top news show. Pick any one. If I tell you what's going on you won't believe me."

Max saved her changes to the deposition and surfed for a link to a news channel.

"The rich and powerful corporate white guys have screwed all of us with a major balls-up, mija," Theresa commented. "They unleashed a science experiment in the Gulf and it ate up that oil spill that happened last week. But it's still hungry. So now it's eating all the petroleum it can find, and they can't figure out how to kick its ass off the planet."

"Wait, what?" Max had a live news stream playing on her computer and it confirmed Theresa's words, but she couldn't wrap her head around it.

"Petroleum, mija. Gas. Oil. All that fossilized prehistoric plant juice we love so much is gonna vanish from the Eastern Seaboard in the time it takes you to make a taco. The rest of the planet soon to follow. Get your sweet self home before the dams bust open and the sky rains hellfire."

"Was that a comment on how long it takes me to make a taco?" Max asked. Theresa laughed.

"I'm gonna lock the dogs inside and go buy all the dog food I can fit in the car. I might even pick up some food for us if I have room for it."

"Gotta love dog food. Hey, buy coffee. I don't think we grow it in this country."

"Listen, Max," Theresa said gently, "I stayed home from the pool because Roo is not doing well. With this mess happening, well, it's inhumane to put an old doxie through an apocalypse, so prepare yourself." Max's stomach lurched. She laughed bitterly.

"What?" Theresa asked, with alarm.

"The human race is teetering on the edge of cataclysmic disaster and to me the tragedy of the moment is losing a geriatric dachshund. Each of us is locked inside our own perspective. Who was it who said 'I create my reality'?"

"That's a little too deep for me, mija. Let's just take things one at a time. Right now, we focus on getting you home safely and stocking up on food," Theresa summarized the plan. Max was viewing a news report on which a map of the country filled the screen. The map illustrated the advance of the petroleum-eating bacteria, which had already consumed the gas and oil in the Southeast region of the country, extending as far north as South Carolina.

"It might take me a while," she warned Theresa. "Traffic will be a holy snarl and, depending on how fast this thing moves, our gas could go. If that happens, I'll walk. Don't dawdle at the store because your gas could disappear while you're inside."

"I don't think it's moving that fast."

Max could see Theresa in her mind's eye, twisting her shiny, black hair around her finger nervously, her head cocked to one side. The image brought a lump to her throat. "In case something unexpected happens, you know you're my life Theresa."

"I love you too, mija. More than I can say in any language." Theresa was crying.

"I'll see you in the time it takes me to make a taco," Max joked. Theresa laughed through her tears. They disconnected.

Max opened the office door and stepped into the hallway. The sense of calm and normalcy in the office surprised her. Then she realized her colleagues probably didn't know. Everyone was working, the news had just broken, they simply didn't know yet. A junior partner emerged from his office across the hall. He looked up from his phone at her in stunned disbelief. Without a word, they proceeded down the hall to Colchester's office, knocked, and entered together. They apprised Colchester (who was the

Colchester in Morgan, Colchester, & Levine LLP) of the situation. Max told Colchester, "Thanks for everything. I've enjoyed working for you and the firm immensely. I hope we're back in the saddle soon, but, if not, stay well." She shook his hand and left. She wondered if she would ever see him again.

Back in her office, she assessed her belongings. What to take? She eyed her bookcase regretfully. She filled a banker's box with a few personal possessions. She picked up a photo of herself and her friends at the reunion, which she had just framed and placed on her desk the previous week. Now it seemed like the reunion had happened a long time ago. With a final scan of her office and a wistful look at the view of the city from her window, she walked out. Perhaps she would return before long. One could hope.

The streets were in turmoil. People ignored the traffic laws, running red lights and barely pausing for stop signs. Fortunately, speeding was out of the question with so much congestion, but tailgating appeared to have been elevated to a national sport. Max saw police officers attempting to enforce the laws, but she didn't think that would last much longer. She figured those loyal officers would quickly rededicate their efforts to protecting and serving their own families and neighborhoods.

A few blocks from the house, Max pulled into the parking lot of a sporting goods store and, with shaking hands, purchased a gun and ammunition for the first time in her life. She had no clue how to operate the firearm. It came with instructions, which she would read later. Just touching the damn thing gave her chills. Brave new world, she thought. She wondered what she was capable of doing to protect Theresa should the need arise. She rounded the corner to her street and sighed with relief when she saw Theresa's car parked in the driveway. She put the gun in the banker's box and replaced the lid. She knew what Theresa would have to say about it and she didn't want to hear it just yet. She gathered her belongings and entered the house. Minnie and Moe bounded to greet her, yipping and shivering with delight. No sign of Roo.

Theresa appeared in the kitchen doorway, wiping her hands on a towel. Max put her things down on the floor. The two women walked wearily into one another's embrace. Theresa patted Max's broad shoulders and then stroked the side of Max's neck with her thumb. "Thank goodness. We're all home."

"But now what?" Max wondered aloud.

"I have more cans of food in the car and we should bring them inside before someone breaks into the car and steals them," Theresa informed her.

"I'll change my clothes and get on it. How's Roo?"

Theresa put a steadying hand on Max's arm. "I stopped at the vet today. Marcy was closing up the office for the time being. She gave me everything we need to end it for the old girl when the time comes. It was kind of her to provide. You get to decide when we do it."

Max nodded sadly and went into the family room to see Roo, who was curled up sweetly in her cozy doggy bed beside the fireplace. Roo lifted her head when she saw Max (or rather smelled her, since Roo's eyesight was long gone). Max stretched out on her stomach on the floor in her good lawyering clothes and rested her chin on her arm, eye-to-eye with Roo. She scratched Roo behind the ears and petted her back while crooning to her softly. Roo cuddled her head against Max's hand and licked Max's fingers.

She could hear Theresa banging around in the garage and remembered the cans of food in the car. She left Roo reluctantly, changed into jeans, and went to help Theresa.

Their garage had not housed a car in such a long time that it had forgotten what a car looked like. Theresa's tangle of possessions spilled off shelves, sprawled across a workbench that ran the length of a wall, and advanced across the floor. Max had no clue what half of the stuff was or what function it served. Theresa used a lot of the tools and materials to maintain the house and yard, including her garden. But much of it was accumulated junk that Theresa would never use. Theresa was a bit of a hoarder. Fortunately, they kept the house fairly tidy, except for Theresa's office, which Max avoided entering because she doubted she could find her way out. Max frequently referred to the garage as a graphic representation of the inside of her wife's brain.

Theresa had cleared a large area of floor space near the door leading to the kitchen, and in that space she had stocked mountains of canned food, including an Everest of both wet and dry dog food. Max was impressed by how much Theresa had accomplished in the time it had taken her to drive home from work. Former work. Max and Theresa finished hauling the food into the garage using a faded and battered radio flyer wagon. ("Does this wagon belong to us?" Max asked. "Sí," Theresa replied with attitude, "I've had it since we lived on McAllister. Don't tell me you don't remember it." Max pretended she did.)

After they finished unloading the car, Theresa made them a Spanish omelet for dinner and they sat in front of the large-screen monitor with their plates on the coffee table to catch the latest news.

"I'm savoring every bite," Max told Theresa, "since the stove will probably quit on us any minute so it could be a long time before I eat one of your super-delicious omelets again." Theresa leaned over and planted an appreciative peck on Max's lips. Her eyes glistened with unshed tears. She loved to cook and she would miss her gas stove when it no longer worked.

Max turned her attention to the screen. Many stations had stopped broadcasting, probably because their staff had abandoned their posts and gone home. Other stations appeared to be set on autopilot and were playing reruns and movies. One mainstream news station was still on, with a red band on the bottom of the screen warning they would discontinue live broadcasting at eight o'clock that evening. They reported that gas and oil in the DC area was beginning to disappear. Images of masses of people walking out of DC and other major cities flashed on the screen. Many of the images had been recorded on personal phones. Max and Theresa had not discussed leaving their home in the suburbs. They would have to think about that.

Max's parents were no longer living and she had no siblings. Theresa's family lived in Puerto Rico and, in any case, they hadn't communicated with her much after she married Max because they didn't approve. Max and Theresa had each other and the dogs. Full stop. When Max thought about who she wanted to call, she thought of Robin. Max wanted to confirm that she was alright. With shaky hands, Max punched in Robin's number. The phone rang quite a few times, and Max was just about to hang up when she heard Robin's breathless voice. "Max? Maxine? Are you OK?"

"It's so good to hear your voice in the midst of all this madness," Maxine burst out. "So far I'm OK, what about you?"

"I'm glad you called. I should have called you earlier. We're digging in for the long haul. You and Theresa should come here before things deteriorate. We'll take care of you like family. The dogs would love it here."

"Things have already deteriorated pretty far. We're going to stay put for now. Too many people are wandering around out there."

"Have you been watching the news?"

"Of course."

"What a disaster," Robin lamented. "I'm not sure how we humans will get out of this."

"How's Willow?"

"Pretty freaked. So am I and everyone else. We feel safe and secure here at Rainbow, but all of us have loved ones elsewhere and we fear for you."

"Hi Robin," Theresa called in the direction of the phone. "Sending lots of love to you guys."

"Tell her I'm sending love back," Robin said, and Max relayed the sentiment.

"It struck me that I don't have any family to call, you know, to see if they're OK. When I thought about who I wanted to call, I thought of you. You're my home girl. In case, well, in case who knows what, I want to say…" Max's voice faltered. "I can't tell you everything I want to say. I can't think how to say it."

Both of them started crying. "We'll see each other again," Robin choked out. "Someone will figure out how to fix this thing before it gets too wild."

"If the phones keep working, I'll call you again soon."

"Take good care of yourself. It could get pretty ugly in the DC area," Robin warned.

"I know it."

"Then think about what I said. Think about making a run for Rainbow."

"We live in a friendly neighborhood," Max reassured her. "People will help each other out."

"I love your optimism. I gotta go. We have a lot to do here to batten down the hatches."

They signed off.

Max took her empty plate to the kitchen, washed it, and placed it in the dish drainer. She filled a glass with water and retrieved the plastic turkey baster from the shelf. She picked Roo up and held her in her lap. Roo had not stirred all evening. Max fed water to Roo using the turkey baster. Roo lapped up a little water and then rested her head on Max's hand. Max was still petting Roo when Theresa tapped her on the shoulder and pointed out, "We should walk Minnie and Moe."

"We can probably take them to the park as usual," Max suggested.

"Do you think it's dangerous out there?" Theresa asked anxiously.

"Could be, depending on whether or not other people from not around here have come into the neighborhood. We'll be cautious." She thought fleetingly of the gun in her banker's box.

Minnie and Moe appeared to have no clue that anything was amiss and they bounded back and forth between Theresa and the front door when they saw her take down their leashes. Theresa snapped them onto the dogs' collars and passed Minnie's leash over to Max. They stepped out onto the porch and Max locked the door behind her.

An eerie quiet permeated the neighborhood. They saw few people as they walked briskly to the park at the end of their street. The proximity to the park had been the deciding factor when they bought the house. A few other dog owners had also stepped out for an evening walk. Max and Theresa knew all of them. They stopped to discuss the crisis and to speculate about what it meant and the implications for their neighborhood and their lives. Theresa talked animatedly with a doctor named Sam, who lived on their street, about organizing a neighborhood meeting and forming a neighborhood association in order to help one another through the days ahead.

While Theresa and Sam conversed, Max scrutinized the perimeter of the park warily. She saw something move at the top of a gentle hill of grass that sloped upward and away from where she and Theresa stood with their neighbor. In among several birch trees she spotted two deer. They stood completely still, ears pricked in guarded attention. They stared straight at Max, acting for all the world as though they thought she could not see them if they did not move.

"Look up there," Max interrupted Theresa and Sam's conversation as she pointed. They turned their gaze up the hill and saw the deer.

"Beautiful," Theresa whispered. Moe sniffed the air and barked, which caused the deer to startle and dart off through the birches.

"I've walked Henry up here for years," Sam commented, "and I've never seen any deer in this park." Max had never seen any deer there before either. The sight of them, wild things, so unexpected and strangely out-of-place, frightened her as if they were a bad sign.

Theresa and Sam made an agreement to go door-to-door in the neighborhood in the morning to enlist people to attend a community meeting to discuss their options and strategies for surviving the crisis by working together and pooling resources.

Max felt relieved when they returned to the house and locked the door behind themselves. Theresa went directly to the kitchen and turned on a burner on the stove to see if they still had gas, which they did. Max found it hard to believe that any minute they wouldn't have gas.

"I'm going to take a hot shower, while I still can," Theresa announced.

"I'll join you," Max piped up with a mischievous smile.

"Ooh, mija, that sounds spicy." Theresa giggled.

The shower was heaven, and one thing led to another. For a brief and luxurious moment they disappeared out of time, forgot about the disaster poised to run amok in the world, and Max and Theresa made love. Theresa cried afterward. Max stroked her hair and her shoulders and held her close. After Theresa drifted off to sleep, Max slipped out of bed, put on her robe, and went to check on Roo. She gently lifted Roo out of her doggie bed and cradled her in her lap. She whispered to her about all the wonderful times they had had in Roo's younger days and thanked her for remaining steadfastly at Max's side through the years. Max wept as she stroked her ears, kissed her age-whitened muzzle, and crooned to her. She cried until the tears came no more. By the time she placed Roo back in her comfy doggie bed and crept back into her own bed, it was past two o'clock.

Theresa stirred next to Max. "Where'd you go?" she asked sleepily.

"I was saying goodbye to Roo. We'll put her down tomorrow."

Theresa put her arm around Max. "She's ready. It's just that we're not. She had a good run. No dog ever enjoyed her life more." Theresa rubbed Max's back.

"I have a confession to make. You should know that I bought a gun." Theresa stiffened. She often quoted statistics that supported the fact that people who owned guns had an astronomically greater chance of getting shot than people who did not own guns. Max felt those stats grossly simplified a complex dynamic and that many factors came into play that skewed that data. But if Theresa quoted the stats now, Max vowed to hold her tongue. Theresa did not.

"I have a confession to make too. I got more euthanasia meds off Marcy than we need for Roo. Much more."

"What do you mean?"

"I mean I have enough meds for all of us, mija. Enough for Roo, Minnie, Moe, me, and you to go quietly into that goodnight if it comes to that."

It didn't come to that for Roo. In the morning they discovered she had gone quietly into that goodnight on her own terms. By the time they finished burying her in the back yard under a dogwood tree, their cars had stopped working, the stove would no longer light, and they had no more hot water.

After burying Roo, Theresa joined Sam and went door-to-door down the block, inviting their neighbors to a community meeting at Sam's house that evening. An irrational panic seized Max after Theresa left the house. She had a gut feeling that the world was unsafe. She reminded herself they needed a plan, and mobilizing the neighborhood seemed like a great place to start. Max went and stood on the front porch so she could watch Theresa and Sam work their way down the street. Her gaze drifted into the distance, where she thought she saw a steady stream of traffic passing by on the cross street. How could that be possible? Cars had ceased to function. Max lived on a quiet side street that branched off a main artery. She could see a great deal of movement on that main artery and decided to investigate. She passed Theresa and Sam, deep in conversation with a cop who lived next door to Sam. She couldn't blame him for staying at home with his family, but if the cops had quit going to work, that left ordinary citizens vulnerable to the lawless.

As she approached the main thoroughfare, she recognized the movement she had seen from her porch as people walking, biking, pushing shopping carts, and pulling wagons loaded with their possessions. She stood at the outlet of her street where it joined the main artery and surveyed the stream of humanity flowing past. A woman and man, each pushing a shopping cart, stopped in front of Max to rearrange the overflowing contents of their carts, which they had pinned down underneath bedspreads tied over the tops. Max tentatively addressed them. "Excuse me, where is everyone going?"

The man laughed. "How should I know?"

Max rephrased the question. "Sorry, where are you going?"

The woman answered, "To our daughter. She lives outside Falls Church in Virginia."

"Why?"

The man answered, "We figure DC will run out of food pretty quick. We're getting out while we can, while we have the energy and a little food with us."

"These other folks are probably thinking the same as us," the woman added.

"Thinking what?" Max asked.

"That our best chance is if we go where people can grow food and hunt, like in the olden days," the man answered.

"We're real lucky," the woman said. "Our daughter has a farm."

"You don't think there will be food around here?" Max asked. She felt a creeping horror as she wondered about the wisdom of sheltering in place.

"Who's going to figure that out? How many congressional representatives does it take to grow a vegetable or shoot a rabbit?" He laughed. "That sounds like a joke, but there's no punchline. Those guys don't know the first thing about that kind of stuff. Who knows if there will even be drinking water, let alone water to grow vegetables."

"I don't see anyone stopping people from doing whatever they damn well please," the woman added.

"You know who are the most helpless, the most useless now?" the man asked, with a note of perverse satisfaction in his voice. "The former leaders. The government. The ones at the top. They don't know how to survive without the hired help to jump when they say jump and without their toys and tools that run on gas. Everything's about to turn upside down. The ones at the bottom who have the street smarts and survival skills will wind up on top and the ones who depend on others to follow orders and do the work for them will sink like lead."

Max didn't argue with him, but it occurred to her that true leaders have leadership skills and could bend the will of others to their wishes in any situation. They would prove more resilient than this smug old man could imagine. The couple moved on. "Good luck," the man called to Max in parting. He saluted her. "I hope you're one of the people with survival skills and not one used to giving orders." The woman waved like the Queen of England with a sideways tilt of her hand.

Max wondered if she and Theresa should walk to Robin's farm in Kentucky after all. She turned away from the stream of people and gazed up at the clear blue sky overhead. Suddenly she thought about winter. What would they do for food and heat when winter came if the situation had not resolved itself? When Theresa returned to the house, Max told her about her conversation with the shopping-cart man and woman, and shared her doubts. "Maybe we should leave."

"I don't think one place will be any safer than another when it comes down to it," Theresa countered. "I would rather die at home in my own bed than go wandering, only to die on the open road among strangers."

Theresa stirred up a chocolate cake mix, baked it in the convection oven, and took it to the community meeting. Sam's living room was packed. Max silently took stock of the skillsets of her neighbors gathered in the room. They had Sam, a doctor, and Jack, a cop; they also had a pharmacist, several engineers (she couldn't remember their fields of expertise), a lot of schoolteachers, and a few business owners. Her own lawyering skills wouldn't count for much now. She thought about the shopping-cart couple and wondered how many people living on her street knew how to grow food. Theresa knew how. Growing food was a mystery to Max.

Jack suggested they start a neighborhood watch group. They set up a schedule for people to patrol the street in shifts. When Jack asked who owned a gun, an awkward silence blanketed the room. Everyone looked around at everyone else hesitantly. Jack reminded them that they were in crisis mode and it was not a good time to refrain from revealing that they had a firearm in their possession. Max raised her hand and was shocked at how many other hands went up. Next Jack asked how many of those who owned a gun had received proper training in how to shoot a gun. Fewer hands went up. Only in America, Max thought. But she couldn't afford to feel superior since she herself had bought a gun without knowing how to use it. Jack announced he would provide firearm training at nine o'clock the following morning in his back yard.

While comforted to be among friends, Max could see that they did not have a viable survival plan for the long-term. But she didn't think they would need one. Some leadership entity, vague in her mind, would find a solution. Some scientists somewhere, also vague, would figure something out. They just had to sit tight for a difficult little time. Nothing would be the same as it was, of course, but a normal, workable life would return. She had to believe that.

Collapse: Melanie

S tory of my life, Melanie thought, as she drove home. The world was unraveling and she was responsible for a classroom of four-year-olds, therefore she could not go home to her own kids because she first had to wait for the parents of the kids in her care to pick them up. Luckily, Ned shook free to collect their children. When she finally handed off the last little one to his mom, it took her forever to navigate the insanely clogged streets in her battered old Toyota.

She had never felt more relieved to pull into the driveway of their rambling house with the leaky roof, sunken porch steps, tricky wiring, and the many other maladies they couldn't afford to fix. As she emerged from the car, she caught a familiar whiff of the nearby cattle feedlot and slaughterhouse. It smelled cat-frighteningly awful, but she had learned to live with it. The proximity of the CAFO (Consolidated Animal Feeding Operation was the technical name for the feedlot) had put the house into their affordability range. She loved that house, despite the stinky neighborhood. The moment she stepped into her comfortable, saggy house, the stench from the feedlot faded, overpowered by the delicious smell of freshly baked chocolate chip cookies. She dropped her canvas bag full of stuff she had grabbed on her way out of the school as well as her enormous handbag on the floor just inside the front door beside a tangle of shoes. She found her family sprawled in front of the large-screen monitor. Well, almost all of them.

"Where's Lisa?" she asked as she surveyed the room and then collapsed into an armchair. Stella immediately ran to her and hopped into her lap. "Jen made cookies," Stella informed her. "Want one?"

"Yeah," Melanie answered. "They smell yummy." Stella went to the platter on the cluttered coffee table and picked up a couple of cookies for Melanie, then returned to sit in her lap.

"Lisa's at Jeremy's," Tracy said. Jeremy was Lisa's boyfriend, who lived a few blocks away.

"They said we might lose our electricity," Jennifer told Melanie, "so I decided I might as well bake that chocolate chip cookie dough in the freezer before the oven cuts off."

"A brilliant idea," Don interjected as he stuffed another cookie into his mouth.

Melanie suddenly felt less anxious. Surrounded by her brood, she thought she could cope with just about anything. She always had. They stared at the news on the screen in continuing astonishment as they decimated the plate of cookies.

"Grammy called," Tracy told her.

"What'd she say?" Melanie asked.

"Family pow-wow at Grammy and Grampy's house at six o'clock tomorrow evening," Don answered. Melanie's parents and her three sisters lived in the immediate vicinity. Between the three of them, her sisters had eleven children (and another one on the way). Counting Melanie's five and her grandson Cody, that added up to a lot of kids. Her parents would get them organized, and the family would help each other weather this storm. Dad was shockingly resourceful and she could depend on him to hatch a plan.

Mention of the family meeting seemed to pull Ned out of his trance of fascination with the images on the screen. "Now that you're home, I want to go to the supermarket," he said. "I'll take Don and Jen with me and we'll take both cars. You stay here with the little ones, OK? Cody's napping."

"What will you get?"

"Everything," Ned replied with a stoic shrug. "A lot of canned food," he added.

"Also candles and matches," Melanie instructed. "And get briquettes so we can use the grill. Get yogurt for the little ones for the calcium. Yogurt should keep in the basement where it's cool. And dried fruit. Soap. Band-Aids. Duct tape. Batteries. Toilet paper. Wait. Let me write a list. Just let me think for a minute."

Ned nodded. "OK, but don't take long. I want to go before the stores empty out."

Melanie disentangled herself from Stella and went into the kitchen where she sat down at the table with a pencil and paper. At first she felt too overwhelmed to write. She took several deep breaths and struggled to clear her mind. Focus on food, she thought, non-perishable food. Food that does not require cooking. Her list got way too long. She rummaged in the utility drawer for a highlighter, and she highlighted the priority items on the list. When Ned and Jen pulled the cars out of the driveway, Melanie felt fear rise in her throat. Please bring them back safely, she prayed. Then her grandson Cody woke up and she gratefully plunged into the distraction of caring for a toddler. The world never comes to a standstill for a two-year-old, she reflected.

 She changed Cody's diaper, fed him a couple cookies with milk, and sent him into the backyard to play with Tracy and Stella. After that she took a moment to call Jo. Thank God she reached her because Jo, alone in a hotel in New York City, had panicked. Melanie talked her down and convinced her to start walking upstate. She told Jo to walk to her in Syracuse. It would probably take her a couple of weeks, but Jo could do it, and she promised to try. They discussed what Jo should do to try to stay safe and they agreed to talk again the following day.

Melanie then went to check on Sylvia, who lived in an apartment on Melanie's street. Sylvia belonged to Melanie's church and she had waged a constant struggle to keep her life together ever since her husband had disappeared a few months earlier. Sylvia suffered from bipolar disorder and she took medication for it. She had three children under the age of five and did not receive enough financial assistance from the government to care for them so Melanie's church stepped in to make sure she could buy food, pay her rent, and keep the electricity on. Since she lived near Melanie, and since Melanie couldn't afford to contribute any money to help out, she made it a point to look in on Sylvia often and to help her with her children. Sylvia had grown up in foster care and had no family of her own. She leaned into the warm love that Melanie beamed toward her like a flower stretching for the sun, turning Melanie into her surrogate mother. Melanie didn't mind assuming this role. Her heart went out to Sylvia and her children. Melanie found the front door to

Sylvia's apartment unlocked and let herself in. Sylvia sat on the couch with the baby asleep next to her while her toddler and four-year-old played with blocks on the floor. She was watching the livestream news on her computer screen in horrified fascination as tears rolled down her cheeks. She turned her bewildered and terrified face to Melanie, who sat down next to her, taking care not to wake the baby.

"Whatever will I do now?" Sylvia asked hoarsely.

"Same as before," Melanie reassured her. "You'll trust in the Lord and rely on the kindness of those who care about you and your little ones. Melanie placed a paper bag on the table beside the couch. "Chocolate chip cookies," she told Sylvia. She sat with her until she quit crying, promised to come back later, and then returned to her own children.

On her way back to the house, Melanie called Jen and told her to add infant formula to Ned's supermarket list. "Tell Dad to get lots and that it's an orange highlight item," she instructed.

Ned, Jen, and Don returned from the store shortly after seven o'clock. In the meantime, Melanie had received a phone call through the church phone tree about a community mobilization meeting that the Neighborhood Association had organized to take place at eight o'clock. The caller assured Melanie there would still be church service on Sunday no matter what.

While the family unloaded the cars, Melanie cooked up a big dinner of spaghetti and meatballs with warm garlic bread and Caesar salad. She sent Lisa over to invite Sylvia, who gratefully accepted. Before eating, they took hands around the table, bowed their heads, and said grace. Melanie and Ned made it a point to say grace before dinner every night, and on this night Ned said a few extra words about entrusting themselves to God's infinite wisdom.

Ned did not linger at the table since he wanted to attend the Neighborhood Association meeting. But Melanie kept the children at the table with ice cream and the last of the chocolate chip cookies, and she went around the table and asked each of them to say something about what they were thinking. The children took the sharing quite seriously, and of course they had a lot of questions. Stella understood that the gas was disappearing and she wanted to know where it was going. Tracy asked if they would get to go back to school. Don wanted to know how much longer they would have electricity. He had looked it up on the internet and learned that one of the primary sources of electricity in their region was gas. Melanie had not known this and tried to hide her alarm. Lisa asked Melanie where their water came from and Melanie said she thought it came from Lake Skaneateles. Don said he would research that on his computer. Jen asked how long Melanie thought the crisis would last. Before Melanie could answer, Don informed his sister, with wide-eyed solemnity, that once the gas had disappeared then it wouldn't come back.

"Don's right," Melanie confirmed, reluctantly. "We'll just have to figure out how to do things differently in the future. It'll be an adventure." She wanted them to stay positive. "The good news for us is that we live in a very special place with a lot of good people and we have resources. In some places, people will start fighting each other and will selfishly look out only for themselves. Here we'll look out for each other so we stand a good chance of solving our problems together. Now let's clear the table and finish putting away our supplies from the store."

It had not escaped Melanie's notice that Sylvia had hardly eaten anything and had remained silent throughout dinner. Melanie took her by the elbow and steered her into the front hallway where they could talk privately. "Hang in there, hon. We're going to get through this. You're not on your own. You're a part of this community and a part of our family."

"I'm so scared. I need some time to think. Maybe the kids could sleep over here tonight?" Sylvia asked hopefully, managing a weak smile as she brushed the tears from her eyes. "Please? To give me a little break so I can get my head straight, you know?"

Melanie didn't really have the energy to look after Sylvia's kids, especially the baby, for the night, but she couldn't ignore Sylvia's fragile state of mind. She knew that her older girls would help out and that Sylvia had no such help, so she agreed to keep Sylvia's kids. Sylvia said she would go home and put together a bag of overnight things for them. "I'll bring that by in a little while. Thanks so much. I don't know what I'd do without you." Sylvia hugged Melanie, clinging to her for an extra-long minute.

Jen and Lisa put up the leftover food, loaded the dishwasher and turned it on, and washed out the big stewpot. Don could not tear himself away from the livestream news. Melanie changed the baby's diaper and enlisted Tracy to help her entertain the little ones with the train set. Just after sunset, Jo called to say she was on her way out of the city on foot and would call again the following night. She sounded in good spirits.

After she talked to Jo, Melanie called her parents. Her dad had some ideas about what the family could do to handle the crisis. Melanie promised him that she and Ned would see him the following evening. "Bring the children," her dad insisted. "Your mother is cooking for the multitudes while her stove still works."

By the time Ned came home at around eleven, Melanie had put the younger children to sleep and joined Jen, Don, and Lisa to watch the news. As more and more news teams had abandoned their posts during the day, fewer and fewer stations had the staff to provide live feeds with real-time information. All the remaining broadcasts pictured people taking to the streets; packing up and leaving their homes or stocking up on supplies to dig in. Eerily, no official government announcements occurred. Don searched the internet and periodically showed the others live feeds of film clips from around the world on his laptop. The bacteria had spread to Cuba and Mexico, and had affected ships in the Gulf as well as the Atlantic Ocean. Many scientists across the globe had remained at work, trying to figure out a solution.

"They could come up with something," Don suggested hopefully. "They have time to invent something that will kill the bacteria before it eats all the oil. Maybe someone in China will solve it."

"Chinese scientists will think of something," Jen said matter-of-factly. "They're smarter than us."

"Everyone is smarter than us," Ned commented. "We're the ones who caused this problem to begin with by dispersing that bacteria. How smart was that?"

"I did some research on it," Don told them. "They didn't have this strain of bacteria perfected yet and they should never have used it."

"Obviously," Jen interjected.

"But the good thing about it," Don continued, "is that it doesn't eat anything made from petroleum-based materials. It only eats the raw stuff. Otherwise it would be eating up so much stuff. Like plastic parts used in about everything, containers used to store stuff, and even nylon thread. Can you imagine people's clothes falling apart because they're made of polyester or sewn with nylon thread? And no one knows how long the bacteria lives. Maybe it will die off when it can't find anything else to eat. The scientists don't know how far it can go underground. It could die off without completely eating up all our gas and oil. Too bad you can't shoot bacteria."

"Thank you, professor," Jen said affectionately.

"What happened at the meeting?" Melanie asked Ned.

"We formed working groups to focus on different areas of concern. Doctor Bennett organized the health professionals in the neighborhood and they're going to have a health clinic at the urgent care center on Ford Street. Bill Thompkins from Public Service was there and he had a lot to say about the water. According to him, Skaneateles is one of the cleanest water sources in the country."

"Way cool," Don interjected.

"They don't even have to filter the stuff, but they do," Ned continued. "They could just put some chlorine in it and it would be safe. I never knew that. We seem good to go with water for the long haul. But we don't know how long it will keep coming from our faucets since they use electricity to pump it and deliver it. We might have to haul it up from the lake by hand. Bill says his guys are working on that problem. It's good to know someone's still at work."

They asked Ned a lot more questions, which he answered as best he could. Melanie thought that the results of the meeting were heartening and that they corroborated her assertion to the kids at the dinner table that they would be OK because they lived in a place where people would help each other.

"I'm determined to stay optimistic," Melanie told Ned that night, as they held each other in the dark in their lumpy, familiar bed.

Her optimism suffered a massive blow the next morning when she went to check up on Sylvia and found her dead.

Sylvia had taken an overdose of her meds, crawled into her bed, and checked out. The note she left for Melanie read SORRY TO PUT THIS ON YOU. I FIGURE THINGS WILL GET PRETTY BAD AND I CAN'T STICK AROUND FOR IT. THEY'RE BETTER OFF WITH YOU. MAKE SURE THEY KNOW HOW MUCH I LOVE THEM. THANKS FOR EVERYTHING. YOU GAVE ME THE CHANCE TO SEE WHAT IT FEELS LIKE TO HAVE A MOM.

By "everything," Sylvia obviously meant adopting her children. Melanie sat down on the edge of the bed and wept.

Collapse: Joanne

J o slept in as usual, waking at one in the afternoon and making coffee in the coffeemaker in her hotel room. She tuned in to the livestream news to keep her company and froze as she watched the stunned reporters try to make sense out of something that didn't make sense. No gas? No transportation? Jo stared at the screen for quite some time before it dawned on her that she didn't know how to get back to Chicago. Short of finding and riding a horse, she had no way to go home.

She tried calling Tim, but he didn't pick up. He had gone to Amsterdam to perform a concert. How would he return to the U.S.? Not via airplane. Maybe he could travel by boat. She had no idea what kind of fuel boats used. What if he never made it back? Ever. She brought a photo of him up on her phone and studied it. Surely she would see him again, right? She thought these things in a strangely detached way. They did not seem real.

Jo had no relatives or close friends in New York, where she had come to perform in concert that night. She only vaguely knew the concert promoters, but she realized that her predicament would mean nothing to them. Not surprisingly, none of her contacts for the gig had called her. They had their own families to consider. She was clearly on her own. She didn't know what to do, where to go, or how to find water, food, and protection. She feared opening the door to her room. When her phone rang she snatched it up greedily, desperate to connect with a person from her life, any person. It was Melanie.

"Thank God I got you," Melanie said with relief. "Where are you?"

"At a hotel near Penn Station in New York," Jo answered, and then she burst into tears. "I don't know what to do. What should I do?"

"OK, OK, take a deep breath," Melanie soothed. "Thank God your phone still works. What's going on there?"

"I don't know. I'm afraid to leave my room," Jo squeaked as she gulped down sobs. "No one answers at the front desk. When I look out the window, I can see the streets below and they're mobbed, Melanie. Everyone is running all over the place. I don't want to go out in that, but I can't stay here. I don't know where to go. I don't have anything to eat. What on earth am I going to do?"

"This is what you're going to do." Melanie took charge. "You're going to dress down in your sweats. You're going to make yourself look as plain and unfamous and nondescript as possible. You're going to leave that hotel and you're going to walk north to Syracuse. You have to find a way to get here. People are leaving the cities in droves on foot. I saw images on Don's computer. They're walking out in groups because, you know, safety in numbers. Find a group heading upstate and join them. Find a group with men, women, and children together. That will be the safest. You come here, Jo," Melanie insisted fiercely. "You come here and live with us until this blows over. We have a strong community and we're going to be OK and you're going to be OK too."

"When I leave this room, what precisely do I do? Give me specific directions. Maybe I shouldn't go out yet."

"You have to go out. The situation will only get worse. You have to get moving right away. Put on your sneakers, the ones you wear on the treadmill. Do you have a backpack?"

"I have the one I use for my laptop."

"Good. Don't take the laptop. Someone might hurt you to steal it. Take anything you have to eat and take water. If there's a bar in the room or alcohol in the mini-fridge then empty the bottles and fill them with water. Take as much water as you can carry. Take something warm to wear, like a sweatshirt or a jacket. Bring extra underwear and socks. The basics, Jo, go for the basics. Take any metal utensils in the room. Any tools."

"I have a Swiss army knife," Jo contributed, hopefully.

"Excellent, honey, that's real good. Take that in your pocket. Listen to me, you're in survival mode now. Think carefully and take the basics. A towel. Spare shoes. Remember that it would be easy for someone to grab your backpack and run. So tie your jacket around your waist and put the Swiss army knife in your pocket. Carry a water bottle in your hand. Go out of the room, use the stairs even if the elevator works. Go down to the street and start walking North."

"How do I know which way is North?"

"By the moss on the trees," Melanie replied with a hysterical giggle. Both of them dissolved into laughter until they cried.

"Oh God," Jo gasped, wiping her eyes. "This is surreal. This is unbelievable."

"Tell me about it," Melanie replied, and for one brief second everything seemed normal again. "When you leave the room, turn your phone off to save the charge. Take the charger with you in your pocket in case you can get electricity again somewhere. But keep the phone off."

"So, seriously, which way is North? I don't have a compass here."

"Your phone has a compass in it. You can look it up on the phone before you turn it off. But, this is what to do, walk up Eighth Avenue toward Upper Manhattan. Then turn left, go to the Hudson River, and follow the river North. As soon as possible, hook up with a group. Just ask people which way they're headed and try to find some folks walking North out of the city. Ask people if they're heading upstate. Don't talk to any men. Just women. If you can't find a group heading to Syracuse, find a group heading toward Albany for now."

"Alright. Best get started." The women fell silent. Jo didn't think she could trust herself to speak. But then, in a choked voice, she said, "I love you Melanie, you and the whole family. Tell Jen thanks for making me godmother. It means everything to me. Hug all the kids for me, especially our precious Cody. You're the best friend ever. You're the best thing in my entire, sorry, celebrity life."

"Get your sorry, celebrity self up here. Call me tomorrow."

"Will do."

"Jo?"

"Yeah?"

"I love you too, girlfriend. Nothing sorry about you at all. You have a gift. Keep singing." Melanie hung up.

Jo did exactly as Melanie had instructed. It hurt her to leave the laptop behind, mainly because it had a lot of music on it. But she agreed with Melanie that taking it would invite trouble. The guitar was another story, though, because she couldn't imagine life without her guitar. When she had packed her things and was ready to leave, she sat down and played one of her favorite songs on her gorgeous and valuable Martin. It broke her heart, but she left the Martin on the bed; even tucked it in under the blankets like a well-fed child. She picked up her old, battered Fender, which she nostalgically hauled around with her everywhere. It didn't have the rich sound of the Martin, but it still sounded good. She had a soft case for it that allowed her to sling it over her shoulder. She put on a floppy hat to protect her face from the sun. She turned her phone off and slid it into her pocket, then took a final look around the hotel room and stepped out into the empty corridor.

The stairwell echoed with her footsteps as she walked down twenty-three flights to the street level. It felt ominous that no one else appeared on the stairs. She should have started out earlier, but she couldn't go back in time and do that. When she reached the sidewalk, people swirled around her, wrapped up in their own concerns, ignoring her. They hurried about carrying suitcases, backpacks, bags, and odd objects; pushing carts or pulling wagons loaded with stuff. A

woman in a purple dress and paisley scarf pushed a shopping
cart full of canned tuna with a cat carrier perched
precariously on top. The cat meowed furiously. People
huddled in groups, talking or gathered together to view
portable electronic devices playing news and pictures or
providing information. She asked a woman for directions to
Eighth Avenue, found it, and began her trek out of the city.
She cut across to the Hudson River as Melanie had
instructed and followed the water.

When she came upon a group of people that included
men (for protection), women (for her personal safety), and
children (whose presence made her feel more comfortable),
she asked where they were headed. At first, each group she
talked to replied that they were leaving the city, but no one
mentioned Syracuse. After a few tries, she latched onto a
friendly group headed upstate. They were three brothers and
their wives and kids. They kindly included her. The children
chatted and called out about what they saw. The brothers
remained silent and grim-faced. The mothers responded to
the children with false cheerfulness. Jo shared chocolate
candy bars she had in her backpack with them. As darkness
fell, Jo and her group turned wearily into a playground
where they could see other travelers settling in for the night
in sleeping bags, wrapped in blankets, or stretched out on the
bare ground with no bedding. They had not walked far
enough to leave the city behind. Jo didn't know where she
was and she wished she had an old-fashioned paper map of
New York State. Where was the AAA when you really
needed them, she thought wryly.

Her traveling companions claimed a section of the playground. The brothers made "sleeping nests" out of blankets for the children, while their wives put together sandwiches of bread, cheese, and lunch meat. They made a sandwich for Jo too. After she ate her sandwich, Jo turned on her phone and called Melanie.

"Where are you?" Melanie demanded.

"I have no idea," Jo answered. "I've walked for miles but I'm still in the city. I'm definitely heading North, though."

"Did you find people to travel with for safety?"

"Sort of. I'm with a family. Three brothers and their wives and kids. We're camping in a playground for the night. There are a lot of other people here. I haven't found anyone heading to Syracuse, but I'll worry about that later. I just want to get out of the city."

"That's good," Melanie affirmed, with a thread of relief in her voice. "We've been watching the news and things are pretty bad in some places. Gangs of young men are roaming in the cities. Stealing and looting. You didn't take your laptop with you, did you?"

"No. I took hardly anything," Jo reassured her. She thought about telling her that she had tucked her Martin into the bed, but then didn't. Too sad.

"I won't rest easy until you get to Syracuse."

"That will take me a minute, girlfriend," Jo reminded her wearily.

"Call me tomorrow evening."

"Will do. I'm wearing my traveling shoes."

"The family sends you love and hugs."

Jo's eyes filled with tears and her voice cracked as she replied, "love to everyone back atcha." Jo sat on the end of a slide and took her guitar out of the soft case. She strummed it a few times and adjusted the tuning. Then she played "You've Got a Friend." The campers fell silent as they listened to Jo's sweet voice carry across the beautiful, clear, summer night that sifted through the playground. Life as they knew it was in the process of unraveling, but it was still the most magnificent thing to sit in a playground and listen to a woman with a spectacular voice play a guitar and sing. Jo tried to make her singing the loveliest it had ever been and the loveliest it would ever be; especially for the family who had so kindly taken her under their wing and shared their food with her. "What do you want to hear?" Jo asked the mother who had made her the sandwich.

"Do you know 'Amazing Grace'?" the woman asked eagerly.

What a cliché, Jo thought, but she launched into the song. The family joined her and other playground campers did as well. When she finished that one, voices called out in the darkness to her with the names of church songs and spirituals. It made sense that these were the tunes that brought comfort in a time of fear and uncertainty. Jo played what the voices requested. She closed her eyes and felt transported back in time to the church of her childhood, where she had first fallen in love with music. She played her guitar and sang with the strangers in the playground for a couple of hours before she lovingly returned the old Fender to its soft case and curled up next to it in the sandbox, wrapped in a thin blanket she had taken from the hotel.

Quite a few people who did not have sleeping bags or proper bedding had elected to sleep in the sand, which was more yielding than the blacktop that covered the rest of the playground.

Jo did not know how long she slept before the intruders awakened her with their racket. A group of young men and teenagers appeared to be stripping the sleep-befuddled playground campers of items the intruders thought valuable and cramming them into bulging duffel bags. Not food or blankets, but watches, phones, laptops, and electronics that, Jo thought, would stop working as soon as the power went out, which it probably would do very soon. She slowly eased her phone out of her pocket and buried it in the sand beneath her.

Four of the hoodlums jumped into the sandbox. They wore baggy pants and baseball caps. Their bright white sneakers gleamed in the light from the nearby streetlamps. The hair on the back of Jo's neck stood up when she noticed that one of the teen boys was waving a gun around. He ordered Jo to stand up and she did as told.

"Check her pockets for her phone," the gunman instructed one of the other boys, who then stepped up and patted Jo down. She noticed in the glow from the streetlamp that his pupils were large and dark, and she wondered what cocktail of drugs he had taken.

He leered at Jo as he stepped back. "This one's kinda cute," he called over his shoulder to his buddies.

"I'm old enough to be your mother and I have AIDS," Jo said quietly.

"You do not," he said with a sharp, false laugh. "But nice try. She's feisty too," he told the others. Then his eyes fell on the guitar case.

"Wow, will ya look at this?" he called out. He bent to pick up the guitar, but Jo stepped in front of it, guarding it fiercely.

"That's not for you," she said between clenched teeth.

The boy with the gun joined his buddy in front of Jo. "You don't get to say what's for me and what's not for me," the boy with the gun informed her. "Nothing has ever been for me. But now it's my time. My family has nothing, princess. We have no guitars. My moms worked cleaning toilets and changing sheets at a lousy hotel for years. She couldn't never afford no guitar for her kids. No food either half the time. Now that the oil tycoons lost their trillions, it's our time. Me and my people will take what's due. We're owed. So don't you tell me what I can and can't have. Hear me?"

"I hear you completely. If you think I'm a privileged princess, then think again. I grew up with nothing, same as you," Jo said in a steely voice. She told the straight truth and she hoped the gunman would hear it in her voice. "When you steal from me, you steal from one of your own. My mom carried bedpans. I worked after school as a waitress to earn enough money to buy this guitar. Do I look like an oil tycoon to you?"

"Oh boo-hoo," said the boy who had patted her down.

"Everything I had is gone. All I have in the world is this guitar. It's all I ever really had." That was the truth. She had forfeited just about every other piece of life that might have mattered to her in order to singularly pursue her musical career.

"You'll get over it," said the boy with the gun. He reached down to pick up Jo's Fender and a wave of overwhelming rage coursed through Jo's body. She kicked the boy with the gun in the face. He fell into a sitting position with a yowl, his nose spouting blood, while the other boy looked on in shocked wonder.

Jo heard the gun go off and felt a hard thud in her chest that knocked her off her feet. She landed on her back in the sand. She gazed up at the stars and the lick of new moon. She was astonished that she had been shot and astonished by the beauty of the sky above her. Both causes of astonishment took her breath away. A song formed in her head. She could hear the notes. It was the best song she had ever composed. She hummed the notes in sweet delight. She couldn't wait to share this beautiful song with other people. It would make them so happy, she thought, as her blood drained into the sand and her voice faded out.

PART THREE: Transition

Transition: Rachel

On the first night of the Systems Collapse, Rachel lay awake for a long time replaying the day in her head, how she had conducted herself, what she had said, and what she had heard. She thought through her conversations with Vince, her parents, and her daughters. She woke at her usual time early the next morning, but she did not feel refreshed. Familiar objects appeared slightly unfamiliar and a bit shiny. It reminded her of her residency, when she had to function on inadequate sleep. Vince called to let her know that he, Angela, and the boys had started walking. She savored the sound of his voice. "Be careful," she begged.

"Extra careful. Give the girls hugs from me and tell them how much I love them. I'll be back in your arms in a few days."

"You have my heart. Bring it home to me."

The Tribe quickly set up a program for the children, housed in the Youth Center. They called it school, even though it was still the summer recess. Rachel appreciated living in a community that valued the care of its children so highly that one of the first things the leaders did was to create a safe and nurturing environment for the children.

After breakfast, she walked the girls over to their new school. Abby and Soph knew all the children there. They had been growing up heaped together at the Rez all their lives. They played with one another, attended celebrations and events together, and participated on basketball teams together. Sophia danced with the Native dancers, even though she was not Native. Not all the children living on the Rez were Native, although most were at least part Native and many were full-blooded. The children seemed to think their new school was more fun than a box of puppies.

After dropping off the girls, Rachel went to the tribal office. She wanted to check in with Chief Firekeeper before opening the clinic for the day. She and Marjorie had always been on a first-name basis, but under the new circumstances, Rachel felt strangely uncomfortable calling the chief by her first name. It was as though Marjorie had transformed overnight and the level of leadership responsibility resting on her shoulders had catapulted her above her previous self. Over the years, Rachel had assumed more and more of a tribal sensibility, and her role as the healer of the community had evolved. She would soon have to step further outside the familiar parameters of practicing scientific medicine and enter even deeper into the spiritual realm of Native culture. It both frightened her and centered her.

She found Chief Firekeeper in the senior center. Christina and the other elders in the new Elders Circle stood in an actual circle with the chief and the other members of the Tribal Council. Rachel waited respectfully just inside the door. Those present had apparently just completed a ritual. Christina held a bundle of smoking sage in her hand, and she was in the process of going around the circle and smudging each of those present. When she finished and returned to her place in the circle, she nodded to the chief, who said, "OH!" The others in the circle repeated "OH!" after her and then dispersed.

Chief Firekeeper approached Rachel and warmly held out her hands to her. Rachel sandwiched them between her own. The chief nodded her head to Rachel slightly and Rachel did the same back. It was as though they were spontaneously inventing new rituals for greeting and meeting; or perhaps reviving old rituals long-abandoned in the flurry of swift-flowing time.

"I thought I'd check in with you before I open the clinic," Rachel explained. "I'll work with my staff to put together a new procedural plan. I anticipate a lot of health issues that will arise that will go beyond the scope of my ability, so we need some contingency plans. Not only do we have people with chronic diseases to manage, but we also have people addicted to drugs they will no longer be able to obtain. Then there are the smokers, who will likely run out of cigarettes."

"It's going to get grisly."

"It will," Rachel concurred. "A big issue will be how to handle the situation with prescription meds. That's an infrastructure issue that should include input from Tom. We have a lot of people dependent on pharmaceuticals that will probably not be available to them much longer." Rachel stopped speaking and swallowed hard, holding back unexpected tears.

"I understand the implications."

"Do you want to give us any guidance before my health services staff and I work out a plan for providing health care?" Rachel asked with stoic resignation.

"Come up with recommendations and bring them before the Spokescouncil and the Elders Circle. We'll go from there," the chief instructed.

"My best idea right now is stepping up education for disease prevention. We'll start classes immediately. The ones who worry me the most are our diabetics. I think I can keep some of them going without insulin if they dramatically change their habits. But we're going to lose some of these people, Chief. Our insulin-dependent diabetics have no more than a three-month supply of insulin on hand. Some have much less."

"You can depend on Terry to teach nutrition classes," Chief Firekeeper pointed out. Terry was a nutritionist who ran the Tribe's farm-to-table program.

Rachel took a deep breath and plunged forward. "The community needs to understand that my skills are limited. People need to know that. For one thing, we don't have any anesthesia, and even if we did, I'm not a surgeon. We are reverting to barefoot medicine now. I can't perform miracles. This must be made clear to everyone," Rachel insisted anxiously.

"I hear you," the chief said, and Rachel felt that she really did and would help Rachel get her message about her limitations across. "Christina knows all about healing herbs, and she's not the only one of our elders who knows. They can help."

"I'm worried about Christina. She's one of the diabetics, and she's been despondent lately and apathetic about her health."

"It hurt her when Crystal lost that baby and then disappeared," Chief Firekeeper replied. Crystal was Christina's sixteen-year-old granddaughter. She had gotten pregnant and then miscarried. After that she ran away.

"That's true. I thought it was the diabetes diagnosis that got her down, but the whole thing with Crystal probably has more to do with it than the diabetes. Some people thought it was a good thing Crystal lost that baby, her being so young."

"Losing a baby is not a good thing. Christina took it hard, and then took it harder when Crystal left. But this new situation has lit a fire under Christina. I can practically feel the energy coming off her skin."

"She must feel useful again," Rachel speculated.

"Useful?" The chief snorted. "She's indispensable. Make sure she manages that diabetes because we can't afford to lose her."

"I'll do my best; and I'll have a conversation with her about herbal medicinals."

"Do that. The gardening committee is revising the planting schedule. We need to put more medicinal herbs into the ground to stock up for winter. It's already late in the season. I have a crew out plowing additional gardening space as we speak, so we can plant more crops." The chief put a steadying hand on Rachel's arm. "The new time has begun. I'm calling it the Vision Time."

"An apt name. Chief, did you sleep last night?"

"A couple of hours," the chief said as she ran a hand over the top of her head wearily.

Rachel reached into her pocket and took out a bottle of Immune Booster, an herbal supplement she recommended to ward off illness, and put it into the chief's hand. "Don't exhaust yourself," she cautioned. "Stress is the number one cause of disease, you know."

"I'll keep that in mind. Thanks."

Rachel met with the clinic staff and the nutritionist, ate a hurried lunch, and saw a few patients with urgent health issues in the afternoon. At four o'clock, Tom came by to inform her that the Tribal Council requested her presence at a meeting that evening. He said the Youth Center would remain open during the meeting, so she could leave her girls there with other children of attendees. This news made her unhappy, even though she had prepared herself for the fact that her role as the community doctor would encroach further on her personal life in the days ahead. She wished it would not start to happen until Vince returned. She was tired and had not seen her children all day.

She left the clinic and collected the girls to spend time with them before the meeting. The resilience of children never ceased to amaze Rachel. Her girls chattered excitedly about their new school at the Youth Center, and what fun they would have with their friends there. They seemed to thrive on the change. They had spent most of the day learning how to make candles from beeswax and melted crayons, and they thought candle-making much more fun than solving math problems.

Rachel made a simple dinner. She called Vince, but his phone went into voicemail and she didn't leave a message. She tried Angela's phone and it, too, went to voicemail. She sent each of them a brief text. What if their phones had been lost or stolen? She left her phone on throughout dinner, hoping for word from Vince. Before leaving, she reluctantly turned her phone off, put it in the drawer of her nightstand, and walked away from it. To think that just the week before, she had trouble sleeping one night because she couldn't decide whether or not to try setting aside more retirement money. She wished that instead of saving for retirement she had spent that money on shoes, dinner at fancy restaurants, buying flowers, and tropical vacations. She regretted paying into a life insurance policy. The concept of life insurance seemed ridiculous now. She should have bought the girls their own horses. It occurred to her that if they had bought an electric car then Vince could drive home from Oakland instead of walking.

When Rachel arrived at the meeting, she studied the parade of flip chart paper taped to the walls. She circled the room slowly, reading the walls. The Green Creek community had been divided into familial groups and an elaborate charting of these groups documented the skills of various groups and individuals. It looked like the Spokescouncil had spent the day inventorying and mapping the human resources at Green Creek. She saw a mind-boggling array of skills and talents listed, including knowing how to make paper, soap, baskets, water barrels, music, and having training/experience in child development, engineering (of all types), gardening, weaving, herbal healing, water purification, hunting, and so-on. Community leaders were taking stock in preparation for reinventing the Green Creek society from the ground up. It comforted Rachel to read the vast array of skillsets and knowledge that they had among them.

For the evening meeting, Chief Firekeeper had assembled the Tribal Council, the Elders Circle, the Spokescouncil, and the heads of department for all the infrastructure components of community life. Tom sat next to Rachel as the chief called the meeting to order. The vice-chairperson of the Tribal Council (technically, Marjorie Firekeeper's title was chairperson, but everyone called her the chief) offered gratitude to the Creator, an appreciation of the ancestors, and a few words about the strength and resilience of the Tribe. He then nodded to the chief.

"The Elders Circle and I have put forth a proposal and the Tribal Council supports it," the chief informed those present. "If adopted, the proposal will impact the survival of each person living at Green Creek. Although the Tribal Council urges the adoption of this proposal in the form of an official Tribal Resolution, we will only adopt it as policy if we receive consensus in the community. I will explain the proposal in a minute. Beginning this evening, we will put this up for discussion for three days. We would like Spokescouncil representatives to share this with your constituent groups in order to bring a response to the Tribal Council in three days." The chief gestured to Christina and invited her to speak. "Christina will describe the proposal."

Christina outlined the discussion that had taken place at the Elders Circle earlier that day. The chief and the elders had considered historical events and concluded that they didn't wish to repeat mistakes. While Native people had been decimated by violence in America, they had also sunk to the level of those who sought to destroy them by engaging in similar violence. The elders proposed that the Green

Creek community make a commitment not to use violence to defend themselves, come what may. Anticipating that eventually intruders might attempt to infiltrate the community, abscond with food, perhaps attempt to enslave or oppress, take control, the elders preferred to die than live under those circumstances or in a situation where the Green Creek people spiritually poisoned themselves by retaliating by murdering the infiltrators. Rachel felt the hair on the back of her neck stand up. Not defend themselves? Die rather than submit or engage in violence? The silence in the room amplified Christina's voice so that it rang out like the song of a bird rising from the depths of a forest.

Instead of matching violence with violence, the elders proposed to invite any intruders to join the community. They would offer to share the community's water, food, and other resources. They would seek to absorb any who came to them into the Green Creek culture, but those who came would have to agree to work and contribute. They would have adequate representation in decision-making, but would also have to participate in the preservation and advancement of the community. To this aim, Christina continued, all firearms in the community would be gathered and placed under lock and key. Tom would keep the key. Weapons would be used only for hunting or the occasional need to put down an animal. Any newcomers who joined the community would be required to relinquish their weapons and abide by the Green Creek governance structure and justice system.

Tom raised his hand and Christina acknowledged him. "What if intruders refuse to agree to these terms?" he asked.

"In that instance," Christina answered firmly, "then they will likely come out shooting and I, for one, do not wish to live in a community dominated by force, built on violence, either theirs or ours. I will not live in fear. I would rather forfeit."

"By forfeit, do you mean die?" Tom interpreted incredulously.

"Yes."

"That's not viable," Tom said quietly. "Forfeit makes it sound like a game. This is not a game."

"Think about it, people. Think it through over the next few days before you answer," Christina exhorted them. "Think through the different potential scenarios. We know all too well what life is like in a culture dominated by violence. We have experienced that for thousands of years, and witness how it has damaged us. There is a better path, and we, the elders, hope our people will burn brightly with wisdom and choose that path. I wish to see my people rise from the ashes and seize this opportunity to reclaim the fundamental values of our culture."

The elders were old, Rachel thought. They would die soon. What about the young people? The children? What about her daughters? How could she agree to allow the possibility that her daughters might lose their lives to support the principle of nonviolence? At the reunion, Angela had asked her if there was something she would lay down her life to preserve, and the only thing she could think of was her girls. Nothing else mattered. Or did it? A way of life mattered. The way they lived, not just that they lived. It was not enough for her daughters to merely survive. She wanted them to love their lives, to have meaningful lives, quality lives. She did not want them to live in fear or to witness violence. Was death a better choice than living a fearful, meaningless life? She would think hard about these questions for the next few days as she decided whether or not to agree to this proposal.

Transition: Angela

They set off for Rosie's house with the boys wheeling their bikes while Angela and Vince each commandeered a shopping cart. Angela felt vulnerable pushing her most precious possessions in a flimsy cart. So this is homelessness, she thought. Few people were on the streets so early. Sulei had propped Big-Dog up in his bicycle basket. Angela wished he would put the stuffed animal into a backpack for safekeeping, but it seemed to give Sulei courage to keep Big-Dog in plain sight. They hurried the few blocks to Rosie's house, where her extended family waited, prepared for departure. Darren greeted them in his jolly, booming voice with the words, "We're all one family from here on out." He provided introductions to his parents, his uncle and aunts, his brother and sister and their families, cousins, a few friends (a couple of them from the police force). Angela could not remember all the names and estimated at least sixty people in Darren's group. She felt grateful for Win-J's insight and brilliant suggestion to enlist

Rosie's family to travel with them. The protection afforded by belonging to this large group made her feel less exposed, less like prey.

Angela's friends Julie and Margaret (and Margaret's husband and children) arrived. Julie had a chocolate Labrador that thoroughly sniffed as many people as possible and elicited more than a few smiles with his candid exuberance. She asked Rosie's older brother to push Sulei's bike, knowing her son wouldn't manage to walk far pushing a bike. Rosie's brother took the bike without complaint and Sulei removed Big-Dog from the basket, hugging him close.

She wondered how much ground they could cover before they would have to pause to rest. Angela observed that some of Rosie's family members were overweight and out-of-shape. She wished she had a stroller for Sulei. Although he would have resisted sitting in a stroller, she knew he would have eventually succumbed when he had walked far enough. But she didn't own a stroller. They hoped to make it to the Richmond-San Rafael Bridge, about fifteen miles, by that evening. With the old folks and the children, and all of them unaccustomed to walking over such distances, plus stopping to eat, she and Vince had calculated that they could make it to the bridge in about twelve hours. At that rate, the whole journey would take about a week. If it took longer, they would run out of food. She hoped they could pick up their pace as they became used to walking.

As they set out, walking East to Highway 580, Rosie's mother Tanisha fell into step beside Angela. "We agreed that we needed to leave the city, but we didn't know where to go," Tanisha told her. "Our lives are completely here; our family and our friends, we all live here. Of course we know people outside the Bay Area, but not well enough to appear on their doorstep. Not well enough to ask if we can sleep in their house or join their community. When all is said and done, we'll look back on this day and say that you saved our lives. And I thank you for it."

"It was Win-J and Rosie," Angela reminded her. "They didn't want to be separated."

"True that. I thought it was just puppy-love between those two, but now I'm beginning to rethink."

Angela glanced to the back of the group, where Vince brought up the rear, pushing one of Angela's loaded shopping carts. Darren had fallen in beside Vince to query him about the Green Creek Pomo and what to expect when they arrived. Vince enthusiastically described life on the Rez. Angela heard Vince exclaim, "You've never had an Indian taco? You're in for a treat." Vince would make Green Creek sound like paradise to the refugees, which was probably a good thing. It would keep everyone motivated over the long journey. However, Angela knew better. In truth, life was about to become exponentially more difficult for everyone, even if they made it to the Green Creek Pomo Rez alive.

She wondered how a Native community would feel about Vince, a white man, not a member of the Tribe, bringing a group of more than sixty African American folks from the inner city to live with them. Rachel was the Tribe's doctor, and knew the leadership, so hopefully that would ease the situation. The Green Creek community trusted Rachel. Go figure how a Jewish woman from Syracuse became the healer for a Native community in California. Life was strange and getting stranger.

They planned to walk on Highway 580, across the Richmond-San Rafael Bridge, and then straight up Highway 101; so they threaded their way through the streets to the highway onramp. Angela had expected to see the highway crowded with refugees, and she and Vince had hoped they could depend on the sense of camaraderie with others fleeing the city to contribute to their safety. But not many people had hit the road for an early start. The sun had barely made its appearance on the horizon when they arrived at the highway onramp, which was eerily empty. It felt peculiar to walk up the ramp and onto the overpass, where she had driven her van so often in the past.

On the overpass, Win-J and Rosie dropped behind the rest of the group as they paused to adjust the straps on Rosie's backpack. Vince helped them. Suddenly, like a swoop of geese appearing in a flap of wings, a group of twenty or more young men swept swiftly up the onramp. Some rode bicycles and others ran. As the young men came alongside Angela's group, one of them reached over and wrested the handlebars of Jamal's bicycle away from him effortlessly, hopped on, and pedaled for all he was worth. Jamal howled in anger. Meanwhile, behind Angela, another assailant grabbed for Win-J's bike. She saw Win-J shove the man and Angela screamed, "Win-J, step down!" His life was more valuable than a bicycle. But the man had already overpowered Angela's boy and taken possession of the bike. She ran toward the isolated group that had dropped behind and been accosted by the thief.

Vince reached for the bike and then everything tumbled into slow-motion. Angela ran as if in a dream, as if she was running in sand and could barely make any progress. The bike thief punched Vince hard in the chest, and a gunshot rang out. Simultaneously, the bike thief crumpled onto the pavement while the blow to Vince's chest knocked him backward and over the guard rail. Vince plummeted to the pavement below while Angela gaped in confused horror. Had Vince been shot? Why had the bike thief fallen on the ground? The young men who had made off with Jamal's bike disappeared in the distance while one of their number remained behind unmoving. Darren materialized at Angela's side with his gun drawn. Someone was screaming in pain. Was it Vince? The bike thief? Was it a dog howling?

Everything came back into focus as Angela looked down from the overpass and saw Vince's lifeless body below. He wore a startled expression on his face as he stared vacantly at the new-morning sky. A pool of blood slowly fanned out from Vince's head in a red halo. "No, no, no," Angela moaned as she hugged herself and rocked back and forth. "Oh Rachel, Rachel, what will you do?" Even as she said these words, she could not refrain from feeling relieved that the body on the ground below was Vince and not Win-J. Her son had been spared. How close they had come, and her son had been spared.

The screaming continued.

Tanisha put her arms around Angela and held her tight, as if to prevent her from coming unraveled. "Your son needs you." Tanisha spoke softly in Angela's ear. The screaming was coming from Win-J. Rosie could not get near him because he was flinging his arms around in a crazy frenzy like a maimed animal. "Take a deep breath," Tanisha said, "and tend to your son."

Angela straightened her spine and, with an outward calm she did not feel inside, she went to Win-J. "Winston Junior," she said to the distraught teenager. "Look at me Winston." She firmly took his face in her hands as he whimpered and dropped his wild arms to his sides. "Winston Junior, you have tremendous strength in you. Bring it."

Win-J collapsed against Angela and wept, his shoulders heaving against her arms. She held him tight until she could feel him begin to uncoil, and then she said firmly, "I have to see to your brothers. Let Rosie comfort you. Don't push her away." He acquiesced when she passed him off to his girlfriend, who put her arms around him. They leaned into one another, weeping.

Angela returned to the rest of the group, hooked an arm around Jamal, and took him with her as she went to Sulei, whom she lifted off his feet and held against her in a tight embrace. While Angela comforted her stricken boys, Darren and several men walked back down the ramp and over to where Vince lay on the roadway below. They checked for a pulse and confirmed that he was dead. With Sulei in her arms, Angela watched them from above on the overpass as Darren closed Vince's eyes, shuttering that startled gaze. Darren went through Vince's pockets and removed his wallet and phone.

As Angela grieved for Vince and bore the weight of the unspeakable loss Rachel would soon suffer, she also grieved for herself and the loss of her own husband. Witnessing

Vince's death snapped something inside her. Vince's death became a surrogate experience for the death of her own husband. She remembered her lovely dream of the night before and hoped Winston would come to her again in her dreams, because she didn't expect him to ever hold her again in real life. Given his situation, in prison, it didn't seem likely. The hard shove that widowed Rachel, widowed her as well. All that mattered now was bringing her sons to a safe place. She would fight to the death for their safety, and the fierce mother-love that would protect her sons would avenge Vince and would be her gift to Winston as his ambassador on Earth.

Rachel and her daughters were waiting for Vince to return home. If Angela made it to Green Creek, she would bring them this devastating news. The weight of it nearly knocked her to her knees. "I don't want this kind of life," she said to Tanisha.

"It's what we've been given, honey. The only way forward is through. No going around," Tanisha replied softly.

Darren checked the bike thief's neck for a pulse and found none. He had shot the thief through the heart. He picked up Win-J's bike, and attempted to hand the bike to Win-J, who refused it with a look of horror. "I don't want it," Win-J blurted. "Leave it."

As Darren wheeled the ill-fated bike to one of his nephews and passed it off without a word, Win-J called after him angrily, "I said leave it!"

Darren did not chastise Win-J for being disrespectful to an elder. Instead he told Win-J, "You never have to touch it again, son, but it's valuable and we'll keep it."

Darren gave Vince's wallet and phone to Angela. She pocketed them reverently, as if they had human qualities. "Shouldn't we take him with us?" Angela asked Darren. "I mean, the body. We should take the body with us to bury it at Green Creek."

Darren glanced at Tanisha, silently soliciting her aid. She stepped closer to the two and placed a comforting hand on Angela's arm. "We can't carry a dead body with us."

"Then we should bury him," Angela insisted stubbornly. "If we can't take him, we should bury him here. How can I tell Rachel we left him out like that?"

For a long moment, no one said anything. Many of the adults in their party had formed a semicircle around Angela and the others as they discussed Vince's body. Darren's mother Josie spoke softly to Angela. "Consider the time we will lose today if we stop to bury Vince. Although it seems wrong to leave him, we have children here to think about. We should get them out of Oakland as quickly as possible. I think Vince would want us to keep moving, to take our children to safety without delay."

Angela thought about the resolution she had just made to protect her sons. Josie was right, of course; but she could not bring herself to step away from Vince, to leave him sprawled below as if his life meant nothing, as if he was unloved.

"He's not in that body anymore, Momma," Sulei said, as he patted her cheek. "He's a spirit now. He can float along with us." Angela hugged her beautiful son close to her as tears ran down her cheeks. She turned her feet reluctantly back to the road. Tanisha walked beside her. Win-J took possession of the shopping cart that Vince had been pushing.

What little gaiety the group had mustered to brighten the launch of their journey had evaporated. They resumed walking in silence punctuated only by the occasional sobbing of some of the women and children. They walked for nearly an hour with no one speaking. Then Rosie started singing a spiritual, a church song, in a high, clear voice, and others joined in. When that one ended, they sang another. And then another. They sang as they walked toward Vince's home, which he would never see again.

Many more refugees appeared on the road as the day progressed. When the sun stood high in the sky, Tanisha brought their caravan to a halt. The old folks needed to rest. Darren's mother, Josie, who was overweight, had fallen far behind. So had several other older members of the family. Darren's brother Michael had remained behind with their mother and the other stragglers. Michael was pulling a wagon in which they had put an elderly uncle who had diabetes and was grossly out of shape from spending his days sitting on the couch watching his shows or playing games. When Angela looked back down the highway, she couldn't even see them anymore in the distance. Tanisha steered the group off the road and they assembled in the shade of a large oak. As Tanisha, Angela, and the other moms distributed sandwiches, fruit, and drinks to the children, Darren's brother Michael rode up on Win-J's ill-fated bicycle. "Momma, and the others are not far back," Michael informed them. "They should catch up in about twenty minutes."

"Go on back and let them know we'll wait up," Tanisha said.

Sulei ate his sandwich wearily and then fell asleep in Angela's lap as the group waited for the rearguard. When they arrived, the slow-moving old folks dropped heavily to the ground, exhausted. Tanisha brought out food and drinks for them. While they ate, they talked quietly with Tanisha, Darren, and some of the other relatives. Angela kept her distance to afford the family their privacy. She noticed with relief that Win-J and Rosie were deep in conversation where they sat, slightly apart from the others. She hoped Win-J would talk his way through the trauma of the bike incident with Rosie.

Sulei slept. Jamal asked Angela what she thought happened to people after they died and she encouraged a conversation in which Jamal could voice his feelings about Vince's murder. Her heart ached with the loss and she was sad that her sons had to cope with assimilating the violence they had witnessed into their young lives. Jamal had a lot to say and she listened carefully. She was a trained therapist and she asked questions that would guide her son to healing. It reminded her that she possessed a useful skill that applied even in this new reality. Eventually, Angela put an arresting hand on Jamal's arm and turned her gaze to Rosie's family. They seemed to be winding down from a heated discussion. Several of the women were crying. Angela didn't want to disturb Sulei by standing up. "Jamal," she instructed, "please find out what's going on and come tell me."

Angela's friend Julie came over and sat down. Julie's dog rested his head on Julie's leg and she petted his ears.

Jamal went to his brother, said something, and then Jamal, Win-J, and Rosie walked over to the adults. Rosie had a conversation with her mother and a look of shock passed across her face. She hugged her grandmother and cried. Win-J and Jamal left Rosie and came to talk to Angela. Rosie's grandmother and some of the other elders and weaker family members insisted that they be left behind to follow the others at their own pace. They argued that it was important to take the children to safety and that the elders would hold the entire group back. A couple of them weren't even sure they could make the trip and they didn't want the children to witness the result if they had to give up by the side of the road, unable to continue. Michael insisted he would travel with the old folks. After Vince's death, everyone felt acutely the danger of their situation and the extent of their vulnerability to the whims of fate. Tanisha had prevailed upon her sister-in-law to stay with the main group in order to see her children to safety, but the woman was nearly hysterical at the prospect of being separated from her husband Michael.

Darren and Michael approached Angela. "We need precise directions to Green Creek for our elders, who have decided to travel behind at a slower pace," Darren told her. "And everyone in our group needs to know how to get there in case we're separated. Would you please explain to everyone how to find Green Creek?"

"Of course." Angela gently transferred the sleeping Sulei to Julie and followed Darren and Michael back to the larger group. The others gathered around to hear.

"Green Creek is off the beaten path but easy to find if you know what you're looking for," Angela reassured them. She explained exactly where they would turn off Highway 101 in Mendocino County and how far they would need to go to reach the tribal lands. She described the landmarks, what road signs they would see, and about how many miles they could expect to cover for each segment of the journey. "The tribal leader is Chief Marjorie Firekeeper and my friend Rachel is the community's doctor. Remember those names," she concluded.

After confirming that everyone in the group had memorized the directions to Green Creek, they prepared to resume their exodus. A tearful parting of the two factions of Darren's family followed. The elders remained huddled under the tree while the rest of the group reluctantly took to the road. They had covered less ground than expected and the lunch stop had taken much longer than Vince had originally calculated. When they resumed walking, people talked in small groups, and before long Rosie started to sing another song. Others joined in. Sulei clutched Big Dog to his chest and smiled tentatively. Angela felt grateful for that tentative smile.

She took out her phone, turned it on, and checked for messages. She had quite a few from friends and family. She had a missed call and a text message from Rachel. She hurriedly turned the phone off. She couldn't imagine communicating with Rachel until she saw her in person at

Green Creek. Her eyes welled with tears. Sulei looked up at her and she wished she could hide her emotions. The tentative smile had left his face. She sang and walked.

Their pace slowed with fatigue as evening approached. The children were subdued. Angela's knees ached. On the Richmond Bridge, Win-J picked Sulei up and carried him piggyback. Rosie carried Big Dog. After a short distance, Darren came up behind Win-J and said, "Give him here, son." Win-J did not argue as he wearily handed Sulei over. The highway had filled with many more people during the course of the day, and the bridge was loaded with foot traffic. Angela admired the beauty of the pink and golden sunset over the bay. She would miss living in the Bay Area. She breathed in a deep gulp of the delicious ocean air, fresh and moist, and wondered how much time would pass before she saw the ocean again.

Darren led their group down the ramp at the Sir Francis Drake exit. Angela couldn't remember ever taking that exit. They sat on a grassy hillside to eat and then bedded down for the night beneath a stand of fir trees. Angela's boys were lucky to have sleeping bags. Not all the children had such a nice outdoor bed. Win-J opened his sleeping bag up double and laid down on top of it with Rosie. Darren and Tanisha didn't protest so Angela said nothing either; but she resolved to have a talk with Tanisha about discussing birth control with their children. She would have to keep an eye on them. Too many things required her vigilance. Exhausted from the long day of walking and the emotional toll of Vince's murder, she fell quickly into sleep. She woke several times during the night. Once when she woke, she heard Darren and Tanisha murmuring softly in conversation. Even though she had slept poorly, she woke as the first pale brush of daylight glimmered on the horizon. Already she could hear people moving on the highway nearby.

She turned her phone on, ignored the missed calls and texts from Rachel, and tried calling her brother. He didn't answer. She turned the phone back off. Every time she saw those texts from Rachel, she wanted to put her head in her hands and weep. She decided to leave the phone off until she arrived at Green Creek where she could wrap Rachel in her arms when she told her. It occurred to her that if something happened to her and the others, and they never made it to Green Creek, then Rachel would never know. But Angela had to take that chance because she couldn't possibly inform Rachel of his death in a phone call. Maybe it would be better if Rachel never knew and kept hoping Vince would return.

All of them were astonished to discover how sore they were from the previous day of walking. There had been a fair amount of uphill and downhill; but it had not seemed daunting at the time. Except for a few among them who worked out at the gym regularly, the travelers were stiff and achy. Even the children had overdone it. Angela couldn't believe that her resilient, athletic sons complained of soreness in their legs. Win-J could barely walk, which particularly surprised her given that he was in the best physical shape of her three sons. Then she remembered her training in treating people who had suffered trauma and it made sense. He had manifested the trauma in his body. The group would need to stop to rest more often than they had the previous day, which made her anxious.

Before they set out, a few people walked to a nearby gas station with a shopping cart full of everyone's water bottles and refilled them from a spigot. The water tasted metallic, but it was wet and that was all that mattered. For breakfast they ate the most perishable food items: hardboiled eggs, milk with cold cereal for the children (served in paper cups), lunch meat, grapes, bread with butter. Angela had saved a little coffee in the bottom of her travel mug and she nursed it with care. She had her boys brush their teeth, using their water sparingly. She wondered if they would have to make do without toothbrushes in the future.

The women took stock of their food supply, estimating how long it would last and what they needed to do to conserve. As they prepared to break camp, Angela's friend Julie piped up. "C'mon people. We should clean up after ourselves. Dumping our trash in nature is what got humans into this mess." She pointed at the ground where they had camped, which was littered with paper cups, napkins, empty egg cartons, and the rest of the waste from their breakfast. Julie produced a plastic bag and opened it. "Trick-or-treat," she said. "Pick it up and put it here." Children and grownups together obediently collected the trash and deposited it in Julie's bag. She tied the bag off and left it neatly propped up against the pole of a road sign. Then they headed up the highway onramp, and Rosie once again started singing as they mingled with the other refugees on the highway. Some of the strangers walking near them sang with them. Music never failed to fulfill its role as the universal language.

When 580 joined 101, everyone cheered because it represented progress. Even Win-J managed a smile. Angela had taken her boys to visit at Green Creek so often that they knew the route. "We walked all the way to 101!" Sulei exclaimed with delight. The journey, which had seemed overwhelming the day before, began to fit into perspective, and Angela, as well as others in their group, could envision eventually arriving at their destination, which heartened them. She wondered how far the rearguard of elders had progressed. When they stopped for lunch, some of the other refugees who had been singing with them on the road stopped to eat as well. These strangers shared food from their stash, including fat chocolate chip cookies, which they passed around to Angela's boys and the other children. Their friendliness and generosity brought tears to Angela's eyes, and renewed her hope that she would encounter goodwill in others during this time of crisis. The kind people with the fat cookies said they were walking to a chicken farm in Petaluma owned by a relative. They joked that they would probably eat nothing but eggs and chickens for the rest of their lives.

"I'm not sure which I would eat first," Darren told them with an impish grin, "the chicken or the egg."

"I have to remember that!" one of the Petaluma travelers remarked with a chuckle.

Darren asked them if his brother could stop at the chicken farm with the old folks for a rest on their way north. He called Michael and introduced him to the chicken-farm-travelers, who gave him directions. Michael's wife spoke to her husband and was relieved to hear that they were still on the march and all was well.

Angela's tribe pushed on, walking during the day and sleeping by the side of the highway at night, a few people going off the road each morning to refill the water bottles, as they inched their way to Green Creek. They talked with other travelers on the road about plans for the future, and coping with the crisis. They and those they met speculated about what life would be like in the days and months ahead. They shared a pervasive sadness for all they had left behind and for the loss of communication with loved ones far away. Many people held out hope that the situation was temporary and someone somewhere would figure it out and return things to a more normal state.

At Cloverdale, they woke in the morning to discover that thieves had made off with their two shopping carts of remaining food during the night. They turned out their pockets, but found precious little to eat. Sulei cried. He couldn't understand why anyone would steal their food.

"They were hungry and they didn't care about whether or not it's wrong to steal," Angela told Sulei. "If they had asked, we would have shared what we had with them, like those nice people who gave you the cookies near Petaluma. We only have a couple more days of walking to get to Green Creek, baby. We'll survive."

"There'll be plenty of food at Green Creek, right?" Jamal asked.

"Of course there will," Angela reassured him. Although she worried, not for the first time, about meeting Jamal's needs on his special diet.

"I just realized," Win-J commented, "that I've never gone a whole day without eating. I guess we're pretty lucky."

He had become more philosophical lately, more inclined to step back from the situations in which he found himself to reflect on them.

"We *have* been lucky," Angela agreed. "A lot of children in this world know what it's like to go hungry and it happens to them often. I'm glad that's not something you boys have ever experienced."

"Until now," Win-J added.

"Until now," Angela confirmed grimly.

Many of the other travelers who had camped out near them also had their food stolen. A few of them still had food, but were reluctant to share their dwindling supply; and Angela could understand. If she had limited food for her sons, she would not feel inclined to give it away. They discussed what to do about food. They could either continue walking, with the strong possibility of no food until they reached Green Creek sometime the following evening, or they could send a group off the highway to forage for food in Cloverdale. Angela feared leaving the highway. She didn't think the towns along the road were safe. She imagined the surrounding countryside as a place where people had guns and dogs, and used them to ruthlessly defend their land. She would have preferred to keep walking, food or no food. But they had to consider the children; plus three of the women in their group were pregnant. They would have to leave the road anyway to get more water. The consensus was for Darren and a few other men to go into Cloverdale to look for food. Angela had a bad feeling about it as she watched them backtrack down the highway to the exit ramp, but she kept her thoughts to herself. The last thing

Tanisha needed was the voice of doom in her ear as Darren disappeared down the road.

Rosie and Win-J went for a walk and came back excited to report that they had found blackberries growing along a creek. All the children and some of the grownups followed them to the berries. Angela stayed with those who remained to guard their possessions. The blackberry hunters were gone for quite some time and returned smeared with berry juice and carrying a couple of bags of berries. Julie's dog was covered in burrs and it took Julie nearly an hour to pick them out of his fur.

Angela thought their time would have been better spent walking to Green Creek. What if the men didn't find anything to eat? Then they would go hungry even longer. Angela could not wait to arrive, while at the same time she dreaded arriving because then she would have to tell Rachel about Vince.

It was nearly noon by the time Darren and the others returned from Cloverdale.

"It's hard to believe," Darren told them, "but everything is picked clean. There was a big grocery store with not a single food item left. There were quick shops at two gas stations, both completely empty. We went to a Burger King and it was emptied out."

"Gives a new meaning to fast food," Angela's friend Julie quipped.

"But we found a few things," Darren informed them. They had stumbled upon an apple orchard and filled several bags with apples. They also discovered a dairy farm. The farmer initially met them at the gate with his shotgun, two dogs, and a scowl as large as Texas, but when Darren explained to him that they were just looking for food, that they were traveling with a group that included children and pregnant women, and that they meant no harm and would leave peacefully if the farmer had nothing to give them, the farmer told them that if they waited at the gate he would bring them something. He returned with a cart filled with chunks of cheese and bottles of fresh milk, which they transferred to Darren's shopping cart.

The pregnant women and the children drank the milk (except lactose-intolerant Jamal). Some of the cheese was goat cheese, which Jamal could stomach better than cow cheese. Angela's boys, who hardly ever ate apples, munched them eagerly with a fresh appreciation. The men who went into town recounted what they had seen. After discovering that the food outlets near the highway had nothing left, they walked further in. Many people remained in their homes. They stopped a woman, told her they were looking for food to feed their families waiting for them on the highway, and asked if she could make any suggestions. She explained that the town had been inundated with travelers looking for food, and said she couldn't help them herself because she had children of her own to feed. She suggested they try the dairy farm and gave them directions. That's how they wound up meeting the generous dairy farmer.

After they ate, the group resumed walking, much to Angela's relief. The road north of Cloverdale required a lot of steep uphill walking. Angela noticed they had more stamina and had become stronger. They didn't need to stop as frequently, they walked faster, and the younger children could walk long distances without tiring so easily. It had been several days since Sulei had agreed to let anyone carry him. They slept alongside the Russian River after a dinner of the remainder of the apples and cheese. Angela was pretty hungry by the time they stopped, and in retrospect she was glad they had taken the time to find food that morning. She had never put her children to bed hungry and she felt grateful that she didn't have to do it that night.

A current of excitement electrified the group as they broke camp the next morning and set out on what they anticipated would be their last day of the journey. Angela felt excrutiatingly empty-handed. They brought nothing to contribute to the community, just more mouths to feed; and they didn't even have Vince with them. How would the Native people of Green Creek receive a destitute group from Oakland, made up mostly of African Americans? Also, upon their arrival, Angela would have to tell Rachel about Vince. The closer they got to Green Creek, the more anxious Angela became. Jamal, walking beside her, intuitively took her hand.

Shortly after noon, they turned off the highway onto the county road that would take them to the entrance of the Green Creek Rez. Darren called the group to a halt. They had no food left, the sun beat down relentlessly, and Angela had a throbbing headache. They stood on the lot of a former gas station on the corner where the highway met the county road. Darren pointed to a water spigot on the side of the gas station building, and they refilled their water bottles and washed their hands and faces. Angela's headache receded after she downed a bottle of water. Angela had come to have a new appreciation for the miraculously restorative power of plain water. Water was more valuable than gold. She wondered how long a person could survive without food if she had plenty of water.

Once the travelers rehydrated, Darren drew everyone together and announced that they would pray. They bowed their heads. Sulei stood in front of Angela and she rested her hands on his shoulders. He held Big Dog tightly in his arms. Jamal put his hands together and held them under his chin, his eyes squinched tightly shut in concentration. Win-J stood next to them with his arm around Rosie. Darren thanked God for preserving them and bringing them to that point on their journey. He prayed the rest of the family would rejoin them soon. He prayed that God would lead them to safety at the Rez and that the Green Creek Pomo would have compassion for them and take them in. He prayed they would find ways to contribute to the Green Creek community so that those living there would never regret offering them sanctuary. Then he called on God to bless the children and to watch over them. When he stopped praying, the group chorused "amen." They stood in silence for a couple of minutes, heads bowed, each person saying their own prayers, until Darren silently took Tanisha's hand and resumed walking on the county road.

Rosie led the group in song as they covered the final few miles of road leading to their destination. Angela couldn't join in the singing because her throat closed every time she thought of the terrible news fast-approaching her dear Rachel. She thought about Sophie and Abigail. Her heart cracked with each step.

Before long, they stood in front of a bright-green road sign that marked the turn-off onto the private road that led to tribal lands. Angela stepped forward to the head of the group as they walked the final stretch onto the Rez. Jamal held one of her hands and Sulei held the other. A teen boy and an old man met them at the entrance gate, which stood invitingly open. The duo had been playing a game of checkers, which they abandoned as they stood to greet the travelers. Angela shook hands with the elderly man and then the boy. She paused to concentrate on keeping her voice steady. "I'm Angela, a friend of Rachel Braverman," she explained. "Rachel and I grew up together. I live in Oakland. I mean that I used to live in Oakland. When this crisis began she told me to come here, with my children. These are my sons." She introduced Sulei, Jamal, and Win-J. The boy and the man did not interrupt. They waited for her to finish. "I invited these friends to come with me. We're refugees from the city with nowhere else to go. We have walked a long way in the hope that you'll allow us to stay here, at least for now." She stopped speaking, not knowing what else to say.

The elderly man replied, "We're the welcome committee for today. I'll take you to Rachel."

"Should I stay here?" the boy asked.

"Naw, c'mon," the man told him. The boy looked relieved.

Angela introduced Darren and Tanisha and a few of the other adults as they started to walk onto the Rez.

The boy explained, "We take turns at the entrance watching for people who turn up, like you. Chief Firekeeper wants us to welcome newcomers. It's part of the philosophy of the Pacific Treaty."

"Enough," the elderly man said and the boy fell silent.

They walked past a series of water towers and a garden in which a number of people were turning soil. The people stopped working to watch them pass. Angela felt self-conscious about the size of the group. It was a lot of people to absorb into a small community with limited resources; and more of them would be coming soon if all went well.

The elderly man pointed to a paved road leading up a hill into a forested area. "The tribal office is up that way," he told Angela and those within earshot, before he fell silent once more. He led them up the paved road, across a gravel parking lot filled with abandoned vehicles, and into a low-slung building. They walked through a short entranceway into a large conference room. A meeting appeared to be in progress. The people in the meeting fell silent as the weary travelers and their escort entered. "They walked from Oakland," their escort announced. He nodded his head in Angela's direction, indicating for her to approach the people meeting at the long table. "This is Angela, a friend of Doc Rachel's." Angela stepped forward, feeling a bit like Dorothy meeting the Wizard. Seated at the table were a dozen people, all Native. A short woman with graying hair and deep brown eyes stood and held her hand out to Angela. "I'm Chief Marjorie Firekeeper. Welcome. Have we met before?"

"Thank you," Angela replied as she took the woman's hand. "Yes, I think we met once or twice when my family visited Rachel." Chief Firekeeper squeezed Angela's hand reassuringly and Angela struggled to keep from dissolving in tears. "I'm Angela Grant. May I have a word with you in private? There's a delicate matter that needs attention."

Chief Firekeeper nodded and took Angela by the elbow. "We'll be right back," she told the others as she steered Angela out of the room, into a corridor covered in colorful posters, and down the hall to her office. She closed the door and turned her expectant gaze on Angela.

Angela opened her mouth to speak and a sob emerged. Chief Firekeeper put her arms around Angela and held her, as if they had known one another a long, long time. Angela wept while Chief Firekeeper held her, saying nothing, until Angela pulled herself together with a shudder. She told the chief, "Vince is dead. He was killed protecting a couple of the children during our journey. Rachel doesn't know, of course. She and I are childhood friends and I'm going to have to tell her this in a few minutes. Vince was staying with me when all this craziness came down. He was at a teachers' conference in Oakland. He and I decided to walk here together. We invited some other people to come with us. Good people. So here we are, without Vince. We hope your Tribe will allow us to join your community. I'm sure there is much to discuss, but first, God help me, I have to break this horrible news to Rachel."

"Understood," Chief Firekeeper said with a nod. She turned toward the door, but Angela stopped her with a hand on her arm.

"There's one more thing you should know," Angela continued. "There are more of us coming. The elders and weaker ones in our group lagged behind. If they survive, if they can make the walk, they may turn up at any time in the coming days. If you agree to let us stay then you must understand that these others, these needy others, will follow."

"The elders, the weak, and the most needy among us often have the most abundant gifts," Chief Firekeeper replied. "Let's find Rachel," the chief said sadly. Angela followed her reluctantly from the office. They returned to the conference room, where her fellow travelers sat at the conference tables eating venison jerky, cheese, and fruit. Angela explained to Darren that she had to find Rachel and tell her about Vince. She said that the situation looked good for them to stay, and a wave of relief crossed Darren's face.

Chief Firekeeper and Angela left the tribal office and walked along a path bordered by enormous agave cactus plants. When they entered the health clinic, the receptionist greeted them cheerfully. It was so late in the afternoon that no more patients remained in the building. They found Rachel in her office, making notes in patient files. When she looked up and saw Angela, she let out a shriek of joy and raced over to embrace her.

"Oh my god! Oh my god! Oh my god!" Rachel exclaimed. "You did it. You walked."

Angela was shaking so hard that her teeth chattered. Chief Firekeeper moved next to Rachel. As Angela stepped back from Rachel's embrace, the chief put a steadying arm around Rachel's waist.

"Where's Vince?"

"He's not with me, Ray. I'm so sorry. He died."

Rachel looked bewildered and Angela recognized that look. She had seen it when people first learned of tragedy. It was the look of stunned disbelief before comprehension. Angela got a grip on herself. She would have to be strong to help Rachel through this.

"He was killed protecting some of the children."

"No, no." Rachel shook her head as if to clear her thoughts. "What do you mean? What are you saying?"

"I'm saying that Vince is dead, honey. He's gone."

"Are you sure?" Rachel asked incongruously.

"I saw him die," Angela confirmed, as tears ran down her cheeks. "I'm absolutely sure."

A rumbling sound started in the back of Rachel's throat, turned into a primitive growl, and then crescendoed into a wail as she collapsed into the chief's arms.

Transition: Robin

Ken left before first light. He took two guns with ammunition from the arsenal and hitched Manzanilla to a wooden horse cart. Manzanilla would pull the cart like a champion and it comforted Robin that the horse would accompany Ken. Willow tearfully begged her dad to be super careful. Fortunately, she would begin her new apprenticeship to Katie that day, which would distract her from worrying about her father. Peter gave Ken a password to re-enter Rainbow should he return at night or under circumstances that prevented him from being recognized by the armed sentries posted at the entrances.

"Come back to me," Robin told him. He promised he would, kissed her deeply, then he was gone. To take her mind off Ken, Robin spent the day building greenhouses with the garden crew, leaving the kitchen in the competent hands of her staff. She wanted to do hard physical work, outdoors in the bright sunshine, so she would collapse into deep sleep come nightfall.

Many years ago, the Rainbow gardeners had taken to starting as many plants as possible in greenhouses instead of outdoors in order to reduce infiltration of drift from genetically modified plants from destroying the viability of their seed stock. Maybe they wouldn't have to worry about that anymore in the future. As she listened to the gardeners discussing this possibility with optimism, Robin reflected that more members of the Rainbow community seemed exhilarated by the disaster than disturbed by it. She did not share their exhilaration. Nevertheless, she felt fortunate to live at Rainbow, with such resourceful people. She was surrounded by problem solvers. For many at Rainbow, the crisis simply presented a higher-level exciting, stimulating problem to solve: how to survive independently from the rest of the world.

Robin had taken a pound of coffee from the community kitchen, hid it in her canvas tote, and snuck it home to supplement Ken's personal stash. But on her lunch break she returned it out of guilt. Others would have to make do and so would Ken. She had no right to take advantage of her position as kitchen manager to sneak coffee. She locked up the coffee and the chocolate to prevent any of her staff from succumbing to the same temptation. They would save the remaining coffee for a special occasion and share it equally among all those who loved a good cup of java.

Her hard day's work on the greenhouse left her sufficiently exhausted that night to fall swiftly into sleep. She woke with a jolt to the sound of gunshots. Her bedside clock said three o'clock. Willow appeared, ghostlike, and slipped into bed beside Robin, shivering, even though it was a warm summer night.

"What is it, do you think, Mom?"

"I don't know, but those are gunshots." She resolved to remain honest with Willow about everything as it happened. She wished that Willow could have finished growing up in peace. At least Willow had enjoyed a blissful childhood at Rainbow, and would carry those memories forever, a gift that no one could take from her.

"Should I go find out about it?" Robin asked.

"You might as well," Willow answered with a sigh. "We're not going to sleep until we know what's going on. Can I come with you?"

The two of them slipped into their clothes, took their flashlights, and went outside. Walking into the uncertainty of the night beside her tall daughter, who towered over her, Robin perceived Willow as an adult rather than a child for the first time. They were two women, walking into the night to face whatever they encountered. They met Rodger on the path to the dining hall and asked him if he knew what was happening.

Rodger hesitated, glancing uncomfortably in Willow's direction.

"My daughter is grown," Robin said resignedly "Whatever it is, she should know just as much as I."

"Intruders attempted to breach the main gate," Rodger informed them. "The sentries shot them."

Robin sucked in her breath. So it begins, she thought. The violence. But the world had become a lawless place and they had to protect themselves at Rainbow. "How many?"

"They're sure it was strangers?" Willow exclaimed in alarm. "Dad's out there somewhere."

It had not occurred to Robin that the sentries might have shot Ken by accident, perhaps not recognizing him as one of their own. Then she remembered the password. "Dad has a password, Willow," she reassured her daughter. "Even if they couldn't see him, he could make himself known to them."

"These were definitely strangers," Rodger confirmed. "It's being taken care of. Go back to bed and you'll find out more in the morning."

"How could they shoot them?" Willow demanded, distraught. "How could they just shoot people?"

"This is how it is now," Rodger asserted gently but firmly, as if instructing Willow in the proper method of pruning an apple tree. "Anyone we don't know could potentially jeopardize the safety of the entire community. If they refuse to turn away at our gate when warned, then we will not hesitate to stand our ground to protect our home and our people. We can survive here; but we can't absorb a large influx of people, particularly people who don't share our way of doing things. We don't have the resources or the inclination for that. We can't allow any stray person who turns up to come in, and if they refuse to leave then we have to remove the threat."

"But it's not right," Willow insisted stubbornly.

"I know it sounds harsh," Robin said, "but Rodger's right. People living at Rainbow are more fully evolved than most of the regular people out there in the world. We've worked hard, sacrificed, and struggled to make Rainbow the way it is. We have certain agreements that constitute the foundation of our community. A stranger, who did not work for this and who does not understand the basic principles of sustainable living or the workings of an intentional community, has no right to come here expecting asylum." In the surreal glow of the flashlight, Robin could see Willow turning these thoughts over in her mind.

"But Grammy is welcome here, right?" Willow asked.

"Of course," Rodger hurried to assure her. "She's your grandmother. We trust one another to bring in a few new people who will fit into our culture. We built Rainbow on trust."

"Come." Robin placed her hand through the crook in Willow's arm. "Let's go back to bed. We have a lot of work to do tomorrow."

Willow nodded her assent; but before they turned back toward their house, Willow told them, "I hear what you're saying, but I don't agree with you. It's wrong to kill. Everyone knows that. You know that. Whoever shot those intruders knows that." Robin did know. Willow was theoretically and morally right, but Robin also knew that in the real world being right could get you killed. Robin wished she could take the moral high ground and survive, both at the same time; but the two seemed mutually exclusive in the context of their current situation.

The next morning, the farm buzzed with discussion about the shootings. Everyone referred to the intruders as "infiltrators." The defenders on guard had called to the infiltrators to retreat, and the infiltrators had refused to comply. In fact, the infiltrators had fired first by all accounts, which somehow made Robin feel better about the resulting shoot-out; as though this fact provided stronger justification for the killing. A group of volunteers from Rainbow went out at first light and dug graves on the outside of the perimeter fence, where they buried the dead. Kristy insisted that a sign be mounted over the fresh graves to warn others that they would share the same fate if they attempted to invade Rainbow.

During the afternoon, while Robin stood at the center island of the kitchen chopping vegetables for dinner with her staff, she overheard two of them discussing the shooting. It was then that she learned that two of those killed were children. She told herself that the safety and security of Rainbow was not her area of responsibility. No one criticized her for the decisions she made about food. They had to trust in one another to make the best decisions they could in the moment in their area of expertise and responsibility. She thought of Ken, outside in that lawless world, and shivered. Her anxiety increased when Ken did not return that evening and did not call. His phone still had a charge when he left, so she wondered why he had not even

texted her or Willow to let them know he was safe. He
should have collected his mother and returned already.
Robin and Willow called and texted both Ken's phone and
Grammy's with no response.

That night, Willow crawled into bed with Robin and fell
asleep instantly. Despite her exhaustion, Robin lay awake
for a long time. Fortunately, when she finally nodded off,
her sleep was not interrupted by gunfire. She woke feeling
less anxious. It was a new day and surely Ken would return.

He didn't.

Worse yet, a group of refugees from nearby Lexington
arrived at the front gate requesting asylum and Kristy turned
them away. The armed guard made them put their hands in
the air and frisked them for weapons, which they did not
have, before Kristy would deign to converse with them.
They were a cluster of desperate families. One of the families
had visited Rainbow Farm the previous year, thinking they
might wish to join the community during one of the rare
occasions when Rainbow had openings and was accepting
applications for membership. The family had not joined the
community at the time, but they remembered it and thought
their children would be fed and they would remain relatively
safe there; so they and some of their extended family and
friends had walked to Rainbow from their homes in the
suburbs. Kristy informed them the community was closed
and ran them off with not so much as a crust of bread. Robin
wondered what the families would do and where they would
go, with little or no skills applicable to the new reality in
which they found themselves. That evening, Willow
speculated that if those families had appeared at the gate

during the night, the defenders might have shot them. Robin
pointed out that was unlikely since they were not aggressive
and had no weapons.

"Those people are not going to make it, are they? They
have no clue. They'll starve to death."

"You're probably right," Robin reluctantly confirmed.

"I don't see why we couldn't let them come in. I'm sure
they would have something to contribute to Rainbow. There
weren't that many of them. And what about the children?
We should have let them come in because of the children."

"And where would that end? Think about it. We can't
take in everyone who shows up at the gate, everyone who
has heard about Rainbow and thinks we'll let them join us
and we'll save them. We can't make even the smallest
impact on the multitudes of desperate people in the world
outside. All those people who never thought ahead and
learned how to grow food or build a sustainable community.
We can't save them, Willow. We're going to have a hard
enough time saving ourselves."

"I know we can't help everyone," Willow persisted, her
eyes welling with tears, "but what if we just helped a few
people? I mean, just a little. Whatever we can manage."

"We *are* going to help a few people. Dad isn't the only
one who went outside to rescue a loved one, remember.
Pretty soon we're going to have a whole bunch of new
people here who are closely related to members of the
community, and we'll have to figure out how to stretch our
resources to include them."

"I guess. But why did Kristy have to be so mean when
she sent those strangers away?"

"Kristy has to be mean because it's hard for her to do what she knows she has to do. If she makes herself mean, then she can do it. She can't afford to go all soft."

"I wish I would wake up and everything would be back to normal."

"I do too, sweetie, I do too."

Robin's anxiety about Ken's safety kept her awake most of the night. Something must have come up that was making it take longer than expected, but why hadn't he called or texted her? Surely all available phones had not gone dead in such a short time. Lack of sleep caused Robin to have brain fog the next day. To make matters worse, the toilet in the bathroom next to the communal kitchen overflowed first thing in the morning. A crew arrived quickly to clear the clogged plumbing and clean up the mess. Fortunately no poo came up from the depths, nevertheless there was a great deal of mopping required, and the paper products sitting on the floor had gotten soaked. Robin set them out in the yard to dry. She couldn't afford to throw them away because they might never see paper towels and toilet tissue again. She imagined there would come a day when people would appreciate having them even if they were stiff, stained, and misshapen.

By mid-afternoon, Robin came to a standstill, paralyzed by exhaustion and worry. Her kitchen staff sent her home to lie down. Her silent house felt overwhelmingly empty. She crawled into bed and cried herself to sleep. She woke several hours later, disoriented and convinced that she heard strange voices in her living room. She went into the bathroom that adjoined her bedroom and brushed her teeth, washed her face with cold water, and combed her hair. She could definitely hear voices in her house and emerged cautiously to investigate.

Ken sat on the couch next to his mother, Diane. He had one arm in a sling, and a butterfly bandage held together a cut above his left eyebrow. Several people she did not recognize sat in her living room. Ignoring the strangers, she flew to Ken, who stood up and caught her as she launched herself at him in an explosion of relief.

"What happened to you? Why didn't you call?"

"We couldn't call, sweetie," Diane informed. "We had our phones stolen."

"Diane," Robin said, as she turned and embraced her mother-in-law, "Thank goodness you're here. I was so worried."

"I can imagine," Diane replied.

"Have you seen Willow?" Robin asked.

"On our way in we saw Willow," Ken answered. "Before we went to the clinic so that I could get this cut stitched up." He gestured toward the wound above his eye. "She went back to Katie after we saw her. We decided to let you sleep."

"Why did it take you so long to come home?"

"Things got complicated," Ken deflected her question, wearily. He waved his hand in the direction of the strangers who populated Robin's living room. "Robin, this is Nancy, Mom's good friend. You remember her?" Robin nodded to indicate that she did. Ken continued, "And these others also live near Mom. This is Cynthia, her wife Ginger, and that's Tom and his wife Anne." Diane had lived in a senior community and she had brought some of her immediate neighbors along with her to Rainbow. They were elders with nowhere safe to go that was within traveling distance. After introductions, Robin offered the new arrivals something to eat, but they said they had been fed at the dining hall while Ken was getting stitched up.

"Did Manzanilla make it back with you?" Robin asked.

"Sure did. He's one tough fellow. Hauled a couple of these ladies in the cart all the way back."

"The rest of us walked," Tom added. "That's one of the reasons why it took us so long. We old-timers don't move real fast."

"And the other reason we took so long is because your hero of a husband looted every pharmacy from here to Lexington," Diane informed her proudly.

"What?" Robin exclaimed.

"I stopped in at a few drug stores to stock up on supplies," Ken explained modestly. "Anne is diabetic, so we started out looking for insulin and test strips and…"

"Which Ken miraculously found," Anne interrupted.

"Not nearly enough," Ken added.

"But enough to last for a little while. None of us knows how much longer we have." Anne shrugged. "I'm grateful for the extra months I'll get out of the supplies Ken found for me."

"He managed to score a lot of meds that will be extremely helpful," Diane told Robin. "He also collected a heap of batteries. Lots of hearing aid batteries."

"Thick-skinned Kristy actually cried when I gave her my stash of hearing aid batteries," Ken said. Kristy was hard of hearing and wore hearing aids in both ears. For the first time, Robin realized that Kristy faced a future in which her ability to communicate would become greatly impaired when the batteries ran out. Their lives were changing so fast that she couldn't keep up. As she glanced around the room at Diane's friends, she noticed that three of them had hearing aids.

No matter how independent they thought they were at Rainbow, their reliance on the world outside would keep coming back to bite them. They were entering a retro-age; and while some of their future would be an advancement, some of it would be a regression. Just how the two directions reconciled with one another and created a new way of life remained for them to discover.

Transition: Max

At breakfast, in the clear light of morning, Max reached across the table and took Theresa's hands in hers. "I think we should make a run for Rainbow Farm. I don't expect the people in this neighborhood to survive the winter if the situation does not improve."

Theresa began to protest as she retrieved her hands from Max's, but Max cut her off, arguing with her most persuasive lawyering logic, "Listen. Who do you think will solve this problem? Scientists in labs? They've gone home to fight for their survival with their families. Governments? Governments have no way to communicate or organize.

Law and order will disintegrate. A few handguns will not protect us from desperate people. Some of the people roaming the world are not nice to begin with and some of the nice people will become not nice when they're hungry. When I try to imagine how we'll stay warm in the winter, all I come up with is burning the furniture in the fireplace until it's all burned up. That's not a viable plan. My biggest worry is food. We have canned goods in the garage, but that will run out. It could be stolen. We don't have the necessary resources, my love. Do you want to stay here and die of starvation with our neighbors?"

Theresa swallowed hard. "How far is it to Rainbow?"

"About five hundred miles," Max told her.

"Is there somewhere closer?"

"If there is, it hasn't come to mind. In fact, I can't think of any other people that I know anywhere who I think have a chance of surviving. If anyone can do it, Robin's people can. Survival is kind of their thing."

"How long do you think it would take us to walk to Rainbow?"

"Maybe about a month," Max replied, "unless we run into problems." She didn't want to imagine possible problems.

"What will we eat for a month?"

"We'll take food with us."

"What if it gets stolen? What will we do when it runs out?"

"We'll go hungry or forage. If we go now, during the first rush of refugees, I think we'll be safer. The roads are loaded with people right now and food and other resources are not yet scarce. You should have seen all the people on Monroe yesterday. I think the cities will empty out soon. People will have to go where food grows. And think about water. What if we turn on the tap and nothing comes out? I don't know how we get water but I imagine it has to get pumped from somewhere and pumping requires energy."

"What if they don't let us in at Rainbow? And it's a survivalist community. I don't really want to live there. That woman Kristy who founded the place is scary. I sat next to her at lunch one day. She's like someone from Waco only without the Jesus factor."

"Robin will make sure we get in. Kristy is not the only one in charge. We don't have a lot of choices here," Max reminded Theresa. "We need food, shelter, protection. Basics, babe."

"I have this feeling, sort of like a premonition, that we'll die on the road." Theresa's voice cracked and she began to cry. Max reached across the table and took her hands again. "I'm trying to stay positive, but I wonder whether we will live through this no matter where we are. I would rather die here in my home surrounded by the things I love. The best death would be to curl up in my bed and go to sleep and not wake up. I can see that your goal is survival, but I'm not sure that my goal is survival, mija. My goal might be peace."

"My goal is you. I've been loving you too long to stop now," Max quoted Otis Redding. "Think about it and we'll decide tomorrow. If you decide to stay, then I'll stay with you until the end because I don't want to live anywhere without you." Theresa took her hands from Max's to wipe the tears from her cheeks.

Max gave Theresa space to ponder the prospect of becoming a refugee. She went to Jack's firearms training and learned how to shoot her gun. She spent an hour on Monroe talking to people in the stream of refugees flowing out of town. She went with a few others from the neighborhood to a nearby pharmacy in search of batteries, but they found the pharmacy stripped. While standing on the sidewalk surveying the plundered pharmacy, Max struck up a conversation with a young woman walking a beautiful, silky, white Pomeranian. The woman wore a bright red T-shirt and had her hair pulled back in a ponytail. She was accompanied by two men, and they had paused in front of the pharmacy to study the wreckage.

"This place was emptied out faster than a movie theater on fire," the ponytail woman commented to Max.

Max admired the dog and kneeled down to pet him. "Are you from around here?"

"Yup. We're on the fourteen-hundred block of Radcliffe," the ponytail woman volunteered. "Near the park."

"That's just a couple of blocks from us," Max said.

"Yeah. But we're getting ready to walk to my Gran's house near Yorkshire. My parents should arrive by tomorrow and we'll go together, before things get too crazy. Are you going to leave?"

"I want to, but my wife is conflicted about it," Max confessed. "I'm waiting for her to make up her mind."

"It sort of doesn't matter, does it?"

"What do you mean?"

"I think us humans are about to get voted off the planet," the woman stated stoically, with a shake of her head that made her ponytail bounce. "I'm not confident we'll survive anywhere and I'd just as soon be with my mom and dad and my Gran, and these guys, my brother and my cousin." She gestured toward the men with her. She shrugged. "I'm not that important. The world will go on without me. It's sad, but I want to enjoy what's left before I check out. Good luck to you and your wife." She waved good-bye. Max wished she could summon the same serenity and humility as the ponytail woman.

She wanted to call Robin, but not until they had reached a decision about staying or traveling to Rainbow. If Theresa refused to go, then Max would have her work cut out for her to make their life at home as sustainable as possible. She knew that many dangers lurked, but she latched onto food and water as the focus of her cumulative anxiety and panic. They had a garage full of canned food that Theresa had stockpiled, but it didn't seem like nearly enough to Max.

That night, Max participated in a security patrol in the neighborhood. She returned to her house around midnight. Theresa was lying on her back staring at the bedroom ceiling in the dim light of the milky moon when Max slipped into bed. Max reached over and took Theresa's hand in hers.

"I've made my decision. I agree that survival here is a long shot, but I don't want to die anywhere else. I don't want to get shot on the road or see the dogs harmed or lose you in a strange place where I have no history and no friends. I would prefer to stay here for as long as it lasts and then, if necessary, take the meds Marcy gave me and end it in peace."

They lay side-by-side in silence until Max finally replied, "So be it."

They made love slowly and tenderly, taking their time and perhaps feeling more comfort than arousal. Theresa cried afterward and then fell asleep in Max's arms. Her rhythmic breathing lulled Max to sleep.

The next morning, Max announced she was going in search of more food. She put her new gun in her jacket pocket, snapped a leash on Minnie, and took a shopping cart in which to put whatever food she could find. A man she had spoken to on Monroe the previous day had told her about a warehouse where they were giving away nonperishable food. It heartened her to learn that someone with a warehouse full of food was willing to share it. She walked purposefully across the dozen blocks to the warehouse. The streets were not as full of people as they had been earlier in the week, but many people were still out and Max felt relatively safe. As she approached the warehouse, she discovered a large crowd gathered in the street in front. Minnie whined and Max pulled the leash tighter. "It's OK, Min," she murmured. The people in front of the warehouse had carts, wagons, wheelbarrows, and strollers in which to transport the anticipated bounty. Max held tightly to the handle of her shopping cart.

"What's going on?" she asked a woman next to her.

"Waiting for it to open," the woman replied.

Max jockeyed for space as she was swept closer to the warehouse by the throng of people. She could feel a thread of anxiety and desperation running through the crowd and she contemplated leaving. But she had come this far and the thought of a warehouse full of food was tantalizing. The grocery store near her house had already been picked clean. Max held Minnie close to her leg. She inched forward in the crush until she stood only a few yards from the entrance. Then the metal roll-top door slid up and the crowd surged forward, lifting Max off her feet for a brief moment in the press of bodies. Minnie yelped as a man lost his balance and stepped on her. Max wanted to put Minnie into the shopping cart to protect her, but the crowd had compressed so tightly that she couldn't bend down. She clung to Minnie's leash. She caught a glimpse of the inside of the warehouse and her heart leapt. She could see rows and rows of canned and boxed food, and she even saw glass cases with brightly colored fruits and vegetables. She wished she had been able to bring two shopping carts.

"Look Minnie," she exclaimed. "Jackpot."

The impatient people swept forward, but the entranceway was too narrow to accommodate all of them shoving and pushing to get inside that warehouse twinkling with bounty. The mob swiftly transformed into a faceless, amorphous mass of bodies forcing its way into a too-small aperture. Some people found themselves pressed hard against the front walls of the building as the frenzied mob pushed. Max's foot became tangled in Minnie's leash and she slipped sideways against the shopping cart. Moments later, Max's leg slid under the cart. She still held the leash in her hand, but she couldn't see Minnie. All she could see was legs, feet, and the horrified faces of two other people on the ground near her. She couldn't breathe. A heavy avalanche of weight crushed her back and collapsed her lungs. Her cheek ground into the pavement. She fought for breath, for air, clawing the concrete. The mob of people swelled and compressed on top of her, stampeding toward the woefully tight entrance to the warehouse. Max felt something inside her chest crack and she heard Theresa's sweet voice, with the clipped Puerto Rican accent she adored, saying softly in her ear, "I love you more than I could ever tell you, mija." Then she blacked out.

After the stampede, after the crush of people seized as much food as they could carry from the warehouse and fled with it, after the street emptied, after the sun disappeared and night spread a blanket of calm darkness over the bodies strewn on the ground in front of the warehouse, Minnie continued to sit next to Max's lifeless form, whimpering. A kind passerby had unclipped Minnie's leash from her collar so that Minnie could find her way home. The other end of the leash remained clutched in Max's stiffened hand. But Minnie had no intention of going home that night. She stretched out beside Max and rested her chin on Max's shoulder. There the dog remained faithfully until just before dawn. In the moments before the sun, oblivious to the infinitesimally small events of human existence, burst over the horizon, Minnie let out a howl of despair and headed back to the house where Theresa would wait in vain for Max during the days ahead, until the light of hope faded to a flicker and finally extinguished.

Transition: Melanie

Ned and some other church members retrieved Sylvia's body and buried her in the cemetery behind the chapel. Melanie stayed home with the kids during the brief memorial service that followed the burial. Even with Jen and Tracy helping out, she was frayed by the time they got the two-year-olds (Jen's Cody and Sylvia's Lucas) and eight-month-old Harper down for afternoon naps. Meanwhile, the four-year-olds, her Stella and Sylvia's Ava, were bouncing off the walls. Don and Tracy mercifully chased the energetic girls around the backyard for a while.

Melanie made a precious pot of coffee and sat down with Jen and Lisa to strategize about dinner and travel plans for the evening's outing to Grammy-and-Grampy's, which was just under three miles away, about an hour's walk. They agreed that Jen and Tracy would stay at home with the little ones while Lisa and Don accompanied Melanie and Ned.

"You better bring us some of whatever Grammy cooks," Jen demanded with a mock pout. "I don't mind staying with the kids, but fix me a plate." Melanie wished they had a family homestead where they all lived in close proximity. The miles between her house and her parents would become a nuisance real fast. She did not relish the thought of the walk home later that night.

When Ned arrived, he accepted a cup of coffee gratefully and described Sylvia's memorial for Melanie. Then he took Jen and Lisa with him to Sylvia's apartment. Sylvia had not owned much, and after several trips back and forth with shopping bags, a wheelbarrow, and the children's wagon, they had transferred the children's clothing as well as everything useful from Sylvia's apartment, including Harper's high chair.

"I'm glad we spent our whole lives winging it, because it makes it easier to keep doing that now," Melanie told Ned, as she put together a dinner for those who would stay behind for the evening. To conserve food, the people going to Grammy-and-Grampy's would eat when they got there.

A lot of people were out and about, all friendly, and their walk to Grammy-and-Grampy's was uneventful, even pleasant, in the warm summer evening. When they arrived, her mom rushed over to hug her and immediately burst into tears, apologizing for being "so weepy."

Melanie told her mother about Sylvia and the children she had inherited, while her mother clucked and shook her head sadly. Don and Lisa crowded around a laptop with their cousins, trying to pick up the latest news from the net, which Don said was becoming patchy and strange. Ned immediately filled a plate and chowed down. Mom had cooked up a storm.

Balancing plates on their knees and sitting wherever they could find space on the furniture or floor, Melanie's family coalesced in the living room where Dad presented his assessment. He outlined the family's most pressing concerns: food, water, shelter, heat when the winter months

came, protection, and communication. Their family, which
had always lived close to one another, suddenly felt spread
out. Dad worried that those few miles separating their
houses could potentially become insurmountable barriers in
a lawless world. He wished he could keep his daughters and
their families under his roof, together; however, he simply
didn't have the space. The family established a
communication protocol for as long as their phones worked.
They shared ideas for maintaining supplies and preparing for
the future; and they agreed to meet again at Grammy-and-
Grampy's in three days. They parted with hugs and tears.

The first week felt peculiarly festive in Melanie's
neighborhood, where people barbecued together every
evening. Once the news about Sylvia had circulated,
Melanie and Ned received quite a bit of support from
neighbors and the church community. They were showered
with clothing, blankets, diapers, food, and many other useful
things to help them care for Sylvia's children. One woman
brought over baby formula she kept for her grandson, who
lived in Albany. Sadly, the woman did not know when (or
if) she would see him again. Melanie would have to get
Harper onto all solid food as soon as she could since she
didn't expect to have much luck getting more baby formula
in the near future. Fortunately, they still had a lot of cloth
diapers since Jen had used them for Cody until recently.
They had a stash of disposable pull-ups for the toddlers, but
Melanie used cloth for the baby. She dreaded running out of
the pull-ups since cloth would not stand up so well with the
older ones. She and Jen would have to potty train them.

They still had electricity, but she wondered how long that would last. She knew that her neighbor Andrea made candles and she asked Andrea if she would teach her how to do it. Andrea said she ordered her candle-making supplies on the internet and didn't know where to get more. Melanie became obsessed with hoarding matches, and had to resist actually counting them. She knew you could rub two sticks together to make a fire, but she had no idea how that actually worked. They had a fireplace in the living room, so they cleared a space in the garage and started collecting firewood for the winter. Don and Lisa collected wood in the wagon and the wheelbarrow, and stashed it in the garage.

The manager of the local grocery store unlocked the store and left it open for anyone to plunder, and the shelves emptied in a few short hours. Don and the older kids brought home shopping carts full of canned and boxed food, which they stored in the garage. Melanie wondered what they would do when it ran out. She didn't know how to grow anything to eat. Maybe they could trade for food, but what did they have worth trading? Babysitting? Her parents grew a large vegetable garden, but they didn't grow nearly enough to feed the whole family. And they didn't have any animals, so there would be no meat, milk, or cheese. Where would they get protein for the children? They could preserve some of the produce from the garden for the winter, but Mom had never done much preserving; just a few jars of relish or some jam to give away at Christmas. They couldn't possibly preserve enough food to last the family through the winter. These worries tramped through her head like a column of thieves robbing her of peace of mind. The most mundane tasks that she did and simple objects that she picked up sent her brain scurrying ahead to a time when things would run out and nothing would work the way it had in the past. She caught herself stopping dead in her tracks and staring in paralyzing panic at soap, toilet paper, thread, trash bags, pencils, batteries, post-its, shoes. Heaven help her – shoes! All those children with growing feet. One afternoon she burst into tears looking at the tangle of worn shoes lying in the entranceway by the front door.

Then, overnight the smell of the CAFO changed. It smelled so bad already that if someone had told her it could get worse, she would not have believed them. Then it did. Don, the family's source of information, learned the situation after talking with some people in the neighborhood. Abandoned by the workers, the CAFO cows had died, and there were acres of carcasses rotting in the summer heat. To make matters worse, either someone had opened the gates and let heaps of the cows loose (perhaps a misguided, well-meaning group of animal-lovers?) or the beasts had stampeded in desperation and broken down the gates. In any event, the dumb creatures made a beeline for Lake Skaneateles, where they promptly crushed each other and drowned, piling up in layers near the shoreline.

"You would think that someone would have figured out how to get some edible meat out of those cows before they started to rot," Ned commented. It just went to show that old-fashioned butchering was a lost art.

The stench of disintegrating dead animals was so nauseating that they had to leave the house. Making several trips to bring the essentials, Melanie and Ned temporarily shifted their household to Grammy-and-Grampy's. They could still smell the rotting cattle from her parents' house, but the odor was not as strong. The older kids slept on the living room floor in sleeping bags, Melanie and Ned bunked in one room with the baby, and they put the four little ones into another room where they slept like a litter of puppies in one big bed. Tracy slept on a cot in the room with the little ones. Once the smell dissipated, she and Ned would move their family back home. She consoled herself with the thought that the CAFO was finished, and she would never have to smell those horrid cows again after they got over this.

On their first night with her parents, Dad made a campfire in a metal firepit on the back patio and they used up Mom's stash of marshmallows, chocolate, and graham crackers making s'mores. It felt festive and took their minds off their worries. Later, while the little ones slept, Melanie, Ned, and the older children sat around the firepit with Mom and Dad. Mom still wore her marshmallow-smeared apron. Dad kept feeding logs into the fire, which glowed and flamed, occasionally sending sparks spiraling upward into the dark sky.

Staring into the flames, Ned remarked that he had been thinking about what he could offer in trade for things the family would need in the future, such as food, shoes, or health services. Ironically, he was a car mechanic by trade. No call for that anymore. The glow from the fire illuminated one side of his face with amber light as he spoke. "Cars are done, but I know how things work and I can fix about anything mechanical. At first, I should probably offer to help people with mechanical problems without expecting anything in return, to build a reputation, you know? Then, after a while, I can barter as the need arises."

"What kinds of things do you know how to fix?" Dad asked. "Nothing that runs on fuel works anymore."

"Don't be negative," Mom chided softly.

"I'm not being negative. I'm being practical."

"That's fine. I don't mind," Ned reassured Mom. "It's a good question. I can fix bicycles."

"OK, that's useful," Dad encouraged Ned.

"And water pumps and solar systems. Wind-up clocks. I dunno. There's stuff."

"Dad," Don said with an amused shake of his head, "no one has a wind-up clock. Everyone uses the clock in their phone."

"I have a wind-up clock," his grandfather informed him.

"We have a grandfather clock in the living room," Mom said. "It will always tell us the correct time." She did not mention that the phones had a limited lifespan or that the power would probably go out soon.

Then Lisa spoke up. "I'm going to apprentice to Dr. Holloway. There's no college anymore, but I still want to be a doctor. Dr. Holloway agreed to teach me what he knows and in exchange I'm going to assist him. There are a few health professionals running a clinic on Apple Street."

Melanie's heart ached to hear her daughter say there would be no college. Lisa had worked so hard only to have this disaster obliterate her dreams. Melanie had no doubt that Lisa would find a pathway to the career she wanted, but that child had loved school. She loved to study. She loved going to classes, discussing things with other students, and learning in that collegial environment. Lisa had lost so much. Tears ran down Melanie's cheeks and she tried to wipe them away without drawing attention, but Lisa saw. "It's OK, Mom," Lisa assured her. "It's not what I wanted, but it will get me where I want to go. Sometimes the wrong train will get you to the right station."

"When did you become so wise?" Mom asked Lisa.

"It could get pretty grisly when the medicine and health supplies run out," Ned noted.

"I know," Lisa told him. "I'll take it as it comes. If I don't continue with my life and the career I wanted, I'll go crazy."

Don snorted.

"What?" Lisa demanded, turning on her brother.

"It's not you. It's me," Don explained. "I wanted to be a computer programmer. So much for that idea." He gestured with his hand to indicate his aspirations dispersing like powder.

"You could be someone who finds information for people," Tracy piped up. "You always know how to find things out."

"That's sweet," Don replied bitterly. "But I can only do that with the internet. Without the internet, I'm as stupid as a blade of grass."

"Well, Don," his grandfather said, clearing his throat, "there is another source of information that functions without electricity. It's called a book. And I happen to have an awful lot of those things lying around."

"Do you have one about raising chickens?" Don asked. "Don't laugh, guys. I'm serious. I want to raise chickens if I can get my hands on some for starters. I have a lead.

Chickens would keep us in eggs and a little meat." The resourcefulness of her children blew Melanie away.

"As it happens, I do have a couple of books on that subject," his grandfather confirmed. "I used to keep chickens. I still have a coop out back we could renovate. Where we'll get our hands on laying hens is going to be a trick, though."

"I told you, I think I have a lead," Don reminded him.

"I remember the chickens," Jen said in a dreamy voice. "I remember going into the hen house and finding warm eggs, and putting them into a basket to carry them into the kitchen, and Grammy scrambled them."

Melanie was so proud of her children for remaining remarkably positive. In their bumbling and disorganized way, she and Ned had managed to raise these extraordinary, resilient young people.

"Everyone's thinking about what their new job will be," Melanie's mother pointed out. "Your dad will be a go-to fix-it guy. Lisa will study to be a doctor and work in the clinic. Don will raise chickens and gather information. What do you think you might do, Jen?"

"Don't put her on the spot, Mom," Melanie intervened on behalf of her daughter.

"It's fine," Jen replied. "Before all this happened I was going to go back to school to study early childhood ed. I'm good with small children. I could watch people's children, you know, so they can do other stuff during the day."

"Seriously?" Lisa exclaimed. "You were going to go to college? Why didn't you tell me?"

"I was going to enroll in a child development class at the JC. I hated high school. But it would have been different studying something that interests me. And maybe, being on campus and all, I might have met a nice guy," she finished wistfully.

"That's what I hate the most about this mess," Lisa burst out. "I wanted to get out into the world and experience different things, different people. That's what would have been the best part of going to college. I might have returned to Syracuse to settle down eventually. But I wanted to see the world. I wanted to travel to New Zealand, France, Thailand." Lisa's voice broke. Melanie reached over and rubbed her daughter's back. Lisa started crying. "I wanted the world and it crashed. What a dirty trick."

"If this had happened about ten years from now, we would have had our chance," Jen speculated. "Why couldn't it have waited just another ten or fifteen years?"

"In fifteen years it would have crashed in on Cody's dreams," their grandmother pointed out.

"Our generation wasn't vigilant," Melanie's father said sadly. "We kept hoping for the best and letting the wheels of destruction turn. People just out to make a buck weren't planning down to the seventh generation and the rest of us acquiesced, let them bulldoze over us. I'm sorry I didn't make more of a hubbub before it was too late."

"I don't know what we could have done to stop those wheels from turning," Ned said. "Us little people haven't had the muscle to slow down the powerful for quite some time. Hell, we couldn't even stop them from building that stupid CAFO, even though we tried real hard on that one."

"That's true," Dad agreed.

Lisa announced she was heading to bed, and the rest of the family soon followed suit. The conversation around the fire had drained Melanie. So many of life's wonders had been snatched from her children. She hoped she would feel better in the morning. She was trying to maintain an optimistic outlook for their sake.

Harper woke Melanie at three for her nighttime feed. As Melanie lifted the baby from the makeshift bed they had made for her in a dresser drawer, she sensed something different. At first she couldn't put her finger on it, but soon the deep silence of the house settled on her and she figured it out. The power had cut off, which meant that she couldn't heat Harper's milk. She carried the fussy baby downstairs to the kitchen. Maybe Harper would take the milk cold and not complain. That seemed unlikely. She decided to mix up some powdered formula because room temperature was a little warmer than refrigerated milk. She thought about the perishables in the fridge.

In the dining room, she discovered Don sitting cross-legged on the floor, with his head in his hands. He turned a face devastated with loss to Melanie.

"That's it," Don announced. "It's gone."

"Maybe it will come back on," she consoled him.

"Even if it does, it won't be back for long. What are we going to do, Mom?" The floodgates opened and her brave son sobbed. "I've lost Anthony. I've totally lost Anthony." Anthony had been his best friend since he was a toddler. When Anthony's family moved to Ohio the previous year, Don had stayed in touch with Anthony daily via screenchat, social media, and phone. Without their electronic devices, they could no longer communicate.

"Your phone still has a charge, Don," Melanie reminded him. "You can at least get Anthony on a screenchat on the phone to say good-bye." Don wiped the tears from his face on his sleeve. "It's not like I didn't expect it," Don said. "I did. I just didn't think it would happen so soon."

Harper produced a hungry wail and Melanie went wearily into the kitchen and took down a canister of powdered baby formula. Suddenly it occurred to her that maybe whatever machine pumped water to the houses in the neighborhood was electric. She turned on the kitchen faucet. Miraculously water came out. Whatever delivery system provided the water was still working, but she wondered for how long.

"I will not panic," Melanie repeated aloud several times as she made up a baby bottle. Harper was so hungry that she sucked viciously at the bottle despite the unexpectedly cool temperature. She made a mental note to discuss the water situation with Ned and her dad as soon as they woke up. Why hadn't they thought of that before?

The family readjusted their daily living in myriad ways, great and small, to live without electricity. Mom set up a laundry schedule, washing clothes and towels by putting them in the bathtub and stomping around on them; then hanging everything up on a web of clotheslines strung between trees. They did diapers every day in a metal trash can in the back yard. Stirring them with a long stick, rinsing them half a dozen times. Dad had a stash of firewood and he kept adding to it, going out daily to find more and bring it back. He kept a fire going in a fire pit in the backyard at all times, and stoked it up for cooking and heating water. The adults and older children took quick cold showers. They washed the younger children using water heated over the fire. Ned designed a solar-heated outdoor shower, but he didn't have all the parts he needed to build it. Melanie loved her family's ingenuity and the sheer force of their perseverance.

One day Lisa came home from the clinic in the middle of the morning to warn the family to start boiling their drinking water. She said the pump system for water appeared to still be working and delivering water to the houses, but Dr. Holloway had learned that the filtration system could be compromised. Those dead cows in the lake were poisoning the water, and no one knew for sure if the nasty bacteria was still being filtered out. "People are coming down with a bad intestinal bug and Dr. Holloway thinks it's from the water."

That evening, Harper started to run a fever. She refused her bottle and, as night came on, she began vomiting. Don walked over to the clinic to get Lisa, who came right home and brought Pedialyte with her. She looked worried. "I don't want to give her the Pedialyte unless she can keep it down. Can we try to get her to drink some water first?"

Dad had been boiling water over the campfire in pots, cooling it, and storing it in mason jars and plastic jugs in the kitchen.

They gave Harper some of Dad's boiled water, but she couldn't keep it down, and soon added diarrhea to her repertoire. Lisa and Melanie stayed awake with the baby throughout the night. They tried to bring her fever down by sponging her with damp washcloths. Lisa gave Harper an injection of antibiotics and Tylenol, but it didn't seem to make any difference. The poor baby was burning up and unable to keep even a teaspoon of boiled water down. Just before sunrise, Dr. Holloway came to the house. By then Harper had turned a grayish color and was barely moving. Every once in a while, she would gag and heave, but nothing came up. Melanie asked the doctor to put the baby on an IV to rehydrate her.

She was so intent on Harper that at first she failed to register the doctor's desperate state. He had dark circles under his eyes and his clothing was creased and disheveled. His shoulders stooped in defeat. "I've been up all night battling this. We should have started boiling our water sooner. We take so many things for granted. Something must have gone amiss in the water filtration system, and that mess of dead animals up at the lake by the CAFO is poisoning our water. I don't think we have cholera here, but it's something akin to it, and we don't have the resources to respond." He paused, licked his lips. "Not on this scale. I'm out of supplies. I can't help you here. All I can tell you is to boil your water." Lisa hugged the doctor, thanking him for coming to the house.

"They need you here. Take your time coming back to the clinic. Harper is probably just the first," the doctor told Lisa quietly. He gave her a bag that contained Pedialyte and Gatorade. When Melanie glimpsed the Gatorade, her heart skipped a beat. Gatorade was for adults, not babies.

Melanie wrapped Harper in her favorite baby blanket and was rocking her back and forth gently in the rocking chair when Harper slipped away. She kept rocking the dead baby while Ned and her father took up shovels and went down to the orchard to dig a little grave. While they were digging, Melanie's father became light-headed. Ned helped him walk back to the house. Her father was no baby. Sure, he was all of sixty-eight, but he was hale and hearty, as strong an older man as they come. Melanie could not process the thought that he could possibly have contracted the same water-borne disease that had taken Harper from them so swiftly. But she was forced to accept it when he began vomiting and running a fever.

While her mother cared for her ailing father, Melanie placed Harper lovingly into an old suitcase. They tucked her favorite stuffed bunny toy in with her. Then they buried the suitcase in the grave under an apple tree. Melanie was so terrified for her father and so numb with grief and dread by the time they finished covering the suitcase with dirt that she didn't even cry. She turned without a word and went straight back to the house to do the best she could with what she had available to go into battle to defend her family from the demon microorganisms.

One of Melanie's sisters arrived to lend support. Her other sister remained at home where her teenager had taken ill. They fastidiously boiled their water, but the bacteria from the CAFO had already staked its claim. During the night, Stella, Cody, and Lucas came down with fever, vomiting, and diarrhea. While Melanie's mother and sister looked after her father, Melanie, Ned, Jen, and Lisa took turns caring for the little ones. At least Tracy and Ava seemed alright, and they slept obliviously through the night.

Melanie snatched a couple of hours of fitful sleep before the sun came up, but she was nearly hallucinatory with exhaustion, anxiety, and grief by daybreak, when she went into the kitchen to eat some crackers and peanut butter. She found Don at the table reading about chickens.

"I kept Grampy's fire going and I made some mint tea," Don said. "Do you want a cup of tea, Mom? It's still warm."

"Thanks, sweetie, yeah, I'd love a cup," Melanie accepted.

"A lot of people are sick from the poisoned water. It's an epidemic. No one knew until it was too late. It sounds like something in the filtering system broke down but the pumping system still works. I don't understand it. Dad probably would. At least water still comes out of the tap, even if we have to boil it to drink it. It would be pretty awful to have to haul our water up from the lake. I hope we keep getting water from the faucet."

"Me too," Melanie agreed despondently. We're so screwed, she thought, but didn't say out loud. She gazed surreptitiously at her beautiful son and prayed with all her heart that he would stay well. "I need a moment," she told Don. She carried her tea to the back porch, where she looked out on the new day, drenched in golden-orange sunlight. The ground was freshly moist with dew and the garden smelled fragrant with late summer tomatoes and rosemary. Her eyes lifted to the tops of the trees and beyond, up, up into the sky. Please don't take my children, she prayed. She couldn't fathom a world without her children. Was it too much to ask to keep her aging father too? How many miracles was she allowed?

When she went back into the kitchen, Tracy and Ava had appeared. They sat at the table eating cereal. Four-year-old Ava turned her solemn brown eyes on Melanie. "Is Lucas sick like Harper?" she asked.

"Lucas, Cody, and Stella got sick last night," Melanie told her.

Ava's face crumpled and she began to cry. "Are they going to die?"

Melanie put her tea cup on the table and sat Ava in her lap, hugging her close. Ava wound her strong, little arms around Melanie's neck. Melanie thought about the other children, how weak they had become during the night, unable to lift their heads. She didn't know what to say to Ava about the others. She wished she could promise they would get well. "They might die," she said finally, "and might not. We don't know yet."

"If they die, Mommy will take care of them," Ava stated. Tracy had started crying also and it was all that Melanie could do to keep herself from breaking down and joining the flood of tears. "I dreamed about Mommy taking care of Harper," Ava told Melanie earnestly.

"They're together now," Melanie reassured the child.

"I'm not going to get sick," Ava insisted. "I made up my mind not to."

"That's good. Just remember not to drink any water unless it's some we boiled. Be sure to ask first before you drink, OK?" Ava nodded solemnly.

"Now I have to go look after the others." Melanie transferred Ava back to her chair. She went into the hallway and discovered her sister and Ned carrying her father out the front door of the house. Had he died? No, she saw him move his arm. She turned a questioning face to her mother, who explained it was impossible to keep him clean in bed and Dad had suggested they lay him out on the lawn. It being summer, the weather would tend to cooperate with that arrangement.

Melanie went up to the children and spent the day cleaning them, cradling them, talking to them, encouraging them. She caught a couple of quick naps. Everyone was equally worn out and took turns nursing the sick. By late afternoon, Melanie's Dad had improved. He was able to keep some Gatorade down and had gone several hours without diarrhea. Lisa said his fever was breaking and he might survive. He was such a determined old coot. They brought him back into the house and he slept deeply, with Melanie's mother stretched out on the bed next to him.

The little ones did not summon the same reserves as Melanie's dad and they succumbed one by one that evening. First Cody, then Lucas, and finally Stella, each of them slipping over into death as simply as if stepping from one room to another. She held Stella in her arms until the very last breath; and then, when Stella was gone, Melanie was overcome with exhaustion. She longed to crawl into her bed, to hide deep in the cocoon of blankets, and never come out; to drift in a dreamworld in which her children played happily, alive and well, laughing and calling to one another. I'll just go lie down for a little while, she thought. Just a short rest, before she had to carry on. "I have to lie down," she told Ned. He hugged her, holding her tightly to him, so that she could feel his heart thumping rhythmically in his chest. We're such fragile creatures, she thought.

Ned kissed her. "Get some rest." He released her. She went to bed and sunk instantly into unconsciousness, far from the weight of her grief. She woke in the night, feeling light-headed and unfocused, her mouth cottony and her limbs heavy as metal weights. She tiptoed out of her room, stumbled into the yard, and hurried across the lawn, through the scrub, and down to the edge of the orchard.

She thought about the blessings she had received in her life, for which she was truly grateful. Her beautiful children and her grandson; her adoring husband and strong marriage; her church community; her rewarding job, which was a constant delight; good friends; good family; the delicious meals she had shared with loved ones, the dances she had danced, the laughter, the love. She had received all she could have hoped for. Well, maybe not the money. They had always struggled financially. But that didn't matter since money was not one of the things she valued most in life. She had been blessed with everything else, and all those blessings had been tainted only, singularly, by the horrid smell of cattle housed in confined quarters and then herded to slaughter. Those diabolical cows had robbed her of a peaceful life and now they had robbed her of her precious Stella and Cody.

She howled with rage and grief amidst the trees. Shouting until her throat ached. She would never, ever again eat beef as long as she lived. She was done with cows forever.

In fact, the thought of eating a hamburger sickened her. She dropped to her knees beneath an apple tree and wretched, heaving up every scrap of food she had forced into herself in order to keep going over the previous couple of days.

At first, she thought it was the overwhelming grief and the idea of the hamburger and dirty cows that nauseated her. But she soon discovered that she could not back-pedal on the nausea. She struggled to stop heaving. She stumbled through the scrub and stretched out on the cool lawn. She lay on her stomach and tried to calm herself. She stopped vomiting, but the nausea remained and she felt too dizzy to stand up. She lay there on the lawn until the sun rose and she heard Ned call to her from the porch.

"Over here," she called back feebly.

She closed her eyes and tried to make the world stop spinning.

Ned knelt beside her. "Melanie, sweetie, can you stand up?" he asked with a desperate edge to his voice.

"I don't think so," she whispered. She felt as flat and thin as paper.

The family had seen what had happened with the children and her father. They thought it best to care for her outside on the lawn, as they had done for her father, because if they put her into a bed she would soil it. Ned put a plastic tarp up to give her some privacy and she let the grass embrace her feverish body. Ned and Jen appeared and disappeared, bringing wet towels and blankets, cleaning her up and moving her from one spot to another, trying to get her to drink Gatorade. She desperately wanted to drink the Gatorade, but she couldn't keep it down.

As the day progressed, only Lisa and Ned came to her aid. Jen did not appear. Melanie's voice had faded to a wisp, but she managed to ask Lisa about Jen, struggling to get the words out loud enough for Lisa to hear her.

"Don't worry about Jen," Lisa told her. But Melanie could tell by the way Lisa said it, and the sadness in her face, that Jen had been taken ill.

Melanie registered darkness and sunlight and knew that time had passed, but she didn't know how much time. She was empty. Ned held her head in his lap and attempted to spoon water into her mouth.

She could not open her eyes. She could not make her body respond to any command issued by her brain. She was not even in her body. She floated above her body and looked down at it, at her head cradled in Ned's lap. She wanted to tell him how much she loved him, but her brain was no longer connected to her mouth and she could not speak. I hope he knows, she thought. I hope he knows how much I love him. Then she no longer felt empty. She felt full to bursting with love for Ned, her children, her family, and all the extraordinary and beautiful people who had touched her life. The abundance of love filled her with warmth and joy, she dissolved into it, and the tiny dim light remaining in Melanie extinguished.

PART FOUR:
Transformation

Transformation: Rachel and Angela

Angela spent an anguished first night at Green Creek. Rachel sobbed inconsolably until a nurse from the clinic administered a sedative. The wrenching task of breaking the news to the girls fell to Angela. She spent the night on Rachel's couch with her arms around the children while they cried, talked, worried about their mom, and eventually fell asleep; Abigail in Angela's lap. In all her years of working with traumatized children, Angela had never suffered empathetically as much as she suffered for Rachel's girls. During that grief-soaked night, she gave up her last shred of hope that Winston had survived. The chance that she would ever know what happened to her husband was about as likely as there ever being another Super Bowl. Believing that Winston could escape prison and walk hundreds of miles in a world where a man could easily be shot over a bicycle was a fantasy.

While allowing herself to grieve, she commanded herself to accept her loss and move forward for the sake of her boys. She had to let go of her old life in order to make a new life at Green Creek. Yet she wanted to keep the myth of Winston's possible survival alive for her sons, at least for the time being. They had suffered so much loss that she didn't want to take that hope away from them. She would remain strong for her boys and for Rachel and the girls. She would compartmentalize her grief, and put her energy into caring for the wellbeing of others, working with Rachel to tend to their newly blended family of two women, five children, no husbands. Over time, her boys would get used to the loss of their father gently, slowly, without drama. It would be a dull ache, not a stab in the chest.

While Sophia and Abby slept on the couch with Angela, Jamal and Sulei slept in the bunkbeds in Abby's room. Win-J looked after them while Angela consoled the girls. He could have slept in Sophia's bed, but he chose instead to sleep in a tent that he found in the garage and pitched in the backyard. She hoped Win-J's anger at Winston would fade and that he would realize how much Winston loved his sons and how completely the arrest and conviction had shattered Winston. Sometimes bad things happened to good people. Angela could attest to that from her years of work with abused children. But it was hard to explain that to an angry adolescent boy, and she had to keep reminding herself that Win-J was still a boy. He had taken on a man's load, even before the Systems Collapse, and he had grown up quickly; but he was still a boy. Angela resolved to try harder to stop depending on Win-J as if he were a man, to give him more space to be a teenager. She would have a conversation with Darren. He could help fill the hole left by Winston's absence for her boys. He would step up. He was that kind of a man. She felt a rush of gratitude for the wonderful people who had come into her life in this crisis.

Angela slept for only a couple of hours and woke stiff and sore from sleeping on the couch with the girls. The heavenly aroma of freshly brewed coffee drifted to her and summoned her like a swami's flute. The first blue-tinged rays of sunlight illuminated the horizon. She gently disentangled herself from Sophia and Abby, taking care not to wake them, and tiptoed into the kitchen where she found Rachel sipping rich coffee from a large green mug with the word VINCE on it. Tears ran down Rachel's cheeks and she brushed them away as she sipped the fragrant brew. She waved her hand in the direction of the coffee maker behind her on the countertop. "We might as well enjoy it while we have it. Vince was a coffee snob so it's the good stuff. I'm not much of a coffee drinker, but it always smells delicious. It's an aroma I associate with him. Won't have that much longer either."

"I haven't had any for two weeks," Angela said, pouring herself a cup. "You're a goddess and this is ambrosia." She added cream and then sat across the table from Rachel. She took a sip, savored it. "This tastes like a miracle."

"A miracle would be if my husband walked through that door."

Angela reached across the table and took Rachel's hand. "A miracle would be if my husband walked through that door with him."

"At least you still have the hope."

Angela shook her head. "I don't think so. I would never say this to my boys, and I trust you to keep this between us, but I would be deluding myself to imagine that Winston is still alive. Think about it. He was locked in a prison cell. He probably died of starvation locked in that cell. Sorry. Too gruesome." She shuddered. "Anyone unfortunate enough to have been in jail when this whole thing came down was doomed. I'll never see him again. I'm grieving for him and Vince both, Ray."

"I don't know what to do. What should I do?"

"Put one foot in front of the other. Get through each hour. Get through each day. And I think you should have a ceremony to honor him and create a way for these people in your community who knew him to say goodbye to him. He was special to a lot of children around here because he was a teacher, right? Children need to acknowledge transitions."

"A memorial service would be good."

"Not a memorial, Ray; a celebration of his life. A remembrance. Do it like that."

Rachel nodded in agreement. "Look at us. Two widows with the world crumbling around us and a house full of children. How can we do this?"

"We'll make it up as we go along."

"I'm willing to fight for a future for the girls. For your boys too and for all the children here at Green Creek, but it's going to get really hard, and scary too. I can't imagine facing this without Vince. He was my rock."

Angela squeezed Rachel's hand. "Well, you have me. A consolation prize. I'm not a rock. More like a squishy blob of moss or something. But I'm here with you."

"I'm grateful for that. And you are not a squishy blob of anything. You're solid. I don't know anyone stronger. I can't believe you walked from Oakland with all these people. You're like Harriet Tubman or something."

"It's an illusion," Angela contradicted. "Underneath the façade I keep up for the kids, I'm all squish. But we'll squish through this together."

Rachel grimaced. "I wish I could skip the next few months and go straight to being used to this enormous hole in my life, his absence. I can't bear this. I don't want to go through this. I want it to be next year."

"Let's hope we're all alive and well next year. You, me, the children." Angela remembered Tanisha's words to her on the overpass. "You know as well as I that there's only one way to get past it and that's going through it."

"I know," Rachel said in a small voice.

They sipped their exquisitely delicious coffee in the heartache of early morning light.

Rachel sighed. "We best look into rearranging the house so that you and the boys have some space."

"Thank you." Angela's voice broke unexpectedly with emotion and she struggled to pull herself together. "We left so much behind. A whole life."

"We're going to make you a new one. Working on that will take my mind off losing Vince. Each of the girls has a bunk bed in her room, you know. They were handy for sleepovers. The girls will share a room and the other room will be for the boys. I have a futon in Abby's closet I can put on the floor for a third bed. You might as well sleep with me. We'll be a comfort to each other."

"Life is pretty unexpected."

"And treacherous."

"That too," Angela agreed.

Rachel was hurting, but calm, and talked with Sophia and Abby about plans for a celebration of their father's life. A popular teacher, Vince was known by many families at the Tribe. He would have continued to be a tremendous asset to the community had he lived. Rachel wanted to make the celebration of his life meaningful for everyone and especially comforting to the grieving children at the Tribe who had loved him, not just an adult-oriented event.

Rosie suggested that she form a children's chorus to sing at the service. Angela was falling in love with Win-J's girlfriend. They were so young that the odds were against them staying together as a couple, but she prayed they would never split up. Rosie was a gem.

The day after their arrival, Angela and the other adults who had walked with her were summoned to a Tribal Council meeting. Before the meeting began, Chief Firekeeper asked those present to stand and she asked an elder named Richard, whom she referred to as the medicine man, to say a few words. He called on the Creator to bless the conversation and to help the group gathered to come to wise and just decisions. Angela had never seen a secular meeting started with a prayer or blessing. The medicine man's words made the gathering feel sacred, like a convocation. They had created a sacred space in which to converse and come to agreement.

Chief Firekeeper addressed the Oakland refugees. "I recognize that you have traveled a long distance to Green Creek and that you have left much behind. I understand that more members of your family will arrive in the coming days and that those still traveling have greater needs. Our Tribal Council hopes that the others of your group arrive safely. You are welcome here and we will work together to grow our community. We welcome the gifts you bring, your various skills and knowledge. We welcome your children and your elders."

Tanisha wiped tears from her cheeks and Angela rubbed her back. Like Tanisha, she felt overwhelmed by the generosity of the Green Creek Natives, and filled with gratitude. How fortunate they were to find a refuge.

"However." The chief paused for effect. "However," she emphasized, "we have terms of agreement on which your acceptance at Green Creek depends. I will lay these out for you at this time. I hope you can appreciate the necessity." She paused, casting her gaze over those seated around the table pointedly before continuing to speak. "First, our community is a sovereign nation ruled by our democratically elected tribal government, seated before you." She nodded to each of the other members of the Tribal Council and they each nodded back. "To live here, you must abide by our government, our laws, our leadership, and our systems. In this crisis situation, we have created a decision-making body we call the Spokescouncil. Representatives from the various family groups within our community have been selected to participate. If you choose a spokesperson from your group, that person is invited to have a vote on the Spokescouncil and to represent your group. Next, if anyone among you breaks our laws, that person will be subject to the justice system we have in place, a system which is a living organism that continues to evolve. You will have input into the evolution of that system through the Spokescouncil. Understood?"

Angela, Darren, Tanisha, and the other Oakland refugees nodded their heads affirmative. Angela's heart beat loudly in her ears, and for a moment she felt a sense of panic. What if one of her sons broke one of the rules of the Tribe? Would she be comfortable agreeing to whatever the punishment for that would be? She didn't know exactly what she was getting herself into.

"Good," Chief Firekeeper stated. "Explain this to your children so they understand that they are subject to our rules and our laws."

"I can agree to this," Darren spoke up, "but I would like to be able to explain more clearly to my children what those rules are, and I would like to understand what they are myself." The others murmured in agreement. Their group had organically come to recognize him as their leader and the one to speak on their behalf. They would certainly select him to represent them on the Spokescouncil.

"That makes sense. We will provide a training session in basic tribal law. Our judge will offer a special training for your teenagers. We'll arrange for this immediately," Chief Firekeeper reassured Darren. Then she turned to the man next to her, a member of the Tribal Council, and indicated for him to speak.

"Quite a few people from the nearby area have come to Green Creek seeking refuge," the man explained. "As of this point in time, we're attempting to absorb everyone who comes to us as long as they agree to respect our governance and follow our laws and rules. This is taxing our systems and will strain our resources. We will need all the ingenuity and hard work we can muster. For instance, we have a lot of folks, like yourselves, who have nowhere to live. We must figure out how to shelter everyone before the weather turns cold. We also have the issue of food. These are foremost among our challenges."

When he paused, Angela's environmentally-conscious friend Julie asked, "What about water? Do you have a good water source?"

"Fortunately, we have plenty of excellent water," Chief Firekeeper assured her with pride. "That's our ace in the hole at Green Creek. We have several springs that produce water in abundance. Good water, flowing out of rock."

"That sounds biblical," Julie replied, eliciting more than a few smiles.

"Our Tribe has remained fairly isolated and private, but there are a number of locals who have a connection with us in some way. This small number of people from around here know about Green Creek, and they know we have an excellent water source and we can grow food because we operate an organic farm and goat dairy. We used to sell every week at the Farmer's Market. Some people have come already and we anticipate more will arrive in the days ahead. We hope to help all those in need who arrive at our gates." Chief Firekeeper paused before switching to another topic. "We are asking all those who choose to join us, yourselves included, to abide by a particular mandate established by our community leaders. The Tribal Council, Spokescouncil, and general membership of the Tribe, as well as all others living at Green Creek, have made an agreement, a pact. If you agree with this pact then you may remain with us and live as equal members of our community and if not then we must ask you to leave. We did not come to this agreement lightly and we understand the consequences. We have agreed that our community will not engage in violence to protect ourselves; and I will explain exactly what that means."

Tanisha sucked in her breath. Darren cast a worried glance at Angela. Angela tried to remain open to the forthcoming explanation, but her first thought was that it sounded impractical. Her next thought was that perhaps she and her children would not be safe at Green Creek after all. She carried the vivid image in her mind of Vince lying dead on the concrete wearing a halo of blood.

"We will not use violence to defend ourselves. We will not barricade ourselves in, arm ourselves, post guards at the entrances to our lands, or respond to armed intruders by escalating hostilities. We are not naïve. We expect strangers to arrive here in the days ahead, and not all of these outsiders will come with good intentions. Not all of them will arrive seeking refuge, willing to live by our laws and customs. We have made a commitment, as a community, to remain open to allowing any who come here to remain in our midst, to participate in our society, and to live here in peace. We will work to find adequate resources and we believe we can survive. We believe we can care for our elders and raise our children. We have the ability to construct more houses. They may be simple, but they will serve. We will figure out how to make our systems work in this new world. But those of us living at Green Creek in this tribal community have made a pact not to use violence to protect ourselves. We will die rather than kill intruders. We have been down the road of violent exchange and have seen that it ends badly for tribal communities. We now have a remarkable opportunity to come to the same crossroads again and to make a different decision this time."

The Oakland refugees sat in stunned silence, trying to comprehend the implications of the chief's words, and what they were being asked to do in order to remain at Green Creek.

"What this means," Chief Firekeeper continued, "is that no one in the community will keep a gun." She motioned to Darren. "We ask that you surrender your weapons. We will only use guns for hunting to provide meat. Guns are stored in a locked armory at the police station. If invaders come with evil intent, we will not fight. We will die rather than fight. It is our hope that we will have the opportunity to sit down and talk with any outsiders who arrive. We live in a remote area and few people know about Green Creek, which we hope will keep us somewhat protected. But if armed intruders arrive, we will attempt to help them understand their choices. They may choose to kill us, eat our food, and then move on, only to search for more food elsewhere. They may choose to pass us by. They may choose to join our community and live by our rules and have enough food, water, shelter, and basic necessities to perhaps survive in this new world. If you choose to remain with us, you must agree to these terms. We call this agreement the Pacific Treaty. To live here, you must sign the Pacific Treaty in good faith. The Tribal Council has decided to give you two days to consider before making your choice. Those who do not agree to the Pacific Treaty will leave." Chief Firekeeper sat back in her chair while the other members of the Tribal Council expressed their approval by intoning "OH!"

Silence blanketed the room. Then Darren slowly pushed his chair out behind him and walked around the table to stand beside Chief Firekeeper. Angela's heart beat so loudly she imagined everyone at the table could hear it. Darren was a career cop. What would he do?

"I don't need two days." He opened his jacket and took his gun out of its holster and set it on the table in front of her. "I'm in. My family is in." Two other men who had traveled with them from Oakland joined Darren at the chief's side and placed their guns on the table.

"We'll bring the rest of our weapons and ammunition to the police station," Darren promised. "Anyone who doesn't want to surrender their weapons will leave."

"I understand you're a policeman, and that there are others in your group in law enforcement. I invite those of you in this profession to join Tom and his team," the chief told Darren. "They're putting together a proposal for law enforcement under the terms of the Pacific Treaty, and they're meeting with our tribal court judge to incorporate peace patrol into our justice system." She laughed abruptly. "Our justice system has been evolving over hundreds of years so, well, at least that's nothing new."

"Thanks for the invite," Darren replied. "We would be honored to participate." He returned to his seat.

Chief Firekeeper did not touch the weapons on the table in front of her. Angela thought perhaps the chief felt that just by touching a gun she'd be contaminated with bad energy.

The chief informed the new arrivals, "In the news streams, in the beginning, they referred to what happened as the Systems Collapse. That's what we call it too. Since we established the Pacific Treaty, we've chosen names for the time before the Systems Collapse and the time we're living in now. We call the before-time the Lost Time. We remain hopeful for our future so we call this living time the Vision Time. One more thing," she added with a half-smile, "even though we've been a self-governing sovereign nation for thousands of years, we continue to change and grow. We're committed to creating an inclusive way of life together. That said, welcome to the Vision Time at Green Creek."

"I applaud your efforts," Darren responded. He gave the chief an impish smile, said "carry on," and saluted the chief, which sent a ripple of laughter through the Tribal Council and around the room.

Angela would not quarrel with the Pacific Treaty, yet she wondered how well it would hold up the first time gangbangers from Oakland or Sacramento stumbled upon Green Creek, isolated in the woods. Such a thing could happen more easily than the tribal leadership imagined. She had witnessed the horror people were capable of inflicting on one another. She had seen the trauma that children had experienced at the hands of those who purported to love them and who were supposed to care for them. She knew the sad results of intergenerational family dysfunction and had seen the lost souls who were the product of childhood trauma. Those damaged, lost souls didn't disappear along with the oil. They still walked in the world. She wished she could muster Chief Firekeeper's optimism but she could not. She would pray for safety, for obscurity, for the ability of Green Creek to remain invisible to the world; because heaven help them if desperate invaders with guns showed up. When that happened, the Pacific Treaty would drag them all down to the bottom of the sea. But she couldn't think of a better alternative for her boys than throwing in their lot with Green Creek. She had nowhere else to go. She would not criticize the Pacific Treaty. She would attempt to explain it to her sons.

Tanisha asked the group if anyone could get a signal for their phone. Signals had been spotty and then nonexistent during the last few days of their journey. A man answered Tanisha's question. "We lost all phone signals about a week ago." They could still generate electricity from some solar panels at Green Creek to recharge electronic devices, but the cell towers had been affected somehow and would not relay messages.

Angela figured the best way to help her sons adjust to the changed circumstances of their lives was to engage them in a project. So she recruited them to help her organize the celebration of Vince's life. They teamed up with other close friends of Vince, a couple members of the Tribal Council, Sophia and Abby, and tribal children who had attended Vince's classes at their former school. Angela told Rachel she didn't have to do any of the work, that they would put something together to honor Vince. Rachel had her hands full at the clinic with people who could no longer access the doctors, medications, and medical care they had utilized in the Lost Time. While Rachel wanted to help organize the celebration, she also wanted to help people stabilize their health. A lot of people, particularly those with chronic conditions, were going through big changes, and they needed Rachel's guidance.

In the midst of their preparations for the celebration, Richard the medicine man approached Angela to talk about the many people he saw suffering from what he called the Distance Sickness. He described this as grief caused by the loss of communication with family and friends not in the immediate vicinity. Richard suggested they perform a ritual at Vince's celebration to acknowledge the grief people felt from their loss of contact with dear ones far away. He described for Angela a guided meditation he wanted to lead for people to send spiritual communication across the miles, culminating in throwing sage on a bonfire as a symbolic gesture. She felt a strong connection to Richard, who demonstrated a deep understanding of human psychology and the spiritual necessities of healing work. She asked him to meet with her after Vince's celebration to talk about further rituals they could devise to help people cope with grief and loss. Because the celebration would include a bonfire, it would take place outdoors.

Richard helped Angela organize and lead the celebration, which they held in the evening. Rosie's children's choir sang in clear and hopeful child-voices. Their children had lost so much in the Systems Collapse, and yet they had retained their sense of wonder and their capacity for delight. Angela and Rachel set up an altar with photographs of Vince from throughout his life as well as objects that they connected with Vince, such as his coffee mug and Oakland As baseball cap. Richard recited an opening blessing. Many people shared memories of Vince. It surprised Angela to see how many children bravely stood up and told stories about Vince. He had made a measurable difference in the lives of so many tribal children. All of Angela's boys said something, even shy Sulei. Richard conducted his guided meditation and at the end of it everyone threw handfuls of dried sage onto a roaring bonfire as part of the closing ceremony. The pungent scent of the sage clung to their clothing and hair. When darkness fell, the sky filled with an explosion of stars. People drew their lawn chairs to the fire and sat talking in small groups. Eventually the children were put to bed and the adults remained clustered around the fire late into the night.

After the ceremony concluded with the burning of the sage, Angela had noticed that Win-J stepped away from the group and headed to a nearby wooded area. She knew that he had taken to walking in this woods and sitting by himself on a particular rock. Angela imagined she would find him there. She padded softly after him. When he saw her coming through the trees to his special place, she asked him, "May I sit with you?"

"Sure," he agreed. They sat in silence, listening to the sounds of the forest; the birds and rustling of branches. It was peaceful and the foliage blocked out noise from the nearby community. Angela could see why Win-J liked the spot.

"I wonder if I'm a jinx," Win-J said.

"Why would you think that?"

"First that stupid situation happened to Dad and he wound up in prison. Then, remember when I started to hang out with Tremel's family and his dad really liked me? Then Tremel's dad had a stroke and they moved to Santa Barbara to be closer to his mom's family. Vince stepped up to the plate for me after Dad went to prison, and he got killed because of that guy trying to steal my bike." Win-J shrugged. "So maybe I'm a jinx for father figures."

"What happened to Vince was random," Angela asserted.

Win-J looked at his feet and then spoke practically inaudibly. "But if I hadn't freaked out over that guy trying to take my bike, Vince would still be alive."

"Winston Junior, you did not cause Vince's death," Angela told him firmly. "Don't you dare put that on yourself. It was a random horrible thing that just happened. It wasn't your fault."

Win-J's eyes filled with tears. "You can't know that."

"I can. I've seen a lot more of life than you've seen. Sometimes random horrible things just happen. Whatever you did or did not do in that moment had no significant impact on the outcome. If you hadn't gotten into it over the bike, it could have been something else, like a shopping cart filled with supplies. I don't believe in fate so I don't think Vince had death coming to him, and that there was nothing anyone could have done to stop it. I like to think there is a mysterious order to the universe, but I also don't think everything happens for a reason. I hate it when people say that. Some things don't happen for a reason. And I am absolutely sure that your actions did not cause Vince's death."

Win-J still appeared worried. "What if I hang out with Rosie's family, I mean like with her father, and then something happens to him? I'm afraid something will happen to Darren if I hang out with him."

"I wish you had been given more time to be a child, Win-J," Angela said, with a sigh. "I'm proud of the young man you've become under the circumstances and I know that Dad would be proud too." Win-J's eyes welled with tears at the compliment. He wiped them away. "But something you need to accept, as a man, is that life is filled with loss and sorrow, and who we are, the measure of our integrity and our ability to make our lives matter, that's built on how we choose to respond to that adversity. If you blame yourself for Vince's death and choose to sink into self-pity and self-doubt then you will hinder your ability to move forward and be productive. If you take the loss into you, make it part of you, and carry it as you continue with your life then you have the potential to make a difference for other people and to improve your life and the lives of others. You hear me?"

"I hear you."

She gave him a hug. "Nothing should prevent you from spending time with Darren. He likes you and he's a good man and a great dad. You're not a jinx."

"Thanks." He sounded relieved so she thought he believed her.

"I'm going back to the fire."

"I think I'll stay here for a little while."

Angela stood. "I'll see you back at the house later."

After their conversation, Win-J visibly regained his spark and optimism. Yet a sliver of that spark had plummeted over the edge of the overpass with Vince and Angela knew from professional experience that her son would never get that sliver back.

During the night following the celebration for Vince, a group of thieves entered the health clinic and stole a large quantity of painkillers. Tom had wanted to lock medications up inside police headquarters, but Rachel had disagreed. He arrived on the scene of the theft wearing his "I told you so" expression.

"What? They could have broken into the police office and stolen them from there just as easily as from here," she defended herself.

"I have several locked safes," Tom countered. "I'm going to find out who did this and get the meds back, and then I'm locking this stuff up in my safe." She couldn't argue. Tom and his officers knew which people in the community were drug addicts and they felt certain they could trace the stolen drugs to them. Those addicted to illicit drugs were struggling. Some had managed to kick their habit, some were desperate, a few had died. True to his word, Tom and his team tracked down the culprits and recovered almost all of the painkillers. The greatest problem posed by the theft was what to do with the thieves. A consequence was in order, but what form should that take? The Tribal Council met with the judge to develop a plan that would bring healing rather than punishment.

Tom locked up the painkillers as well as quite a few other pharmaceuticals at the police office. This made extra steps for Rachel when she wanted to prescribe the drugs, but she couldn't argue with him about it anymore after what had happened. She had to admit that having the meds out of reach made her think more carefully about whether or not to prescribe them. She hated withholding drugs from people who would feel better if she could dispense the drugs, but she had to save them for those instances when the need was truly great. There would come a time when she wouldn't have them at all. For anyone.

The evening after the stolen drugs were recovered, Rachel sat down for a scheduled screen chat with Callie. She held her breath, hoping her friend would be there. To her relief, Callie appeared right on time. "When you actually turn up on the screen it feels like a miracle," Rachel said, immensely grateful that the connection had gone through.

"I wonder how many more times it will work. So far we've been lucky." Callie wore her favorite faded-yellow sundress. Her dreadlocks were tied back with a piece of jute. Rachel fixed the image of Callie in her mind, as she always did now when they chatted, preparing herself to lose her friend at any time.

"I have someone here who wants to say hi."

"Seriously?" Callie's eyebrows shot up in anticipation.

Angela revealed her presence beside Rachel. "Oh my god!" Callie shouted. "I mean if I believed in god then, well, but, oh my god! How did you get there? It's so great to see you."

Angela took Rachel's hand in hers and told Callie an abridged version of her exodus from Oakland. As Rachel cried silently beside her, she broke the news about Vince.

Callie held her hand up to the screen, fingers splayed, "I wish I could touch you. Oh Ray, I wish I could give you a hug. I'm so far away."

"You're so far away. You really are," Rachel replied.

"And I'm not coming back. We should dial up on the computer more often. While it still works."

"I know," Rachel agreed. "We should try every other evening. Sometimes it won't work, but we should at least try. It has to be later than this because I'm usually needed at the clinic." They agreed on a time that they would check in for as long as they could. Angela commented on the irony that she and Rachel had lost contact with the other girlfriends, Jo, Melanie, Max, Robin, who were in the same country with them, but they had managed to stay in communication with Callie in Latin America. Dear Callie, grounded while at the same time inspired by an advanced spiritual sensibility, talked with Rachel for a long time, helping her navigate the landscape of her grief, before they disconnected.

Rachel threw herself into her work. She and her clinical staff had a lot of educating to do, not to mention the need for their emotional support as they tried to help people change their lifestyle habits so they might survive. Many people were not going to make the adjustment, and it would cost them their lives. Some had already died.

One late afternoon, while wrapping up a long day at the clinic, meeting with her last patient, Rachel saw a powder-blue vintage Volkswagen van towing a metal camper pass by the window of the examination room. She and her patient fell silent in mid-conversation and stared out the window in disbelief. They had not seen any automotive vehicles on the move since the Systems Collapse, so the camper and the van seemed as real as a unicorn walking down the street.

"What do you think it runs on?" Rachel asked her patient.

"No clue," he replied.

"We'll find out soon enough, I suppose."

Burning with curiosity, Rachel left the clinic the minute she finished with her patient, and walked over to the tribal office. Parked just down the street, in front of Christina's house, the camper glinted like a giant tin can in the amber late-day sun. When she encountered Tom on the porch of the tribal office, she didn't even need to formulate a question before he informed her, "It runs on a combination of electrical charge and used vegetable oil. Ain't that something?"

"Seriously?" Rachel exclaimed.

"I kid you not," Tom confirmed.

"Who does it belong to?"

"Crystal is back."

"Christina's Crystal?"

"Yup. That very one. And she's pregnant again," Tom stated with an unmistakable tone of judgment. "She brought the baby's daddy with her. That French-fry-powered contraption belongs to him."

"French fries?"

"He says he starts the engine up with an electrical charge from a solar-powered battery and then he switches it over to a tank of used vegetable grease. They been stopping at fast food joints along the way to load up on used grease. They stopped at that burger place just off the highway right before they drove into the Rez and raided the abandoned deep fat fryer. Craziest thing I ever heard."

"I wonder if Crystal's baby-daddy knows how to build another one."

"Now that's a concept," Tom replied with quickened interest. "What if he can convert my cruiser? That would be pretty damn cool."

"So Crystal is over at Christina's?" The previous year, Crystal had turned up pregnant at sixteen, and just when everyone was finally getting used to the idea of her having a baby, she miscarried. Then Crystal burned out on hearing that losing the baby was "for the better" since she was so young, and she ran away. She wanted that baby fiercely and saw nothing "for the better" about her loss.

"Sure is."

Rachel walked over to Christina's to welcome Crystal home and to satisfy her curiosity about the baby's daddy. She made a silent vow to remain extra vigilant through Crystal's pregnancy this time around; to do everything in her power to see this baby into the world safely. Becoming a teen mom no longer seemed like such an unfortunate choice for Crystal as it once had. What other alternatives did Crystal have now? Not college, career, or travel.

Rachel knocked on the doorframe and entered. In recent days, people did this more and more often; they didn't wait for an invitation or formal greeting, but simply notified each other of their presence and walked right into each other's homes as if they all lived in all of the houses. Callie would have relished studying the anthropological dimension of changes in the dynamic of the community since the Systems Collapse. Oh Callie.

"We must have conjured you up," Christina announced delightedly as Rachel entered the living room. Crystal sat on the couch next to her grandmother, who held Crystal's hand sandwiched between both of hers. How Christina had missed her wild girl. Two men with deep-chocolate-brown skin sat on the floor. One of them was tall and willowy, while the other was shorter, compact, and dense, with a muscular upper body. On the worn, rose-colored armchair across the room sat a woman who Rachel guessed was in her early sixties. She had shoulder-length, straight, white hair with thick bangs across her forehead and a spray of lovely laugh lines fanning out from the corners of her eyes.

Crystal bounced up from the couch and hurried over to give Rachel a hug. "I'm so sorry about Vince," Crystal said softly in Rachel's ear. Rachel's eyes welled with tears. "It's OK," Crystal said as she rubbed Rachel's back. It wasn't OK, but she knew that Crystal meant well. Rachel's face contorted for a moment before she managed to beat the grief back, focusing on Crystal instead of her own bottomless loss. She stepped back from Crystal to have a look at her, wiping her eyes, and commented, "By the size of you, young lady, you must be about six months along."

"Almost," Crystal replied, pleased. "And we know it's a boy."

"We had a sonogram," said the shorter, more muscular man. A pleasant African accent encased his velvety-deep voice.

"This is my husband, Sanyu," Crystal introduced him. "Sanyu, this is Rachel."

Sanyu stood and held his hand out to Rachel. "I've heard a lot about you. I hope I can be of assistance to you."

Christina piped up, "Sanyu is a nurse practitioner."

"Oh my god!" Rachel exclaimed. "I'm the only doctor at Green Creek."

"So I hear," Sanyu said.

"And this is Bernadette," Crystal said as she pointed to the older woman in the armchair, who did not rise, but nodded and smiled.

"This is my friend, Musoke," Sanyu introduced the other man. Musoke unfolded his stork-like legs, rose from the floor, catapulted himself to his full lean and lanky height of well over six feet, and approached Rachel to shake her hand.

"I will be no help," Musoke said with a giggle. "I faint at the sight of blood. I don't suppose there's much need for an interior decorator here." He had a similar African accent to Sanyu's.

"I hope you don't mind my asking, what country do you men come from originally?" Rachel inquired.

"Uganda," Sanyu informed her, while Musoke grimaced, raised two fingers, and pretended to spit between the fingers. "Don't mind him," Sanyu continued. "He does that whenever I mention Uganda."

Crystal explained, "Musoke and Sanyu grew up together, like brothers. Sanyu helped him escape Uganda about six inches ahead of a homophobic government that would have executed him for being gay if he hadn't left."

"I do not miss my murderous backward homeland. I was having a blast in the Castro until the wheels came off and then these guys called me and told me to stay put and they came to get me and brought me up here. There must be at least a few gay guys living on the Rez. One can always hope."

"Shut up," Crystal said with a laugh, as she slapped Musoke's arm playfully.

"We call it two-spirit," Christina informed him.

"Queer," Crystal clarified. "Here we call it two-spirit."

Bernadette piped up, "I'm neither Ugandan nor two-spirit, honey. I'm Shoshone, from Idaho, where all my children and grandchildren live, so I will probably never see them again." She said several words, probably in Shoshone, that Rachel did not recognize before she shrugged with resignation.

"What are you doing in Cali?" Rachel asked Bernadette.

"Followed a man, what else would bring me so far from home?" Bernadette replied. "I worked in medical records as a data entry clerk up until a few weeks ago. I know Sanyu from the medical center."

Rachel turned to Sanyu. "I hear you have a vehicle that runs on used vegetable grease. That works? I'm amazed you got here in that thing."

"It does work," Sanyu confirmed. "It was a bit tricky traveling since we needed to use back roads and reduce our exposure to people who might try to steal it from us. But we figured it out. The hardest part was getting it out of town since a lot of the streets in the city are completely clogged with dead cars."

"We got some incredible lucky breaks," Crystal added.

"And wait until you see what they brought in Bernadette's trailer," Christina told Rachel.

"What is that?"

"I'll show you," Bernadette offered. She heaved herself up from the chair. "I want that chair. It's about the most comfy chair ever."

"Good energy in that chair," Christina muttered.

"Excellent," Bernadette agreed. "If it vanishes, you will find it in my camper." Clearly Christina had an affinity with Bernadette.

"You come to the clinic first thing tomorrow and I'll fit you in to check you out," Rachel told Crystal before she and Bernadette stepped out of the house.

Bernadette opened the back door to her tin can of a mobile house and unfolded two steps. "After you," she said. Rachel stepped up into the little camper. There was barely space to turn around inside. The camper had a bed, a fold-down table, and a tiny counter with a gas stove. There was a sink and even a chemical toilet. The surfaces of everything except a corner of the bed were covered in stacks of medical supplies. Rachel picked up a package close to hand. It contained an insulin pump. Then she noticed that there were coolers stacked all over the bed. She half-turned to Bernadette and raised an inquiring eyebrow.

"Insulin in the coolers. It's all diabetes supplies. A boatload of them."

Rachel nearly cried. The supplies in Bernadette's trailer would keep dozens of people alive for many months, maybe years. "Why?" Rachel asked, as the two women left the hot camper and stepped out onto the street.

Bernadette gazed off into the distance. She shuddered. She turned back to Rachel. "My husband was diabetic. I had access to supplies at the hospital. Sanyu helped me load up. I figured I had enough to keep Arnie alive for a long time. But when Sanyu and I got back to my house, we found Arnie barely conscious. I had a truckload of diabetes medical supplies and Arnie, at home alone, had let his blood sugar drop so low he had flat-lined and he was foaming at the mouth, having seizures, the whole show. We had been gone for hours. He had probably been extremely low for a very long time. I'm surprised he was even alive when we got there."

"Did you have glucagon?" Rachel asked.

"Of course. I have boxes of it." she waved her arm in the direction of the camper. "Sanyu got one and administered it, but by then Arnie had died in my arms. We couldn't get him back. I tell you, we humans make plans and God laughs. I'm a widow with a camper full of diabetes medical supplies."

"I'm a widow too."

"So I heard. I'm a widow and my children are beyond my reach. I could never make it to Idaho from here." Bernadette shrugged. "The oil barons robbed me of everything that matters in my life."

"I'm sorry."

"The catastrophic level of events did Arnie in. I imagine him sitting and watching the news in horror and disbelief and not paying attention to his blood sugar. After all the close scrapes we have had over the years, it took this magnitude of insanity in the world to take him from me."

"I have a job for you if you want it."

"What is that?"

"I need help training the diabetics at Green Creek to manage their blood sugar better. We don't have access to lab tests or an endocrinologist anymore. We only have our own best guesses. Someone who knows the disease like you do is a tremendous asset. I have people in all stages and a lot of them could kick the disease altogether with diet and lifestyle changes. They're a lot more motivated in the Vision Time because with dwindling availability of meds, they feel death breathing down their necks."

"The Vision Time?"

"That's what we call the time we live in now. Our chief named it."

"Good name."

"Our chief is a visionary woman."

"What did she name the time before?"

"The Lost Time."

"I'd like to meet your chief."

Rachel had a feeling that Chief Firekeeper and Bernadette would become fast friends.

A few days after Crystal and her entourage arrived, and after Angela had lived at Green Creek for nearly three weeks, Win-J burst into the kitchen, where his mother and Rachel were preparing dinner for their blended family. He practically bounced off the walls with excitement. He had become so serious since they had left Oakland and resettled at Green Creek that Angela savored the sight of him so animated and grinning widely.

"Guess what, Mom. You will never guess!"

"Something good?" Angela replied as she wiped her damp hands on a towel.

"Super-good! Michael, you know, Darren's brother, and the rest of Rosie's family have arrived. Rosie's grandmother Josie made it."

Angela threw a joyful glance in Rachel's direction and told her, "Gotta go. I'll be back soon. It's the rest of our people from Oakland. The elders and the sick ones, the ones who had to walk more slowly."

"Go, go." Rachel shooed Angela out of the kitchen. "I'll finish making dinner." As Angela hurried out the door, Rachel sighed, thinking of how much more work was coming her way with additional elderly and sick people arriving.

Angela took off at a run beside Win-J. Rosie's extended family had assembled on the patch of dry weeds and wild grasses that pretended to be a reminder of a lawn in front of the doublewide trailer that the Tribe had relegated to Darren's family. On that little patch of parched ground, a great deal of hugging and tearful reunion was underway. Angela recognized Josie at once, even though the woman had lost a lot of weight. Darren had his arm around her in a proprietary manner, and he would not let her go. Rosie, Jamal, Sulei, and the other children who had walked from Oakland circulated in the crowd, celebrating the arrival. It surprised Angela that she felt so connected to these others who had fallen behind so early on their journey. They had separated from Angela's group so soon after leaving Oakland that she barely knew them, and yet they felt like family. Her feelings had a lot to do with the fact that she and her group from Oakland were virtually the only African Americans in the Green Creek community. It felt like reinforcements had arrived. After all, what was an African American community without its elders?

As Angela approached, Josie disengaged herself from her son and stepped forward to embrace Angela. Over Josie's shoulder, Angela glimpsed Darren's sister-in-law, who had become hysterical when her husband Michael informed her he would stay behind with his mother and the others. The woman wept with relief as she clung to her husband. Angela felt a pang of envy and heartache rear its ugly head. She didn't think she would ever shake her anger and grief at her own loss. She did not begrudge the other woman her good fortune, she simply felt rage that fortune had not smiled so kindly on her. Tears sprang to her eyes.

"Hey baby," Josie crooned softly, "you are the sweetest. Thank you for rescuing our family." She had misinterpreted Angela's tears, and Angela didn't set her straight.

"I'm so glad you made it. You look terrific."

"It's amazing what living on apples and water and walking six miles a day can do for a woman's figure," Josie joked. Then she became more serious as she said quietly, "Not all of us survived."

"Who did you lose?"

Josie named four names. The only one Angela recognized was the aging uncle whom Michael had pulled in the wagon. "We have a couple people who need medical attention," she added.

"My friend Rachel is the doctor here. I'm sure she'll go to the clinic and meet with those in need this evening if necessary. We also have medicine. It'll run out eventually, but we're not hoarding it, we're using it for as long as it lasts."

"I ran out of my blood pressure meds," Josie said, as Darren came up behind her and threw his arm over her shoulders again. He could not get enough of laying hands on his mother, as if he had to convince himself that she was still alive by touching her.

"Rachel might have more," Darren suggested.

"I don't think I need them. I have my cuff and I took my blood pressure every day. It went down to normal. Must have been all that walking. I intend to keep walking for exercise. I like it. Walking clears my head. What was I thinking spending so much of my life indoors sitting around on my fat ass before?"

Angela laughed.

"They have an organic farm here, Momma," Darren said. "You could help out at the farm if you want to spend time outdoors. It's beautiful. Tanisha works there every day."

"Sounds wonderful."

"And they're expanding it," Darren continued enthusiastically. "They have livestock too. Goats, poultry, rabbits. Momma loves to cook her some rabbit," Darren told Angela.

"The garden is getting bigger every day," Angela added. They had more animals than Darren had mentioned. They also kept cows, sheep, and pigs. They even had some horses and a couple of donkeys on the Rez. Some people had kept their own farm animals on their own property, mostly rabbits, chickens, and an occasional goat. But most of the farm animals in the community were now cared for communally at the farm. "I'll ask the children to give you a tour of Green Creek tomorrow," Angela promised Josie. "That will keep you walking."

"Terrific. Right now, I could really go for some chicken. I haven't eaten meat in weeks. What you got in your refrigerator?" Josie asked her son.

"Momma needs her some chicken, Tanisha," Darren hollered over his shoulder, chuckling merrily.

"Y'all better cut me in on some of that," Michael interjected.

"I'm on it," Tanisha replied, laughing.

"Eating over here, tonight," Win-J said to Angela as he came up beside her.

"This may be about to turn into a Stone Soup potluck up in here," Angela rejoined. "I better go get Rachel and the girls. If some chickens are about to be sacrificed then they will want to get a piece of the action."

Darren would have to go to the garden director to discuss the chickens, but Angela already knew they would be forthcoming. It was going to be a late night of celebration.

"Take those in need of medical attention over to the clinic," Angela instructed Darren. "Rachel can take care of that while you folks wrangle some chicken."

"Right," Darren replied.

Angela wove through the crowd, greeting other newcomers and sharing the festive mood. Win-J headed home to fetch Rachel to the clinic for consultations with those experiencing health issues, while Jamal organized the girls and Sulei to carry food over from their house to Tanisha's. As the party unfolded, Angela realized how desperately people had needed a reason to celebrate. She sought out Richard and in the context of a conversation about the healing properties of community events, they cooked up the idea to have a bonfire once a month on the new moon.

During the first week in September, Rachel received the answer to one of her silent prayers. A dentist arrived at Green Creek. Rachel knew Dr. Chaudhary because his two daughters were close in age to Abby and Sophia and the girls were friends. Rachel had thought about taking Tom and a couple other guys for protection and going to Vinod Chaudhary's house to recruit him to move to Green Creek because she was not trained or equipped to provide anything more than the most rudimentary dental care. A burden lifted from her shoulders when Vinod and his wife and daughters arrived with their four horses, six goats, two border collies, and a large, orange cat. The horses and goats were another boon for the community.

Rachel hurried to the chief's office the instant she could shake free after she learned of the Chaudhary family's arrival. She saw the family's horses tied to the front porch railing of the tribal office building and felt as if she had been transported in a time machine to the old days of the West.

Vinod flashed Rachel a delighted grin when she entered the room and his wife Rani burst into tears. Rachel hugged Rani reassuringly. "You're a sight for sore eyes! Or should I say for sore mouths? We need you here desperately, Vinod."

He appeared taken aback. "Well, yes, OK. You don't have a dentist here?"

"Now we do. I hope you brought your instruments."

"I only brought what I could carry, just the basics."

"Why did you come to Green Creek?"

"The well ran dry," Vinod told her, with a little shrug. "It's been doing that every summer for the past few years, with the drought and all. We knew it would happen. Usually at this time of year we stay at the cottage behind my office in town until the rains raise the water table in the fall. We have city water there. But it's not safe in town these days. I don't want my girls in town where I can't protect them. We stayed at home as long as we could and then we had to leave. We can't survive on our ranch without water. I guess you folks are not on a well here."

"That we are not," the chief confirmed. "We have excellent gravity-flow springs."

"Even if the well was producing," Rani added in a quavering voice, "we were afraid to stay at the ranch alone. Marauding groups from the cities are roaming in the countryside now. It's not safe to be isolated. We were pretty well hidden out in the woods, but you never know who will find you."

"We would be deeply grateful if you would let us stay at Green Creek," Vinod said.

"Are you crazy?" Rachel exclaimed. "Do you have any idea how valuable a dentist is? Of course you can stay. Right, chief?"

"Absolutely," the chief agreed. "We just need to figure out where to put you. But we'll come up with something. We always do."

"Too bad we don't have our cars," Vinod said wistfully. "There's a RV sales lot near here on Compton Springs Road. A heap of RVs are sitting on that lot. If we could bring some of them over here, then people could live in them."

Rachel and the chief exchanged a glance, both of them thinking of Sanyu's electric-and-French-fry-grease VW.

"Thanks for that information. We actually do have a way to drag them over here," the chief told Vinod.

"A guy here has a van that runs mainly on used vegetable oil," Rachel said.

"Seriously?!"

"Oh yeah," the chief confirmed.

RVs aside, Rachel moved on with her own agenda. "I don't suppose you have any anesthetic, do you?"

"I can help with that," Rani answered in Vinod's stead. "I had a cottage botanicals business before all this happened."

"I remember that."

"I grew flowers and I distilled flower essences. I made essential oils and medicinal flower extracts," Rani continued. "I saved seeds and I still have them." Rachel didn't see the connection with anesthesia, but she didn't say so, instead waiting for Rani to finish. "I can distill opium from poppies."

"Opium?" Rachel echoed, mystified.

"Rani can take your average California poppy," Vinod explained, "that grows wild all over the hills, and make opium from it. We can use opium to knock people out to treat them." Rachel was stunned at the simplicity of it.

"I also have some lovely cultivated poppy seeds that should germinate. So I don't have to depend entirely on wild poppies," Rani added. "But I can use wild poppies too. If I can have access to some arable land, I can grow flowers and make many useful essences from them. You'd be surprised. I just have to figure out where to store the botanicals after I brew them because I couldn't bring very many bottles."

"Do you have more bottles back at your house?" the chief asked.

"Some," Rani answered, "but even if I can bring them over here, they'll run out eventually."

"Like everything else," Vinod added with resignation.

"How long will it take to make a batch of opium?" Rachel asked. "I'm dreading the first time that someone needs surgery. I don't see how I can perform surgery if I can't knock the person out. But it's going to happen eventually, and it terrifies me. How long would it take you to make opium?"

"Let's not get ahead of ourselves," Rani replied. "First I need the poppies. It takes time to grow flowers."

"We have wild California poppies growing around here," the chief said. "I'll send the children out to pick."

"I have a little anesthetic at my office," Vinod informed them. "I also have a lot of dental and medical supplies at the office. But I don't have a way to transport them; and on top of that, it's getting dangerous in town. I would rather not go back out there now that we made it here safely."

"Let me work on that," the chief said. She stuck her head out the door and called to her assistant to fetch Tom.

"Safety is relative," Rachel stated quietly. "My husband was killed while walking up here from Oakland. He was away at a teacher's conference. Rotten luck. The group he was with walked for two weeks after he died and found us without him. There's no telling who else will find us." Rachel paused before continuing to share her thoughts. "I'm the only doctor in the community, although I have a trained staff of health care providers. But I've worried about how to handle dental care. I'm so relieved to have you aboard."

"I assure you that my skill set is of lesser consequence than Rani's." He exchanged a glance with his wife. "Rani is a nutritionist. She can help prevent people from getting sick in the first place."

"You mean a registered dietician?"

"No," Rani replied, "that's not quite what I do. I'm a holistic nutritionist. I take a different approach; but I do teach people how to eat clean food to stay healthy."

"She makes miracles. I've seen her do it."

"Honey, please; too much hype," Rani protested in embarrassment.

Tom appeared in the doorway. "What's up?"

"I've got a job for you and you're gonna love this one." The chief outlined her plan for Tom to assemble a team of trained officers to accompany Sanyu (in the van) and Vinod into town to collect equipment and supplies from Vinod's office. Tom refused flat out to go into town unarmed. The chief did not like this, but she capitulated. She also wanted them to haul RVs from the site Vinod had mentioned.

Housing for the people who arrived at Green Creek seeking refuge was one of the chief's biggest concerns. They sent for Sanyu, who greeted their plan with enthusiasm.

"Please don't send Vinod back out," Rani pleaded. "He's no police officer. There are dangerous and desperate people out there. People not from around here, not from a rural community; people who never grew anything to eat, who don't know the first thing about horses, but think they can figure it out if they could get their hands on one; people with few survival skills in this situation are out there looking to take whatever they can from others. People who have no reverence for life are out there." Rani's voice wavered as she fought back tears.

Vinod put his arms around his wife. "Lord knows I don't want to go back out. But I have to do this. I'll be OK," he reassured her. Rachel thought about Vince. Rani was right. The men who went out would risk their lives, and Vinod might not come back OK.

"Please bring books back with you," Rachel told Vinod. "Because you need to start teaching dentistry to other people. I've taken young apprentices myself. If the community survives, if it continues, and for the sake of our children I hope it does, then our young people need to have medical and dental knowledge passed down because those of us who had the benefit of formal training won't live forever. The community needs more than one doctor and more than one dentist. Life is even more tenuous in the Vision Time and we must prepare for what lies ahead."

"I'll bring reference books," Vinod promised.

"Vision Time?" Rani asked.

"That's what we call the new era, since the Systems Collapse," the chief explained.

"Crystal won't like this," Sanyu noted. He winced, imagining how he would break the news to her that he was going out.

"Crystal?" Vinod asked.

"My pregnant wife," Sanyu informed him.

"You shouldn't go," Rani blurted. "Not with a baby on the way."

"The baby is not due this week," Sanyu told her.

"Does anyone else know how to run that VW?" the chief asked.

"Nope," Sanyu replied. "Musoke knows a little bit. But he's no engineer; he couldn't haul RVs with it. Frankly, I wouldn't want him or anyone else driving it. We can't afford to destroy it."

"And we can't afford to have it stolen," Tom added. "I need to take a substantial armed guard. We'll go on horseback and use the VW exclusively for transporting supplies when we go to Vinod's office, and exclusively for hauling RVs after that." Tom had started organizing the mission in his head. Rachel smiled to see how happy it made him to jump back into action as the police chief.

"Works for me," Sanyu agreed.

Chief Firekeeper assigned an abandoned house with a backyard garden area to the Chaudhary family and introduced Rani to the farming leaders. Meanwhile, Tom assembled his team for their first foray into the outside world, scheduled in two days' time at dawn. Despite the danger of going out, and the trepidation of those they left behind, Tom and his security force (which included Darren, Michael, and their Oakland Police friends) could not conceal their delight at the prospect of getting back on the job and packing their guns. Tom drilled into his force the importance of not divulging to anyone where they came from or how to get there. Their obscurity and remote location was the most significant protective factor they had going for them.

On the night of their arrival at Green Creek, the Chaudhary family accepted an invitation to eat dinner with Angela, Rachel, and their children. Their girls bubbled with excitement to see their friends Abby and Sophia again.

Jamal, who had developed an interest in cooking, brought home vegetables and cheese from the farm every day for the family's dinner and helped prepare it with either Angela or Rachel, who shared responsibility for family dinners. But since Angela lacked culinary skills and Rachel enjoyed cooking to help her relax, Rachel wound up involved in the cooking more often than Angela did. If Rachel had to work late, she would send for Jamal and give him instructions about what to do in her absence.

For dinner that night, Rachel and Jamal cooked a vegetable stew of squashes, peppers, onions, garlic, and tomatoes. They served it over baked potatoes and topped it all off with goat cheese. Angela missed meat, but she felt grateful to have nourishing food for herself and her boys. They still ate meat from time to time, but not often. At least the meat she ate when she could get it was delicious because it came directly from the farm.

Rachel had initiated a ritual of joining hands before dinner and saying a few words of thanks. She wanted to consciously practice gratitude in all aspects of her life since losing Vince. Thus, when the family sat down to their vegetable stew with the Chaudhary family, Rachel asked everyone to join hands and she said a few words of thanks for the safety of the new arrivals. The girls burst into happy chatter immediately thereafter, and the families enjoyed a lively conversation over their meal. Jamal expressed an interest in learning more about nutrition from Rani, who promised to teach him. Angela had made a pear and apple custard for dessert, sweetened with honey. With sugar dwindling at Green Creek, the farming contingent had started expanding their beekeeping operation. Halfway through dessert, the lights went out and the low-level electrical hum of the house fell silent.

The children rushed to the windows to look for lights from other houses. Rachel's house was not on the Rez proper, but adjacent to the road leading into Green Creek. The twinkling of lights from structures on the Rez was usually visible from her house, but they could not see any lights coming from the Rez. Rachel tried to wrestle her panic to the mat for the sake of the children, but grief had left her in such a fragile emotional state that she failed. She started to cry. She had dreaded the loss of electricity, not so much for the impact this would have on her home life, but more for the impact on her work and the health of others. She faced the prospect of running a medical clinic in which many of her most important tools and instruments would no longer operate. Angela put a steadying hand on Rachel's shoulder.

Rani took Rachel's hand in hers. "A great deal of healing happened before electricity and a great deal of it will happen after it too," she said.

Fortunately, the children didn't realize the greater ramifications, and they took this new development in stride. They had become astonishingly resilient and adaptable. Angela often marveled over their ability to accept each new challenge, to adjust, to transform their thinking and move forward. They hunted for candles and flashlights, came up with the idea of constructing a tent in the living room with their blankets, and enlisted Vinod to crawl into the tent with them and tell them ghost stories. Angela, Win-J, and Rosie cleared the table, washed the dishes in the sink (no dishwasher) by candlelight, and surveyed the food in the refrigerator to determine what they needed to eat before it went bad. As they stood at the open refrigerator, the lights flashed on and the appliances roared back to life as suddenly as they had gone silent.

The restoration of power transformed the blackout from an immediate challenge to a harsh forecast of their future. Rachel resolved to meet with her team to make contingency plans in preparation for the eventual permanent loss of power. Clearly, they already could not depend on it. They would need backup plans to follow in the event that they lost power while in the middle of a power-dependent medical procedure. She would talk to the chief about directing power from the Rez's small solar array to the clinic. She knew they had some power from the panels, but she didn't know how much. She ran a load of laundry and recharged her computer, along with everything else in the house that worked on a battery charge, such as Vince's electric drill, the phones (which were useless for just about anything other than looking at pictures or listening to music), and her toothbrush.

The power outage reminded Angela that there would come a day when she would have no way to listen to the Pointer Sisters singing "Sisters Are Doin' It for Themselves." She had so many beloved songs on her tablet, which would fall silent when the electricity failed for good. She wished she knew how to play a musical instrument.

Two days later, Tom and his men left on horseback with Sanyu in his VW at sunrise. Tom loved every minute of this mission. Not only did he have his gun on his hip again, but he was doing real security work. Just about all of the policing that he and his officers had been doing for the past few weeks had been mediation. They helped people settle ridiculous disputes that had escalated, related to things such as noise at night and dogs getting loose. Since there was little alcohol left on the Rez, and therefore less drunkenness, everyone was getting along better. Rachel imagined that Tom sometimes felt useless. But now he had a purpose and he was all fired up.

Richard held a drumming circle during the afternoon to send the intention out to the universe, through their drumming, for the safe return of those who had ventured into the world. As Angela watched the drumming, she reflected on how much she was learning about healing and mental health from this tribal medicine man.

On the day that the men set out on their mission, Rachel hurried home from the clinic for a screen chat with Callie. She never knew if Callie would appear at the scheduled time (often she didn't), so she was relieved when she saw Callie's face. She told Callie about the blackout. "We have a small solar array here, so I hope I can continue to charge my computer from time to time after the power grid goes dark. But I'll have to get in line for that. I don't know if the Tribal Council will consider charging computers a high priority for use of the limited power we can generate."

Callie turned her gaze off into the jungle beside her for a moment. When she turned back, she said, "For quite a while now my solar setup has been in and out. I like the idea of quietly fading out, not having to say good-bye."

"You're my touchstone, girlfriend. All my life. I can't..." Rachel choked up.

"You still have Angela," Callie reminded her.

"Thank goodness for that."

"Listen, I'll try to connect according to our schedule. But if I don't turn up, I have a backup plan. When my system fails, maybe at some future time I can get it running again or an alternative opportunity will present itself, and then I'll try the screen chat at sunset, my time, on the night of the full moon. So look for me then. At sunset, OK?"

"Absolutely. When we get cut off, I'll look for you on the evening of the full moon whenever I can charge the computer," Rachel assured her. "I've tried to imagine what it's like for you to never go home again."

"It's certainly not what I expected. But I've adapted. I've spent so much time studying the Quarana that I've slipped easily into their ways, their worldview, as if into a dream. The Quarana live in the present. They remember the past and they plan for the future, but these activities take up only a tiny slice of their time." Callie held up her arm to show Rachel her wrist. "I buried my watch."

"Then how did you know when I would call?"

"By the sun. I'm in Quarana time, and here we measure in seasons, the cycles of nature, and the arcs of journey of the sun and moon. Days and hours serve no purpose."

"I wonder if we could live in Quarana time here."

"You eventually will. Trust me on that. So. Now. I have a few things I want to share with you. I should have said them before." She shrugged. "I hope we have some more good calls, but just in case."

"Of course." Rachel's throat suddenly went dry.

"I bailed from my role as the anthropologist here, of course. I'm not 'studying' the Quarana. I'm one of them. I'm still learning from them and I think they're learning from me, at least I hope I have some things to offer. But I've joined them."

"What exactly does that mean?"

"I've been taken as a wife." Callie's voice quavered. She looked down shyly.

"Poiry?" Rachel knew it had to be Poiry. She had seen that Callie loved him, and she knew that he had tried to convince her to marry him several times already.

"Yeah. Poiry. He asked me again if he could take me into his hut and I agreed to it. What else would there be for me here? I'm no longer who I was. A professor. An anthropologist. An academic. A well-respected researcher.

All that means nothing. Now I'm a woman in a forest. I'm lucky to find myself here, in a place where I can survive. So I'm becoming one with the subjects of my anthropological study, which is an interesting concept, that I would have liked to write about, but that's not going to happen. I'm becoming an anthropologee." Callie giggled. Then she grew serious. "Also, I'm pretty sure I'm pregnant, Ray. I'm late. I'm never late. It's cool. I'm excited. I want children. I want to belong somewhere and be happy. Poiry will be a good husband and a good father, and he'll give me a some ordinary happiness."

"That's so great! I can't wait to tell Angela. You and Poiry will make such a beautiful child. Who will deliver the baby?"

"Babies are born here all the time. There are women who know midwifery. They'll help me. I'll be fine."

"Are you safe there? Will you and the baby be safe?"

"As safe as anywhere. We're safer now than before the oil dried up. The despicable big-oil barons disappeared along with the oil. The handful of company people stationed near here have disappeared. We assume they died. We haven't seen any of them for quite some time, and they had no idea how to survive in a jungle. So the forest belongs to the Quarana again. We're free to live by Quarana ways, for all the good of it and all the bad of it. I can hang with that, Ray. I can raise a child here. The forest is vicious and beneficent and glorious. I learn more about how to coexist with it every day. It's an incredible place to raise children."

"I'll always think of you there in the lush jungle with Poiry. I'll imagine you with a couple of children of your own, gossiping around the campfire with the other women, making music and drumming. I'll imagine you growing old, loving your grandchildren, and telling astonishing stories about life as we knew it before. They won't believe those stories, but tell them anyway." Tears slid down Rachel's cheeks.

"That sounds like a good life to me. Hey. Ray. There's something I want to tell you. Maybe I kept it to myself for so long because it means so much to me and I didn't want to share. The name of my Tribe, 'Quarana', it means 'guardians of water' in Quarani."

"Why guardians of water?"

"Because we live beside a perfect spring that feeds a stream that eventually flows into the Amazon. The water from our spring is the most delicious water in the world. It tastes like love. The Quarana have protected this spring for generations, for thousands of years. Many indigenous people died fighting the oil companies to keep them from polluting this spring. If everything hadn't gone to hell when it did, those oil companies would have won. They would have destroyed one of the purest, most sacred water sources on the planet. But oil lost and water won. We have ceremonies to honor this spring. Sometimes I imagine that the best in us, what some call the human spirit, resides in the part of us that is water, which makes up about 60% of the human body. Did you know three-quarters of the brain is water?"

Rachel bowed her head as if in prayer and swallowed hard. Both women were silent for a minute. "My people are also guardians of water. That could be the name of this Tribe too. Our beautiful water comes from several springs, which we cherish and protect. I fear for our safety because of our water. People from outside might come and want to control it, own it, kill us for that pure water," Rachel confessed. "I hope they never find us."

"Try to live in Quarana time, in the present. The future is a fantasy."

"I'll try. Please do something for me."

"What can I do from here?" Callie asked with an ironic laugh.

"Every month on the full moon, look up at the moon and send me the love, girlfriend, and I'll send it back to you."

"I can do that," Callie agreed softly. She kissed her fingertips and touched them to the screen. Rachel did the same.

"Loving you, always."

"Loving you back," Callie responded. "Until we meet again."

"Until then."

Soon after the screen chat with Callie, Rachel heard Angela come in the front door of the house. She felt a little guilty that she had talked to Callie without Angela, but she needed that private conversation. She had a feeling about her conversation with Callie; that perhaps it was the last time the screen chat would work. It felt like an ending. She couldn't know for sure. There were so many things she had done and would be doing for the last time without knowing it was the last time. She reminded herself to make the best of the living moment because of that never-knowing. She was heading into Callie's Quarana time.

"I'm in here," she called to Angela, who followed her voice into the bedroom.

"I just talked to Callie. She married Poiry, or whatever the Quarana version of that looks like, she's pregnant, and she buried her watch."

"Whoa, do they make you bury your watch when you get married down there?" Angela asked drily. Rachel laughed. "I hope she'll find happiness and peace in the Amazon," Angela added.

"I think she will."

The men had not returned from their mission yet when Rani and her girls joined Angela, Rachel, and their children for dinner. Rani, who had spent the better part of the day at the drumming circle, still needed to figure out how to collect food daily from the farm, and how to prepare it in her new circumstances. The house she had been assigned by the chief had a gas stove, which, of course, no longer worked. Many people tended their own garden plots at their own houses. Rani would plant a garden of her own, but first she and Vinod would have to deal with necessary cleaning and repairs for the house, which had stood abandoned for more than a year after the previous owner, a tribal elder, had passed away. Rachel had visited the Chaudhary's beautiful farmhouse on a remote forty acres of forest and could barely imagine what Rani must have felt as the family rode away from that cherished home among the tall trees, a home with no water.

Rani remained quietly introspective at dinner. She glanced out the window often, watching the fading light anxiously while her daughters chirped back and forth with the other children, marveling over the new things they had experienced at Green Creek. The resiliency of the children continued to inspire Angela. She felt sure she would not have survived the Systems Collapse if not for her sons, and she remained optimistic for the future, in spite of everything, because of the continued enthusiasm for the adventure of life demonstrated by the children sitting at her dinner table every evening and surrounding her at Green Creek. Suddenly, Rani bolted from the table and raced out the front door.

Looking out the window, Angela saw what Rani had seen: her husband and the other men on the entrance road. The expedition returned safely, with no casualties, and they had some things to report about the world outside that gave them a clearer picture of how to protect themselves when they went back out to raid the RV park, which they proceeded to do in earnest the very next day. Vinod did not go with the others to fetch RVs. Setting up a barebones dental office kept him busy. He also spearheaded a campaign to coax people into the office to have their teeth cleaned to prevent the occurrence of dental problems down the road that he would not have the means to fix.

The electrical power shuddered on and off erratically, sometimes going out only for a moment before turning back on, while at other times staying off for several hours; and on more than one occasion for a day or two. Rachel and Angela found alternative ways of doing things. Read-aloud before bed became a family affair that required only one battery-powered lantern. They read one book together instead of cach of them reading their own book before bed, which would require individual lights.

Rachel could not reach Callie again. The net was rapidly disintegrating, and she figured the screen chat service they had used had probably collapsed. She kept her computer battery fully charged and took care not to deplete it. She would continue to try Callie once a month on the full moon as they had agreed, but she felt in her heart that she would not see her again. One more loss to assimilate.

As the green of summer dissolved into the gold of autumn, the community turned its full attention to harvesting the last of the summer crops and planting a fall garden. Although many infrastructure concerns required attention, and many different work groups concentrated on these various concerns, the most pressing concern was food. Without food nothing else would matter. Unable to use their tractors and earth movers, they had to plough the gardens for the fall planting by hand. Christina saved the day with her astonishing ingenuity. She and a group of elders enlisted a few young people to help them raid the Green Creek Cultural Center, which had fallen into disuse more than a decade earlier. This museum housed "artifacts" from bygone days in the history of the Tribe.

Few people at Green Creek even remembered they had a dim and dusty museum. Christina remembered. The museum contained tools from the distant past, such as plows that could be pulled by horses (or people), grinding stones once used to grind corn into flour and acorns into meal (they had access to both corn and acorns in abundance, as well as amaranth and rice), cradle boards for carrying babies, baskets of all shapes and sizes intended for many practical uses, and even two wooden wagons (complete with spare wagon wheels). The antique plows were still quite sturdy and they worked efficiently to till the earth when hitched to the horses and donkeys using yokes, also found in the museum.

Two tribal elders, who were masterful basket weavers, taught well-attended classes in the ancient art. These master-weavers knew how to weave baskets tight enough to hold water, strong enough to carry a child, and large enough to serve as feast platters. They knew the roots, reeds, grasses, and other materials used in basket weaving, where to find them, how to recognize the plants that yielded these materials, how to cure and treat the materials so they would bend to the weaver's hand, and, finally, how to weave an astonishing variety of shapes and forms. Their craft, which had nearly died out before the Systems Collapse, charged back in full force.

With the erratic on-and-off of their power, which moved rapidly to being more off than on, the Green Creek community mobilized to solve the problems presented by their new way of life. They struggled to remember back and back and back to how people had made things from scratch, such as candles, soap, paper, and cooking oil. They relearned how to start a fire without matches. They rethought even the most simple tasks. The community inched forward as if feeling its way along a dark corridor, hoping to come out into a sunlit clearing at the end. Each day brought fresh challenges, fresh triumphs, fresh adventures, fresh frustrations, fresh fears, fresh knowledge, fresh losses, fresh ideas, fresh relationships, fresh struggles, and fresh rewards. Richard claimed that people were using more of their brain capacity than they had in the Lost Time. Crime in the community practically vanished as people came together to work on the more important issues at hand that would impact their survival. The judge helped resolve disputes and they used a method of working out disagreements based on restorative justice that had come down to them through the generations from their ancestors.

Rachel and Angela fell into a pattern of everyday life with their blended family. They felt comforted by the sibling relationships that formed between their children because they could see their children would have each other to lean on in the future. Their family developed routines for such things as who used the bathrooms when, who cooked which meals and who cleaned up afterward, who did the laundry and on which day, who read at the family read-aloud before bed at night, and who stopped at the communal gardens to bring home food. They adopted a cat named Pepper, who took turns sleeping with Abby and Sulei at night. They started a Friday drumming jam that swelled beyond the confines of their own home. Their family routines fit with those of the tribal community, revolving around Spokescouncil meetings that Rachel attended and monthly bonfires at the new moon, as well as community feasts and celebrations (such as the traditional Pomo event of putting the bear to sleep in the autumn), and lifecycle events (such as births, weddings, and deaths).

Win-J and Rosie lived in Win-J's tent together until the RVs arrived, and then they received their own RV parked under a stand of madrone trees near Rachel's house. Rachel taught Rosie how to avoid getting pregnant. She supplied her with a diaphragm and several tubes of spermicide. When the spermicide ran out, they would either figure out a Plan B (such as charting her cycles to know when it was safe) or Rosie would get pregnant. In the Vision Time, teen pregnancy no longer seemed like such a problem as it once had. Attitudes, perceptions, and values were changing.

The power finally went out permanently a couple of weeks before Thanksgiving. Early on the morning that they lost the power for good, in the dim milky light of the hour before dawn, Christina awakened Rachel to fetch her to her house because Crystal had gone into labor. By that time Rachel had already delivered five babies at Green Creek without benefit of a hospital and things had gone well. Sanyu had assisted her, and he would probably be alright to assist her with his own baby, but just in case something went awry and she needed a less emotionally invested health professional on the team, she sent Christina to wake Cindy, her clinical nurse, to attend the birth.

Rachel dressed quietly and slipped out of the house. Angela knew where she had gone and would tell the children. She figured Christina would feed her breakfast and sure enough she found warm apple amaranth muffins and a pot of chamomile tea on the countertop in the kitchen when she arrived.

Christina, Crystal's mother Susan, and Sanyu had attended Crystal through the night and had waited until she was in active labor to fetch Rachel. By the time Rachel arrived, Crystal was nearly fully dilated. While Crystal's labor seemed to be going well, Rachel sensed something was off and she couldn't define it until Crystal leaned close to

Rachel and whispered confidentially in her ear that she should "tell the elves to leave the room" because she didn't like them staring at her.

After some stern questioning, she discovered that Sanyu had given Crystal Demerol for the pain. Rachel figured the drug was causing hallucinations. She, Susan, and Christina pretended to herd elves out of the bedroom. This calmed Crystal, but Rachel still couldn't get her to focus on the delivery of the baby. Crystal rambled on about purple lights flashing and various sounds she heard coming from outside the house, and despite Rachel's best efforts to get her to breathe through the contractions, Crystal lost control in the continuous swell of pain that washed over her in waves. She would need to push soon, and the effects of the Demerol, though fading, were still inhibiting her ability to function.

Wiping tears from his eyes, Sanyu apologized for administering the Demerol. Rachel abandoned any effort to relate to him as a medical colleague and approached him as she would any father at the birth of his own child. She assured him that she understood he had meant to make things easier for Crystal. "Now, however," she insisted, "we need to help Crystal concentrate. She has to push a baby out."

Suddenly, the house shook violently and the floor rolled beneath them. Two framed pictures fell off the walls, items jumped off a dresser and crashed to the floor, and Christina grabbed a lamp on the nightstand to steady it. Sanyu jumped into the bed with Crystal and shielded her from falling objects. Fortunately, nothing fell onto the bed. As the house creaked and trembled before settling back to stillness, Rachel wondered for a fleeting moment if she, too, had started hallucinating.

"Earthquake," Cindy said matter-of-factly. The lights fizzled and went out, and the hum of electricity fell silent (for the last time, they would soon discover). Fortunately, the sun had burst above the horizon, so cheerful sunlight flooded through the open windows.

"It's all shaking. Everything is shattered," Crystal shouted in a panic.

Rachel took Crystal's face gently but firmly between her hands. "Look at me. Are you ready to have a baby?" Crystal nodded mutely.

"OK then. You made this choice to have a child and it's a choice you will make every day for the rest of your life. So put on your can-do hat and push this baby out," Rachel commanded. "I'm going to tell you when to push and when to breathe and you're going to do as I say and we're going to have a baby here. Are you with me?"

"Yes," Crystal moaned, as another contraction seized her. Sanyu climbed behind her and propped her up, holding her lovingly against his chest. Cindy thoughtfully lifted a mirror off the wall (blessedly it had not fallen to the ground and broken in the earthquake) and held it at the foot of the bed so Crystal and Sanyu could watch their baby crown. Susan stood next to Cindy. Following Rachel's directions, Crystal pushed and the baby's head, covered in thick dark hair, emerged. With the next push, out came the shoulders, and the rest of the body soon followed. Rachel and Christina together caught the slippery boy in a thick, thirsty towel.

"We have our boy!" Christina announced joyfully.

Sanyu cut his son's cord. They put the baby, wrapped in the towel, in Crystal's arms. She and Sanyu cried and kissed each other and cooed over the perfect brown baby with abundant hair. Then Cindy took the baby to clean him up and swaddle him while Rachel waited for the placenta and the afterbirth. Crystal had emerged from the ill effects of the Demerol and she was lucid and elated. Sanyu wanted to call the baby Tremor because he was born during an earthquake.

Tremor, like a contemporary archangel, heralded the end of the era of electricity and the advent of the next hurdle in their survival gauntlet with his arrival. As time went by, the community accepted the fact that the wires had gone dead forever. The birth of Tremor marked another life-changing milestone in the journey of remaking reality in the Vision Time.

Transformation: Robin

On Ken's first night back, Robin made love to him with a frantic passion, then slept as if hit in the head with a rock. She woke up energized and hopped out of bed ready to tackle the latest challenges of running the communal kitchen.

It was up to Robin and Ken to house the refugees he had brought to Rainbow. Robin settled Diane and her friend Nancy in the guest room. She put Tom and Anne into a camper parked beside the house, which would work for them until the weather turned cold. They would have to think of some other arrangement for the winter, but for the time being this would do. Ginger and Cynthia would sleep in Ken's wall tent, which he pitched on the small patch of lawn behind their house with assistance from them since he had only one good arm. The tent was tall enough for them to stand inside. They had brought few possessions with them, and they disappeared into the tent for the evening, emerging to join the others at the dining hall for dinner. Later that night, Robin heard the murmur of their voices in deep debate coming from the tent. When she came home from work the next day, she found Ken and Diane embroiled in a heart-to-heart with Ginger and Cynthia. Diane was clearly upset.

"What's going on?" Robin asked, as she put a comforting hand on Diane's shoulder.

Ken waved his good arm in Ginger's direction, indicating that she should explain. "Cynthia and I have decided to leave. We'll see if we can make it to my granddaughter's place near Roanoke."

Robin could not believe that these two women in their eighties planned to walk nearly five hundred miles, uphill and down dale, through country crawling with desperate people. "That strikes me as suicidal," Robin said bluntly. "I can appreciate your desire to reunite with your granddaughter, but you do understand what's out there between here and Roanoke, don't you?"

"Mom and I have been trying to dissuade them, but these are two stubborn women."

"You can stay with us," Robin reassured them. "Rainbow is limiting how many new people we take in, but you have received a welcome. You'll be safe here. I think your granddaughter would want that for you."

"Our safety is not our chief concern," Cynthia said softly, her mouth set in a grim line.

"They take exception to the weapons," Diane informed Robin.

"We take exception to murder," Ginger corrected her friend.

"Oh. That," Robin said.

"Yes. That," Ginger confirmed. "We saw the graves, featured prominently at the entrance; and today one of your leaders named Kristy, who we understand is a founding mother of this community, put a sign up threatening uninvited visitors. It looks to me like your people intend to run off any strangers who arrive at your gate seeking assistance, and will not hesitate to kill them if they refuse to leave."

"We won't live like that," Cynthia said. "We're deeply grateful to you for opening your home to us and offering us a safe haven. You have done us a great kindness. But..." Cynthia looked down at her hands sadly.

Ginger continued Cynthia's line of thought for her. "But we could never live in a place that condones that violence. We're pacifists."

"Longtime committed pacifists," Cynthia explained further. "We have gone to jail to protest more than one war during our lives. We're war tax resisters. Ginger camped out with Cindy Sheehan at Bush's ranch in 2005 after Cindy's son died in Iraq. Rainbow is not the right home for us."

"We live in difficult times that require extreme measures," Ken reminded them. Robin saw the set of his jaw and inferred that he supported the Rainbow policy.

"We have always lived in difficult times that require extreme measures," Cynthia countered. "I just disagree with you about what extreme measures are acceptable and ethical."

Ken continued. "Go ahead, take the moral high ground, but you must realize that, practically speaking, we will survive here at Rainbow and you will die out there, crucified on your high ideals."

"Maybe and maybe not. No one can read the future. We would rather take our chances on the road. We would rather die without compromising our reverence for life than live in a community built on violence," Ginger snapped, her eyes afire.

"Do not fear for us," Cynthia told them. "We are prepared to accept the consequences of our choices. We always have been."

Unlike Ken and Diane, Robin did not argue with the couple, who had obviously made up their minds. "So when do you plan to leave?" she asked.

"Tomorrow morning," Cynthia replied.

"I'll fix you some food for the road. Will you wait until after breakfast? We can put together supplies for you then," Robin offered.

"That's it?" Diane exclaimed, turning on her daughter-in-law. "You won't try to talk sense into them?"

"I'm sorry Diane, but they've decided and it's their choice."

"Thank you," Ginger replied curtly, as she folded her arms across her chest.

Robin didn't confess to Ken that she had misgivings about the shootings and the policy of non-admittance. She felt even more like she had blood on her hands after the conversation with Ginger and Cynthia. At the same time, she felt powerless to change things. Rainbow was fundamentally a survivalist community. She had known that when she entered into it. She had never thought they would actually have to fight for their survival. But here they were. Robin didn't have the luxury of taking the moral high ground, like Ginger and Cynthia. She had a family at Rainbow, a young daughter, a life. She had nowhere to go if she walked away from the bloodshed. She would have to inure herself to it. She wanted Ginger and Cynthia gone quickly so she didn't have to listen to them give voice to her own conscience. She doubted that the aging pacifist couple would last a week after they left the safety of Rainbow; and she figured they pretty much knew it too, as did Diane, who threw her arms around Cynthia and sobbed while Ginger murmured, "Don't cry for us." The moment felt almost biblical and Robin fled to the sanctuary of her kitchen.

After Ginger and Cynthia walked out of Rainbow the next morning, Diane collapsed inward. She became subdued. Meanwhile, her other friends, eager to contribute to the community that had so kindly taken them in, tried to make themselves useful. Nancy worked several hours each morning in the garden and tutored children at the school in the afternoon. Anne, a writer by trade, organized a storytelling hour after dinner in the evenings, and she read aloud to children at the preschool in the mornings. Tom, who loved animals, went with Willow to learn veterinary skills each day. By comparison, Diane sat on the porch, sipping tea and staring into space. After nearly two weeks of painfully watching his mother sink into depression, Ken persuaded her to assist at the health clinic. Having worked as a nurse for over forty years, Diane had valuable skills, and making herself useful finally lifted her out of her funk.

Meanwhile, Robin worked in the kitchen and the gardens as if driven by wolves. She planned late into the evenings with the gardeners and her kitchen staff to secure food for the winter and strategized how to perpetuate the garden to provide food into the future. She rose early in the morning each day and threw herself into her work. She and her staff had traditionally dedicated time to canning and preserving during the summer harvest, but the need to put up enough food to last the community through the winter forced them to take the canning and preserving to a higher level. This added much more work than usual for the season. In addition to putting food by for the winter, Robin managed daily meals at the dining hall. Rainbow kept bees and had its own flour mill to grind corn, wheat, oats, and rye, which they grew on their land. They had always saved seeds to support the sustainable organic gardening methods used at Rainbow, but they stepped up their efforts, knowing that they had no outside source for seeds to back them up. If they failed to sustain a vegetable to the next season, they would likely never eat it again. Robin dealt with the weight on her shoulders by working harder, and the strenuous physical work wore her out so she slept hard at night and woke with her energy restored.

With Robin working long hours, Ken took the initiative in reinventing their family life to include Diane and her friends. He made tea and toast for everyone in the morning, and they sat on the screened-in porch together to eat it before going to their various jobs and activities. Willow went to the dining hall for a more hearty breakfast, but she would check in with the elders on the porch first, and often ate a slice of toast. Robin arrived at the dining hall at first light, missing the tea-and-toast starters. The family reconvened in the evenings before bed to wind down together. Robin relaxed for perhaps the only time all day during those late evenings with her family. Creating a routine kept them centered and steady.

The sentries at the front gate frequently rebuffed people who sought asylum, but fortunately no further bloodshed occurred. Robin was relieved by the absence of violence at the gate. Then a new turn of events disrupted their lives and sent her into a quandary about her approval rating for the moral fiber of Rainbow. The Decision Association decided to have all medications pooled at the clinic pharmacy, and they created a task force, comprised mostly of health professionals, that would determine which people would receive meds and how much they would receive at one time and how often they could receive more. They then required everyone to turn in their stash of medications to the pharmacy. This included insulin.

Ken had risked his life to retrieve insulin and diabetes-related supplies for Anne when he had gone to fetch his mother. Anne's supplies were confiscated with all the others, and she had to go to the pharmacy every other day to replenish her stock. The system forced her to go off her insulin pump and revert to injections, and as a result she was having difficulty keeping her blood sugar stable. Anne assumed a Zen-like calm about the situation and declared that she was at peace and felt prepared to die at any time; but the family did not share her attitude. Tom stopped assisting Katie with the animals and instead accompanied Anne everywhere she went to keep an eye on her.

Ken crashed a meeting of the meds task force, and insisted that the task force include representation from insulin-dependent diabetics as well as people dependent on other meds. Kristy informed him that he was out of line and making inappropriate demands. She reminded him that when he joined Rainbow, he agreed to abide by the determinations of the Decision Association, and that the community's governance system didn't work if individuals took it upon themselves to oppose it. Ken lost his temper and demanded they hand over Anne's insulin and supplies she needed to use her pump, supplies he had brought into Rainbow specifically for her. Kristy impressed upon him that he lived at a commune where theoretically no one individually owned anything. Ken accused Kristy of hoarding hearing aid batteries and Kristy argued that hearing aid batteries were not meds and did not fall within the jurisdiction of the meds task force. Ken called Kristy a

fascist, informed her that he would "out" her about the
hearing aid batteries to the community, and stalked off.

Robin heard about all of this secondhand from Ken, who
appeared at the dining hall and asked her if she would walk
with him on the hill path. After he played the conversation
back for her, Robin reminded him that he needed to exercise
caution because the Decision Association had the power to
send their family into exile. "You're in the right, Ken. Peter
and Kristy probably know it, but they won't admit it. With
things as they are in the world outside, exile is not just a bad
thing that can happen anymore. If they were to vote us into
exile, we would die out there."

"I will not live in fear. Besides, they would never vote
you into exile. You're the food guru. They need you."

"That doesn't mean they can't send you away."

"How could they possibly send me away without you?"

"They certainly could exile you and not me. They know
I couldn't go with you because of Willow. I could never
leave her here alone and I couldn't take her out with us to
die. We have no options and they have all the power."

"We came here to escape from a society controlled by a
handful of power-mongers. Look at what we have become?"

"When I think back to the beginning, when we started
Rainbow," Robin replied. "I think about what Peter and
Kristy and the others were like back then. We had such pure
and lofty ideals."

"You had lofty ideals. Kristy, Peter, and a lot of the
others always had this tyranny in them. They had this
murder in them, but they didn't need to use it before. They
have no qualms about using it now. Rainbow has always

been a survivalist community. We've been heading to this moment from the beginning. I see it so clearly. I didn't see it before because I didn't want to see it. We should have left when Willow was born. We should have started something else, a different intentional community, a better one. I was lazy. I stayed here because it was easy."

"You're not lazy. You work harder than anybody I know. You're valuable to the community too. What would we do without your engineering knowledge? It's important for people to speak up when they disagree with the Decision Association, but please be careful. Don't say anything about Kristy's hearing aid batteries. She'll find a way to get back at you. She's dangerous."

"What if they kill Anne with this insulin distribution thing?"

"Be realistic. The insulin will run out eventually so the insulin-dependent diabetics are on borrowed time already. They know that. I mean, seriously Ken, where would we get more insulin? Where would we get any meds? Blood pressure meds, heart meds, asthma inhalers, all of it. Honestly, anyone on meds of any kind is going to have to learn to live without them very soon and if they have a life-threatening condition then their prospects don't look good. Kristy's hearing aid batteries will run out eventually too so don't think she isn't scared."

Ken cast Robin a defeated look. "So I will live in a dictatorship. I will exercise caution. I will not speak out about what is right or wrong or what is just or true." They had reached a look-out point on the hillside and had a view of Rainbow in one direction and a view of the world beyond

Rainbow in the other, all the way to the blue-purple mountains, hooded and watchful as monks, assembled in the distance. Ken gazed at the view, taking in the panorama, then he turned Robin to him, took her in his arms, and kissed her deeply. He searched her eyes, brushed her hair back from her face, and kissed her on the nose. Tears filled Robin's eyes.

"Insects are the most persistent creatures on the planet, surviving over centuries while other living beings succumb to extinction. The reason why insects survive so well is because they are adaptable," Ken said with a note of bitterness.

"Then we will be insects. For Willow's sake. And we will generate as much love as we can under the circumstances."

"Love!" Ken exclaimed with a snort of derision. "Rainbow is not built on love. It's built on paranoia, anger, resourcefulness, and fierce independence."

"There is always room for love, even in a dictatorship."

They returned to the house hand-in-hand. Ken remained subdued throughout the evening. It appeared that Kristy, Peter, and the others who witnessed Ken's outburst had made a tacit agreement to keep quiet about the incident. Perhaps they feared stirring up further dissent in the community. To Ken's satisfaction, they did invite a couple of insulin-dependent diabetics to join the meds task force. Ken said nothing further about Kristy's hearing aid batteries. Anne continued to struggle with regulating her blood sugar, and Tom's attention to his ailing wife broke Robin's heart. Tom knew he would lose her soon, and he was savoring every moment he had with her.

Robin didn't have time to dwell on the politics of power struggles and governance at Rainbow. Resigned to the fact that she had no influence over decisions unrelated to the food supply, she focused on that. They had planted a number of extra crops in the garden late in the summer to increase the harvest, and they were beginning starts in the greenhouses for the fall planting. Robin supervised massive canning and preserving efforts every single day. A flock of teenagers assigned to her to help with this work took it seriously. She enjoyed training them to put up food, as well as teaching them about nutrition and cooking. The survival of the community through the winter depended on her ability to organize her staff and helpers to secure enough food to keep them going. Sometimes the responsibility overwhelmed her and she had to pause to take a deep breath and go for a walk to quiet her soul. She could only do her best and hope it was enough.

One morning in early September, Robin discovered that the bell pepper seeds they had saved had molded because one of her workers had ignorantly placed them in plastic-wrap. She did not chastise the woman, who already felt terrible when she learned that she had ruined the seeds. Instead, she harvested some late peppers and stored the seeds from them correctly. But the incident frightened her and she started obsessively checking stored seeds. She was engrossed in checking seeds when the sound of gunshots penetrated her consciousness and set off an alarm in her brain. She hurried to the front porch of the dining hall.

The Decision Association had developed what they termed the "Emergency Defense Plan," and all Rainbow residents participated in weekly drills to practice implementing the EDP. From her vantage point on the porch, Robin could see that the EDP was in full swing, and this was not a drill. Elders swept children to safe locations while able-bodied adults rushed to the entrance gate armed and prepared for battle. The medical staff was setting up the clinic to triage casualties.

Because a lot of people knew about Rainbow, strangers continued to come knocking to gain entrance into what they perceived as a refuge where they would be protected and fed. They were bitterly disappointed to be turned away. After the initial influx of friends and relatives of community members, the gates were closed and locked, and remained carefully guarded. Unfortunately, however, Rainbow had a far-reaching reputation that it could not erase. The sentries at the Rainbow entrance had turned away many strangers and potential intruders. Outsiders usually came in small groups that left without incident. The sentries had fired their guns to disperse a threatening group of marauders the week before, but had not hit any of them. The marauders had scattered. Since they had triggered the EDP, Robin assumed the current situation presented a more serious threat, probably a larger group of potential invaders. It felt dangerous.

According to the EDP, armed residents would descend on the kitchen any minute to ensure the safety of the food supply. Robin had arranged for her role in the EDP to involve protection of the farm animals so she could be near Willow. Her pulse racing, she hurried to the rabbit hutches and chicken coops. More shots rang out at the main gate behind her. She found Willow herding goats into a barn. Having her daughter in sight made her feel less panicked. Willow waved to her and she waved back before helping Kate corral the poultry. She was grateful that the attack had occurred in daylight. Dangerous situations always seemed more dire when they happened in the dark. Once they secured the chickens and geese, Robin and Kate joined some of the others in the horse barn where they attempted to calm the horses and dogs, particularly those that had a fear of gunshots. Robin and Willow sat in the hay with a few border collies and labs, petting them and crooning to them as they shivered. The incident felt as though it went on for a long time, but in fact the would-be intruders were vanquished quickly.

Feeling shaky, Robin returned to the kitchen. While some people drifted to the entrance to gawk at the dead bodies lying beyond the gate, Robin meticulously avoided exposing herself to the scene. She began chopping vegetables for dinner and gave orders to her staff as they drifted into the kitchen to help. She felt like a coiled wire. A light touch in the small of her back caused her to whirl around as if bitten by a snake to find herself face-to-face with Ken. She fell into his arms and started crying. Ken led her out to the herb garden and sat with her on a bench until she composed herself.

Ken had participated in a delegation chosen by lottery to bury the dead beyond the gate. He returned in the evening with a puppy, which he plopped into Willow's arms. "He's yours now," he told her. Willow named him Loyalty and she and Diane took the puppy to Kate for a health inspection. After they left, Ken confided in Robin that Loyalty was found curled against the body of a boy of maybe twelve or thirteen years of age.

"So we have taken to killing children now?"

"Well," Ken replied, "they have also taken to trying to kill us. The boy had a loaded rifle. It gives us a glimpse into what's going on outside." Ken ran a hand through his hair and grimaced. "I need to take a shower."

Robin felt infinitely exhausted and wanted to lie down in a cool, dark, quiet place far away from people and the madness that walked in the world. She thought about the gardens at Rainbow and her kitchen. She thought about the rows upon rows of beautifully packed jars of fruit and vegetables in storage for the winter, lined up on the pantry shelves like sparkling jewels. Green, red, yellow, orange, purple – all the colors nature offered. In the lost past, she would have surveyed those shelves of bounty and felt a tremendous sense of peace. She could no longer feel peaceful. She did not feel safe or at-home. She would never feel safe, peaceful, or completely happy again. A poison had infected her community and infiltrated her soul.

In the days following the shoot-out, Robin carried on with her duties with grim determination and little joy. Only watching Willow play with Loyalty lifted her spirits. When she caught herself laughing over Loyalty's antics, she felt grateful to feel a moment of delight. In the evenings, Robin sat wearily on her back step with Willow, who threw a tennis ball for Loyalty, who ran after it with puppy abandon. He brought the ball back, covered in slobber, and dropped it at Willow's feet, gazing at her with such anticipation, watching her every move, and emitting the occasional yip if she didn't pick the ball up fast enough for him. He fetched that ball as if he had studied fetching in college and perfected the art of it. That silly, enthusiastic, little puppy cheered Robin up more than anything else.

When they turned the corner into October, the chilly air of autumn nipped at Robin's cheeks and fingers. It comforted her to bundle herself into her oversized sweaters. She felt as though she could hide from life in them. She had fallen silent, not chatting much anymore with others. Willow, on the other hand, blossomed as Kate's veterinary assistant. She shared stories from her work with the animals when the family came together in the evening and early morning. Willow's exuberance reeled in some of the slack from Robin's reticence. Ken had a steely edge to him that Robin had never seen before. He had become hardened and bitter; but accepting of the authority of the regime under which they lived.

Anne's health deteriorated during the weeks after she went off her insulin pump. She had used the insulin pump for so many years that she couldn't adjust to gauging how much insulin to take with injections. She kept taking too little or too much. Tom, Diane, and Nancy fretted over her. Anne had become muddled in her new surroundings with her brain dulled from her fluctuating blood sugar. She became easily disoriented. Diane told Robin and Ken that, in her opinion, Anne showed signs of dementia; but they said nothing about this to Tom. They moved Tom and Anne in from the trailer and settled them in Willow's room for the winter. Willow took a thermal sleeping bag and moved out to the trailer without complaint. She claimed she liked living in the trailer and that she kept plenty warm with Loyalty sleeping in her bed. Robin wondered how she could have raised such a resilient and generous young woman. Her love for Willow gave her the strength to carry on more than anything else did.

The gardeners lovingly cared for their beds of greens, broccoli, cabbage, carrots, peas, and other cold-weather crops; while Robin and her crew started cooking and storing the soups and stews that she hoped would sustain the community through the winter. Unsure if she had enough food to last until the next summer harvest began, she used her ingenuity to stretch what she had available. Sometimes she considered what she would do the following year, when she would not have any clean, unused canning lids, and could therefore not safely preserve food in jars. Next summer she would have to smoke and dry everything instead. She thought about this in the abstract, because she did not know if she believed in the future anymore. She wanted to, for Willow's sake, but she couldn't quite envision it.

Three weeks before Thanksgiving, the community awakened in the middle of the night to an explosive volley of gunshots. Ken leapt out of bed and hastily pulled on his pants. As he headed toward the door, Robin caught him by the arm and pulled him toward her. "Be careful," she said. "Always," Ken replied. He kissed her quickly and hurried out. Robin left her elders sitting anxiously in the living room where they spoke to one another in hushed voices, and she started out for the health clinic. She discovered Willow on the front porch, putting on her sneakers. "I'm going to the barns," Willow told her.

She kissed Willow on the cheek. "Be careful. I think they will need me more at the clinic than the barns, but if not I'll be over to help you and Kate shortly."

"Did Dad go to the front gate?"

"Yeah."

"He'll be OK, Mom. See you soon."

The gunshots sounded extraordinarily loud to Robin as she navigated the path to the clinic through the chilly night. The air smelled of fire and iron. The clinic still had anesthetics, but Robin knew the medical staff was struggling to come up with a plan for what to do when their anesthetics ran out. For a supposedly self-contained survivalist community, Rainbow had been more dependent on the outside world than they had ever imagined before everything changed.

After about twenty minutes, silence indicated that the firefight at the entrance had ended, and everyone at the clinic assembled anxiously on the front porch. From out of the silence, Robin heard the call of voices and the moaning of people in pain. The hair on the back of her neck stood on end as the voices and moans came closer. She took a deep breath, anticipating the onslaught. The fighters arrived and engulfed the medical staff. Peter and Roger pushed a flat cart up to the front steps of the clinic. Peter's eyes met Robin's briefly, held her in his gaze. Such pain, such compassion, Robin thought. It surprised her coming from Peter. Then she looked down at the cart where Ken lay unconscious, his right leg a mangle of blood and torn flesh. Robin stumbled down the steps, and attempted to reach Ken, but strong arms restrained her. Ken was gently lifted and carried inside the clinic, while Peter repeated several times in Robin's ear, "It's his leg. He's still alive. He's wounded, but he's still alive. It's only his leg."

The tension of the recent months and her growing fear and anxiety bubbled over and Robin took leave of her senses. She could not control the low-pitched moans coming from deep within her. When Peter attempted to embrace her, she pushed him away viciously and shouted "no, no, no." She didn't want him to touch her. She held him partly responsible for Ken's injury, for the violence that permeated their lives. One of the nurses from the clinic quickly came to her aid and she allowed the woman to guide her to a private room inside as she continued to moan and whimper, while her entire body shook uncontrollably. The nurse sat down with her, held her hands, and spoke calmly, telling Robin to take deep breaths. "Breathe," the nurse repeated with each breath. Robin breathed in rhythm with the nurse. As she regained control of herself, she thought, sarcastically, that of course she was breathing, because if she wasn't breathing she would be dead. But she continued to breathe in rhythm with the nurse because she didn't know what else to do. After she had recovered an adequate measure of self control, and no longer whimpered involuntarily, the nurse walked her home.

"I'll come with news as soon as he comes out of surgery," the nurse promised.

She entered the house, where the elders continued to sit in the living room. Anne had nodded off to sleep with her head on Tom's shoulder. Nancy talked quietly with Diane, who held Loyalty in her lap and stroked the dog's back. Willow had not returned from the barns. Robin's eyes locked with Diane's and she could tell that Diane knew instantly that something had happened to her son.

"Ken was shot in the leg, Mom. He's in surgery. It looks pretty awful. But that's the only wound he has. Fortunately none of his internal organs were injured." Robin turned a chair in toward the group and sat down heavily. She reached over and petted Loyalty on the head and scratched behind his ears, and then she took Diane's hand and squeezed.

Nancy softly sang a church song and then she sang another. Tom joined in with his lovely baritone. Anne woke and sang with them for a few songs and then nodded off to sleep again. When Willow came in, she announced that she knew about her father. A nurse had walked over to the barn to tell her. She was exhausted. She hugged Robin and Diane, scooped up Loyalty, and went straight to bed.

At dawn, a nurse came by with news. Ken was resting comfortably and his life was not in danger. Whatever type of bullet had entered Ken's shin, it had exploded on contact and shattered his leg. No one on the medical staff at Rainbow had the expertise to rebuild the leg so they were forced to amputate just below the knee. In the old days, Ken would have been airlifted to a hospital where a specialist might have saved the leg. But in the old days, Ken would never have been shot with an exploding bullet. Robin and Diane asked how soon they could see him. The nurse replied that he was heavily sedated and suggested they get some sleep and check in on him when they woke up. Only then did Robin and the elders part ways and go to their separate beds. Robin didn't think she would sleep, but she did, hard and heavy until the early afternoon.

She woke disoriented and it took her a moment to remember what had happened. She felt annoyed at herself for sleeping so late, and she showered and dressed quickly, ate scrambled eggs, then went to the clinic. She assumed that her staff at the dining hall had been informed and would prepare the day's meals without her. At the clinic, she found Diane and Nancy sitting beside Ken's bed while he slept.

"He's still doped up," Diane told her.

"Does he know he lost his leg?" Robin asked anxiously.

"He came out of the anesthesia, but they put him on morphine right away. He doesn't know what happened. He probably won't know for a couple of days while they keep him sedated. Thank God we still have morphine on hand."

"I can't bring myself to thank God for anything right now, Mom," Robin replied. She continued in a low voice, afraid to be overheard speaking treasonous words. "To be honest, I wish we had thrown in our lot with a different group of people before everything came crashing down. These shoot-'em-ups are wrong."

"What would you have your people do instead?" Diane asked. "Let invaders take over the community? Some very bad people populate the world, and I certainly don't want them getting in here."

"We are some very bad people," Robin hissed. "I don't know what I would have Rainbow do instead. Can't I just hate this without coming up with a solution?" She took Ken's limp hand and held it to her cheek.

Diane went over to her and put her arm around Robin's shoulders, "Of course you can, honey. Of course. I hate it too."

"Where's Willow?" Robin asked.

"She came over earlier and then went to work. There's no reason for her to sit here. The doctor says Ken's going to be knocked out for a couple of days. You might as well go to work. It will take your mind off it."

Diane was right. But she wanted to sit for a while and look at Ken. She wanted to watch him breathe. She wanted to remember that he could have lost his life and to feel grateful that he had lost only his leg, but she was having trouble feeling grateful. She felt angry, depressed, and, most of all, disempowered. She had lost control over her life and the lives of her family. She lived in a dictatorship and she had no viable alternatives. It did not improve her mood to learn that one member of the Rainbow community had been killed and several others wounded, one of them so seriously that it did not seem likely that she would live.

Later, while she cut up carrots for dinner, Robin had a visit from Willow, who told her, while munching on a carrot swiped from the cutting board, that she heard that Peter's "troops" had captured a prisoner from among the attackers. After Willow returned to work, Robin went in search of Peter, whom she found at the administration office. In fact, she encountered him and Kristy together on their way out of the building. Robin allowed Kristy to give her a hug and a commiserative squeeze of the arm in greeting. Peter hung back, probably remembering how Robin had recoiled from him the previous night when he attempted to comfort her.

She did not waste time on trivialities. "I hear you have a prisoner."

"That's true," Peter replied cautiously.

"And I suppose you have questioned him. Or her. And that you will do so again, correct?"

"We have not questioned him yet," Kristy divulged. "We put him in one of the community house guest rooms with a guard posted. We have treated him decently if that's what worries you."

"I'm glad to hear that. I came to request that you appoint a panel of observers to be present in the room while you question him. Emotions are running high and I would like to ensure that we act in a humane manner." She did not expect them to take her seriously so it surprised her when Peter nodded in agreement. Did she have more credibility now that her husband had lost a leg fighting to protect Rainbow?

"That's a good suggestion and we will do it," Peter said. "You should participate on the panel of observers."

"I agree," Kristy added, nodding vigorously.

Robin was taken aback by how easy it had been to approach Peter and Kristy and how quickly they had agreed with her. Maybe she was not as disempowered as she had thought. "What do you plan to do with the prisoner once you're satisfied that you have wrung him dry of any valuable information?"

"That's still under discussion," Kristy replied.

Peter's jaw hardened. "We don't know if he will cooperate."

"I accept your offer to observe," Robin told him. She couldn't imagine that the prisoner would refuse to cooperate, but in case he did, she wanted to be in a position to ensure that he did not come to harm. All of them were treading on new territory for Rainbow and had no rule book to guide them other than common decency; and Robin wondered if the Rainbow leadership still had enough of that. "When do you plan to question him? Or should I call it an interrogation?" Peter flinched at her use of the word.

"We're all pretty tired after last night and not at our best, and we want to be at our best for our conversation with this man," Kristy answered. "Plus we should consult with the Decision Association about who else to include on the panel of observers. But you will definitely be on. Pete and I will make sure of that." She glanced at Peter for confirmation.

"So when?" Robin repeated.

"Let's say we'll question him after breakfast tomorrow. Maybe at nine. We'll let you know for sure. Will that work for you?" Peter asked.

She would want to look in on Ken before the interrogation, but she figured she could make that timing work so she agreed to it. She walked over to the clinic where she found Ken still sleeping. Robin sat with him and held his hand while Diane and Nancy went to get something to eat. She was relieved that the doctor planned to keep Ken knocked out for a couple days. She dreaded the moment when he regained consciousness and understood he had lost his leg. She wondered if they could fit him with some sort of prosthesis; maybe something they could make out of wood. Ken could probably design it himself. He had such ingenuity when it came to that sort of thing. The medical staff sent Ken's family home at the end of the day, assuring them he would remain drugged through the night and that someone would fetch them if anything changed. Robin didn't argue since she desperately needed a good night's sleep.

The next morning, Ken's condition had not changed. The staff at the clinic were subdued and spoke quietly. The critically injured member of the community in their care had died during the night.

Robin left the clinic and walked to the community meeting room for the interrogation. The prisoner was seated at a table, flanked by two armed Rainbow security patrol members. The panel of observers included six people, and one of them was Ken's close friend Frank, who hurried over to Robin to fold her in a hug and ask about Ken. She sat next to him and he took her hand in his.

The prisoner whom Peter had referred to as a man was merely a boy not much older than Willow; probably still a teenager. His large head rested on a spindly neck that appeared too frail to support the weight of it. He was skinny and he chewed on his fingernails anxiously. She reminded herself that this vulnerable, frightened youth had carried a gun against Rainbow, and could have been the person who shot off Ken's leg. She had trouble wrapping her head around that possibility.

The members of the Decision Association filed into the room and sat across the table from the prisoner. The proceedings seemed ridiculously formal to Robin. It felt like a tribunal when it was just the Rainbow leaders asking some kid some questions to which he probably would not even know the answers. She almost laughed.

Peter asked the boy his name and where he came from.

"I'm Mike Roundstone," the boy answered obediently. "Do you mean where do I come from now or from before everything fell apart?"

"Tell us both."

The boy nodded his head and took a deep breath. "OK. Well, in July, you know, when the wheels came off, I was in a summer program at the University of Kentucky in Lexington, where I was studying agriculture. I finished my sophomore year. That seems like a real long time ago. My family is in New Orleans, I mean, you know, if they're still alive." His voice wavered and he stopped talking. Robin thought he might start crying. He looked dreadfully forlorn. He swallowed hard and continued. "I was too far away to go home so I had to figure out where to go. As part of my summer program, I was doing an internship at Agrico, and the bosses there invited people working for them to stay to harvest the crops, but we had to agree to do what they said otherwise they would run us off. I saw them run some people off. I didn't know where else I could go so I stayed. They gave me a room and food. I felt like I could survive there as long as I did what they said. They have a lot of weapons at Agrico. They have a security system." Then he added, in a quiet voice, so that Robin could barely hear him, "I didn't know if I wanted to survive or not." He ran a hand through his unruly, dark, curly hair. "Sorry," he murmured.

Kristy asked him to repeat what he had said because she couldn't hear it. So the boy repeated in a louder voice, "I didn't know if I wanted to survive."

"By Agrico, you mean the agribusiness giant?" Peter asked.

"Yeah. That one. I worked as a research assistant for them. But they shut all the labs down when everything happened and they sent everyone out to the fields to harvest. There are a lot of people over at Agrico. It's like a whole city. When their irrigation system quit on them, we had to harvest a lot of food real quick and preserve it for the winter. There wasn't enough rain to make up for the failure of the irrigation system. Now harvest is done. Of course, you can see why we had to come over here," Mike finished, as if it was as obvious to everyone else in the room as it was to him.

"No," Peter said, "we can't see that. Please tell us why you had to come over here."

"Everyone knows about you guys. Everyone knows you're a survivalist community and you grow your own food. Food is what it's all about now. Food and water. And med supplies, but those are getting impossible to find."

"Do you still have electricity at Agrico?" Peter asked.

Kristy put a hand on her husband's arm and said, "Let him explain about the food first, Peter." Then she asked Mike, "What is the big deal about Rainbow growing food? Agrico grows way more food than we do."

Robin knew, before Mike opened his mouth to explain, what was coming next. The whole picture instantly became clear to her and she realized with a wave of horror that

Rainbow was in deep trouble precisely because they had prepared so well.

"You have seeds," Mike said, as he leaned forward, resting his elbows on the table that separated him from his interrogators. "You can save seeds. Agrico can't. By-the-way, Peter," Mike's voice had a hint of amusement in it when he said Peter's name, which he had registered when Kristy spoke, "we don't have electricity anymore, but Agrico is working on that."

"What do you mean about the seeds?" Peter asked, bewildered. Robin wondered how he could be so stupid.

"Agrico seeds are genetically modified. They're nicknamed 'killer seeds' because they can't grow plants. All the plants they grow at Agrico are one-season only. It does no good for them to save their seeds because they're genetically engineered to fail. I thought you guys knew everything about agriculture over here." Mike sounded disappointed in them.

Peter turned in his seat and looked pointedly at Robin. "Robin, what does he mean?" The entire Decision Association turned to Robin, and she could see from their expressions which ones among them already understood exactly what it meant and which ones had no clue.

"The large agribusinesses, like Agrico, developed plants that make seeds that won't propagate. They did this for profit and to keep control of their products. If you sell a farmer seeds that grow vegetables that make seeds that won't grow again, then the farmer has to go back to the agribusiness to buy more seeds every year because they can't save seeds and use them the next year. The seeds we have in our organic gardens can be saved and used to grow plants again the next year. We've saved seeds every year since Rainbow began; this year more than ever."

"That lady gets it." Mike interjected. He seemed to grow bolder with his sense that he had valuable information to share. "Anyone working in agriculture in this whole area knows you guys have good seeds. You can bet that Agrico isn't the only one out there that wants your seeds. I'm surprised you guys are even still here, like, you know, that you haven't been blown sky high by one of the roaming gangs."

"Roaming gangs?" someone on the Decision Association echoed.

"You don't get out much, do you?" Mike asked with a hint of a smile. "Of course not. Yeah, well, there are these armed gangs foraging for food and water. At Agrico we call them roaming gangs. In my opinion..."

"We didn't ask for your opinion," Kristy interrupted Mike coldly. "You and your buddies killed two of our people and cost our chief civil engineer one of his legs."

Mike stared down at the table in shame. "They're not my buddies. It wasn't me. Really."

"You had a gun on you," Kristy reminded him.

He looked at Kristy and raked a hand through his hair again. "They make me go out with the raiding parties. You know, I'm a young man, a prime recruit. They taught me how to shoot a gun. They would run me off if I didn't agree to go with the raiding parties. But I fire the gun into the ground. A lot of us do. I could never shoot a person. I mean, jeez, I'm a vegan." His eyes glistened with unshed tears.

One of the women on the Decision Association asked, "In your opinion, what? You started to say something in your opinion." Robin could have hugged her because she wanted to know what Mike had been about to say when Kristy cut him off. Mike wiped his eyes on the hem of his T-shirt, which was bright green and sported an image of a pelican below the words BRETON WILDLIFE REFUGE. He gulped. "I was going to say I think you guys should go over to Agrico to negotiate with them. Offer them seeds so they won't bother you and keep enough of your seeds for yourselves. Do it before they come and shoot you and take what they want."

"We don't negotiate with armed robbers," Kristy asserted.

"Suit yourselves. But my guess is that if you don't negotiate then whoever's ammo holds out the longest will wind up in charge of the seeds and everything else." He looked Kristy in the eye. "I hope you have a lot of ammo, 'cause you're gonna need it."

Although the Decision Association continued to question Mike for quite some time to find out more about Agrico and what the world had become beyond the borders of their isolated community, Robin had heard all she needed to hear. After the questioning, the security guards escorted Mike back to his room and the people on the Decision Association stood, stretched, talked in small groups. It would take time to digest what they had learned and they would need to decide how and when to share the information with the rest of the community.

Robin approached Peter. "Peter," she said to get his attention. Several other members of the Decision Association heard her and fell silent as they turned in her direction. Kristy was speaking to a couple of people and when she noticed the silence, she stopped talking. The swirl of activity and conversation parted and Robin stepped into the silence. "Peter," she repeated, "and the rest of you guys," she added with a wave of her arm to encompass the entire decision-making body. "Mike's just a sad, scared young man who lost his family and has no idea what to do next. I'd like to take him home to stay with us, if you don't mind. He doesn't have anywhere to go. He's harmless. If you send him out, he'll wind up back at Agrico and they'll just send him here to shoot at us again."

"He said he shot his gun into the ground, away from people," Peter reminded her. "I'd rather have someone like that coming at us than someone more bloodthirsty."

"Peter, really?" Robin chided.

"How do we know he's telling the truth? How do we know he's not dangerous?" Kristy suggested suspiciously.

"Look at him. He's a lost kid," Robin replied.

Uncharacteristically, Kristy backed down. "Maybe so."

"You guys talk about it. I'm fine having him stay with us. We have half my mother-in-law's neighborhood at our house plus a stray puppy, what's one more lost soul? We'll find somewhere for him to bunk and we'll look after him. He needs a family and we could definitely put a former ag student to good use in the community garden. Also, please consider the fact that I'm going to need help with Ken when he comes home. Assigning Mike to look after Ken would be restorative justice. That's not something you have the opportunity to implement every day."

Peter promised that the Decision Association would discuss Robin's proposition, but she could tell from their faces that she had them at "lost kid." She had already started working out in her head how to rearrange the household to assimilate Mike, who would have to sleep in the living room.

That afternoon, when the doctor reduced Ken's pain meds and he swam up to consciousness, Robin, Diane, and Willow were at his bedside to lift him out of the swamp. He didn't remember anything from the moment he went down during the shoot-out. "What's all this?" Ken asked, with a wan smile, as he waved his hand to encompass his family, the doctor, and the hospital bed. Robin thought the doctor did an excellent job of breaking the news to Ken gently that he had lost a leg. Even so, it tore her up to see his face change as he began to comprehend. He kept saying, "no, what? no, what?" He ripped the blankets off and studied the empty place below his knee.

"Please don't try to move your leg yet," the doctor said.

Ken looked at Robin in utter astonishment. "I don't understand."

"You don't have to understand, sweetie," Diane told her son. "Take as much time understanding as you need. We're grateful you're alive."

Crying steadily through the whole scene, Willow climbed into the bed with Ken and mumbled "Oh Daddy" soggily into his chest.

Robin took his hand. "You're going to be OK."

"Explain to me what happened." Robin gave the doctor an entreating look and he proceeded to give Ken more details about the shooting, the type of bullet that had exploded Ken's leg, the fact that they were not equipped to deal with this kind of medical emergency at Rainbow, and all the rest. Ken listened to all of it with focused concentration.

"What if they come back?" Ken asked.

"Let's let the Decision Association worry about that," the doctor answered.

Robin thought, grimly, that it was not a matter of if but when they came back. They needed viable seeds. But until they returned, she would love her life fiercely and as completely as possible, every moment of it, every day. She would take delight in her daughter, her husband, her family, her friends, and her work; savoring it all for as long as it lasted.

Robin would never have imagined that her role at Rainbow would become so pivotal. It had always been about food and water, even before everything had gone to pieces, but now it was completely about that for survival. Their lives depended on her work and the work of the director of the community's farm.

By the time Ken came home from the clinic, Mike had settled into the living room. Willow and Diane hung India bedspreads from the ceiling with carpet tacks as a partition to make a separate little space for Mike, who had no possessions and slept on the floor in a sleeping bag. They moved the couch to the other side of the fabric partition, so they still had a living room for the family to gather in, but it was much smaller. Mike was shamelessly happy with his new living situation. He loved everything and everybody. Diane said it was as if they had acquired another puppy. Loyalty thought Mike actually was another puppy and gave him slurpy puppy kisses (on the lips, ugh) at every opportunity. No other human in Loyalty's acquaintance allowed the pooch to bestow so much slurpy doggy love.

Mike turned out to be a boon for the whole family.

First there was Anne, who had sunk into semi-dementia. Ken held the Decision Association responsible for Anne's deteriorated cognition, and believed that she could have had many more good months if they had let her keep the supplies she needed to support the system familiar to her for her blood sugar regulation. When Mike moved in, Anne, in her befuddled state, mistook Mike for her absent son. She called him Randy and he kindly answered to that name. She perked up and became more lively with Mike's arrival. She made Mike his lunch every day (Randy's favorite, an egg salad sandwich) and chatted brightly with him while he ate. Mike indulged her and she functioned better in his presence.

Second there was Willow. Mike had lived with them for only a couple of days, and Ken had not come home from the clinic yet, when Robin, returning home after dark from a long, weary day in the kitchen, discovered Mike and Willow locked in a passionate kiss on the glider on the front porch. They didn't notice her and she felt like a voyeur. She padded quietly back up the road and turned on her flashlight, which she rarely used since she knew the path so well. She made some noise and swung the flashlight to alert the couple of her approach. This time when she arrived at the front porch, they sat primly with their hands in their laps. They chatted with her for a few minutes, and then Willow went to bed in the trailer while Mike followed Robin into the house to sack out in his corner of the living room. Robin wondered when Willow intended to tell her about the romance. She supposed she should feel grateful for it. Everyone in Willow's peer group at Rainbow had grown up with Willow, so she wasn't likely to develop a romantic interest in any of those brotherly boys. It made sense that she was attracted to Mike, from the outside, a handsome young former college student. Robin wanted to be happy that Willow had a chance at love. But if things didn't work out, what then?

Then there was Ken. When he came home from the clinic grumpy and morose, frustrated by his limitations since he couldn't stand without something to lean on and couldn't walk, Mike proved invaluable. He remained at Ken's beck and call, willing to help as needed. Ken often behaved gruffly and even rudely toward Mike. Robin worried about him, but Diane said to give him time to adjust. She said she had nursed many people who had to accept similar losses, and they worked through it eventually. "He'll have a turning point and then he'll start to come out of it," Diane assured Robin.

The engineers who managed infrastructure at Rainbow missed Ken's input into figuring out the puzzles they had to solve and they couldn't wait to get him back on the team. They generated most of the electricity at Rainbow using solar power, but their solar systems consisted of equipment they could no longer replace when it wore out because they had purchased it from a solar company outside Rainbow.

Plus they stored energy in batteries, which had a finite shelf life. Maintaining the flow of water presented the most pressing problem. Rainbow's water came from four wells and two springs. The wells used pumps that ran on solar-generated electricity. In preparation for a time with little or no electric power, Ken's colleagues were working on expanding the spring-fed water systems to carry the full load when the wells failed, but the springs were not fully capable of doing so. Ken had previously contributed to this effort; but after he lost his leg, he made no move to resume working on it. His doctor instructed him to rest, the other engineers tread softly, and no one pressured him to return to work.

Robin dreaded a future without her electric stoves. Some of the engineers at Rainbow had converted a couple of stoves to wood-burning. They asked Robin to practice cooking on their prototypes. She dutifully attempted to cook a hot lunch using the damn things twice a week and she hated it. She had imagined that Ken would figure something out, but not if he continued to wallow in self-pity and refused to work. Maybe it wouldn't matter. She could feel Agrico breathing down her neck, coveting their seeds.

The week after Ken returned home, Willow announced to the family that she and Mike were "seeing each other, you know, as more than friends." Ken did not like it and that put him in an awkward position since he depended on Mike to aid him in daily functioning. Of course he felt protective of Willow. Fortunately, Mike's undaunted good humor and unabashed joy at being part of the family and freed from Agrico was endearing.

Robin no longer worked during the evening meal at the dining hall. Instead, she sat down and ate with her own extended family. Only a few months ago, their family had consisted of Robin, Ken, and Willow. In those days they sat at dinner with other families. Now their household took up a whole table all by themselves. Mike pushed Ken to the dining hall for dinner in a wheelchair every evening. The first time Ken returned to the dining hall for dinner, he received a standing ovation, much to his amazement and embarrassment. Robin hoped that the recognition from the community would help him begin to take an interest in life again.

After a conversation with the doctor about prosthetics, Mike informed Ken that he would make him a wooden leg.

"You'll be like a pirate, Daddy," Willow said excitedly.

"I'll need an eye patch and a parrot," he replied, with a lopsided smile.

"I can work on the parrot," she offered. "Grammy will have to do the eye patch."

"You can't wear the wooden leg until your stump heals," Mike said earnestly. "But I'll make the leg and then you'll have it waiting when you're ready for it. I hope you'll come to the carpentry shop with me to work on it," Mike suggested. "I could use some training on using the woodworking tools."

"Maybe," Ken replied.

Robin glanced at Diane, who raised her eyebrows as if to say, "He'll come around."

Mike and Willow went for a walk together every evening after dinner, even as the days grew shorter and the evenings darker. They took a lantern and walked to the barns to say goodnight to the animals, or followed some of the trails in the woods. Although they had only just met, it seemed as though they had known each other for a long time. Nancy told Diane and Robin that she thought Willow and Mike had been married in a previous life. That was the kind of stuff Nancy believed. Robin considered that sort of thing a bunch of argle-bargle; nevertheless, she agreed that the two were a good match. Thrilled to watch her daughter falling in love, she marveled at such an unexpected turn of events.

Another unexpected turn of events was the daily visits from Peter. After Ken's brush with death, Peter began to visit him every morning after breakfast. At first he'd just stop by to say hey. Then he started to sit on one of the porch steps for a few minutes to chat. Before long, he had taken to sitting with Ken on the porch to drink a cup of tea and have a conversation every morning. One night, as they settled into bed, Robin asked Ken what was up with Peter and his visits.

"He's lost his way. And so have I. We empathize with each other. We remember together."

"Explain."

"Peter's a regular guy from Iowa who got scared about the state of the world, the environment, and everything. He got scared and he imagined this intentional community where he would feel safe. A lot of it had to do with Kristy. She had a survivalist vision, and Peter thought it coincided with his intentional community vision, but it didn't exactly. Well it did for a while, most of the time, but now, with everything mixed up and crazy, he doesn't know what he thinks anymore. He says he still felt generally OK about

things until I lost my leg. Something about that night and
that fight deeply disturbed him. He and Kristy have had a lot
of differences of opinion since then. He says he doesn't know
if he's making good decisions anymore."

"That's intense. And not something I want to hear from
one of our supposed leaders."

"For sure. I like talking to him, though. We tell each
other stories from when we were growing up. Today I told
him about my grandfather George. Do you remember that
George went to Canada to avoid the draft so he wouldn't
have to fight in Vietnam?"

"I had forgotten that."

"Grandpa George was a conscientious objector. I've
always considered myself a pacifist. So what in hell was I
doing shooting a gun at people? I told Peter that I'm through.
I should have refused to participate in that shootout, and I
deserved to lose a leg because maybe I killed someone out
there that night. I'll never know. No matter how much good
I have done in my life, if I killed a person that night, then...."

"Sweetie, these are difficult and unprecedented times,
and we have entered uncharted waters. Who knows what
might have happened if we had not defended ourselves, if
you had not gone out there that night to defend Rainbow?"

"Do you think it's OK for us to kill people who come to
our gates?"

Robin looked at the wooden leg that Mike had made for
Ken, which leaned against the wall by the bureau like a
promise. She carefully considered her answer while Ken
waited patiently. "I don't think it was right for us to turn
away the people who came during those first weeks, the

people who were lost and needed a safe place where they could take refuge. We should have let them in. But if people come shooting at us, if they want to kill us to get in here and take our seeds or whatever else we have, I think we have to defend ourselves," Robin said carefully.

"What if we fired on them first? What if we didn't give them a chance to declare their intentions, if we just started shooting at them and they shot back?"

"Is that what happened. Did we fire on them first?"

"I'm not saying that's what happened. As far as I could tell, it wasn't. But I can't stop thinking about it. I think about why we came to Rainbow in the first place, what we thought this community would accomplish, and I'm thinking about everything we've lost, not just personally, not just as a community, but as a world. A whole world. We screwed it up. We trashed the earth and hijacked the future of the young people, like Willow and Mike."

"Maybe we shouldn't have come here at all. Maybe we should have stayed out in the world and tried harder to make things turn out better than they did," Robin speculated.

"Obviously it wasn't only on us. A lot of people would have had to quit their normal lives and dedicated themselves to fixing the world."

"That didn't happen."

"No, it didn't. And here we are. For how much longer?"

"Yeah," Robin agreed. "Here we are. I have this idea that I want to make a big deal out of Christmas. I'm going to talk to the Decision Association about it. I think we ought to celebrate that we made it this far, that we survived to now. We need a time-out-of-time to join together and reaffirm."

Ken put his arms around Robin and pulled her to him. "I love the way you turn a good meal into a healing, an affirmation, a spiritual experience. Food as epiphany. That's my wife. I'm lucky I married you." What can a woman do when a man says something like that? Robin kissed Ken long and deep. For the first time in weeks, she had a feeling they might be OK, that everything might be OK.

As Christmas approached, Robin threw herself into preparing a feast for the community. The farming crew fattened up chickens, turkeys, and pigs, while Robin retrieved a few delicacies she had squirreled away for a special occasion. She fired up her staff and the community to prepare for a Christmas dinner they would remember. It lifted everyone's spirits to have something to look forward to when life remained overshadowed by a future so frighteningly unpredictable. She desperately wanted to make the event amazingly special.

In preparation for Christmas dinner, the young people made decorations for the dining hall and fixed it up to look festive. Willow and Mike joined the fun, climbing ladders with a crew of enthusiastic teenagers who festooned the ceiling with brightly colored paper chains, creating centerpieces with dried flowers and gourds, and taping pictures made by the little children to the walls. They carved jack-o-lanterns for the porch and made headdresses for the kitchen crew to wear.

Robin's staff baked pumpkin pies, apple pies, breads, biscuits, cheesecakes, and cookies. Members of the community went out of their way to pass by outside the kitchen windows just to sniff at the air and drool in anticipation. They roasted meat in shifts for several days and then stored it in the walk-in to be reheated for the feast. They made green beans and collards in butter and garlic, cornbread dressing, cranberry sauce, sweet potatoes dusted with some of the last precious cinnamon and topped with the very last of the canned pineapples, mashed potatoes fluffy and loaded with cream, gravy, and more delights. Spirits ran high when they finally gathered for the Christmas feast. Robin invited the community to dress up for the occasion. They never had anything to get dressed up for anymore, and Robin thought it made a difference for people to dress up now and then. So people turned out in their finest with bright colors, dashing hats, high heels, cloaks, and gowns. Some of the men wore tuxedos.

Candles glowed on the tables. Robin produced bottles of wine from far-away places that might no longer exist for all they knew. When she removed her apron and stepped out of the kitchen, she received a standing ovation. She called her staff to stand with her and they took a little bow before seating themselves with their respective families at the long tables loaded with the bounty from their gardens.

"This will not be a long speech," Kristy said, as she rose to her feet at the head table where she sat with the Decision Association and their immediate family members. "I don't want to let this gorgeous food get cold." Everyone cheered. "But it's important for us to pause for a moment to express our gratitude for our continued ability to thrive as a community in these difficult times. We have come a long way." She raised her glass, and others did the same around the room. "We are grateful for this abundant spread of food and we acknowledge the hard work from many hands that has gone into making this feast possible. We are grateful for the love and friendship that we share at Rainbow. I feel blessed and honored to live among you. To Rainbow."

"To Rainbow!" everyone shouted. Robin felt annoyed at herself for the tears that welled up in her eyes and the pride that swelled in her chest. She knew that in twenty-four hours she would once again be angry at the Decision Association; but for one evening, she was happy to live at Rainbow. People filled their plates and ate heartily, while the dining room filled with joyful conversation, laughter, and delight. The gleeful shouts of the children rang out. Dogs barked. All was right with the world.

Until it wasn't.

An explosion of gunshots pierced the air.

Everyone stopped with loaded forks halfway to mouths and smiles frozen on faces in the second before happy thoughts changed to fear.

Robin hugged Willow to her fiercely while she ordered Mike, "Take her. Take Willow, go out through the kitchen, and run up to the ridge. I can't leave Ken. But Mike, you have to save our daughter. I'm counting on you." She released Willow and threw her into Mike's arms.

Willow sobbed. "I love you Mom, Dad." Mike took her arm and tugged her in the direction of the kitchen. Willow scooped Loyalty up in her arms and hugged him to her chest.

"I love you my dearest one," Robin called after her extraordinary and beautiful daughter, whom she and Ken had made together from their love for one another; the greatest blessing of their lives.

"I've got this. I promise you, I'll keep her safe. We'll find a way," Mike hollered as the two young people fled. Mike and Willow (with Loyalty held tight) ran to the kitchen door and disappeared from view only moments before a swarm of armed invaders burst through the front doors of the dining hall. It made perfect sense for them to attack on Christmas, when Rainbow had not remained as vigilant as usual, not posted as many to guard the gate.

In the first instant of the invasion, grief and terror overwhelmed Robin, but then she felt her soul drift out of her body, away from the scene, and she watched the situation as if from afar. Events slowed and happened in a hallucinogenic, altered zone outside of time. Peter, Kristy, and others in the room pulled out guns and fired at the intruders, who wore black clothing and a boatload of leather. The intruders far outnumbered the community, and they continued to pour into the dining hall, firing semiautomatic weapons rapidly in all directions. Ken grabbed Robin and pulled her under the table, where he lay on top of her, his heart pounding against her back. She peered out from under his arm to see the still forms of Peter and Kristy, their blood draining out across the floor under the head table. Robin stared into the lifeless eyes of the founders of Rainbow.

Their attackers had certainly come from Agrico, had come for Rainbow's good seeds. Rainbow could never have held off the deluge of intruders pouring into the dining hall, even if her people had not been caught in a moment of weakness, eating their last Christmas supper. Even if they had stood in full force at the gate, they would not have withstood this barrage.

Ken brushed his lips against her neck. Then whump, whump, whump, she felt Ken jolt. His weight shifted against her, pressing heavily. He sighed deeply, still shielding her with his body even as the life flowed out of him. Robin squeezed out from under Ken and sat up, cradling his head in her lap. A hint of life remained in his eyes yet. "I love you so much my darling," she said, and she could see that he heard her, and his lips curved in a smile as he transitioned out of their known world. She kissed his eyes shut, moving in slow motion. The gunshots continued to reverberate around her, while a few people from Rainbow tucked away behind barricades of furniture continued to shoot at their assailants; but anyone could see that it would be over in a few minutes.

Robin imagined Mike would sweep Willow to safety, that they would be resourceful and live in a new way. She had faith. She envisioned the two of them escaping into an enchanted forest, deep and sheltered, where they would find food and water and invent a better way of life. They would build a cabin and have children with soft Asian eyes like Robin's mother's. Her beautiful, beloved Willow. Robin stood up, stood her ground in her home, her dining hall. She presented an easy target, she knew, but she felt impervious because she no longer cared whether she lived or died. She had nothing left and nowhere to go. She shouted into the crossfire, "Do you want to live like this? Is this what you want? You have the power to create your life, your world; and you choose to make it this?"

She ranted. A Cassandra, a prophetess, a lunatic, screaming into the roar of gunfire. Hot white lightning burst through her brain and Robin crumpled beside her husband, following him out of reach, beyond the mire of human existence, transformed.

PART FIVE: Renewal

Rachel and Angela

Celebrating the holidays without their husbands could have crushed Angela and Rachel, but the enthusiasm and optimism of their resilient children rescued them. Rachel and Vince had celebrated both Christmas and Hanukkah in their home. Rachel had come to love Christmas, with its pervasive spirit of generosity and kindness, its hopeful message of belief in the fundamental goodness of humankind. She had made an effort to create memorable Christmas traditions in their family, even though she came into the marriage with none of her own. One of those traditions was that Vince made chocolate chip pancakes for Christmas dinner. Rachel would have given it her best shot but they didn't have any chocolate chips. When she discovered she also didn't have enough candles to light her Hanukkah menorah for the whole week, she cried. Angela made "a great miracle happen there" (words evoked on every dreidel) by collecting enough birthday candles from the neighbors to carry Rachel and her girls through Hanukkah. A Christmas tree was another matter. Good forestry stewardship dictated the plan for tree cutting. Individual households would have a spindly young fir sapling if desired and they cut one large tree for the community center.

Angela and Rachel went to work creating new traditions for their children, which would perhaps continue in future years if they survived. They made a bonfire in the yard on Christmas Eve and the children told stories about their missing fathers around its glow. They sang together on Christmas morning, then ate fresh-baked apple muffins with butter and honey for breakfast, and joined in a community dance and music jam on Christmas afternoon. On each night of Hanukkah, they lit candles and then they went around the family and each of them told one thing for which they felt grateful.

Rachel used the charge saved in her computer to try to reach Callie on a screen chat on Christmas Day at about the time of sunset in the Amazon, but the screen chat program no longer worked. She wondered if Callie knew it was Christmas. She took a look around the internet while she had the computer turned on and discovered hardly anything out there. All those memory banks loaded with digital information running in acres of rooms somewhere had whirred to a stop. Data on "the cloud" had dissipated as quickly as a cloud.

Chief Firekeeper allowed community members to use the solar energy resources to charge phones and computers prior to New Year's Day so that people could attempt to reach distant family and friends. Even though Rachel had lost contact with her parents in the first month after the Systems Collapse, she charged her phone to try calling them. But she, as well as everyone else at Green Creek, soon discovered that the telecommunications systems of the Lost Time had entirely collapsed. Both the phones and computers were useless as communication tools. Nevertheless, it cheered people up to have access to the archived material on their devices. Rachel and Angela's children had a wonderful time looking at photographs, listening to music, and playing vids. Jamal had the entire Hayao Miyazaki film *Nausicaa of the Valley of the Wind* on his computer, and the children watched it with intense focus from beginning to end. The theme of the imminent destruction of the planet, nearly taken over completely by the Toxic Jungle, resonated with them. They identified with the persistence of the characters, their hope for the future, and their efforts to save the planet. The girls and Sulei cried during the harsher scenes.

At sunset on New Year's Day, Richard lit a bonfire in a fire ring behind the community center. At the lighting of the fire, he led a ceremony at which he burned sage and bowed in each of the four directions. Those in attendance called out the names of the people they held in their thoughts. The children's chorus, which Rosie had dubbed the Vince Chorus, performed as the fire took and the sun sank behind the hills. Sanyu (who played the drums and saxophone) and an elder from the Tribe (who played the piano) had stepped up to help her lead the chorus. Many more children had joined since the initial performance, put together so quickly to honor Vince.

After the Vince Chorus performed, the community shifted their attention to drumming, dancing, and deep, fire-lit conversations, all of which eased the loss and grief felt by all as they ushered in a new year in the absence of loved ones and without the benefit of cherished, familiar traditions from the Lost Time. At midnight, Richard shook his medicine man's gourd filled with rattling dry seeds to command the silence and attention of the crowd. The amber glow of the fire cast one side of his body in gold light while the other side remained in darkness. He appeared half-man, half-shadow. When he spoke, his voice carried to the outer edges of the crowd, as clear as an owl calling on a winter's night.

"The Vision Time has transformed us," Richard declared. "We, the people of Green Creek, no longer live outside a society that co-opted our land and devalued our culture. No more must our children attend the conquerer's school and learn the distorted history of this land put forward by the dominant culture. Our children are free to learn the true history. We will teach them our ways, our values, our traditions, which have greater importance now that we must depend on them for survival. In the Vision Time, we return to our core beliefs, our core being. The spirit-energy that flows from the Creator infuses all creatures and all things, living and dead, past and present; connecting everything with everything else. We reach back into our past and pull forward the knowledge we once had about living in partnership with the natural world surrounding us. Here, in our ancestral home, once again our justice is the only justice, our laws the only laws, our healing the only healing, our water our only water, our food our only food. Oh Green Creek people, my people, we have regained ownership of our lives. We have such abundance. As we welcome those in need who come to us in this time in a different way from the history of past encounters, we create the opportunity to build a society that honors difference, values diversity, and establishes ways for us to benefit from learning from one another. We belong once again to the land, which belongs once again to no person. No person owns the trees, the air, the water, and the earth. If you mourn loved ones you have lost, if you mourn lost connections, know that your grief is honored in this sacred space we have created. My people, my old people and my new people, people of Green Creek living together in the Vision Time, know that I rejoice that I lived to see this day. May you rejoice in it too."

A resounding "OH!" reverberated around the fire and swelled into the night, in the place where they assembled to celebrate the turning of the year.

Angela had taken Rachel's hand during Richard's speech; and when he finished speaking, her friend turned toward her with tears sparkling in her eyes like the crest of waves in the sunlight. "Even though we have lost so much, we still have so much else for which I am grateful. We still have each other."

"We do. You saved me, my boys, and my friends from Oakland, woman."

"You save me every day. Happy new year, girlfriend."

"Happy new year."

It had not occurred to Angela until she heard Richard speak on New Year's that the elders at Green Creek might perceive the Systems Collapse as the answer to a prayer, a mechanism that would catapult the Tribe into a golden age, beyond the reach of the devastation of colonialism, invasion, and genocide. She lived in a community in which some people viewed the Systems Collapse as a positive development. This realization stunned her and propelled her into thinking differently about all that had transpired, and about how the new future had changed everything in the past, everything that had gone before, by casting it in a new light.

After New Year's, the cold, wet winter seized the land in earnest, challenging the community to stay warm and dry. Many homes needed adaptation to create a heat source. A team began working on figuring out how to make boots from animal skins so the community would be prepared when the boots they had wore out. They had to find winter footwear for all the growing children. Chief Firekeeper appointed a team of hunters to use guns and ammunition from the armory to hunt for deer, wild turkeys, wild boar, and rabbits. The hunting party went out regularly and returned with game, which was cooked and distributed or smoked and stored. The skins were used by the boot makers.

The gardeners, whose ranks had swelled as the importance of producing food had gained priority over all things, had set aside fruit, vegetables, herbs, and spices for the winter from the summer and autumn gardens. They still had many cold-weather crops growing; but those proficient in gardening knew that the next summer would bring far greater challenges to food production than they had ever experienced. In the meantime, their ace in the hole was their excellent water source; those magnificent springs that did not run dry, delivering pure water. During January they constructed greenhouses, and in February the gardeners began planting and lovingly tending the first seedlings for the upcoming growing season.

Thus, Green Creek was focused on food, not security, on the breezy February day when the New Brothers Gang sauntered onto tribal lands, holding Annie and Joseph (who had been posted at the entrance gate to watch for incoming refugees) hostage at gunpoint. At the precise moment that the New Brothers made their fateful entrance, Rachel was on her lunch break, sipping a cup of tea while she chatted with Tom in his office. Tom's receptionist appeared in the doorway with an expression of such fear and alarm that Tom leapt to his feet. Rachel saw him pat his hip where his gun used to live, in a subconscious gesture of habit. His hand dropped to his side, empty. His gun had not rested on his hip for many months.

"Come quick," the receptionist said urgently.

Rachel put her tea mug on the edge of Tom's desk and hurried out the door one step behind him. From the windows in the reception area, they could see the intruders, who appeared rough and urban. They were muscular and wore heavy boots and copious leather. They had elaborate tattoos running up their necks and pouring out of their sleeves along their hands and forearms. All of them were men, and they were heavily armed. They examined their surroundings through cold, hard eyes; hyper-alert, wary, and without a hint of a smile.

"Stay inside," Tom told Rachel in a low voice, saturated with protective caution. "You're our only doctor. Keep yourself safe. Slip out the back and go to the clinic. Warn the others. I hope that once they realize you're a doctor they'll value your life." His voice had taken on the same tone that she had heard in it one hot day at the end of the summer when he had asked people to stand back while he killed a rattler with a long-handled axe, cleanly chopping off its head with one pure, well-aimed stroke.

Rachel nodded. "Be careful. Stay safe," she begged Tom. She hugged him fiercely before turning toward the hallway leading to the back door.

Tom took a deep breath and stepped onto the porch. Even though he had agreed to the Pacific Treaty, and left both his police gun and his personal gun locked inside the store room, which he had converted into their armory, he continued to wear his uniform. He speculated that some people might still have a gun hidden in their home, but the common narrative was that everyone had turned in their weapons when they signed the Pacific Treaty, so, theoretically, no one in the community had an available firearm. Chief Firekeeper had proudly hung the signed Pacific Treaty on the wall of her office. Everyone over the age of fourteen had signed it, and as a community, they held liars in low esteem so perhaps there really were no contraband guns out there. He doubted it.

Rachel crept out the back door and hurried to the clinic, where she, her staff, and patients who had arrived for afternoon appointments waited tensely to see what would happen.

Because Angela's consultation room was down the hall from Chief Firekeeper's office, she was one of the first to discover that the community was under siege. After having spent so many hours of her professional life conversing with unstable individuals, she lacked a healthy sense of alarm at the appearance of the thugs at Green Creek. The guns made the back of her neck prickle, but the men who held the guns reminded her of guys she had seen regularly in the grocery store in Oakland, and she figured that now as then food was probably the first thing on their agenda. It worried her they had no women or children with them, which was a bad sign. It meant they could be after sex as well as food. Angela moved closer to Chief Firekeeper where they stood on the front porch of the tribal office beside the other members of the Tribal Council and Tom.

Their spokesperson (probably their leader) trained his ludicrously large semi-automatic weapon on Chief Firekeeper when she identified herself as the chief. Angela imagined the gang leader saying to Annie and Joseph at the gate, "Take me to your leader," like in a Sixties sci-fi movie. She identified the invaders as a gang by the colors they displayed, their hats, and the patterns in the tattoos on visible skin. She recognized their symbology. She had worked in CPS with families affiliated with gangs. At first their gang symbology confused her because she saw conflicting gang markings and some of the intruders were Asian while others were Latino. Gangs did not usually cross racial lines. Then she realized that probably two different gangs, remarkably, must have joined forces, which was fascinating from an anthropological standpoint. She filed her observation away for later because it could prove helpful in handling them; and handle them they must if they wished to live. Angela had a better chance than others at Green Creek of talking with the intruders and working out a deal both because of her psychology training and her familiarity with the former lives these men had led in the city. She would bet good money that they had come up from the Bay Area, maybe even from Oakland. All these thoughts crossed Angela's mind in the space of a few seconds as she took in the scene.

The gang leader approached the porch. He smirked. "You're the chief? Where's your feathers? Where's your warriors? How come you people chose an old woman to be the chief? That's messed up."

"I will respect you and your people if you will respect me and mine," Chief Firekeeper replied evenly.

"News flash. My people have all the muscle," he threatened.

"I see your guns," Chief Firekeeper responded. "I suppose you think those are useful to you. Your mistake. You can't eat guns. I have food, which I think you want, because I very much doubt you know how to grow anything."

"My guns will get me that food and anything else I want," the man asserted, with a belligerent jut of his chin. Angela recognized his style of speech as that of someone who spoke Spanish as his first language.

"Food runs out," the chief reminded him. "You can kill every one of us and eat all our food. Then what? Move on? Starve again until you find more food? Not much of a plan. We know how to grow food." She pointed to her head with her finger. "My knowledge is more valuable to you than anything you can imagine. Don't squander your resources."

The man looked bemused, then quizzical, then suspicious. Angela suppressed a smile. He had never encountered someone like the chief. Angela thought that, despite his bad attitude and poor manners, he was handsome. He had honey-colored skin and deep brown eyes. Consciously cultivated muscles defined his chest and upper arms. His straight, blue-black hair glinted in the sunlight. But it was shaggy. He needed a haircut. She guessed his age as late thirties, possibly forty; close to her own age. The other men appeared to be mostly younger than the leader; probably in their twenties and thirties.

The gang leader gestured toward Annie and Joseph. "You didn't post an impressive guard at the entrance to your precious empire."

Tom spoke for the first time. "They aren't a guard. They're a welcoming committee. You're welcome." The intruders laughed and shook their heads in disbelief.

The leader turned his attention to Tom, without moving the aim of his gun from Chief Firekeeper. "A welcoming committee? You Injuns are crazy."

"That's a derogatory term," Tom replied with noticeable restraint. "Please don't use it."

The man looked as though he couldn't believe he had heard Tom right. "You have got to be kidding me. Who are you?"

"I'm the police chief for Green Creek. You are on Green Creek land and subject to Green Creek justice," Tom replied determinedly.

"Lee, Oscar, pat him down," the gang leader ordered as he waved a hand over his shoulder at a couple of his companions, both of whom brandished firearms. He trained his gun on Tom instead of the chief. "Do her too while you're at it," he said as he pointed toward the chief. Angela wondered why she had escaped notice. Maybe she didn't seem dangerous to them. This amused her because she believed she posed more danger to the gang members than anyone on that porch since she knew best how to get inside their heads.

Lee, a stout and muscular Asian, patted down Tom, while Oscar, a tall and broad Latino, patted down the chief. Then they stepped off the porch to flank their leader. "He's clean," Lee mumbled.

"I like the uniform," the leader complimented Tom sarcastically. "All dressed up and nowhere to go. What kind of police chief doesn't carry a gun?"

"The kind of police chief who's a better man than you," Angela said. "We don't wave guns around here. It's not that kind of place."

"It is now," the gang leader replied with a condescending chuckle. "And who might you be?"

"I might be Angela. This is Chief Marjorie Firekeeper and Police Chief Tom Kaweyo. Your friends appear to be Lee and Oscar, and who might you be?" Angela asked, meeting his gaze unwaveringly, attempting to lure him into forming relationships with the people he sought to victimize.

"Chava," he replied haltingly, warily, thrown off guard for a second.

"Pleased to meet you," Angela said as she held out her hand, which he ignored, so she withdrew it. "So. Chava. I invite you to come inside to have a conversation with our Tribal Council. Obviously you want something and you mean to take it, but perhaps it's something we would freely offer without the need for you to shoot anyone to get it."

Chava hesitated. Angela thought she saw a tiny crack in his armor, and she had the distinct impression that he was much smarter than he at first appeared, behind the swagger and the weapons. She took a quick head count of the men with him, about twenty. She wondered if there were more of them who didn't come onto the Rez, and just how many people Chava had under his leadership. It impressed her that they were not a homogenous group. This showed evidence that Chava, as their leader, had the skills to keep a diverse group of Latinos and Asians functioning in harmony.

"I could do that," Chava replied. He left most of his men outside holding Annie and Joseph hostage while he took several men, including Lee and Oscar, with him inside the tribal office building with their guns still drawn. Angela, Tom, Chief Firekeeper, and the Tribal Council members filed into the conference room, followed by Chava and his men, who kept them in their sights. Chief Firekeeper sat at a circular table.

"Would you like me to call my assistant to bring some drinks?" Chief Firekeeper asked Chava. Angela appreciated the chief's calm, and the way her body language and speech suggested strength and maintenance of control.

"What kind of drinks?" Chava asked cautiously, as if he thought she might have the refreshments poisoned.

"Non-alcoholic apple cider and herbal tea," the chief answered. "I'm sorry we can't offer you coffee, but we finished that long ago."

"Apple cider," Chava chose.

Chief Firekeeper turned to Angela and asked, "Would you please tell Nikki to bring us glasses and a couple of pitchers? Some apple cider and some mint tea."

Angela found Nikki, submitted the request, and returned to the room promptly, where she took a seat near the door next to Tom. The Tribal Council assembled around the table with Chava, Lee, and Oscar.

"This is a table of peace," the chief told Chava. "Please put your weapons away."

"We're not going to do that," Chava replied.

"The guns are not in your best interest," the chief said evenly.

Chava laughed.

Unruffled, the chief continued, "Let me explain how we do things here. The people who live here have made an agreement that we call the Pacific Treaty. According to the Pacific Treaty, we do not engage in violence. This means that we will not use force to defend ourselves against you or any other intruders. So you can shoot every blessed one of us and we won't fight back. But consider your options carefully before you act."

"Our options?" Chava replied, incredulously. "I don't see how you're in a position to offer us options here."

Tom blurted, "Just because we won't shoot you doesn't mean we won't resist. We can be incredibly uncooperative, especially if you harm any of our people. I suggest that..."

"Tom," the chief interrupted with a raised hand. "Let me handle this." Tom sat back and crossed his arms over his chest, restraining himself only with great effort.

"Are you threatening me?" Chava bristled.

Nikki entered with the cider and tea. She poured cups and distributed drinks. Her appearance distracted Chava and Tom from their confrontation.

"We were discussing options." Chief Firekeeper set the discussion back on track. "One choice for you is to shoot us to get what you want. Or some of us, anyway. If you do that, you will soon discover just how many people live in this community and that we will resist you in ways you cannot imagine. But let's consider for a moment what you want. I'm thinking food tops your list. We're willing to share our food with you. You don't have to force us to do that. Unlike you, we know how to grow vegetables and fruit; how to care for, slaughter, and cook animals; how to hunt and how to cure venison; how to preserve food, save seeds, and plant through the seasons. If you kill us, you lose our knowledge about these things. You get all the food to yourselves until it runs out, and then you will have to move on, returning to the dangers, discomfort, hungers, and insecurity of the road. When you reach that point, your choice to kill us may not seem like it was such a great idea in retrospect."

"Why would you share your food with us?" Chava asked suspiciously.

"Why wouldn't we?" replied one of the Tribal Council members.

"You have an option that I doubt you have considered," Chief Firekeeper continued. "You could surrender your weapons and join us. I am offering right now to take your people in. We'll figure out how to provide homes for you and to include you in our community. You can settle here.

But only if you relinquish the weapons, sign the Pacific Treaty, and agree to abide by our laws."

"And what? Become your servants?"

"Who said anything about servants?" A Tribal Council member answered. "You would choose a representative to participate in governance and your group would have a vote on our Spokescouncil."

"We have a respectful, egalitarian, shared system of decision-making," the chief explained. "There's no place in this system for force or violence, however. Our people have gone down that road before and have seen precisely, in painful detail, over centuries, how completely that fails."

"Violence makes more violence, so no one is ever safe," Angela interjected. "Our chief invites you to join our community as equal partners. If you choose instead to use force to bend us to your will then people will die, you'll cause fathomless grief, and you'll come up emptyhanded in the end, I assure you. Once you exhaust our supplies, what will you do and where will you go? Seriously, Chava, do you know how to grow a potato?"

Chava replied to Angela sarcastically, "A potato? Angela you're adorable." Then he turned to the chief. "Now I'm going to tell you what's going to happen. Oscar and Lee are going to walk you home and keep you company at your house to make sure we all stay on the same page. Some of my men will go with some of your people to collect food for us, which we will take to our camp. Yes, we have more people you haven't had the pleasure to meet yet."

"How many of you?" Tom asked.

Chava ignored him and asked Chief Firekeeper, "Do you have a doctor here?"

"We have a health clinic with a doctor and other medical staff," the chief informed him calmly, despite his rudeness.

"One of our people needs medical attention. Let's get moving." Chava waved his gun over his head, stood, and headed toward the door. Oscar and Lee trained their guns on the chief as those assembled followed Chava out.

On the porch, Chava selected a few of his men and sent them with Annie and Joseph to gather food. He sent a few of others to get the injured one who needed medical care.

"Where's the clinic?" he asked the chief.

She pointed to the health center and informed him, "The clinic is that building over there and you will find Rachel, our doctor, on duty."

"Are you kidding me?" Chava replied, shaking his head in amusement. "You have a woman chief and a woman doctor? This is like one of those weird women's tribes of the Amazon or something."

Angela noticed Tom's jaw clench in anger.

"What's wrong with the person who needs medical care?" the chief asked.

"That's none of your business," Chava replied.

"Just so you know, we have no anesthesia and limited medical supplies. Surgery under these conditions is problematic. Our doctor is good but she doesn't work miracles, certainly not at gunpoint."

"Escort madam chief home and stay with her," Chava commanded Oscar and Lee.

"Angela and Tom will take you to the clinic," the chief informed Chava. "I trust you recognize the value of our only doctor and will treat her well." Angela noted that Chava dropped his swagger for a split second and looked unsure before he motioned several of his men to accompany him, while Oscar and Lee followed the chief down the road toward her house.

As Angela preceded Chava on the path to the clinic, she wondered how Darren and other men among her people from Oakland would respond in this situation. Would they stick to the Pacific Treaty? Even if it meant watching Chava's gang kill people? She thought not. Would Chava hurt Rachel if she didn't obey him? Then the thought struck her that he might think Rachel was someone worth kidnapping. As they approached the clinic, Rachel stepped out on the front porch flanked by Musoke, Bernadette, and her longstanding physician's assistant Cindy. She wore her white coat and looked the very picture of professionalism. "What's all this about?" she greeted them.

"We're bringing you one of our men who needs medical attention," Chava answered, with that belligerent jut of his chin that Angela had seen several times already.

Rachel held out her right hand to Chava to shake by way of introduction. "I'm Doctor Rachel Braverman, pleased to meet you."

Flustered, Chava had to switch his gun to his left hand to shake hands with Rachel. "Salvador Wong," he said. "Call me Chava." He shook her hand. Angela found it curious that he had given Rachel his full name.

"What's the problem with your man, Chava?"

"He was shot," Chava informed her.

"That's not surprising with all these guns waving around," Rachel said with no effort to hide her judgement.

"Obviously he wasn't shot by one of our own guys," Chava said. It seemed as though Rachel had somehow thrown him off balance. Angela found that interesting.

"Why obviously? It's a fact that people who own guns are more likely to get shot than people who don't own guns. If I were you, I wouldn't want to take my chances," she told him. Angela was enjoying the conversation and could tell from Chava's body language that he didn't know what to make of Rachel, and he felt less sure of himself. Angela wondered about that. Did Rachel remind him of someone? A female authority figure in his past, perhaps? Her social worker's instincts on high beam, Angela observed the dynamic unfolding before her with a clinical eye piqued by curiosity.

"Where was he shot?" Rachel asked.

"Back there in Cloverdale," Chava answered, waving a hand over his shoulder.

"Not the town. I mean where did the bullet lodge in his body?" Rachel responded impatiently. Tom glanced surreptitiously at Angela with a twinkle in his eye. She returned his glance with a tiny nod and the slightest smile. He was enjoying Rachel's effect as well.

"One bullet in the hand and one in the thigh," Chava answered, flushing slightly with embarrassment about having misinterpreted Rachel's question.

"How long ago?"

"Yesterday morning. They're bringing him here now, so we should go inside and wait."

"You may not go inside with guns" Rachel crossed her arms over her chest. "This is a house of healing. No weapons allowed."

Chava threw his head back and laughed before saying, "Damn if you ain't the feistiest doctor I ever met. What if I want to bring my gun in there?"

"How good are you at removing bullets?"

"I could shoot you and be done with you and your smart mouth," Chava threatened with a flare of anger.

"That would be brilliant, wouldn't it? Shoot the only doctor. I could really do some doctoring once I'm dead." Rachel pitched a flare of anger right back at Chava. "You have a lot of nerve coming into our home and waving your fat guns around. Giving orders like Christopher Columbus. A please and thank-you would serve you a lot better than bullying. If you want to come inside then leave your gun out here. I have never had a gun in my clinic and I never will."

Rachel and Chava glared at each other for perhaps a full minute. Rachel stood her ground. Angela held her breath. "Fine," Chava said curtly as he handed his gun to one of his men and ordered four other men to leave their guns outside with their companions and to accompany him inside Rachel's weapons-free clinic. His men grumbled, but Chava shut them up with a fierce look. Rachel and her medical staff, Tom, Angela, Chava, and Chava's four men entered the clinic to wait for the wounded man to arrive.

Rachel asked Chava where he and his people came from.

"What's that supposed to mean?" Chava replied defensively, with a scowl. "We're American."

Rachel rolled her eyes. "Don't give me that crap. You know what I mean. I'm not asking to see your passport. Where were you when the systems collapsed? Where did you live before?"

"Oakland." Angela allowed herself a smug smile. She had been right about that.

"You're an interesting mix of people," Rachel commented.

Chava shrugged. Angela could see that Rachel had made an impression on him. He allowed Rachel to engage him in conversation and he had noticeably dialed his gang-thug persona down a notch in her presence. "We're the New Brothers."

"Is that the name of your gang?" Rachel asked.

"Our family. We're not a gang."

Angela succumbed to her curiosity and interjected, "I lived in Oakland before too, and I never heard of the New Brothers."

"Most of our people belonged to two different gangs back when that was a thing. We joined together after the crash. It's all different now. We're a group of people, a family."

"And so you guys are Chinese and Mexican?" Angela pressed.

"Mostly, yeah," Chava confirmed. "I'm half Chinese, half Mexican. It doesn't get more American than that, does it?" He flashed a genuine smile. Rachel and Angela both noticed that when he smiled he was extraordinarily handsome. He had a dimple in his cheek, and clear, golden skin. His straight black hair glinted with a healthy shine. He had deep brown eyes and an expressive face. Angela knew Rachel so well, had known her since childhood, and could read her. Chava was exactly the kind of dangerous-gorgeous man that Rachel had gone for back in the day before she met safe, reliable, parent-approved Vince. Angela could tell that Rachel found Chava attractive. Admitting such an attraction to herself when so recently widowed would throw her, especially an attraction to a dangerous, bad-boy, gangsta-type. Angela resolved to tread lightly with her observations.

A contingent of New Brothers arrived just then with the wounded man, who was twenty-something. They carried him into the clinic on a litter constructed from canvas stretched across two tree trunks. A girl with straight blonde hair, blue eyes, and a prominent pregnant belly accompanied him. She was young, maybe still a teenager. Angela felt relieved to see the girl. She wondered how many others, women and children, perhaps elders too, were in the New Brothers "family."

At the arrival of the patient, Rachel became her professional self. She instructed them to carry the wounded man into her procedure room (equipped for light surgical procedures in a relatively sterile environment), which had access to electrical power from a solar array. She kept Cindy and Musoke with her and shooed everyone else out, except for Chava and the pregnant girl. Rachel introduced herself to the injured man, but he didn't respond. He was high on something. One bullet had entered his left hand and the other his right thigh. Rachel was relieved that no internal organs had been compromised. She instructed Cindy to start an IV. Then she turned to Chava, who lingered in the doorway. "Please bring four of your men, strong guys who aren't squeamish, and wait outside the door here with them. I will need you to restrain him. We'll give him whiskey to try to knock him out, but I need to keep him absolutely immobile. Taking bullets out should be straightforward if no bones are shattered, but it's an unpleasant business."

"He's pretty stoned. We've kept him high on marijuana to help him out. Also gave him some Vicodin."

"How much and how long ago?"

Chava thought for a minute. "Last time about three hours ago and I'll have Lee bring the bottle to show you. I don't know how much. It says on the bottle. We gave him two tabs." The injured man moaned softly.

"What's his name?"

"Raphael. His sister was my wife. She was shot and killed last year during a gang dispute, before the oil crash. I feel responsible for him, especially with Susan expecting the baby." Rachel flinched when Chava said his wife was shot. Her reaction did not escape him and he raised an eyebrow. "What?"

"Nothing."

"Yeah, something," he eyed her shrewdly. "What?"

"Hit a nerve," she admitted. "My husband was shot and killed in July in Oakland in a pointless dispute over a bicycle." Chava gave her an unequivocally empathetic look. Lightly brushing her arm with the back of his hand, he said, "I'm sorry." Tears welled in her eyes at his surprising kindness, but she managed to gain control quickly. She needed to focus. She gestured toward Susan and asked, "Raphael is the father?"

Both Susan and Chava nodded.

"OK. Go round up some guys and bring me the Vicodin bottle. We'll look after him." After Chava left, she spoke to Susan. Rachel asked her how far along she was in her pregnancy and she said she didn't know. She thought she had gotten pregnant right after the oil disappeared, but she had not been able to see a doctor.

"After we take care of Raphael, I'm going to have a look at you, young lady," Rachel told her sternly. The girl seemed thin. She and the baby would benefit from a prenatal vitamin complex, and Rachel still had some. She wondered what these people had been eating. The term "feral" came to mind. How many humans had become feral?

Cindy started Raphael on an IV while Musoke fetched the whiskey. Rachel set up her instruments. Susan wiped tears from her cheeks with her hands and Cindy handed her a box of tissues.

"He should be fine," Rachel consoled the girl, smiling kindly. "It doesn't look like he has suffered any serious damage. I'm going to chase you out of here. Please tell Chava that I will call him and his guys in when I need them."

"To hold him down?" Susan asked, wide-eyed.

"He's a big boy. Stop worrying. You'll scare that baby in there. Ask my friend Angela to bring you some tea and a plate of scrambled eggs. Tell her I said so. She's that African American woman who was just in here and I'll bet you she's right outside or in the lobby." Rachel pointed to the door. "Out." She knew she could depend on Angela to take care of Susan, and felt a rush of love for her super-social-worker friend.

Musoke lifted Raphael's head and encouraged him to drink the whiskey. Rachel put Benadryl in the IV to make Raphael sleepy. She hoped for no more shootings because removing bullets without anesthesia would get old real fast.

She decided to work on the thigh first, since that site appeared more difficult. She called in Chava and his men and had them wash their hands with disinfectant. She positioned them where she needed them and then she made an incision. Raphael leapt out of his stupor, screaming and struggling; but Chava and his men grimly did their job and the thigh remained steady under Rachel's expert hand. To everyone's relief, Raphael passed out about a minute into the surgery. She felt rushed and had to force herself to slow down, take her time, and do the work correctly. Raphael stirred and moaned occasionally, but did not regain consciousness. Chava and his men remained at the ready throughout the procedure.

By the time she stitched Raphael up and settled him in a room with Musoke monitoring him, she was exhausted. Apart from the stress of working on someone who wasn't completely knocked out, she was not accustomed to performing for an audience of strangers. She dismissed Chava and his men with a weary "thank you," but Chava would not be brushed off so easily.

"Whoa, whoa," he said. "we'll be done here when I say we're done here."

Rachel put a hand on her hip and cocked her head to one side. "Seriously? I'm bone-weary from dealing with your shoot-em-up mess, but I still have to take a look at Susan, who I think is malnourished. Also, I have a couple of people who were scheduled to see me today who got bounced because of your emergency, and they still need to see me. Today. So go perform your thug show somewhere else because I have a clinic to run."

"Feisty lady doctor, I have more important business to attend to now that Raphael is squared away, so I'm going to go, but not because you ordered me to. Are we clear?"

"No, we're not clear," Rachel snapped back, eyes flashing. "And I'm not giving orders. No one gives orders at Green Creek. We're not that kind of place. You're in for a rude awakening Señor Macho."

"We'll see who's in for a rude awakening." Chava turned abruptly on his heel and left.

Rachel settled Susan in a chair next to Raphael and went to talk with Angela, to find out what she had learned. Angela told her that when she got Susan alone, the girl rambled in a stream of consciousness, her words tumbling out like marbles strewn across the floor. "She kept apologizing for leading the New Brothers to Green Creek and said her father had a friend who lived here, and that when she was a little girl her family came here to visit. Her dad would go hunting with his friend. She remembered how to get here."

"I wonder who the friend was and if he still lives here. Do you know what happened to Susan's dad?"

"She wouldn't say. She led the New Brothers here after Raphael was shot, hoping she could find help for him. She apologized over and over again for leading the New Brothers to Green Creek. She said she never would have done it if

Raphael hadn't been shot. She doesn't want to cause trouble for us."

"So what did you say?"

"I told her he probably would've died if she hadn't come to Green Creek. I mean, what else could I say? She's already beating herself up over revealing the community to the New Brothers. Ray, she wasn't exactly sure how to find us, but she said she followed the road signs from the highway. We're so stupid."

"Oh boy. We should have taken down the signs, huh? If we survive this invasion, we need to send some people out to take down the road signs pointing to Green Creek."

"Unfortunately, the horse has already left the barn on that one."

"We're going to be OK. We can turn this around. I have faith we can salvage this situation. There's something about Chava. He's not all thug. I think we can reach him."

"You mean *you* can reach him," Angela suggested with a sly smile.

Rachel gave her a stern look. "I just think he's not all he pretends to be. He's not all that tough."

"I hope you're right."

"I'm going to have a consultation with Susan. She looks malnourished. And I have to send Musoke to bring in a couple of folks I was supposed to see today who need immediate attention. Can you look after the kids? I'm going to be late this evening."

"No worries, I have it covered. At least, I do if things stay relatively normal. If things get squirrelly then come home. The girls will need you. Who knows what's going to happen now that these New Brothers think they're in charge?"

"I hope they don't shoot anybody. I so do not want to remove more bullets from people. We'll see what the chief has to say about all this. She's more than Chava can handle. He doesn't realize that yet, but he'll figure it out soon enough."

"Hey, better to remove bullets than bury people."

"You've got that right."

Rachel examined Susan and gave her a prenatal vitamin supplement. She recommended that Susan join a yoga class that met every evening in the community center. Then she saw her two priority appointments for the day. One of them was an older man with chronic conditions who resisted making changes to his lifestyle. He didn't know what to do with himself without his e-games and programs to stream on his monitor. She recommended that he talk to Angela, but he said he didn't need anyone "messing with his head." She didn't expect him to live much longer.

She looked in on Raphael before leaving the clinic. Cindy would spend the night at the clinic to keep an eye on him, and they had set up a cot for Susan in his room.

Night cloaked her path through the woods and the family had eaten dinner by the time Rachel arrived at home. They took turns reading aloud in the evenings by the light of a battery-powered lantern, and that night was Rosie's turn. (She and Win-J lived comfortably in the trailer parked in Rachel's driveway.) Rosie had just found the place where Jamal had left off in *Harry Potter and the Prisoner of Azkaban* the previous night when Rachel walked in. Angela brought her a plate with amaranth-and-cornmeal-crust pizza and a bowl of lukewarm soup. Angela offered to heat the soup up over the fire pit in the back yard, but Rachel told her not to bother. She listened to Rosie read while she ate. Tom had sunk into his customary easy chair. In recent weeks he spent most of his off-hours at their house. She couldn't say if he had adopted them or they had adopted him. Either way, he was part of the family, a welcome male presence in a household of women and children bereft of fathers.

Tom, still quite fit at fifty-seven, had lost his wife to cancer several years earlier. His two children lived in Southern California and, before, in the Lost Time, he saw them often since they frequently came to visit him or he flew down to see them. He would certainly never see them again. Rachel welcomed him into her home. His presence benefitted the children.

After the read-aloud, bedtime rituals, and settling the children for the night, Rachel and Angela sat in the kitchen with Tom and drank a cup of tea. Tom told them that the New Brothers had plundered the farm, spiriting away large bags of kale and potatoes, and requiring the slaughter and plucking of a sizable number of chickens. While they appeared to take turns at guard duty to allow men to go to their mysterious encampment to eat, in the end many New Brothers men remained at Green Creek for the night. They guarded the chief and Tribal Council members in their homes as hostages, and posted sentries at the clinic (where Raphael and Susan slept), making their threatening presence felt. Tom reckoned the New Brothers people had camped out nearby. "I wonder how many of them are out there, and if any are more trigger-happy than those we've encountered so far," Tom worried.

"I wanna bet they have women and children with them," Angela replied. "If they have families then they're likely to show more compassion and more caution."

"Well, I consider it a good sign that they haven't shot anyone," Rachel added, wearily.

"Yet," Tom pointed out. "Haven't shot anyone yet."

"Darren and his brother and his cop friends better restrain themselves. If they confront these guys we could have a bloodbath," Angela noted. "I had a talk with Darren this evening. He's having a hard time leaving his gun locked up in your broom closet, Tom."

"I'm having a hard time leaving my gun locked up in my broom closet. If Darren and his men see their families threatened, I doubt they'll honor the Pacific Treaty."

"The chief has it right, though," Rachel emphasized. "She never thought it would be easy to take the high road, she just knows it's the right way to go. Otherwise we sink into the mire of violence, and it never ends. It never, never ends."

"I get it," Tom said. "Do you see me running for my gun? I haven't done it, have I?"

"Good man," Angela encouraged him as she patted his arm. "The problem with this country has always been that it was built on violence, which is the absolutely worst foundation for a society. It's why it was so dysfunctional for so long and it's why everything eventually fell apart."

"What country wasn't built on violence?" Rachel asked softly.

Tom stood. "I'm going to sleep on your couch tonight if you don't mind, ladies," he informed them. "Gun or no gun, I don't like the idea of leaving you and all these children alone in this house."

Rachel thanked him with a kiss on the cheek. "I don't know what I would do without you."

Angela found a pillow and some blankets for Tom, while Rachel brushed her teeth and changed into her nightgown. Rachel wanted badly to fall into a deep, restorative sleep. Since losing Vince, she never felt completely rested when she woke in the morning. She dreamed of him often and then, during that first instant after she woke, she didn't remember that he had died. A moment later, when she remembered, she didn't want to get out of bed and face another day without him.

When she woke up on the morning after the New Brothers arrived, and looked out the window, she felt even more like putting the covers over her head. A relentless drizzle trickled out of a dreary gray sky. Angela was already up and getting breakfast for the children. Rachel put on her bathrobe and walked over to the window. She glanced at the road leading into Green Creek and caught her breath in surprise. A parade of damp and bedraggled women and children filed into Green Creek. Accompanied by a number of armed men, and pushing shopping carts and pulling wagons, the rest of the New Brothers clan had been flushed out by the weather and were making themselves visible. Rachel hurried into the kitchen and asked Angela, "Did you see?"

Busy getting the children up and fed, Angela had not noticed. Rachel led her into the living room, where Tom sat on the sofa lacing up his boots, and she pulled back the curtain from the picture window. She pointed to the road. Angela, Tom, and the children gazed out at the stream of nomads entering their community.

"You got your wish," Tom said to Angela softly. "Women and children. I had better get my woefully unarmed self over to the tribal office."

"Use the forest path around back," Rachel suggested.

"You betcha," Tom replied as he threw on his jacket, and then he was gone.

"Did he eat breakfast?" Rachel asked Angela, who nodded in the affirmative.

"How many d'you think are out there?" Win-J asked.

"Not sure," Angela replied. "Maybe about thirty women and children? I can't tell how many guys are with the gang."

"You should stop calling them a gang," Rosie said. "It makes them sound creepy. They're not a gang anymore. That's from the Lost Time. They're just some random people. They're like a Tribe kind of. They call themselves a family."

"You're right, girl," Angela told her approvingly. "Except they're a Tribe with guns and we're a Tribe without guns."

"I like our Tribe better," Sulei piped up, hugging Big Dog to his chest.

"Me too, baby," Angela agreed.

"I don't think it's safe for you kids to go to school today," Rachel said, trembling. If anything happened to Sophia and

Abby, it would kill her. "I think you should stay in the house."

"Mommmmm," Sophia whined, unhappy at the idea of spending a boring day in the house away from her friends. "The most fun thing we get to do is go to school. Why can't we go? What's gonna happen?"

"Sophia, just do as I say," Rachel snapped. "There are men with guns on the Rez and I want you safe at home." Sophia pouted.

"It's raining anyway," Rosie pointed out cheerfully. "Win-J and I will stay here with you guys. We'll build a fort in the living room and make popcorn over the fire. It'll be fun." Rosie tugged affectionately at the end of one of Sophia's pigtails.

"You're an angel," Rachel told Rosie with relief, before she hurried to her room to get dressed. Angela insisted that Rachel eat a square of cold cornbread and a hunk of cheese before she left the house.

"I'll be right behind you," Angela promised as Rachel pulled on her boots. "Just have to make sure the kids are set up with something for lunch."

"See you on the deck," Rachel called over her shoulder as she ran out the door.

She checked on Raphael and Susan first when she arrived at the clinic. They still had Raphael on painkillers provided by Chava, but he was conscious enough to understand where he was and that the bullets had been removed. Fortunately, she still had antibiotics on hand. Practicing medicine in the Vision Time was like jumping off a cliff. As her arsenal of medications dwindled, she was dropping into free-fall. A lot of people would die from treatable ailments in the near future when she ran out of pharmaceuticals. She had already lost quite a few diabetics and several elders with cardiovascular disease. On the other hand, there were those, like Christina, who had embraced the opportunity to change their lifestyle.

In the early afternoon, Angela appeared at the clinic and assembled the clinic staff in the lobby. She somberly shared the news that the New Brothers had taken the children hostage at the Youth Center at gunpoint as a consequence of some sort of argument in progress with Tom about weapons.

"Thank goodness we kept our children at home today," Rachel commented.

Angela took a deep breath and then informed Rachel, "We did our best. When I went home for lunch I discovered that Sophia snuck out this morning and went to school."

Rachel gasped and clutched at a table to steady herself. It felt like her heart had stopped. "Sophia is at the school?"

"Tom is dealing with the situation."

"I'm going over there."

"No, that would make the situation even more volatile. Parents have to stay away. We need to let Tom do his job," Angela insisted.

"I should go home to the children, then," Rachel suggested.

"I didn't tell them about this. They're safe at the house. Hopefully everything will be resolved soon and the children won't have to know until it's all over."

Rachel couldn't concentrate on work and sent her afternoon patients home with an apology. She and Angela sat on the couch in Rachel's office, talking softly, remembering old times to preoccupy their minds. The rain pounded on the roof like a family of dancing gorillas.Throughout the afternoon, Rachel started at every sudden noise. A flock of quail lifting from the Bottlebrush tree outside the window of her office made her jump. She had one ear cocked for the sound of gunshots. How would she survive removing bullets from children without anesthesia? How would she survive if she lost Sophia? She couldn't think that. She had to stay positive. She struggled to contain her fury at Chava and the New Brothers for bringing such anguish to her and others at Green Creek.

At around four o'clock, Bernadette blew in on the damp gusts of the storm with the news that all the children had been released unharmed. Rachel's eyes welled with tears of relief. "Sophia is on her way home," Bernadette told her.

Angela noted wearily, "I'll go to the school tomorrow, talk to the children, run damage control."

"Those children will not be at school tomorrow," Bernadette pointed out. "Their parents won't send them."

"Of course."

"I'm sure the chief will close the school now that we realize we can't afford to make ourselves that vulnerable again by putting our children together in one place. We shouldn't have even had the school open today," Bernadette said.

Rachel and Angela were about to leave the clinic when a messenger from the New Brothers arrived to inform Rachel that some of their people would come to see her the following morning about health issues. She met him on the

porch and kept him standing awkwardly outside in the rain
during their conversation because he was packing a gun. "I
have appointments tomorrow morning," Rachel informed
him icily. She could barely contain her fury.

"Then cancel them," the man told her, with a belligerent
shrug.

"Your people can wait their turn like everyone else," she
replied stubbornly. "Is anyone suffering from something that
requires urgent attention? I'll see someone if they have an
urgent issue. Otherwise have them set up appointments with
my receptionist."

"Chava will not be pleased," he warned.

"I am not pleased with Chava," Rachel snapped back.
"He pointed a gun at my daughter today." End of
conversation. She and Angela hurried home from the clinic
through the rain.

Their children had no idea what had happened. They
were shocked when a soaked and bedraggled Sophia
appeared and fell into Rachel's arms sobbing. Rachel
clutched her daughter to her fiercely. Then she started
hollering at her to never, never, never disobey her mother
again. Sophia gulped for air while Angela tried to calm
Rachel.

"Your mom was scared to death, Sophia," Angela told
the child. "She's just relieved that you're safe." Rachel
struggled to get herself under control while Angela explained
to the other children what had happened. That set Abby off
crying and she clung to Sophia.

"It's over now, let's go see what we can scrounge up for
dinner," Angela said, as she opened the door and headed for

the kitchen. As it turned out, Rosie and Jamal had enlisted the other children to help and they had a good pot of goat and vegetable stew simmering over the fire in the fire pit.

"It has a little rain in it," Sulei informed them cheerfully.

Later, when they were halfway through devouring their stew, Tom showed up. Although Rachel and Angela were anxious to hear details about what had happened at the school, they didn't want to discuss it in front of the children, so they waited patiently until they put the young ones to bed. When Rosie and Win-J said good-night and prepared to head off to their trailer, Angela told them to stay for the conversation with Tom. Then they all sat down at the kitchen table to get the full story.

Tom explained that the New Brothers women and children had moved into the community center that morning. Once Chava had seen them settled, he sought Tom and asked him where he kept the Green Creek guns. Chava figured that they had guns stored somewhere, and he wanted at them. Tom reluctantly led him to the storage closet (that he had taken to calling the armory), only to discover that someone had broken into the closet during the night and removed every single gun and all the ammunition. Not even a lone bullet remained.

Enraged, Chava accused Tom of staging the break-in and hiding the guns. After some discussion, Tom successfully convinced Chava that he had no idea where the weapons had gone. Chava declared he would find out who had moved them, demand their return, and confiscate them. He marched Tom to the school, taking a group of armed New Brothers with him. They pulled the children out of class and assembled them in the gymnasium. Chava gave Tom one hour to spread the word at Green Creek that the New Brothers would shoot one child every five minutes until the guns and ammo reappeared.

Tom swiftly enlisted his police officers to help him figure out what was going on. Darren and Michael immediately confessed to Tom that they had hidden the guns in the hay in a barn on the farm. They accompanied Tom to the school, where they agreed to take Chava to the weapons if he would release the children. Chava said he would release the children when he had possession of the weapons. Tom, Darren, and Michael led him and his men to the barn and uncovered the guns and ammo. After that they let the terrified children and teachers go home.

Remarkably restrained under the circumstances, Tom made a point of telling Chava that the Green Creek community needed those guns to hunt for wild game to eat. He asked Chava if any of his people knew how to hunt deer, wild turkeys, or rabbits. He explained that the hunter had to know how to hit an animal just right to kill it instantly, otherwise it would release hormones (from the pain and terror) into its body that would render the meat substandard. Chava suggested with a bemused smile that the community use bows and arrows to hunt instead of guns. Tom informed him that was a racist comment and explained that it took a great deal of hard work to make bows and arrows, and that the people at Green Creek were still learning how to use them to hunt, hoping they would develop the necessary skill with bows and arrows by the time the bullets ran out. Just because they were Natives didn't mean they automatically knew how to shoot an arrow. Tom and Chava got into a shouting match and were hollering at each other in front of Chief Firekeeper's house when she appeared on her porch. Oscar and the other New Brothers who held her under house arrest aimed their guns at her. She waved them off like a swarm of inconsequential gnats, and commanded them to lower their weapons, which they surprisingly did. She ushered Tom and Chava inside.

"Marjorie never ceases to amaze me," Tom said, shaking his head in wonderment. "That woman has an extremely old spirit." Angela and Rachel nodded in agreement as Tom continued his account.

The chief surmised that if Chava's people planned on staying at Green Creek, then they would likely welcome the meat that could be procured using the weapons they had taken. She suggested that perhaps they could work out an agreement for skilled Green Creek hunters to use the guns under the supervision of New Brothers to go on hunting expeditions. Chava conceded, guardedly, that he would take it under advisement, but Tom could see that the chief's words had reached him. She thanked Tom for turning over the weaponry. She said she didn't care who kept the guns or where they were kept so long as they were used appropriately. She looked pointedly at Chava, who Tom claimed squirmed noticeably under her gaze. She then asked Chava to make her a promise that he would not point guns at children again.

He said he was not prepared to commit to that.

She told him she had something to give him in return if he could do that.

He boasted that anything she could give him he could take without her consent.

She disagreed. He could not take her hospitality unless she chose to offer it. She warned him that there were too many things he did not know and did not understand. "Without the guidance of me and my people, you will look straight at resources, benefits, assets, and the means to accomplish things without even realizing that these are in front of you. You won't recognize them or comprehend how to use them."

Chava studied the chief in silence for a long time. Then he agreed not to use the children as hostages again and not to point guns at them. The chief thanked him for agreeing, and held her hand out for him to shake it. When he took her hand, she held his firmly, placed her other hand on top of his, and looked him in the eye. "I hold you to this oath. We honor our promises at Green Creek. Promises are sacred. We do not break promises like those who sought to destroy us and exploit us throughout history." Tom said they should have seen Chava's expression. It was as if the chief had put a spell on him. Angela, Rachel, Win-J, and Rosie listened to Tom's description of the conversation with rapt attention.

When Chava stood to leave, the chief told him to sit back down and he did. She said that she had heard that the New Brothers had brought their families to Green Creek and that they were camping out in the community center. Chava asked her if she had a problem with that and she said she did. She said that was no place for women and children to live.

Tom shook his head and grinned. The amazement he had experienced in the chief's house still clung to him when he told the others that the chief then offered the New Brothers the use of some of the trailers that Musoke had dragged out to Green Creek with his electro-vegetable-grease van. Musoke had spent many long days dragging trailers, and they had a lot of them parked in a field above the cow pasture. They had run water over there from the springs that fed Green Creek and a few of the families who had come up from Oakland with Angela were living there along with some of the locals who had turned up looking for shelter.

The chief told Chava where to find the trailers and that his people were welcome to claim any of them that were not taken. She requested that his people share as much as possible to keep trailers available to make room for more people who would need shelter in the future. Chava could not conceal his astonishment at the chief's generosity, her implication that the New Brothers were welcome to make a home at Green Creek. He told the chief that they had been sleeping out in the open, in tents and makeshift shelters. The women would be grateful to be able to put their children to sleep in beds in those trailers. Then he appeared embarrassed, as if he had said too much and regretted it.

At that point, Tom couldn't resist reminding Chava that he and his men had pointed guns at the children of Green Creek and their chief had responded by putting a roof over the heads of the New Brothers' children. The chief told Tom he needed to work on having a more generous heart. "Can you believe it?" he asked his listeners. "She's really something."

The chief then asked Tom to walk Chava over to the trailers and to make sure the families were settled into them and fed before it got dark. "I swear I could hear the gears turning in Chava's head," Tom told his kitchen-table audience with a chuckle. "He didn't know what to make of our chief. It was interesting. I saw something happen with him that's hard to explain. When she offered him the trailers for his people, it was as if he rebooted, as if he shut something off and restarted it fresh. He left her house a little different from who he was when he went in."

"So that's what my day was like," Tom concluded, with an ironic laugh. After he wrapped up his account, Rachel and Angela said good-night to Win-J and Rosie, who thanked them for including them in hearing Tom's story. The youngsters left the kitchen and walked across the yard to the trailer hand-in-hand. Angela started to go into the living room to get some bedding for Tom, but he called her back to the table.

"I didn't want to say anything with the kids in here, but there's one more thing of interest from this surprising day."

"What is that?" Rachel asked curiously.

"When we uncovered the guns in the hay to hand them over to the New Brothers, not all of the weapons were there."

"What do you mean not all of them were there?" Angela asked.

"I mean that some of the guns were missing. I know what I had in the armory. All of our tribal police weapons were there and so were most of the personal weapons that people had turned in (as far as I could tell). But I didn't see any of the firearms issued by the Oakland Police Department. Darren, Michael, and their people kept those out. They put them somewhere else. The guys who came up here from Oakland with you, Angela, well, they hid their own weapons somewhere else and they still have them. Chava doesn't know it and I'm sure not going to tell him. I wouldn't tell the chief because I feel absolutely certain she would make Darren and his folks surrender them. I'm telling you because I trust that you won't tell anyone either."

"So you're saying that some of our people have guns," Angela repeated. "You're saying we could be in for a shoot-out."

"Not necessarily a shoot-out, but,yes, some of our guys are armed and prepared to defend their families," Tom affirmed.

"Is that good or bad?" Angela asked.

"I don't know," Tom answered. "At this point, I just... I really don't know."

"It sounds like a bad idea to me," Rachel said. "But I'm not going to be the one to snitch about it." Rachel stood. "It's getting late. We need to get some sleep so we are at our best in the morning. I'm keeping the children home tomorrow."

"Everyone is," Tom noted.

"I don't know what we'd do without Rosie," Angela added.

"And you too, Tom," Rachel said. "It's comforting to have you staying with us. I do appreciate it."

"Not a big deal. You guys are my family now. I don't have anyone else."

"Then it's not just the attraction of our solar-electric hot water heater," Rachel teased as she hugged him before heading off to bed.

Sophia woke during the night in the grip of a nightmare and Angela and Rachel took her into the bed with them. Angela would have a therapeutic conversation with her the next day and work to mitigate the trauma the child had suffered. She would put the word out to Green Creek parents that they could bring their children to her if they wished, to mop up from the mess Chava had made.

The next couple of days remained quiet at Green Creek. It rained most of the time. Rachel and Angela went to work and the children stayed home with Rosie and Win-J. A contrite Sophia did her best to be super well-behaved. The Chaudhary girls came over to the house so their mother could work in the gardens on the farm. Their house was messy and chaotic, but the children seemed happy and, most of all, relatively safe.

Musoke helped Raphael move into a trailer with Susan. Cindy visited them every day to change the dressings on Raphael's wounds. Raphael was recovering quickly and Susan perked up after a few sessions with Angela. She joined the yoga class Rachel had recommended as well as an exercise class for pregnant women that met in the community center.

Chava maintained an armed guard at Chief Firekeeper's house and at the homes of the other Tribal Council members. But he and his men didn't prevent people from coming in and going out of the houses to confer with the chief or the other leaders. The farm continued to produce enough food to feed the expanded community, and the established infrastructure systems ran without interference from the New Brothers, who had settled into their trailers. Some of the Green Creek women visited the New Brothers women and they began to get to know one another. Angela learned from Tanisha that a woman named Claudia, who was in her late fifties, was essentially the New Brothers matriarch. Apparently Claudia went to the chief's house to share a pot of tea every morning.

After a couple weeks, Chava came to the clinic one afternoon. He waited until Rachel finished with the patient she was seeing, but then he jumped the queue and insisted that she see his daughter, Soledad. He didn't bring his gun into the clinic, but he didn't bother to make an appointment either. Out of concern for the skinny girl presented to her, Rachel let him disrupt her schedule. She ushered Soledad into her examination room and curtly ordered Chava to wait outside when he tried to join them.

"I'm her father. She's a minor," Chava protested.

"I'll come for you when we're ready for you." Rachel shut the door firmly.

She invited Soledad to take a seat in a chair, rather than putting her up on the examination table. Rachel determined that Soledad was eleven years old. She had straight hair as black as a raven's wing that fell to her waist, and green eyes with flecks of gold in them. Rachel thought if the child were an animal she would be a cat. She told her that anything she said in that room was confidential and that Rachel was sworn as a doctor not to share it with anyone without the patient's permission.

"You mean you won't tell my dad what I say if I tell you not to?" Soledad asked earnestly, her eyes large and wary.

"That's right. Anything we say here is between us. Before we let your dad join us, we'll talk about what you want to keep private and what I can share. So tell me why your dad brought you to a doctor."

"I can't eat. I mean, yeah, I eat. Obviously, or I'd be dead. But a lot of times my stomach hurts or I feel like I'm going to throw up and I have to force myself to eat."

"Where does it hurt?"

She circled her belly with her hand. Rachel could see it wasn't actually her stomach that was bothering her but her intestines. In children, this was often caused by stress. It could also be a food allergy, but she suspected it had more to do with trauma manifesting in the child's body.

"When it hurts a lot, what do you do?"

"My dad gives me like an aspirin or something."

"Does that help?" Rachel filed away the "or something" and would ask Chava if he was giving the child stronger painkillers.

"Sometimes. If it's at night then yeah coz it helps me sleep. Claudia gives me chamomile and spearmint tea and that's good. Sometimes nothing helps."

"What is the pain like? Is it constant or does it come in waves of cramps?"

"Cramps."

"On a scale of one to ten, how intense is it usually?"

She thought for a moment. "Different. Sometimes about two or three and sometimes like, I don't know, maybe seven or eight? Sometimes it makes me cry."

Rachel asked her for more health information, and determined that the child had not started her period yet. "When did you start having these cramps?"

"When Mami died. Before everything went crazy. When everything went crazy and we had to leave our home, the cramps got worse. I had them all the time. Especially when we were traveling. They put me in a shopping cart and pushed me because I couldn't walk."

"Why do you think you get sick like this?"

The child spoke almost inaudibly, "I think some things make me sick to my stomach."

"What kinds of things?" Rachel prodded gently.

Soledad said nothing and Rachel gave her space. Then she blurted vehemently, "Papi was in a gang and the gangs got in a fight and Mami got killed. If Papi had stayed away from those gangs then Mami would still be alive. He knows it. He knows it's his fault. Then all the gas disappeared and he made us leave our house and my friends and everything. That was stupid. Why did we have to leave everything? Now he thinks he has to protect me and other people, and that the way to do that is to shoot anyone who won't do what he says. He always has a gun. So do all the guys. They could shoot me by accident. They say Mami got shot by accident. How do they know they won't shoot me by accident?"

"Have you talked to your dad about how you feel?"

Soledad gave Rachel a withering look. "You see what he's like. I could never talk to him about it. He wouldn't listen to my point of view. He would tell me I'm weak. He's so stupid. He can't figure out why I'm sick and unhappy but isn't it obvious? He doesn't care."

"Well he brought you to see me, didn't he?"

She mumbled something inaudible.

"Does he criticize you for being weak?"

"He doesn't have to say it. I see how he looks at me. He wants me to be strong, courageous, and fierce. He wants me to have a lot of fight, like some of the other kids. But I'm not brave and I don't want to fight. I just want to go home." Her voice trembled. "I want to climb into my bed and read a book. My dad doesn't get me. I'm a disappointment and he's ashamed of me." Soledad crossed her arms in front of her and bent forward slightly, wincing. "He's a bully. He used to be different when Mami was alive. I loved him then." She broke off abruptly, terrified of what she had revealed.

"And now?" Rachel prodded.

"Now I don't know," Soledad whispered and she began to cry. "You won't say anything, right?'

"Of course not," Rachel assured her. "You're a big girl so I'm going to tell you honestly what I think is the problem. I think you're sad." At this, Soledad began sobbing, and Rachel pulled her chair next to the child's chair and put her arms around her. Rachel handed her a tissue. "Are you listening to me?" she asked. Soledad nodded. "You're sad, and you're frightened, and you've been through a lot of terrible experiences. A lot of things have happened to you that have upset you and shocked you. The technical term for this is trauma. These kinds of traumatic experiences make a lasting impact on us, all of us, adults too, and we hold the feelings from these hard experiences locked in our bodies. I think you have a lot of hard experiences locked in your body that are giving you pain. Does that make sense?"

"You mean the pain in my thoughts and my heart goes into my stomach and turns into real pain I can feel in my body?"

Rachel rubbed Soledad's back. "That's exactly what I mean. You're very smart."

"So my stomach ache is from my head?"

"No. I don't want you to think I told you that. That's not what I said. That makes it sound like you could stop it if you would just think differently. Your stomach ache is real. I know it's real. It could be partially connected to the way you are eating, which could certainly have something to do with it. But I think it's mostly caused by stress, sadness, and fear; by trauma. Just knowing what causes it, though, is not going to make the pain stop. I have a friend here at Green Creek. She's a therapist. She helps children like you who suffer from trauma. I think she could help you feel better, if you're willing to talk to her. Her name is Angela and she is also required to keep everything you say to her confidential."

"I would talk to her."

"I also want you to keep coming to me to see if we can find out if you're eating something that doesn't agree with you. And first of all, I want you to stop eating any cow's milk or anything made from cow's milk, like cheese. I want to see if you are having trouble digesting cow dairy right now. We have excellent goat milk and goat cheese here at Green Creek and I think you could keep eating that, but do you think you could give up cow milk and cheese for a couple of weeks?"

"Sure. I'm never hungry anyway. But do you think I'm going to be here for a couple of weeks?" she asked incredulously.

"I have a feeling you are and that you and I are going to become friends. And I think that tomorrow you should come to my house and spend the day with my girls. They're around your age. Someone shot and killed their father in July, down in Oakland, so they have sadness from that like you do for your mami. But they do a lot of fun things to try to stay as happy as they can, because they know that their dad would have wanted them to be happy and not to feel sad all the time about losing him. I'm sure your mami would have wanted you to be happy again too."

"What are their names?"

"Abby and Sophia. Do we have a plan?"

"I think so. But I have to ask permission."

"Can I get a hug?" Rachel asked. Soledad gave her the hug with a bonus smile to go with it. "Are we ready to talk to your big, mean papi?"

"Yeah. You won't tell him what I said about him, right?"

"Of course not. I'll tell you a secret if you promise to keep this really secret, OK?"

"I promise," Soledad vowed solemnly.

"Really secret. I think your mean papi is a soft Teddy bear who acts tough and bossy because he's scared and because he's sad about your mami. I think he has no idea what to do next and underneath everything, under all that mean-ness, he could be very sweet if he would try." Rachel leaned close and whispered in Soledad's ear, "I also think he loves you very much and you are the most important thing

in his life, but he doesn't know how to show you that."
Soledad nodded and tears welled in her eyes.

"Now I'm going to go let the mean papi in," Rachel
warned. She had not examined Soledad, but she didn't need
to. She had seen enough children suffering digestive issues
caused by stress and trauma to recognize it. Plus, she could
tell from observing the child that she was basically healthy;
a bit malnourished from not eating, but healthy. Rachel
went out to the lobby and invited Chava into the
examination room.

When he was seated next to his silent daughter, who
carefully studied her feet, Rachel sat and put her hands into
the pockets of her white coat. "In my estimation, Soledad's
digestive issues are caused by trauma, stress, and grief
resulting primarily from the loss of her mother and her
home." Chava glanced at Soledad and back at Rachel, his
forehead tense and knotted. "I have discussed this with
Soledad and she is old enough to understand how this
sometimes happens and that it's happening to her."

"Are you telling me her stomach pain is psychological?
I've seen her in pain. Something is wrong and I want to
know what it is," Chava demanded.

"Listen to her, Papi," Soledad said quietly. "She's right."

Chava appeared taken aback.

"I'm not saying the pain is imagined. I understand it's
real. Your daughter has been through an extremely difficult
time. She lost her mother, her home, her friends, everything
familiar to her. She has been on the move, in a hostile
environment, surrounded by violence or potential violence.

This is frightening and stressful. She is a textbook study in what happens to children who suffer trauma."

"But I protect her. I..." Chava began, but he stopped speaking abruptly when Soledad took his hand and looked pleadingly at him. She wanted him to listen, and she clearly agreed with Rachel's assessment.

"Here is my recommendation. Soledad should see Angela, who is a qualified, trained children's therapist. She has been providing therapy to people of all ages at Green Creek. But her specialty is working with children. I think she can help Soledad work through the difficult feelings she is experiencing. I also talked to Soledad about not eating cow's milk products for a while to see if this helps her digestion improve. We have a lot of goat products at Green Creek that she can eat instead." Chava appeared to approve of the dietary restriction. It sounded like a concrete medical recommendation. "And I have invited Soledad to come to my house tomorrow to play with my daughters, who are also grieving for a dead parent as it happens, but who manage to have a lot of fun in spite of their loss." Rachel did not make reference to the closure of the school or Chava's role in causing this to happen, even though what he had done infuriated her. She took the high road for Soledad's sake. "Soledad and I have discussed these things and she has agreed to this."

"Will Angela see her?" Chava asked. "She doesn't like me."

"It's not that she doesn't like you. She disapproves of what you do; but that has nothing to do with this," Rachel replied with a sigh. "She's a professional and of course she'll see Soledad."

"We can do the goat cheese thing." Chava turned to Soledad, "We can do that, right, mija?"

"I don't know if I like goat cheese, but I'll try it," Soledad replied.

"Spending the day at your house tomorrow is a bad idea," Chava informed them. Soledad rolled her eyes and said something to Chava in clipped Spanish. He looked uncertain. Rachel glanced back and forth from father to daughter. He reluctantly agreed to let her go to Rachel's house.

"One more thing," Rachel told him. "Stop giving her painkillers. They're aggravating her digestive issues. Claudia has been giving her mint and chamomile tea, which is a much better remedy. Tell Claudia to see Christina if she needs more herbs for tea. We grow both mint and chamomile. If Soledad can't sleep from pain, rub her tummy. That should help her relax." Rachel turned to Soledad and asked, "Will you let your papi rub your tummy if it hurts at bedtime?" She nodded affirmative and surprisingly Chava sent Rachel a look so loaded with gratitude that it nearly knocked her off her seat.

"OK then," Rachel said as she stood up. "I'm going to walk Soledad over to Angela's office and set up an appointment. Then I'm going to get back to my patients who have been waiting through this interruption."

Before handing Soledad off to Angela, she briefed Angela privately about all that had transpired. Angela set up a time to meet with Soledad the next day. But then she complained, "I don't like the idea of having Chava's daughter at our house, Ray. I wish you had asked me before you invited her. You're drawing attention to us. Now he knows where we live and where he can find a group of children together if he wants to take children hostage again. The school's closed, but you tipped him off to a group of children he can use."

"He promised the chief he wouldn't hold children hostage again," Rachel reminded her.

Angela snorted. "He promised? I don't trust him."

"Besides," Rachel argued, "he would be a lot less likely to target a group of children who are his daughter's friends. I think it affords them greater protection."

"You can't fool me. I know you. You have a thing for him, don't you? That's why you invited his daughter over." Angela was annoyed and couldn't hold her tongue. "He's a fine-looking man and I see how you act around him. Remember he's as dangerous as a scorpion. He's not one of your high school bad boys. He's an Oakland gang leader having a field day in a new anarchy. He's a different creature from what you've ever encountered."

"Don't be so negative. And FYI, I'm a recently widowed mommy. I have no interest in a romance with him or anyone else, Ms. Know-it-all."

"I see what I see." Angela shrugged.

Rachel threw Angela a look of disdain. As she turned to leave she flung a few parting words over her shoulder. "Whatever. Just help out here with Soledad. She's suffering."

"Suffering children are my specialty," Angela replied wryly to Rachel's back.

Despite her denials, Rachel knew Angela's accusations held a grain of truth. If she was being honest, she liked Chava and she was attracted to him; even though he was exactly as dangerous as Angela said he was. What was she thinking? She needed to get a grip. She felt guilty even thinking about a man in that way so soon after losing Vince. And yet, she was so tired of her grief, so burned out on getting up in the morning and hoisting the weight of the tragedy of her lost marriage onto her shoulders. Don't think about it, she told herself, just go back to work.

Spending time with Angela's and Rachel's children was the best medicine for Soledad. She thrived in their busy household, where she found kindred spirits in Rachel's girls, who mourned the loss of Vince, and Angela's boys, who had begun to accept the fact that they would probably never see Winston again. Within the space of a few days, she formed a strong connection with Sophia. The Chaudhary girls stayed at the house most days as well. Rosie and Win-J looked after the younger children, doing projects with them, playing games, preparing the family dinner, often walking en masse to the farm to work in the gardens. The children formed an attachment to the goats, which had distinct and funny personalities.

The resilience of the children often overwhelmed Rachel with emotion. They adapted astonishingly well. Most afternoons, Rosie and Jamal made corn cakes over the back yard fire pit in a couple of large skillets. The community had grown an enormous crop of corn and a smaller crop of amaranth. They milled the grains using grinding stones salvaged from the museum, as well as new grinding stones made to match the museum relics. One group of community members spent their days milling grain for the whole community. Crystal had developed a recipe for corn cakes that had spread instantly throughout the community. All the families made them, and they were the staple in everyone's diet. They ate them for breakfast with butter and jam. They made sandwiches with them for lunch. They ate them with soup or stew for dinner, and never seemed to tire of them. Soledad became a fan of them as well, and she claimed they settled her stomach.

After a few days at Rachel's house, Soledad asked if she could sleep over. She spent that night in bed with Sophia, and then the next night, and then she simply moved in with them. Chava soon appeared at Rachel's house to see his daughter, who never failed to make sure that he had not brought any weapons, because Rachel stood her ground and banned guns from her house. Chava meekly complied with the ban. Finding a place where she felt at home and safe did even more good for Soledad than her therapy sessions with Angela, and her stomach aches subsided. Rachel fed the girl chamomile tea with a spoonful of honey before bed each night. Angela said it made sense that Soledad had improved because what she needed most of all was some semblance of a stable, normal life.

Meanwhile, the Green Creek community fell into an odd complacence on the surface of things. The New Brothers continued to hold the Tribal Council members under house arrest, with an armed guard at each house; and continued to issue orders. The demands of the New Brothers decreased as they began to blend into Green Creek, making friends and falling into the rhythm of community life. They had shelter, food, water, medical care, and they felt safer than they had in a long time. While things generally flowed along more or less as they had before the arrival of the New Brothers, the structure of governance at Green Creek remained on hold. It was impossible for the Tribal Council, the Spokescouncil, or the elders to meet and organize the continuation of community systems necessary for their survival while in the presence of the New Brothers, their guns, and their pseudo-leadership. In the privacy of their bedroom at night, Rachel and Angela deconstructed the situation and speculated about where it would take them. Whichever way they looked at it, they did not think it would end well.

Rachel implemented her own stealthy plan to undermine the New Brothers by engaging Chava (their leader), enmeshing him in an attachment to her family, hooking him through his daughter. Or at least, that's what she told herself she was doing. She invited Chava to join them for dinner whenever he came by to see Soledad late in the day. So he came by in the evening more and more often, anticipating the dinner invitation.

Soledad clearly did not want to return to the New Brothers community in the trailer park section of Green Creek. She went there to see Claudia, but she didn't appear to feel any allegiance to the people with whom she had arrived. Angela thought Soledad's disapproval of Chava's strong-arm way of doing things was keeping him in check. But she didn't expect it to last. The community was sitting on dynamite. All it would take was one unfortunate incident, and Darren might come out shooting, provoking the New Brothers. While knowing that Darren had guns stashed somewhere made Angela feel safer, it made Rachel feel more vulnerable. If Chava shot Rosie's father, or visa-versa, it would shatter the little kingdom of children at Rachel's house. They were barely functioning at an acceptable level as it was, with all the deprivations and creative improvising they lived with daily, such as children outgrowing shoes and the need to start making candles from scratch. A burst of violence would be devastating.

Angela did not like Chava coming for dinner, and only put up with it for Soledad's sake. If not for the fact that Tom ate with them most nights at the long, crowded dining room table, she might have made more of a fuss about it. Angela felt comforted and protected by Tom's presence. Interestingly, Chava and Tom got along rather well when all the guns remained out of sight.

Angela learned from her sessions with Soledad that Claudia was putting a lot of pressure on Chava to dial down the swagger and to negotiate with the Tribal Council for a mutual agreement that would establish the foundation for the New Brothers people to stay at Green Creek without placing the Green Creek leaders under siege. Claudia had befriended the chief, and the two women discussed how to engineer a viable future for the community. Theirs was not the only friendship forming between New Brothers people and Green Creek people. Things were getting tricky for Chava and his gun-toting buddies as relationships formed.

Angela felt about ready to make popcorn and pull up a chair to observe the psychology of the situation as it unfolded.

One Sunday afternoon, Chava appeared at her house and asked Rachel if she would take a walk with him. He said he wanted to talk with her about Soledad. As she pulled on her jacket to join Chava on her front porch, Angela gave her the look.

"What?" she demanded.

Angela crossed her arms over her chest. "He didn't ask *me* to talk with him about Soledad. And he could have done it in your office, but no, he wants to go for a walk. Be on your guard" Angela rolled her eyes.

"He didn't ask you because you disapprove of him. He wants to walk because it's a beautiful day and it beats sitting still. Don't be so suspicious," Rachel chided as she headed for the door.

It was indeed a beautiful March day, with a deep blue sky serving as a backdrop for enormous fluffy clouds. The air was crisp and fresh with a touch of spring around the edges. It was still chilly, however, and Rachel slipped her hands into her gloves as they walked down the driveway.

"I heard through the grapevine that you work out in the Fitness Center every morning. I wish I could get more people to do that," Rachel observed, making conversation.

"I'm turning forty in October. I never thought I would live this long. Never in a million years. Not when I lived in Oakland. Not now. I don't expect to live a long life with everything messed up the way it is. But it spooks me to think about getting old so I work out to keep in shape."

They walked in silence for a minute.

"I thought my wife would always be around for Soledad. I thought I'd get killed and she'd always be around. She was a good mom. I don't know what to do with a girl, how to take care of her, what to say to her."

"You love her very much."

"I love her more than anyone and more than anything. I think she's OK here. I think this place is a good home for her. What do you think, Doc?"

"She's not having so much trouble with her digestion lately. She's not in pain very often anymore. She's attached to Claudia. She likes it at my house with the other kids. I don't think she feels comfortable with the young people her age in your gang so it has been helpful for her to spend time with children she likes."

"Don't call us a gang. That's from before. And even then we weren't a gang. We're an extended family. Our family has people in it who used to be in two different gangs and people who were never in any gang. I don't even know how we came together. It just happened. And somehow I'm the one responsible for making decisions."

"Probably because you have leadership skills."

"Yeah. OK." He laughed wryly. "I'll take that. I like having control, but I don't like having to make all the decisions."

"Seriously? You seem to love making all the decisions. Bossing everyone. Stomping around in your big boots." She had not meant to criticize him. She was trying to gain his trust so she could influence him. But her anger got the best of her. She bit her lip to stop herself from saying more.

Surprisingly, he did not bristle. "So that's how you see me?"

"That's how pretty much everyone sees you," she replied truthfully.

"But we're doing OK here. Things are going steady and running smoothly. We have plenty of water. Everyone is getting enough to eat. Roof over everyone's head. People feel safe."

"Is that what you think?" Rachel stopped walking and cast him a look of disbelief.

"What?"

"First of all, no one feels safe with you and your guys waving your guns around. Least of all your daughter. She hates those guns. That's how her mother died, from people waving guns around. Secondly, we only have food because the farm is functioning according to plans made earlier this year. We haven't hunted game in weeks because you won't give us access to our guns and you haven't rustled up any venison because you and your guys don't know how to hunt. Our dried and smoked meat will run out soon. Every day that you prevent our Tribal Council from meeting and our Spokescouncil from meeting, every day that you prevent us from finding solutions to the enormous infrastructure issues that threaten us, you're driving our whole community, yourself and your daughter and your people included, closer to disaster."

He stared at her, his mouth slightly open. "What solutions? What needs to be figured out?"

"I don't believe you are really this stupid. We'll eventually run out of things like paper, matches, pharmaceuticals, batteries. Our children will outgrow shoes, wear out clothing. We have no access to anything synthetic. We can't make plastic. We can't replace fishing line or PVC pipe. We need to develop contingency plans for the future, plans for making tools, repurposing metal, building more houses, conserving the materials we have, securing more food, creating heat. I have apprentices working with me at the clinic every day to learn how to practice medicine because I'm the only one here with a medical degree. What happens when I die? The veterinarian has apprentices as well. The dentist has apprentices; the engineers, the farmers and gardeners, even our medicine man Richard—they all have apprentices. We need to plan ahead or our children will perish. You don't have the capability to deal with all the things we, as a community, will have to deal with. None of us has that capability on our own. But working together, pooling our skills, we have resources. Unfortunately, you've halted the work of our leaders, organizers, managers, and decision-makers. You've interrupted our efforts to solve the problems that need solving." She had so much pent up inside of her that once she opened the door a crack, it all poured out like molten lava.

"I see," he said. She wondered if he did.

"I hope you do. Our chief is a wise, resourceful, and determined woman. So far, she has been giving you time."

"*She* has been giving *me* time?" He laughed.

"You have no idea. When she loses patience with you, I guarantee you won't know what hit you. She's a spiritual linebacker and you're a spiritual Ping-Pong ball compared to her."

"If you say so, Doc."

"Quit being so smug. Something's going to give soon."

They had walked along a path through a forested area between Rachel's house and the Green Creek tribal office. If they kept going on the path, they would come to the clinic and the community center. While some of the trees were bare, many of them still had their leaves, such as the manzanita, madrone, fir, and even varieties of oaks. Chalk-green lichens trailed like lace from the branches that webbed around them.

"My daughter is not the only one in this family who likes you, Doc. I'm not being smug. I'm listening to what you have to say." He cast a dazzling smile in her direction as he turned to look at her, his eyes deep pools, and paid her a sincere compliment. "You're brave."

Desire and fear flowed into Rachel's bloodstream simultaneously. Desire because Chava was a fine-looking man, and she believed he was a good man when it came down to essentials, if given the chance to prove himself. Fear because she felt her attraction to him was a betrayal of Vince and also that she was in danger of placing herself in a problematic situation with an unknown quantity. She wanted Chava to like her and trust her. She had assured Angela that it was all part of her plan to overthrow his grip on the community, but Rachel knew there was more to it.

Chava studied Rachel carefully, and he saw her confusion and conflicted feelings in her face. He also saw her desire. He took her shoulder gently, turned her toward him, and leaned in slightly.

She put a finger to his lips. "That is not a good idea."

"Probably not. But I don't seem to be thinking it through."

"I'll think it through for both of us." She turned abruptly and hurried back down the path in the direction of her house. He did not follow.

The day after she took the walk in the woods with Chava, Tom arrived at the house in the evening with surprising news. "Guess what?" he burst out, as he came through the door, unable to contain himself. "Chava gave the Tribal Council permission to meet again. He won't let them meet privately, and he insists on attending the Tribal Council meetings with those guys Oscar and Lee. They brought their guns into the first meeting."

"And the chief didn't say anything about the guns?" Rachel asked.

"Not today," Tom confirmed.

"I wonder how long that will last."

"She probably thinks it's more important to get the Tribal Council meetings going again. She picks her battles. She insisted that the Spokescouncil start meeting again too, and she invited Chava to send a representative from the New Brothers to those meetings. So get this." Tom flashed a satisfied grin. "Chava assumed he would be the rep for his people at the Spokescouncil, but when his people found out about the Spokescouncil, they sent a delegation to inform him that they didn't want him to represent them to the Spokescouncil. That ruffled his feathers. They want Claudia to represent them instead."

"Did he go for it?" Angela asked.

"He was angry. He got his people together and took a vote by show of hands. I heard that Claudia won easily, with only a scant few of Chava's men voting in his favor. They voted him off the Spokescouncil." Tom had a good guffaw at that. Rachel wondered if there would be unfortunate repercussions. She hoped Chava could accept the mandate of his people graciously, but he didn't seem like the kind of person who could do that.

Once she had leadership back up and running, the chief swiftly reinstated the work groups she had formed to focus on various components of community infrastructure, such as water, waste management, health, agriculture, hunting, justice systems, materials development, conservation, and housing. After three days, when she had systems management and planning back in motion, she called Chava to meet with her privately. After the meeting, word spread quickly at Green Creek about their conversation. The chief informed Chava that she was going on a hunger strike. She would only drink water until Chava and his men either relinquished their weapons and agreed to the Pacific Treaty, left the community, or she died. She invited Chava and his people to remain at Green Creek, to join the community, but only if they agreed to the Pacific Treaty and swore they would uphold the principles of nonviolence. She asked him to surrender his weapons to Tom so they could be locked in the armory.

The instant Rachel heard the news, she dropped everything and hurried to the chief's house. "Chief, you're seventy-four years old. This is a dangerous course of action to take. If you even survive a hunger strike at all, you're risking permanent damage to your kidneys. They could fail. Please don't do this," Rachel begged.

"You won't change my mind so stop trying. I need to press the issue. If our community is going to survive, then this siege has to end. I will not live surrounded by violence. I am prepared to die."

"But no one else is prepared for you to die."

To make matters worse, the rest of the Tribal Council joined in the hunger strike. Some of them were also elders and not in good enough physical shape to withstand such deprivation. They took to their beds, where they were tended by family and friends.

On the first evening of the hunger strike, Rachel barred Chava from her house when he arrived to eat dinner with them. "Do you really think I'll feed you while our tribal leaders are starving themselves because of your guns and your obsession with power? The chief is an old woman. She won't live long if she doesn't eat. You need to evolve that pea-brain of yours pretty fast or we're going to lose her," Rachel hollered at Chava from her front porch.

Chava clenched his jaw and scowled. Previously, when he came to Rachel's house, he left his gun by the front steps. Now he drew it and pointed it at Rachel. "Where's my daughter?" he demanded.

The gun did not scare Rachel. She didn't think he would shoot her.

"Soledad!" Chava shouted. "Come out here. Now."

Angela emerged from the house with Soledad. The other children held the curtains aside and peered out the windows, wide-eyed.

Chava waved the gun in the direction of the driveway. "We're going home," he ordered his daughter.

"We don't have a home," Soledad reminded him quietly.

"You know what I mean. You belong with me."

"I don't want to." Soledad defied her father, with a jut of her chin that exactly mirrored the jut of his chin when he was displeased, as at that moment. Father and daughter glared at one another.

"Come here now," Chava ordered, pointing the gun at the ground beside him.

"Or what?" Soledad demanded. "You'll shoot me? She would have hated the way you are. You know she would have hated it. Who is Chava, the bully, the boss-man? I want Sal back. Where did he go? What did you do with my papi?" The child began sobbing hysterically, gulping for air. Angela put rubbed her back.

"Shut up!" Chava yelled.

"I hate Chava!" Soledad shouted with frightening venom. "I hate you!"

"You don't hate your father," Angela told the child. "You're mad at him but you know he loves you."

In frustration, Chava shot out one of the tires in Rachel's Mazda, which squatted in the yard like a paralyzed prehistoric animal. Then he turned and strode off, as if he didn't trust himself and had to remove himself quickly from his daughter's presence.

Angela turned Soledad's face to hers and instructed, "Breathe, baby, OK? Take a breath. Breathe." Soledad did as told, breathing in rhythm with Angela.

"We're going to sit here on the porch for a little while," Angela said to Rachel, as she guided Soledad to the porch swing. Rachel went into the house to see about dinner. It was a good thing Tom was not around. She shuddered at the thought of what he might have done in the heat of the moment, with Chava pointing a gun at Rachel. She wondered if perhaps the chief had the best plan, if everyone should go on a hunger strike until Chava surrendered his guns. Her thoughts turned to the story of the ancient Hebrews of Masada who had committed suicide, all 960 of them, when the Roman army stormed their fortress with the intention of raping, murdering, torturing, and enslaving the rebels inside. She wondered if Green Creek would end up like Masada. Triumphant but dead. There would be no one to read and remember their history the way generations of people had read the history of Masada.

Later that night, alone in their bedroom after they had settled the children down with great difficulty, Rachel asked Angela if she had managed to find out from Soledad what that business about Sal and Chava meant. Angela explained, "Soledad's mother called him Sal. When he became more involved in the gangs, he started to go by the name Chava with the gangbangers who looked up to him as their leader. That's not a gang name or anything. It's just a typical nickname for people named Salvador. After Soledad's mother died, he never referred to himself as Sal again. As his Chava persona, he became consumed with gang activity and with avenging his wife's murder. Soledad says he changed after her mother died, and she doesn't recognize him anymore. She misses the good dad he used to be. I told her that good dad is still in there somewhere. What else could I say?"

"Do you think there's hope for him?" Rachel asked. "As a psychologist, do you think he can go back to being that good dad, that good man?"

"That good husband?"

"Don't go there," Rachel warned. "I asked a simple question. Can he reform?"

"I don't know. When people suffer trauma they can recover if they want to recover. But sometimes they can't find their way to a good life again, to happiness. Sometimes they're permanently damaged. It depends on so many factors. But if I didn't believe that people can change then I would never have gone into this profession. I believe that people are capable of astonishing transformation."

Rachel hugged Angela. "I don't know how I would have survived all of this without you, girlfriend. You save my life every day."

"As you save mine."

The health of the elders on hunger strike deteriorated quickly over the next few days. Rachel managed to convince them to put lemon juice and a little salt into the water they drank. It was a small success. Many people in the community joined the hunger strike. Rachel spent her mornings visiting strikers to monitor their condition. The Green Creek community was under a great deal of stress as they feared for the lives of their elders and struggled to calm their terrified children. Along with the Green Creek community, the New Brothers women and children shunned Chava and his armed men. Even though these men had started to become part of the community and had made friends among the Green Creek people, once their presence with their weapons came to symbolize the oppression and violence that the chief and others on hunger strike opposed, the New Brothers men became pariahs. Everyone avoided them. The children hid from them. They ate alone, slept alone, walked alone. Even New Brothers women and children avoided interaction with the men who carried the guns. Claudia camped out at the chief's house with the chief's family, participating in prayer circles throughout the day. She had heatedly given Chava a piece of her mind.

On the fourth day of the hunger strike, Angela consulted with Richard about organizing a spiritual intervention. She was the queen of counter-crisis, but the situation they faced took her deep into uncharted territory. She and Richard came up with an idea. They gathered the drummers who usually performed ritual drumming for the Green Creek Tribe. The drummers assembled at the communal fire pit behind the tribal office building and they drummed. Richard lit a ritual fire. Dancers donned their ceremonial regalia and danced. Before long, community members converged on the event, bringing their drums and other instruments. The drumming circle grew. Many people sat on their own porches or in their front yards and drummed along. The drummers paused from time to time to eat and sleep, but they staggered their breaks so the drumming remained continuous. The drumming raised the people up, reminded them that spirit infused each of them and all creation, and allowed them to transcend the current moment. The drumming held each and every one of them in the loving embrace of community.

The New Brothers men maintained an armed guard at the homes of Tribal Council members, as if these elders and leaders weakened by starvation posed a physical threat requiring subjugation. While the Tribal Council and Elders Circle no longer met, the Spokescouncil continued to meet, and Chava as well as some of his men, always armed, sat in on these meetings, despite the fact that he was not the New Brothers' chosen representative.

Chava did not return to Rachel's house or attempt to pry his daughter from her clutches. Soledad's stomach aches returned. Sulei became confused at first and thought Soledad was on a hunger strike too because she wasn't eating. "I might as well go on a hunger strike," Soledad told Angela. But she continued to sip the broth and tea they fed her and nibbled on corn cakes. If she stayed in bed, hiding from the world, she felt a little better. Sophia cuddled up with her and read aloud to her.

Angela suggested Rachel try to talk sense into Chava. Rachel obviously had a strong influence on him. After all, he reconvened the Tribal Council and Spokescouncil after their talk in the woods. But Rachel stubbornly refused to have anything to do with him. "I'm too angry at him to have a civilized conversation. Let him stew in his own toxic juices and maybe he'll realize how wrong he is," she told Angela. Besides, she had her hands full with the health consequences of the hunger strike, not only for those fasting, but for those who worried about them.

The drumming went continuously for nearly forty-eight hours before Chava and his followers attempted to put a stop to it. He had lost the support of the New Brothers women and children completely, and many of them had joined the drumming. Angela knew that for Chava and his men, the drumming represented agreement with the chief's ultimatum, to which they refused to submit. They apparently believed that if they turned in their guns, they would hand power over to the chief and the Tribal Council. They didn't yet realize that their guns had no power in this community, had never had any power in this community. What would it take to make them see this?

Chava, Oscar, Lee, and other armed New Brothers invaded the drumming circle in the late afternoon. While they referred to it as a drumming circle, it was not a circle by any stretch of the imagination. It was a crowd of people congregated around a fire. Chava interrupted the drumming by firing a round of bullets into the air. The drumming came to a halt and silence spread over the crowd. Angela noticed Darren, his brother, and a couple of their police buddies slip away from the crowd. She remembered the missing guns and feared the situation would not end well. But she had harbored a foreboding from the moment the New Brothers swaggered into Green Creek. Perhaps the situation would have defused over time as the New Brothers became assimilated into the community, without the chief pressing the issue. They would never know. She wondered who would still be alive at the end of the day and the thought sent a shiver through her.

Members of the chief's family had carried her to the fire on a stretcher and had placed her gently on a mattress set on top of a plastic tarp. She was extremely weak, but her presence carried tremendous weight with those assembled. What if the chief died? Tears welled in Angela's eyes. She had never known anyone more wise or courageous than Chief Firekeeper. She looked for Rachel in the crowd; her rock, her sister-girl. She saw her on the other side of the fire pit with Win-J, Rosie, and Abby. Fortunately, Sophia had stayed at home with Soledad, who did not need to witness her father making this spectacle of himself. Brushing her tears away, Angela moved next to Sulei and Jamal, to protect them with her body if necessary. Her boys sat with their drums in their laps, watching Chava. They could not reconcile this dangerous threat with their image of the man who sometimes ate dinner with them, this man who was Soledad's father. Angela's children and Rachel's had seen a different side of him; they had seen the possibility of who he could be. Also, they had come to love his daughter and to accept her as part of the family. They were having as much difficulty as Angela and Rachel accepting the fact that this wild-eyed villain who stood before them brandishing a loaded gun was the same daddy who had laughed with them at the dinner table.

Locked inside his gang-leader persona, Chava moved to the fire pit flanked by Oscar and Lee, while his other men circled the edges of the crowd threateningly. "This is over," Chava announced. "You will disperse. Go home. And you," he pointed his gun at the chief where she lay unmoving on the mattress, "will eat."

Claudia stepped up to challenge him. "What if we don't disperse? What if the chief doesn't eat until you hand over that gun? Will you shoot her to keep her from starving herself to death? Think that one over Chava Wong. Take a good look at yourself. You're ridiculous." She raised her voice so the other New Brothers could hear her more clearly. "All you boys are ridiculous. You shame me. Grow up. Be men." She then lay down on the mattress next to the chief and embraced her, shielding her body from the guns with her own.

Rachel walked over to Chava. She reached out and grasped his hand, which held the gun. She placed the barrel of the gun against her own chest. People gasped. Angela cried out. Abby hid her face in Rosie's side and wept. Sulei cast his mother a terrified look, his eyes huge.

"Enough Sal," Rachel said. The brilliance of Rachel's words, of her choice to call him back to his true self with the use of the name that Soledad had divulged, the name from when he was his best self, filled Angela with admiration for her friend. Rachel and I are healers, Angela thought. And she was proud to count herself as a member of Rachel's Tribe, whatever it was, whatever it had become, whatever it would be.

Chava, Sal, Salvador Wong, whoever this man was, stood thinking for the longest minute of his life, while a woman he had grown to love and admire held the barrel of his gun against her heart. Silence hung over the crowd while he thought. Then he slowly lowered his arm and dropped his gun in the dirt. Stunned, no one moved at first. Claudia released the chief and sat on the edge of the mattress. The chief gazed up weakly at Chava. "Thank you," Chief Firekeeper said quietly. "Where's Tom?"

"I'm right here chief."

She lifted a hand weakly and waved it in the direction of the gun.

"I'm on it," Tom told her. "We'll put the weapons in the armory."

Out of the corner of her eye, Angela saw Darren and his guys slip back into the group. She figured they were packing forbidden guns. She also figured that the chief had no idea. She wasn't going to say anything either. The chief might be a saint, pure of heart, but Angela was not. Tom was not. Darren was not. It looked like they would be able to simply whisper their guns away to wherever they had hidden them, no one the wiser, now that Chava had caved.

"New Brothers, we will stay at Green Creek," Chava announced to his people. "We will surrender our guns like the chief requests, and we will live here and agree to abide by the decisions of the Tribal Council." Claudia stood beside him and took his hand to demonstrate her approval. "Anyone who doesn't want to agree to this should leave now," Chava concluded. Other than burying his wife, it was the hardest thing he had ever done. Claudia raised his hand and hers triumphantly above their heads in solidarity.

Oscar, Lee, and the other New Brothers men looked around at one another, unsure of themselves, conflicted, confused. Angela could see these men struggling, deciding their path forward. She could see Darren and his brother and police buddies watching, poised, ready to spring into action if they saw one provocative move. She gave herself over to the moment, to whatever would happen. Then Lee stepped forward and placed his gun on the ground next to Chava's. "I'm with you, man."

Oscar exploded. "You disgust me!" He rattled off a string of angry invective in Spanish at Chava. Then he switched to English. "You're an embarrassment. You're agreeing to this because you want to get that lady doctor into bed. You're a traitor to the Hermanos. I'm out of here, man. Gone. You're crazy, these people are crazy, and I don't want any part of it. You're all gonna die here. I'm out. Who's with me?"

"I'm sorry," Chava said to Oscar. "I need a safe place for my daughter. I have to stop running."

Oscar stepped carefully and deliberately away from the group. Other men joined him, all of them with guns cocked at the ready, aimed in the direction of the crowd of people. Oscar pointed his gun at Chava, then at Rachel, then back at Chava. Angela was terrified that he would shoot Rachel on his way out, a parting shot to hurt Chava. Chava spoke to Oscar in Spanish. Angela understood that he was trying to convince Oscar to stay. But Oscar lowered his gun and then he and the others who had decided to leave walked off in the direction of their trailers. They would gather their things and be gone within the hour.

A commotion at the back of the crowd caught everyone's attention. Raphael called out, "Where's the doc? We need the doc."

What now? Angela thought. She was burning out on so much drama.

Raphael pushed his way through the press of people to where Rachel stood next to Chava. He bent over and put his hands on his knees while he tried to catch his breath. Then he stood up straight, gulping air, and announced, "Susan's in labor."

Rachel laughed joyfully, with more joy than she had felt in some time. "We'll be there soon," she assured Raphael. "Go back and keep an eye on her. And boil some water." Raphael nodded and then disappeared as quickly as he had arrived. Rachel beckoned Musoke to her. She asked him to stop at the clinic to pick up their birthing supplies and promised she'd meet him at Raphael and Susan's trailer shortly. Then Rachel spoke to Claudia, explaining to her how to feed the chief to help her ease back from her week of fasting. A group of men had already lifted the chief onto the litter and were carrying her back to her house through the parted throng.

"All of those who went on the hunger strike need to ease back into eating," Rachel said. "Can you explain to their families what to do now that I have explained it to you?" she asked Claudia.

"Of course," Claudia assured her, "but I don't know who they are or where they live."

Richard stepped forward. "I will help with that."

Rachel put her hand on Chava's arm and said, "Come with me. We should go tell Soledad about your decision. She has been unwell ever since you two exchanged words." Rachel waved to Angela, who waved back, before she and Chava hurried off down the road to Rachel's house.

Sulei looked up at Angela, his face glowing. "I want to drum to celebrate," he said.

"Then I think you should drum, baby. Maybe some other people feel the same way."

Sulei sat down next to Jamal and the brothers began to tap their drums again and other drummers joined in and then dancers danced and a new drumming circle celebrated the ability of the community to move forward again on its mysterious path in pursuit of survival.

Angela kept her thoughts to herself. She wondered if she was the only one at Green Creek to realize that if Oscar and his pals left, then he would quite possibly return in the future with more men and more guns, and that he would kill every man, woman, and child. She sought Tom and walked with him to his office. He was the only person to whom she felt she could voice her concerns. He shared them, but didn't know what to do about it. He also told her he still wasn't going to say anything about Darren's secret. He also suspected that some of the New Brothers would keep hidden guns. But he felt it best to let sleeping dogs lie. She agreed.

"We should send a crew out to take down the signage pointing to Green Creek immediately," Angela told him. "We need to make an effort to remain hidden. This is such a remote location that without any signs to show the way, someone would have to be looking hard to find us. A stray person may stumble upon us. But other than that, only people who have been here and know where we are will find us. I would go so far as to falsify the signage so it leads away from Green Creek. Being a secret protects us. Our excellent water source could make us a target. We have to guard the secret of our water." Tom said he would get on it right away.

Maybe if Oscar tried to find the community again to do them harm he would get lost. One could always hope.

While Angela talked to Tom about signage, while the drumming resumed, while Musoke went to look after Susan, Rachel and Chava walked to Rachel's house to give the good news about Chava's change of heart to Soledad. "If you insist on calling me Doc, then I'm going to call you Sal," Rachel informed him.

"I can live with that, Doc," Chava replied wearily.

"You know that the chief will ask you to sign the Pacific Treaty, and if intruders turn up here with weapons you will not have yours. You understand what you have agreed to, right?"

"My head knows it," Chava answered. "When that situation actually happens, I'm not sure what I will do. I picked up a gun because I decided not to be a victim anymore."

"Then what made you decide to stay here and agree to the chief's terms?"

"Soledad means more to me than anything in the world, more than my life. This is a good place for her to live and she likes it here. If I have to change myself to give her this home, then I will."

"You are about to make one little girl very happy."

They were in the forest on the path to her house. She stopped, turned toward him, and brushed his lips with her fingertips. He stepped back and regarded her with astonishment.

"You said you thought that was a bad idea."

"Maybe we both can change."

Chava pulled her toward him and kissed her deeply, searchingly, longingly. She gave herself permission to live in the moment, with no thoughts. Only the kiss.

She broke away, breathless, filled with wanting him.

"I have to deliver a baby."

Chava threw his head back and laughed. She had never seen him lose himself in laughter quite like that. He took her hand and they continued walking to her house.

"Have you ever seen a baby be born?"

He shook his head.

"First time for everything. You're about to become a great-uncle. Raphael could use your support."

Susan gave birth to a boy, and they named him Salvador. Chava bent everyone's ear for days recounting the story of Chavito's birth. He cut the baby's umbilical cord himself under Musoke's direction. Soledad referred to Chavito as her brother. She was working on forgiving her father for his transgressions and the two of them were both trying to get along better. Her stomach aches subsided.

The days following the capitulation of the New Brothers were eventful throughout the community. The chief and other hunger strikers regained their strength, and the Tribal Council and Elders Circle resumed meeting. Rachel considered it a small miracle that no one had died during the hunger strike. The remaining New Brothers signed the Pacific Treaty and the chief hung the copy with their signatures in her office. Tom, Darren, and a crew ventured out of Green Creek to remove or falsify the signage pointing to the Rez. The children went back to school. Hunting resumed to bring in venison, rabbit, wild turkey, quail, and other game to be eaten as well as preserved by smoking and drying. They started transitioning from hunting with guns to hunting with bows and arrows made by hand, which was a tedious process. But the bullets wouldn't last forever so they needed to work on their Plan B. An archery range was set up, and as the first functional arrows were completed, aspiring archers practiced with them to build their skills. The garden crew put out a call for all hands on deck to prepare the garden beds and complete spring planting. They built another greenhouse where they would start more vegetables to plant further into the season.

Musoke hauled Chava's trailer to Rachel's property with his van. When Chava realized that the van actually worked, he was furious that the community had kept this a secret from him and he stomped out to the archery range where he practiced shooting arrows for hours before he cooled down. They put a futon mattress on the floor of Abby and Sophia's room for Soledad so she didn't have to keep sleeping with Sophia.

Rachel and Chava shared a bed in his trailer. Angela offered to move into the trailer so that Rachel could have her own bed. But Rachel convinced her that she preferred the privacy of the trailer. She insisted it was all good. It wasn't exactly all good for Angela, however, who felt abandoned when Rachel moved into the trailer, but she didn't say anything about this because she was genuinely happy for her friend. She had seen many people recover from grief and loss. It was her profession to help people recover so they could move forward and experience joy once again. So in the end, she approved of Rachel's relationship with Chava.

Rachel had said yes to the opportunity to be happy again. Angela knew that was what you had to do because you couldn't afford to let that kind of opportunity pass you by. It might not come around a second time.

Chava still called Rachel "Doc." She and Soledad were the only ones at Green Creek who referred to him as Sal, but the fact that they chose to see him as his better self helped him work on changing and growing. He tried every day to be that better self so he wouldn't let them down. Rachel's girls approached Chava's presence in their family with caution. He certainly would never replace their father. Soledad timidly asked Rachel if she could call her "Mom."

The lively, blended family thrived. Tom joined them for dinner most evenings. He had started seeing Bernadette, and she usually came over to eat with him. Rosie and Win-J were like a longtime married couple in their cozy trailer. Even though they often ate dinner with Darren and Tanisha, they made their home at Rachel's house. A couple of weeks after she moved into the trailer with Chava, Rachel started a dinner game she called "Again." After they said a few words of thanks for their food, they went around the table and each person said one thing from the Lost Time that they would like to do again. Sharing remembrances of things they used to have and used to do eased their loss.

One evening, Angela started the game by pointing at Win-J to say his Again.

"Eating Mexican pizza at Tortilla Flats," Win-J said. His brothers made yummy sounds, remembering the delicious cheesy, meaty, greasy taste of that pizza.

"Swimming in the ocean," Rosie chose for her turn.

Chava was next. "Watching a Raiders football game."

"Good one!" Angela complimented him, while her boys and Tom hooted in agreement.

"Shopping for new shoes" was Soledad's Again.

"What she said." Sophia pointed to Soledad and everyone laughed.

"Bananas," came from Abby.

"Soaking in a hot bath," Rachel said as she pointed to Jamal who sat next to her.

"Christmas tree-lighting at Jack London Square," Jamal contributed.

Sulei was next and he was so excited to take his turn that he popped up and down in his chair. "Introducing Big Dog to Chavito!" he shouted gleefully.

Angela couldn't speak for the lump that rose in her throat. Her eyes welled with tears. Her boys looked at her with confusion and concern.

"What is it?" Rachel asked.

Angela reached over and took Sulei's hand and kissed him on the top of the head. "You are an old soul, baby."

"What I do?" Sulei asked with a crooked smile.

Comprehension bloomed on the faces of the adults while Angela explained to the children what had moved her. "Sulei's Again is something that happened in the Vision Time. It isn't something from the Lost Time. He reminded me that we have lots of good things yet to come and we are making more good memories every day." Sulei, who had the fewest memories from the Lost Time of anyone in the family, had embraced their present life faster and more completely than any of them, and, despite their losses, he was having a happy childhood. Angela felt triumphant.

"But it's still OK to remember from the Lost Time, right?" Abby asked anxiously.

"Absolutely," Angela reassured her. "Let's remember all the good things from all the good times. Let's especially remember Vince and Winston and things we used to do with our dads. So. My Again is having a mocha latte with Winston at the corner café."

"Mooommmm," Win-J complained, "coffee was your Again last night."

"Last night it was an Italian espresso," Angela defended her choice. "I can remember coffee as often as I want."

Later, when they were alone in the kitchen washing dishes, Win-J told his mom conspiratorially, "I have the perfect gift for Chava."

"What's that?"

"I have that Raiders game where they trampled the Patriots in the championships the year the Raiders went on to win the Super Bowl saved on my computer. The whole game. If I can recharge the computer then Chava can watch a Raiders game again," he confided smugly.

"I want to watch that too! Give that to Chava for his fortieth birthday. It's the perfect present. We'll all watch it together."

As spring advanced, the community focused intensely on the farm, where the work was endless and critically important to their survival. The children attended school for half days only and spent their afternoons on the farm where they weeded, helped prepare more garden beds, turned compost into the soil, planted starts, and made themselves useful performing chores at the direction of the gardeners.

One Sunday late in May, while Rachel and Chava worked with some of the children on the small personal garden patch behind their house, Tom appeared with the news that Oscar had returned and he had a child with him.

"Bring them here, we'll take care of them," Rachel told Tom. While they waited for Tom to return with Oscar, Rachel cautioned Chava, "Forgiveness is a virtue. Anger damages no one more than the one who holds the anger."

"I'm working on it."

When Oscar arrived, he shook Chava's hand formally and apologized to him for parting on such bad terms. He was extremely thin, his clothing was soiled and torn, he was filthy, and the small boy with him appeared even more starved and bedraggled than Oscar. Oscar no longer had his precious gun. Rachel brought them food, which they devoured like wild beasts. They gulped water as if they had just crawled through a desert. Chava did not reproach Oscar for leaving or for the venomous words he had spoken before his departure. He did not press him to tell them what had happened to him in the interim.

Rachel pointed Oscar toward the shower and brought him fresh clothing. He took the child into the shower with him and they washed together. Angela found some of Sulei's outgrown clothing for the boy, who was perhaps five years old. Rachel examined him after he was cleaned up and felt satisfied that he was only malnourished and not diseased. Oscar put the boy to sleep. Angela and Rachel shooed their children out of the room and sat at the kitchen table with

Chava and Oscar. Chava poured Oscar a small glass of hard apple cider while casting an expectant look in his direction. "So what happened to you out there, man?"

Oscar told them that the other New Brothers men who had left with him were dead. He choked on his words, said he wasn't ready to talk about what happened to them. He described a frightening, vicious, and chaotic world. He had encountered many different people, some kind enough to feed him and give him a place to sleep, some so dangerous he feared they would kill him to eat his flesh. He said water was scarce, that it had become the most precious commodity of all. He had seen a man kill someone for a bottle of water. He found the child, Fernando, hiding in a deserted barn. Fernando spoke only Spanish.

"He trusts me because I speak Spanish," Oscar confided. "His family came here from Mexico just before the Systems Collapse. From what I can tell, they came for a visit and then couldn't get back. Fernando won't tell me what happened to his family. It must be too painful for him to talk about."

"I'll work with him," Angela offered. "That's what I do, and I speak Spanish. I can help."

"Gracias. I have never seen him smile. Imagine a child who never smiles. What horror has he seen that he will not smile? He barely speaks. He's the kindest, most gentle boy. He's so generous to others. I knew I had to swallow my pride and come back here when I found him. I wanted to help him, to take him to a safe place. I kept hearing your voice in my head, hermano," Oscar told Chava, "when you said you needed a safe place for Soledad."

"So far, it is still safe. We hope it stays this way. Did you tell anyone about Green Creek while you were out there?" Chava asked anxiously.

"I swear I didn't tell anyone. I saw you changed the signs to lead people away from here. That's good."

"We hope no one with evil intent finds us. Dios help us if they do because the chief will insist on no guns and we have agreed to be shot and killed rather than fight back. I don't like it, but I gave her my word and life has been good to me here. Soledad is happy." Chava reached over and took Rachel's hand. He smiled at Oscar. "And I did get my pretty lady doc into bed, like you said."

Rachel blushed. "Sal," she cautioned him. "Watch it or you'll be sleeping in that trailer alone tonight."

Oscar smiled.

"It's good to see you smile, hermano."

Oscar's eyes welled with tears. "It's good to hear you say it."

Oscar and Fernando were given a trailer near the other New Brothers people. Claudia, who spoke Spanish, embraced little Fernando and he quickly became attached to her. He met with Angela twice a week, but her work with him was slow going. The child had experienced extreme trauma.

In mid-June, Rachel and Angela ceremoniously picked the very first Early Girl tomatoes to ripen in their little garden behind their house. As they stood side-by-side in the garden, Angela reflected on the fact that it had been one year since the girlfriends reunion.

"Stay right there," Rachel exclaimed suddenly. "I'll be right back." She ran into the house and from the back of her closet produced the pole with the colorful ribbons they had entwined that day at the beach. She took it outside. When Angela saw it she laughed. Rachel fetched a hammer and a step-ladder and together they pounded the pole of ribbons into the rich earth at the end of a row of pert, young tomato plants.

"I wonder what happened to the others," Rachel said. "I hope they're alright."

"We'll never know, so let's imagine them alive and well with their families," Angela replied.

Rachel held her hands up in the air next to the pole of ribbons and waved them above her head. "Sending you love and light, ladies. Robin, Max, Jo, Melanie. Sending you our thoughts for happiness and health."

"Amen to that." Angela waved her hands in the air too.

"And Callie too," Rachel added. "I hope you get that baby you wanted soon, girlfriend," she called to the sky.

"We should say something. A prayer or something," Angela suggested.

"Yeah, sure."

"I'm not good at that kind of thing."

"I know. I'll say something." Rachel took a moment to gather her thoughts before addressing the pole of ribbons. "We are still here. We live at the whim of the seasons, dependent on the continued abundance of water, the success of our gardens and our hunters. We will remain alive by the measure of each year's harvest. We live by chance, by luck, by who may find us here on our land and who may pass us by with their guns and their hardened hearts. Should those with weapons and desperation find us, then our lives depend on whether or not we can touch their hearts and change them as we did with the New Brothers so that they choose to join us rather than annihilate us. But life has always gone like this. In the Lost Time, we fooled ourselves into thinking it was different from this. It was never any different. Life is fragile and tenuous. We live one season to the next, celebrating the miracle of our community, our family, and our friendships; delighting in our brilliant children; mourning our losses in the embrace of community. We hope to raise our children with love, to provide them with food, water, shelter, and a quality life. We hope to die peacefully in our sleep surrounded by our grandchildren, secure in the knowledge of having accomplished something worthy of our work. Things are less complicated these days. We focus on essentials. Perhaps, if our luck holds for enough seasons passing, if our ingenuity and resourcefulness continue, we'll become the keepers of one of the few places on Earth where humans thrive, in spite of our failings, because we've found a way to perpetuate the best within us."

As she had learned from the Green Creek Natives, Angela voiced a heartfelt "OH!"

Afterward, Angela couldn't get Rachel's words out of her mind, but that was fine with her because she didn't want to forget them. She tried to remember them to write them down. The next day she spent her afternoon working in the gardens of the Green Creek farm. The community had worked so hard, cleared so much land, and planted so much food. She wondered if it would be enough to see them through the winter. She felt proud to belong to an on-task, conscientious community. They came from many different cultures, but the diverse people of Green Creek were now one Tribe.

Angela wondered how she had ever lived in a place where she could just stop at the store and pick up some vegetables without a second thought to the effort that had gone into producing them. Staying fed was hard work. She felt bone weary from her afternoon digging in the dirt and spreading mulch, but Rachel had been called to the clinic for an emergency so Angela had to put together a dinner for their enormous family, bursting at the seams with all those growing children. Fortunately, Rosie and Jamal had made a fresh batch of corn cakes.

Grateful for the warm, dry weather, Angela stirred up the fire in the fire pit and stoked it. She could make vegetable and cheese omelets over the fire. She went inside and cut up asparagus to put in the eggs. She set red and yellow fingerling potatoes on the grate over the hot coals.

Despite her fatigue, she felt happy. Summer was around the corner and they had abundance in the gardens. She sang as she cooked. Things could have turned out much worse for her and her boys. Somehow, astonishingly, she had found her way to safety. Even though she knew there were no guarantees and even though she knew that the Green Creek community lived precariously from one season to the next, vulnerable to the unpredictable patterns of the weather and infiltration from invasive predators from outside, even though all this and more, she felt blessed. She and Rachel had made a viable home for their children.

Rachel returned from the clinic in time to join the family as they assembled around the table. Angela dished up dinner in good spirits. The children teased and tussled like a den of cubs. Before eating, they took hands, their usual ritual, and Tom said a blessing over the food. Rachel and Angela wanted their children to realize how lucky they were every single day so that whatever the future brought, they would never feel that they had squandered the gift of days they had received.

Their cat Pepper stood at the front door and meowed. Jamal hopped up and went to open the door to let Pepper out. He stood transfixed in the doorway, staring ahead, and did not return to the table. Holding the door ajar with one hand he called to Angela urgently in a tone that made the alarm bells go off in her head. "Mama," he yelped, without turning from the door. "Mama, come quick!"

Angela bolted from the table and ran to his side. Looking over Jamal's shoulder, seeing what he saw, she stopped breathing.

Winston stood in the driveway with a knapsack over his shoulder. She took in the real and overwhelming presence of him, as wide and bright as hope for the future. Dreadlocks flopped past his shoulders, his boots were caked with mud, and he smiled brilliantly. He held in his right hand that ridiculous Raiders football she had left on top of the note for him on their bed in another lifetime. Angela screamed. Winston threw the football to Jamal, who caught it and hugged it to him as Sulei, Win-J, and the others raced to the doorway.

"You guys need to do something about your signage. This place is impossible to find," Winston commented.

Angela laughed joyously as she and her incredulous boys scrambled off the porch and hurled themselves at Winston, knocking him to the ground.

"Where have you been all this time?" Angela demanded.

"That's a long story," Winston answered.

"I want to hear every word."

Acknowledgements

People sometimes ask me why I like to read post-apocalyptic fiction. "Don't you find it depressing?" they ask. I read fiction about the end of life as we know it because I'm rehearsing for the future. I read all sorts of speculative fiction; it's a broad genre. Speculative fiction is generally defined as narrative that does not remain within the confines of true life (whatever that is) set in the real world (whatever that is). Speculative fiction bends reality (whatever that is) and often diverges from the laws of physics and hard science (whatever that is). We seem to make our own laws of science these days. If someone doesn't "believe in" climate change, it doesn't exist for them. If someone doesn't "believe in" acupuncture, it has no impact on the body as far as they are concerned. I suppose if someone doesn't "believe in" trees, they don't exist; at least not for them. Whatever people choose to believe is apparently scientific fact in their worldview. People make their own reality. You can't argue with that. I can't tell you what's in your head.

Guardians of Water is my fantasy about how humans might survive on this planet and have a chance at a future of some quality and value. The idea that humans could vote ourselves off the planet saddens me. I hope some version of us will survive and perpetuate the beauty that often lives in the human spirit and moves me so deeply. Perhaps there is a way we can drag our technology into the future with us and continue on Earth. But I'm more inclined to think that Earth cannot sustain our technology and our future lies in a different direction. Perhaps our future lies in our past. Thank you for indulging me in this thought and where it takes us in this story.

I thank my circle of family and friends for supporting me as a creative and believing in me as a writer through long years of rejection from the publishing industrial machine. I thank my book group of many years in Ukiah for reading an early version of this book and giving me excellent input. I thank Cynthia Frank and the folks at Cypress House for helping me with the nitty-gritty of publishing a book. I thank Anjelica for help with the cover design. I have been blessed throughout my life with extraordinary women friends and I thank all of you, living and now gone, for the exchange of ideas, laughter, and love. I thank my children, daughters-in-law, and grandchildren for the hours you spend with me. You are everything. I thank my mother, Natalie, for igniting the spark that grew into this story while she was on her deathbed too many years ago. I wish you could have read this one, Mom.

Thank you, Ron, for this dance.